JM

B

# THE THRIVING THORN

# THE THRIVING THORN

Jeanne Whitmee

CHIVERS
**THORNDIKE**

This Large Print book is published by BBC Audiobooks Ltd, Bath, England and by Thorndike Press®, Waterville, Maine, USA.

Published in 2005 in the U.K. by arrangement with the Author.

Published in 2005 in the U.S. by arrangement with Dorian Literary Agency.

U.K. Hardcover   ISBN 1–4056–3417–0  (Chivers Large Print)
U.K. Softcover   ISBN 1–4056–3418–9  (Camden Large Print)
U.S. Softcover   ISBN 0–7862–7788–2  (Buckinghams)

The text of this Large Print edition is unabridged.
Other aspects of the book may vary from the original edition.

Set in 16 pt. New Times Roman.

Printed in Great Britain on acid-free paper.

**British Library Cataloguing in Publication Data available**

**Library of Congress Cataloging-in-Publication Data**

Whitmee, Jeanne.
    The thriving thorn / by Jeanne Whitmee.
        p.   cm.
    "Thorndike Press large print Buckinghams."—T.p. verso.
    ISBN 0–7862–7788–2 (lg. print : sc : alk. paper)
    1. Women domestics—Fiction. 2. Young women—Fiction.
3. Boston (Mass.)—History—19th century—Fiction. 4. Large type books. 5. Historical fiction. gsafd 6. Love stories. gsafd
I. Title.
PR6073.H65T48 2005
823'.914—dc22                              2005010236

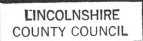

# Part One
# The Reardons

# CHAPTER ONE

*March 1838*

Seamus Reardon stood on the wharf and watched as the herring boat sailed slowly downstream towards him. The March wind stung his leathery old face and he pulled up the collar of his coat, sinking his head into it. Pray God the childer would be on this one, for wasn't it the seventh boat he'd met this week?

As the *Mary Ann* slid alongside and the crew began to make her fast, Seamus searched the faces on deck, his quick brown eyes darting, and his little monkey's face wrinkled anxiously. Suddenly a voice hailed him.

'Ahoy there! Seamus Reardon!'

He turned to see Tom Craven, the *Mary Ann*'s master, coming ashore, his weather-beaten face beaming good-naturedly under his shock of sandy hair.

'I've a package for you, boy!' he roared. 'Or, to be more truthful—*two* packages.'

Seamus relaxed visibly. 'Ah—thanks be to God, Tom. So ye kept an eye on 'em like I asked you to. God bless ye!'

Tom clapped the little man on the shoulder, laughing heartily. 'I did that. Found 'em waiting on Boston docks, looking like two lost souls. They've had a long trip of it, Seamus.

3

Nigh on a month since they left Dublin.'

Seamus knew only too well. Sending money to his dead brother's children had been a risky business. So had the many messages he'd sent, both by hand and by mouth, to ensure their safe arrival on English soil. But he had good honest friends among the sea captains and barge masters who plied their trade around the East Coast and up the river to Elvemere. He hadn't really doubted—but all the same, it was a relief to him that they were here at last.

'Two young 'uns, eh?' Tom said, looking at him speculatively. 'Never had a family of your own, have you, Seamus? What will you do with them, eh?'

Seamus looked up at the big man. 'Why they'll work for their livin',' he said. 'Sure it's cost me a fortune bringin' 'em over from the old country. But it was the least I could do for me poor brother, Michael, God rest his soul.' He crossed himself briefly and stamped his feet on the cobblestones to warm them.

'Work, eh?' Tom cocked an eyebrow. 'So you'll be lookin' for jobs for the young 'uns then?'

'Ah, no. Sure I've all that arranged,' Seamus said smugly. 'Haven't I got the pair o' them fixed up at Denmark House?'

Tom looked suitably impressed. 'Oh! Well, that's the benefit of being coachman to Mr Henry Quincey himself, I don't doubt!'

Seamus nodded. He liked people to think

4

he was in favour with his master, though in actual fact, the permission to bring over his niece and nephew owed more to the compassion of Mrs Quincey. He raised his eyes and scanned the deck of the *Mary Ann* again. The crew had lost no time and were busy unloading the catch of herring on the wharf.

'Where are they?' he asked impatiently. 'I haven't all day to stand here.'

'Here's the missus with 'em now.' Tom pointed as three figures came up from below. 'A fine, strong lad you've got there, Seamus. And as pretty a little lass as I've seen in many a day. The missus'll be quite sad partin' with them.'

Seamus sniffed as he watched the boy and girl disembark. Well, at least they looked healthy, unlike their parents. He shook his head as he thought of his imprudent and luckless brother. What a mess he had made of his life. His first wife had died when the girl, Kathleen, was a baby of two years, then what must the fellow do but go and marry the village whore—and her with a bastard child of her own; a boy, got through a sinful alliance with some travelling tinker or other.

'Ah, poor Michael.' He shook his head. 'More sinned against than sinnin'. I only hope these two'll make a better go of it than he did—God rest his soul.' He sank his chin on to his chest and Tom slapped him heartily on the

5

shoulder.

'Oh cheer up and put on a smile of welcome for the poor devils, you old misery.' He laughed. 'You've a face that'd sour the milk in the cow!' He held his hands out to the two youngsters. 'Well now, come and meet your old Uncle Seamus,' he boomed. 'He's just been telling me, you're as welcome as the flowers in May. Isn't that so, old fellow?'

Seamus nodded unconvincingly. 'It is— it is, to be sure. Come now and I'll take you to your new place. Have you a box or anything?'

But all the two had between them was a bundle tied up in a brown cloth, which the boy now picked up and shouldered. He stepped forward and looked at Seamus eye to eye—for he was already as tall as the coachman.

'I'm Patrick, Uncle Seamus. And this here is me sister, Kathleen,' he said gravely.

'I know—I know,' said Seamus. 'But we'd better be moving now. There's work to be done.' He looked at Tom Craven. 'Am I anything in your debt, Tom?'

The big man shook his head. 'Bless you, no! The lad worked like a beaver—more'n paid for the trip.'

Seamus nodded and turned away. 'Thank ye. I'll bid ye good day then.' He nodded to his niece and nephew. 'Follow me—and look sharp.'

Patrick turned to Tom Craven and his wife, Meg, who stood on the *Mary Ann*'s deck.

6

'Goodbye, sir—and thank you.'

Kathleen grasped her brother's hand tightly, tears pricking at her eyelids. The kindness shown by the captain and his wife was the first she had known since her father's death, and she would miss them. She and Patrick had had a hard and seemingly endless journey across the sea to Liverpool and then by road, canal and river to Boston where they had met the captain. Now they were finally at Elvemere and before them lay a new life in a strange foreign country. She knew she would never have done it all without Patrick.

'Goodbye,' she whispered. 'And I hope we meet again some day.'

But Seamus was growing irritable. 'Make haste for God's sake,' he snapped. 'You've a master to serve now, same as me, and he don't pay folk to stand yapping!'

They followed his hurrying figure through the throng of people on the wharf, almost running to keep sight of the long brown coat and hard hat as Seamus threaded deftly in and out between the barrels of fish. Leaving the wharf they went along a narrow street and across a bridge higher up the river. When Seamus reached the far side of the bridge he turned to wait for them, surveying the pair as they came towards him. Tom had been right: the lad looked strong enough. Aged about fifteen, he was tall for his age and broad of shoulder. The coachman shook his head as he

7

noted the head of thick black curling hair and the dark eyes, inherited, no doubt, from his gipsy father. The boy was really no relation of his, he reminded himself grudgingly, but he owed it to his dead brother to continue the responsibilities he had taken on; besides, the two of them might well be a comfort to him in his childless old age. His beady brown eyes took in their ragged clothes, the frayed shawl which the girl, Kathleen, wore over her head and shoulders and the brown skin of the boy's almost bare chest, where his buttonless shirt gaped. They swept down to the two pairs of bare legs and feet. He pushed his hat on to the back of his head and scratched his grizzled hair.

'Have ye no shoes t'your feet?' he asked.

The boy, Patrick, straightened his shoulders proudly. 'No, Uncle, we have not.'

Kathleen blushed and hung her head as the strange man who called himself 'Uncle' scrutinised her closely.

'Huh!' he said at last. 'You're hardly a sight t'be proud of, but it can't be helped, I suppose. Come on, I'll have to give ye both a good talkin' to before I can take ye anywheres.'

Without another word they followed Seamus, Patrick walking very straight and tall with the look on his face that Kathleen knew all too well. He was angry. If only he wasn't so proud. It had been the cause of all the fights he'd ever got into, and there had been many.

As she ran to keep up with him, Kathleen hoped he would be able to hold his tongue and his temper now that they were come to this fine new life. It would be terrible if it were spoilt after coming all this way from home.

But Patrick's boiling thoughts were quickly diverted by the sight which now lay before them. On their left, the wide river was teeming with boats of every type and size from schooners to fishing smacks. On the far bank, where they themselves had docked in the *Mary Ann*, were the wharves and warehouses, bustling with life, whilst in contrast, on this side stood many fine houses, finer than Patrick had ever seen in his life. He lifted his eyes to the tall windows—three, sometimes four rows of them. There were elegant doorways too, with richly gleaming paint and brasswork. In front stood tall iron railings, sometimes enclosing miniature green lawns and small conical trees in painted tubs. Patrick's dark eyes shone. It was grand—very grand indeed.

Seamus motioned to them that they must cross the road and they stood back waiting for a carriage to pass. Kathleen's hand groped for her brother's as she gazed in awe at the gleaming polished coachwork, the liveried coachman and postillion. Patrick was gazing in wonder too, but at the fine, prancing horses, perfectly matched for their satin chestnut coats and creamy manes.

Seamus looked at the boy, noting with

satisfaction his admiration of the animals.

'D'ye like horses then, lad?'

Patrick nodded. 'Indeed I do, Uncle.'

Seamus smiled, his walnut face breaking into a mass of wrinkles. 'Well it's glad I am to hear it. We'll see if we can make a tiger out o' ye.' He inclined his head towards the retreating carriage and pair. 'Sure them beasts couldn't hold a candle to the ones we have in our stable,' he said proudly. 'For you're to be employed by the richest man in Elvemere town!'

Denmark House was the finest house of them all. Set well back from the busy street it was square and three-storeyed, built in the middle of the previous century. Inside the tall, pillared gates manicured lawns were bordered by box hedges, and the sun reflected from the many fine windows. A flight of steps, white as snow, led up to the front door but Seamus hurried his niece and nephew past the gates. Further along the street a pair of tall wooden gates led into a yard and Seamus ushered them through. They found themselves in an oblong cobbled yard with an open coach-house facing them at one end. Stabling for up to a dozen horses ranged on either side of them. Seamus pointed to a wooden staircase at the side of the coach-house.

'Them's me quarters. Ye'd better come up with me.'

At the top of the stairs he let them into a

large, comfortable room under the rafters. A wood fire burned dully in a stone fireplace in front of which was a table and bench. To one side of the fireplace a high-backed wooden chair stood, with a leather cushion on its seat. On the far side of the room, under a round window, stood a chest and a truckle bed. The floor was covered with clean straw. Seamus turned to them proudly.

'Sit ye down. Could ye drink a cup o' tea?'

The two nodded eagerly and seated themselves on the bench while Seamus stirred the fire and pressed a large blackened kettle into the heart of it. He took a clay pipe from the mantel-shelf and seated himself in the chair.

'I'll say one thing,' he said as he filled the pipe and reached for a spill. 'I'll have to get the pair o' ye cleaned up a might before I can let anyone see ye!'

Kathleen reddened and looked at Patrick who said: 'We've been a long time travellin', Uncle. 'Tis not our habit to be dirty, even though we're poor.'

Seamus nodded, sucking at his pipe. 'To be sure—to be sure.' He looked at the brown bundle which Patrick had placed on the floor beside him. He pointed at it with the stem of his pipe. 'What's in there? Have ye a change o' clothes?'

'We have not, Uncle,' Patrick said briefly.

Kathleen glanced at her brother and added

quickly: 'Da had been sick for a long time when he died, Uncle. He hadn't been able to work. We owed money and rent. When he died everything was taken by them we owed it to.' She glanced at the bundle. 'In there are a few things that belonged to Da—that we hid.' She bent down and untied the bundle revealing a shabby suit of clothes, a clasp-knife and a neckerchief. Seamus cleared his throat as he looked at the pathetic relics.

'They took the clothes from your back, child?' Kathleen nodded and he cursed under his breath. 'Sure 'tis a hard country and it's glad I am t'be out of it. Poverty makes animals out of decent men!' He leaned forward to pour the boiling water from the kettle into the earthenware teapot warming on the hearth. 'Well, that's all behind ye now, me young 'uns. Ye'll have a good place here as long as ye work hard and do as ye're told.' He poured the thick, strong tea into tin mugs and handed them one each. 'Now—there's one or two things ye must understand to begin with. It'd be best if ye didn't call me "Uncle" in front of the other servants—and don't let on ye're Catholic. People in these parts have no time for popery. Then ye must learn to hold your tongues and speak only when ye're spoken to. D'ye see?'

They nodded, Kathleen eagerly—Patrick reluctantly.

'What will we have to do, Uncle?' Kathleen

asked.

'Well—' Seamus leaned back, sucking at his pipe. 'I've permission to take on a "tiger".' He looked at the two puzzled faces. 'That's a lad to travel with the carriage,' he explained. 'To hold the horses' heads and hand the ladies in and out. Of course there'd be other jobs around the stables and the kitchen for ye to do, lad,' he said to Patrick. 'As for you, Kathleen, it'll be up to Mrs Brown, the housekeeper. She's wantin' a scullery maid and I dare say ye'll do, but she'll be wantin' to look ye over.' He frowned, looking thoughtfully at the ragged dress and dirty face. 'The pair o' yous'll have to get some o' that muck off before we goes any further. Patrick can swill off at the pump in the yard but I'll have to see what I can fix for you.' He nodded at Kathleen and rose from his chair but Patrick spoke as he did so.

'An' will we get paid for our services, Uncle?'

Seamus thrust his thumbs into his braces as he looked at the lad. 'Paid is it? I was about your age when I came into service, lad. All I got then was me bed and board and a sound thrashin' when I put a foot wrong!' He shook his head. 'But things is different now. You'll be bonded for a year and your payment for that time will be five pounds.' He paused to let this piece of information sink in, then added: 'You'll get your livery too and by the look o' ye

13

I'm thinkin' it'll have to be a new one. Sure ye're twice the size o' the last 'tiger'. It'll be made by the finest tailor in town, lad, so ye see you'll be well off—eatin' the same food as the gentry an' no worries about the roof leakin' eh?'

Kathleen nodded with a sigh. It sounded blissful to her. She well remembered the crude cabin where she had been born, with its earth floor, smoking fireplace and leaking roof. Looking round, her uncle's quarters looked like a little palace to her, so snug and warm. She thought sadly of her father. If only he could have spent his last days in such comfort. Patrick touched her arm. 'There's a comb in the bundle. Will you tidy your hair?'

But Seamus waved a hand at him. 'Never mind. I'll take her over to the house—to Sarah. She's the kitchen maid and a grand lass. She'll see to her.' He held out a rough brown hand to Kathleen. 'Make haste now, girl. Patrick'll have to stay here with me, but you'll see him again later.'

Sarah sat dozing by the kitchen fire, a pile of rough mending at her side on a table. She was the lowest member of the household and this was the only peaceful moment of her day, when Cook and Mrs Brown were having their afternoon rest and the rest of the servants were about their business. When Seamus came in at the back door she started and snatched up a stocking, bending her head over it in an attempt to look diligent.

Seamus laughed. ' 'Tis all right, Sarah. 'Tis only me.'

The girl flushed and looked up, laughing. 'Oh, Mr Reardon, you frightened the life out of me!' She caught sight of Kathleen and broke off. 'Oh—is this—?'

'Me niece, Kathleen.' Seamus pushed Kathleen forward. 'She's been travellin' for over a month and in a sorry state as ye can see. I'd be grateful if ye could clean her up a bit, Sarah. If Mrs Brown sees her like this—'

'Say no more, Mr Reardon!' Sarah threw her hands up. 'Don't worry. I'll see she's fit.' Her broad, shiny face was compassionate and Kathleen liked her on sight. 'You leave her with me now. Cook won't stir for another hour. I'll get the tub out.' She eyed Kathleen swiftly. 'Have you got another frock, duck?' Kathleen shook her head, blushing with shame again, but Sarah patted her shoulder. She had come to Denmark House three years ago from the workhouse and poverty was no novelty to her. 'Never you mind. I'll find something clean and decent for you to put on.'

With Seamus out of the way, Sarah lost no time in hauling the tin bath out of the laundry and filling it from cans heated on the range fire. The whole exercise took almost half an hour but at last the bath was ready. She tied a large apron round her plump waist and rolled up her sleeves, looking expectantly at Kathleen.

15

'In with you then, duck, and I'll have you clean in no time.'

Kathleen looked apprehensively at the steaming water in the tub and at Sarah's large hands and arms. 'Have I to—get in—*right* in—with all me clothes off?' she asked fearfully.

Sarah's broad face beamed with amusement. 'O' course—unless you want to get in with 'em on! Come on, make haste, duck. We don't want Cook or Mrs Brown to walk in, do we?'

Slipping the dirt-caked dress and shawl to the floor Kathleen stepped into the warm water and sat down, allowing Sarah's capable hands to soap and wash her with surprising gentleness, lathering also the long hair that hung down her back. When she stepped out, Sarah wrapped her in a large rough towel which had been placed before the fire, and rubbed her dry.

'I found this old dress of Miss Caroline's,' Sarah said, slipping the garment over Kathleen's head. 'It was given to me a long time ago but it was always too small for me. There!' She sat back on her heels to survey her handiwork. Kathleen's damp hair, now combed and free of tangles, hung in soft waves to her waist and as it dried, Sarah could see that it was a delightful bronze colour. Her skin was the colour of rich cream and her eyes were a deep violet blue. Inside Sarah's breast there was a soft, full feeling—a feeling of maternal tenderness.

16

'There, you look right handsome now,' she said, smiling. 'Don't you worry about nothing. Sarah'll take care o' you.' She rose to her feet and began to gather up the wet towels. 'Come on, now. Help me put away the bath and things, then I'll let Mrs Brown know you're here.'

Outside the housekeeper's room Sarah gave Kathleen's arm a squeeze.

'Don't worry now. Her bark's worse than her bite. Just remember to speak up. I'll be in the kitchen when you're done. You know the way back, don't you?'

Although Kathleen nodded, she wasn't at all sure. They scemed to have walked along miles of twisting passages and up and down many steps to get here. Sarah tapped on the door and entered the room, bobbing respectfully to someone out of Kathleen's line of vision.

'Please, Mrs Brown, here's Mr Reardon's niece come for the post of scullery maid. Her name's Kathleen, if you please.'

'Bring her in, then you may go, Sarah.' The voice was deep and sounded to Kathleen like rumbling thunder. She felt a sick churning in her stomach as Sarah put out a hand and drew her into the room. Then she was gone, closing the door and leaving her standing in the middle of the floor feeling lost and alone.

The room was the finest she had ever seen. The floor she stood upon was covered in a rich red carpet whilst the table at which the

17

formidable Mrs Brown sat was of shining polished wood. In the fireplace a bright fire burned, reflecting its light on the brass fender and irons.

Mrs Brown eyed Kathleen through steel-rimmed spectacles which seemed precariously perched on her thin nose. She wore a snowy lace cap on her greying hair, and her board-like bosom, which was all Kathleen could see of her person, was hung about with jet beads, glowing dully against the black bombazine of her dress.

'Well child—and what have you to say for yourself?' she asked Kathleen, who stood rooted to the floor with fear. She swallowed twice and tried to find her voice, but it refused to come. Her face flushed and her eyes filled with tears.

Mrs Brown leaned forward and peered at her short-sightedly. 'Come child, speak up! Has the cat got your tongue? Do you not know that it is extremely impolite to remain silent when you are spoken to?'

Kathleen took a deep breath. 'Yes,' she squeaked.

The housekeeper nodded. 'Then pray tell me what household experience you have.'

'I looked after me Da and me brother Patrick ever since me Ma died,' she said.

Mrs Brown blinked at her from behind the spectacles. Really! The girl spoke like a foreigner. One could scarcely understand her.

18

'When you address me you call me ma'am, girl.'

'Yes—ma'am.'

'And when did your unfortunate mother die?'

'Four years ago—ma'am.'

'And how old are you now, girl?'

'Fourteen, ma'am.'

Mrs Brown sniffed disapprovingly. She had heard stories about the Irish: wild, uncivilised people who lived like animals in hovels—indeed *shared* their homes with animals as often as not! Anything this girl may have learned in the way of household matters would more than likely have to be *un*learned! She stared at the girl, standing there in a cast-off dress and slippers too large for her. At least the child seemed docile. That at least was something to be thankful for. However much she would have wished the mistress to leave the choosing of kitchen girls to her entirely, she had to admit that the girl seemed willing to please.

'No doubt you are acquainted with the method of lighting a fire, girl?' she boomed. Kathleen nodded. 'And that of scrubbing floors and washing up dishes?' Another nod from Kathleen brought a rebuke: 'Answer properly, child!'

'Yes—I mean, yes, ma'am.' Kathleen flushed painfully.

'That is better. I shall give you a trial,

19

Kathleen, and we shall see how quickly you will learn,' the housekeeper said. 'You will take your orders from Cook and help Sarah. You will be provided with two dresses for which you will be responsible and at all times you must appear clean and tidy. Do you understand, girl?'

'Yes, ma'am.'

'Then you may go.'

Somehow Kathleen was out in the passage again. She felt dazed. It seemed the job was hers! She drew a sigh of relief. What would she have done if she had been turned away—parted from Patrick? She walked along the passage, turned a corner and descended a flight of stairs. At the bottom was a green-lined door standing half open. Unsure, she hesitated. Was this the way? She did not remember this door, but then she had been too nervous to take much notice of anything.

She pushed the door open and stepped through on to the other side and at once her eyes opened wide. She might have stepped into another world. She found herself standing in an elegant hallway, the like of which she had never set eyes on. The floor was of black and white marble squares and a wide staircase curved upwards from it with a beautifully carved banister. The furniture was also richly carved, heavy and ornate. On her right a door stood open and she moved to the threshold, gazing in wonder at a blue and white drawing-room. There was a white marble fireplace in which a fire burned brightly. Blue brocade curtains hung at the long windows which looked out over smooth green lawns, and a soft blue carpet lay under her feet. The furniture was like something from a dream and in one corner a girl a few years older than herself was playing on a piano, a sound that Kathleen had never heard before but thought the most beautiful she had ever heard.

Suddenly a voice spoke sharply behind her: 'Who are you, pray? And what do you think you are doing?'

Kathleen spun round to see another girl eyeing her indignantly. She wore a beautiful pink gown with tiny black kid slippers and her fair hair hung in two dainty bunches of ringlets over her ears. Kathleen stared at her in amazement.

'I—I'm Kathleen Reardon, please, miss. I'm to be the new scullery maid.'

'Then what, pray, are you doing in the drawing-room?' the girl asked shrilly. 'Get out—do you hear? And don't let anyone catch you gawping about up here again.'

Kathleen's eyes were wide with fear as she looked around for some means of escape. The door through which she had come was part of the pale wood panelling and now that it was shut she could not see where it had been. Suddenly another voice spoke. The girl who had been playing the piano had stopped and

21

was walking towards them across the elegant room.

'Caroline—please. Can you not see that you are frightening the girl?' She looked kindly at Kathleen and said: 'You must be Reardon's niece, from Ireland.'

Kathleen nodded, then remembered her manners and said: 'Yes—if you please, miss.'

'Well I am Miss Melissa Quincey and this is my sister, Caroline. What is your name?'

'Kathleen, miss.'

'Are you lost, Kathleen?' Kathleen nodded, blushing. 'Come with me then, and I will show you the way back to the kitchen.' She opened the door in the panelling and together they stepped through into the passage beyond. Kathleen followed Miss Melissa, thinking how lovely she was, tall and slim, moving with such grace, like a dancer. She wore her brown hair in a smooth chignon which showed off the beauty of her classic features and her cream silk gown was perfection in Kathleen's eyes. At last she stopped and pointed.

'If you go down those stairs you will find the kitchen door at the bottom.' She stood aside for Kathleen to pass. 'I hope you will be happy working here at Denmark House,' she said.

Kathleen flushed with pleasure and dropped a curtsy in the way she had seen Sarah do. 'Thank you, miss,' she mumbled, then watched as Miss Melissa walked back along the passage. At that moment she would

22

happily have died for her.

The hours that followed were a confusing blur to Kathleen. To her, Cook was a red-faced, bustling virago while Mr Simpson, the tall man in the black suit who Sarah told her was the butler, seemed terrifyingly stern and forbidding. Sarah told her to keep out of the way but watch as much as she could and as she did so her heart sank lower and lower with every minute. She would surely never remember where everything was kept and would just as surely earn the disapproval of everyone with her incompetence.

When the first rush of serving dinner was over she was kept busy in the scullery at the shallow stone sink, helping Sarah to wash up. Finally the last dish was put away and the candles were lit for retiring. She was to share Sarah's room over the laundry and one of the grooms had already set up another truckle bed there for her.

To her delight she found her dresses laid out for her—two, just as Mrs Brown had promised, made of blue cotton material along with mob-caps and aprons. She fell upon them with a cry of pleasure. Never in her whole life had she had anything so fine to wear.

'Look Sarah, new dresses! And did ye ever see such a grand blue?'

But Sarah could only yawn. 'Better get into bed and get some sleep,' she advised sensibly. 'We've to be up at five. You've a lot to learn tomorrow.'

And so she would; though just now she didn't know how she would learn it with her head already so full of new things. When she closed her eyes it was as though a kaleidoscope whirled inside her brain. A kaleidoscope of sights and sounds—ships and fine houses, red hurrying faces and black bombazine, dirty dishes and grand new blue cotton dresses. But through it all shone the face of Miss Melissa and the sound of the piano playing in the blue and white drawing-room upstairs.

\*     \*     \*

Sarah's was not the only room in which an extra bed had been erected. Patrick was to share his uncle's quarters above the coach-house. All the grooms and the gardeners 'lived out' and Seamus's room was the only accommodation for outside staff at Denmark House. There had been no warm bath before the kitchen fire for Patrick. He had stripped and washed himself at the pump in the yard, then Seamus had found him a shirt and an old pair of breeches. He was a small man and this tall lad more than filled his clothes.

As he'd watched the boy dress, Seamus had sucked his pipe thoughtfully. The rippling muscles under the dusky skin and the promise of power in the broadening shoulders augured well. Seamus would train him thoroughly—

24

first as groom and 'tiger', later as coachman, perhaps to replace himself when the time came. True, the lad was not of his blood, but his brother Michael had been fond of him, he had heard, and wasn't he the nearest that Seamus would ever have to a son of his own? All the same, there was something about the boy that made him uneasy—a certain set of the mouth, a hint of fire in those gipsy eyes. He hoped he'd not turn out to be a wild one. The old man sighed. Ah well, it would all be as God willed. And anyway, hadn't he tamed and broken many a fiery stallion in his time?

As they lay in their beds in the light of the dying fire Patrick asked: 'Who is Mr Quincey, Uncle? Is he a lord?'

Seamus laughed softly. 'Henry Quincey—a lord? That's a good one to be sure! Though there's times I'm sure he thinks he is!' There was a creak as he rolled over to peer through the dim light at his nephew. 'Henry Quincey's a businessman and a clever one. His father was a farmer and Mr Henry inherited from him, but he didn't let it rest at that. He owns four farms now, a fine mill and a ropewalk over the other side o' the river. Then there's a fleet o' barges—and two years ago he started a brewery too. Oh yes, a fine headpiece has Mr Quincey.'

'A farmer's son!' breathed Patrick. 'Then he was no better than me when he started!'

But Seamus shook his head. 'Not a tenant

25

farmer, lad, like your Da, but a man who owned his own land. Ah, there was money there at the start, make no mistake.' He raised himself on one elbow and glared across at Patrick. 'I don't want to hear no talk about servants bein' as good as their masters either!' he growled. 'Henry Quincey may not be a lord but he's as good as one in this town. He has money and power and he can crush his enemies as if they was beetles—so make sure you don't become one of them. D'ye understand, lad?'

But Patrick lay with his hands behind his head, thinking of all he had seen today: the stables full of beautiful animals, the two fine carriages, the scurrying grooms and the brigade of servants. He had glimpsed the gardens and beyond them, a great park. There would be more too. Luxury and splendour inside the house such as he and Kathy had never dreamed of and all of it belonging to the son of a humble farmer.

'This house—' he asked. 'Did he build it himself?'

Seamus gave a short bark of laughter. 'Huh! Ignorant boy. This house is more'n a hundred years old! No, he came into it when the mistress's father died. Mrs Quincey was the daughter of Sir Edward Graves before she married. He was Member of Parliament for these parts for years and the mistress was his only child.'

Patrick's eyes glowed. 'Ah, so he married into money too?'

Seamus turned over, his feeling of uneasiness growing. 'He did not! Old Sir Edward wasn't well off for all his fine house and position. Sure I should know, for I served him before I served Mr Quincey. No, all he got out of the marriage was the position. They do say that the mistress is related to the nobility. But it was Quincey money that put Denmark House to rights and made it the grand place it is today.' He peered at his nephew through the gathering darkness. 'But none o' this is any o' your business, lad. 'Tis ours to serve—not to ask questions.'

But Patrick knew that he *must* ask questions. He had been asking questions all his life. Wasn't his very existence a question? He knew he would never rest until he knew the answers to them all.

'Uncle,' he whispered. 'Can you read and write?'

Seamus grunted impatiently. 'No I can*not*. And 'tis wishin' for things like that as brings the downfall o' the likes o' us. If ye take my advice, ye'll keep to your station in life—know it, keep to it and be proud of it. Anything else is folly.'

But Patrick smiled in the darkness. It was not a smile of pleasure but one of grim determination. He made up his mind there and then that he would better himself or die in the attempt, and now he knew what must be the first step. Inside him burned a fire of fierce resentment. All his life he had been looked down on. He lacked something that others— even the poorest of them—had: a name of his own, for he had always known that Michael Reardon was not his true father. At times it had seemed to him that there was nothing in the world that he could truly call his own— even Kathleen was not his sister by blood tie. All he had was himself; his person; his body and strength and he knew that each day he was growing bigger and stronger. One day, he promised himself fiercely—one day he would be powerful in other ways too. He would own a fine house and land and he would show people that Patrick Reardon was a force to be reckoned with. He would—by God he would!

## CHAPTER TWO

'Oh, Patrick, you'll never believe how grand it is!'

Kathleen sat on a pile of straw in one corner of the stable watching her brother groom Bonny, Miss Caroline's pony. 'Stevens, she's the parlour maid, took me round yesterday when everyone was out visitin'. Oh, I wish you could see it all!'

Patrick smiled affectionately at her. 'So you

like it here. Do they treat you well?'

Kathleen nodded doubtfully. 'Cook's a bit fierce—so is Mrs Brown. She's the housekeeper. She comes down to the kitchen every mornin' to inspect us all and if there's as much as a speck of dirt on you—' she rolled her eyes. 'Oh, she's a tongue on her that would shrivel you up, Patrick.'

He laughed. 'Then you'd better watch out.'

'All the others are nice, though,' she went on. 'Specially Sarah. She's me best friend. You haven't said I look nice.' She stood up and pirouetted for him. 'Don't I look grand? I've *two* dresses like this. Aren't they a grand colour blue?'

He looked at the cotton dress and the calico apron she wore over it. She had pulled off the mob-cap when she came into the stable and her bronze hair hung down her back, clean and shining. Her cheeks were pink and her blue eyes sparkled. His heart contracted. To him she looked prettier than all the grand ladies in the land, though he'd never have told her so. He nodded.

'You'll do well enough.' He put down his curry-comb and came over to her. 'Now, Kathleen, you know well enough that I like to see you, but are you sure you should be here? We don't want any trouble.'

She pouted. 'Ah, Patrick. We've been here more than three weeks now and this is the first time I've seen ye to speak to.'

29

He nodded patiently. 'Sure I know that. But did ye ask if ye could come?'

She bit her lip and reached out a hand to pat the pony's shining flank. 'Is this Miss Caroline's pony, did ye say?' she asked, changing the subject. 'Sure she's a terrible temper on her, that one. She shouted at me on me first day here and Sarah said she threw a shoe at her once. Have you seen her?'

Patrick nodded. 'Don't I see them all every mornin' when they go for their ride?'

Kathleen looked at him sideways. 'She's pretty, I suppose—do you think so?'

His eyes sparkled wickedly. 'Sure she must be the most beautiful young lady in the world,' he said fervently.

Her eyes opened wide. 'Do you think so? Is she—is she prettier than me?'

He frowned. 'Oh *far* prettier.' He looked at her crestfallen face for a moment, then, unable to keep his face straight he burst out laughing, his dark eyes dancing with merriment and his white teeth gleaming. Kathleen threw herself at him, a small bundle of bronze fury.

'Why Patrick Reardon, you're a devil—a *devil!*' She pummelled her small fists against his chest and reached up to pull his curly hair whilst he protested, laughing. At last he caught both her hands on one of his and held her fast.

'You're a little she-cat, Kathleen Reardon. And you'll have to learn that there are far finer and prettier girls than you in the world.

Sure you're too vain be half!'

She stared at him and for a moment he thought she was going to cry, but instead she said in a small voice:

'It's not what I am, but what you think of me, Patrick. That's all I care about.'

His heart softened as he looked into the great blue eyes and he patted her shoulder awkwardly.

'Sure I'm only teasin',' he said gruffly. 'Haven't ye the sense to see that, you great baby?'

'So *here* you are!' Sarah spoke from the doorway, her plain face shining pink with exertion. 'I've been looking everywhere for you. Cook's goin' mad! There's a pile of vegetables a mile high to do for tonight's dinner. You'd better make haste and come wi' me.' She glanced shyly at Patrick and muttered: 'Good-day.'

He nodded and turned away, resuming his grooming. 'Get along now, Kathleen,' he said gravely. 'And see ye don't come out here again without askin' first. D'ye want to lose your place?'

As the girls hurried across the stable-yard and through the gate into the kitchen garden, Sarah looked at Kathleen.

'I'd put that cap on if I was you and tidy yourself up a bit,' she advised. 'What have you been up to?'

Kathleen smiled. 'Patrick was teasin' me—

sayin' how pretty he thought Miss Caroline was. But he only said it to make me mad.'

Sarah smiled too. 'It must be nice to have a brother, and such a good-lookin' one. How old is he?'

'Almost sixteen,' Kathleen told her proudly. 'But he's not really me brother.'

Sarah stared at her. 'But I thought he *was.*'

'No. Me Da married *his* Ma after *mine* died—but she'd already got him,' Kathleen explained. 'So he's no relation at all except that we was brought up by the same man and woman.' She lifted her chin. 'Sure one day I'm goin' to marry Patrick.'

Sarah laughed. 'Oh—and does *he* know that?'

'He does not—and don't you dare tell him!' Kathleen stopped to tuck the last strand of hair under her mob-cap. 'I love Patrick and I could never marry any other man, but he must never know it!'

Sarah shook her head. 'Then I don't see how it can happen.'

'It'll happen sure enough,' said Kathleen with a secret smile. 'When the time comes he'll know it all by himself.'

Although the Reardons had been at Denmark House for close on a month, Patrick had seen little of his employer, Henry Quincey. Each morning he went to his office in the town, driven by Seamus in the new brougham. Occasionally he rode in the park in the early morning with his daughters, but Patrick had seen him only at a distance: a large, broad-shouldered man with the build and the ruddy complexion of a farmer. He was a handsome man in his way, but there was a ruthlessness about him that made his fellow businessmen admire him, and his subordinates cringe. He fascinated Patrick, as indeed the whole family fascinated him: Mrs Quincey, whom he seldom saw, with her delicate fair colouring and queenly manner; the daughters, Miss Caroline and Miss Melissa, the former haughty and spirited, while the latter was quiet and gentle. Then there was the baby of the family, Master Paul, a little boy of seven who sometimes came to the stables with his governess, a small mouse-like young woman of about eighteen, whose name, he soon learned, was Miss Agnes Dale. It was on this young woman that Patrick concentrated his attention—for the moment, at least. For it was she who had, and could impart, something he desired very much indeed. Moreover, there was no time to be lost in getting it. Master Paul, he had heard, was to go away to school next year. He must move quickly if he were to carry out the plan which was evolving in his mind.

So it was that the next time little Paul Quincey came to the stables with his governess they found Patrick busying himself in the yard. He made himself agreeable to the boy, walking him round on his father's huge hunter and letting him help to polish the saddles in the tackroom. But all the time his eyes were on Agnes Dale, small and insignificant in her plain grey dress with its neat white collar. She had a pale, oval face in which hazel eyes watched warily and he noticed the nervous way in which her hands kept fluttering to her hair. At last he spoke to her:

'Would you be from these parts, miss?'

She flushed painfully. 'I? Yes. I am from a village eight miles from Elvemere—Malfrey Chapel. My father is vicar there.'

'I see. I come from Ireland meself,' he told her. 'From Bansha village in County Limerick.'

She nodded. 'That is a great way off. You must miss your country and your family very much.'

He shook his head. 'Sure I have no home or family, miss. Me father died and me an' me sister was thrown off our farm.'

She bit her lip. 'Oh—how dreadful for you.'

He nodded. 'If me father hadn't managed to get word to me uncle I'm sure I don't know what would have become of us.'

'I'm—glad it all turned out well for you.' She blushed again and turned away awkwardly.

'Oh, I don't ask for sympathy, miss,' Patrick said boldly. 'Now that I've got me chance I'm goin' to take it. I've no intention of stayin' a poor man all me life!'

She turned again to look at him in surprise. He spoke with such firmness, such resolution;

not like a penniless orphan at all! 'I am glad to hear it,' she said with a smile.

He smiled back at her, his dark eyes alight with charm and his teeth showing white against his brown skin. 'Sure it'd be nice if we could be friends, miss,' he said firmly. 'You're just the kind of young woman I admire.'

Agnes felt her cheeks burn. She knew she should really be indignant. Surely this stable-lad realised that she was above him in station. But he seemed to have no such notion, or if he did he ignored it. The way his eyes swept over her, openly admiring. No one—no *man* had ever . . . She cleared her throat delicately.

'It is time I took Master Paul back to the nursery for tea,' she said breathlessly.

Patrick shook his head, smiling disarmingly. 'Look at the boy. He's enjoyin' himself. Sure you can spare a moment or two longer.'

'No, really—I must go.' She called to the child: 'Paul! Come now, it's time for tea. Nurse will be cross if we are late.' She looked up to find that Patrick was still smiling at her.

'Will ye come again tomorrow, miss?'

She hesitated, lowering her eyes, but the little boy who had heard, cried:

'Oh yes, please, Miss Dale—Agnes please!'

'Agnes—what a pretty name to be sure. Well—will ye come—Agnes?' Patrick asked softly.

She took the child by the hand briskly. 'We shall see,' she said. And looking at her pink cheeks Patrick knew that she would do more than 'see'.

After that Agnes came to the stables almost every day with her charge. The little boy took a great fancy to Patrick who constantly thought up new ways of amusing him and when, one day about two weeks later, he saw him go out with his mother in the carriage, he saw his opportunity. By now he knew that Agnes was fond of the garden and he guessed that being a fine day, that was where she would spend her free time. When all was quiet he set off to find her.

She was, as he had suspected, in the rose garden, seated in one of the arbours reading a book. She looked up, quite startled at his approach.

'Oh! I didn't know—'

'I thought you might be here,' he said. 'May I join you?'

She bit her lip, looking round. 'But—are you allowed? If you were discovered might it mean trouble for you? I would hate—' She stopped as he stepped into the arbour and sat down on the bench beside her looking into her eyes.

'It's good of you to worry about me, Agnes, but to tell the truth it's worse trouble for me not to see you. Please—may I stay a moment?'

She nodded, confused. 'Well—yes—if you think—' She broke off, rendered suddenly speechless by the brilliance of his smile. When he looked at her like that something very strange happened to her breathing, making speech difficult. It was really most foolish of her. She had made discreet enquiries and she knew that he was two years younger than she—yet he seemed such a man. They really should not be alone together like this. It was quite outrageous!

'What's that you're readin'?' Patrick asked, breaking through her disquieting thoughts. She handed him the small, leather-bound volume, but he shook his head, smiling wryly.

'Sure don't you know, Agnes, that I'm only a poor ignorant Irish boy? I can't read. You'll have to tell me what it is.'

'Oh—I'm sorry, Patrick.' She cleared her throat nervously. 'It is poetry—the poetry of poor dear Mr Shelley.'

He smiled at her. 'Is that right? Would ye do me a great kindness, Agnes—would you read some of it to me?'

She shook her head, blushing with embarrassment, but he took the book gently from her and opened it at random.

'Ah, please—' he held it out to her. 'Read me that one.'

She glanced at the poem he had chosen, *The Indian Serenade*, and her cheeks burned crimson. 'Oh—I—I couldn't!'

'Go on, Agnes. It'd be such a treat for me an' sure I can't read it for meself, now can I?'

She looked into his imploring eyes and

37

moistened her lips with the tip of her tongue. 'Oh—very well then.' She cleared her throat and began:

I arise from dreams of thee
In the first sweet sleep of night,
When the winds are breathing low,
And the stars are burning bright.
I arise from dreams of thee,
And a spirit in my feet
Hath led me—who knows how?
To thy chamber window, sweet.

She stopped, her eyes still on the page, and he let out a long breath.

'Ah, isn't that beautiful? Is that truly what it says—there on that page?' She nodded and he put his finger under her chin and raised her face to look at him. 'Isn't it strange that I should have chosen that one—an' me not knowin'? Because it's just what I feel, Agnes. I do dream of you when I sleep at night. And wouldn't I like to do just as it says there: Come to your window—sweet?' He bent his head and gently kissed her on the lips. He knew that he was taking a chance—that she might thrust him from her and run away, ruining everything. But something—some instinct beyond his years told him that he was safe. The next moment he was proved right. Agnes lifted both her arms and wound them around his neck, kissing him with a passion that set her small, ladylike body trembling. The book of poems fell to the ground with a soft thud and Patrick slid his arms round Agnes and held her close while his heart raced triumphantly.

'Will—will you do something for me, Agnes?' he whispered huskily. She looked up at him through half-closed eyes, her lips softly parted. 'Anything, dearest—anything. Only ask.'

'Will you teach me to read?'

Her eyes flew open and he added quickly: 'So that I can read the poems too—so that we can read them together.'

She sighed and drew his head onto her breast. 'Of course I will, my darling. I should love to do it.'

It was arranged between them that every evening after Master Paul was in bed and while the family was at dinner, they would steal away to a disused potting-shed which Patrick had discovered behind the glasshouse at the end of the kitchen garden. Together there they each learned happily—Patrick, to read and write and Agnes, to love, with every fibre of her small quivering being.

It was not until the middle of July that the two younger Reardons learned that there was another member of the Quincey family, one of whom they had so far been unaware. It was Kathleen who first gave Patrick the news on one of her morning visits to him, on the way to the kitchen garden. It was one of her jobs to take Cook's list to Mr Hobson, the gardener, first thing after breakfast and she had fallen into the habit of visiting Patrick while she waited for the vegetables to be gathered.

'They're all talkin' about young Mr Charles comin' home,' she told him, selecting a straw to chew.

He straightened his back to look at her. 'Mr Charles? Who's he when he's at home?'

'Don't ye know?' She seated herself comfortably on a pile of straw, delighted to tell him something new. 'He's the eldest son—the heir, Cook calls him. He's away at a grand school and he's comin' home for the holidays. They say he's very fond of riding and there's a new horse comin' for him, so I dare say you'll see a lot of him.' She regarded him, her head on one side. 'Fancy you not knowin'.'

He shrugged. 'Why should anyone tell me?' But nevertheless, he asked Seamus the next time he saw him, feeling it was odd that there had been no mention of the young gentleman.

Seamus nodded. 'Mr Charles? Right enough. It must soon be time for him comin' home.'

'I hear there's to be a new horse for him,' Patrick said.

A frown crossed the coachman's face. 'That's right. A fine bay gelding. It was bought some time ago. 'Tis a good thing you reminded me. We'd better make ready for the creature.' He glanced at Patrick. 'You'd best watch out

40

for Mr Charles,' he warned. 'A very well set up young gentleman and very fussy about his mounts. He'll keep ye on your toes right enough!'

'What age would he be?' Patrick asked uneasily.

Seamus closed his eyes and screwed up his face in concentration. 'Well now, let me think—he must have been born in 1820 because it was the year that the Prince Regent became King George. I was workin' for Sir Edward Graves then, when he had his estate in the old country and I remember what rejoicin' there was when it was known that the only child, Mrs Quincey, had given birth to a son.' He shook his head sadly. 'Poor Sir Edward died a few years after that and the estate in County Wicklow had to be sold to pay off his debts. Mr Quincey, he come over and bought up some o' the fine furniture and it was then that he offered me the job o' coachman to himself.'

'Yes, but how *old* is Mr Charles?' Patrick asked, impatient with the old man's reminiscent ramblings.

Seamus's eyes snapped open. 'Why, he'd be eighteen at that rate. Can ye not count, lad?' He nodded. 'Yes, eighteen this August and the new horse is to be a birthday present.'

\*     \*     \*

It was a week later that Charles Quincey

41

arrived home. Seamus went off to collect him from the Stage which was due at the White Hart Inn at four in the afternoon and the whole house seemed to be in a turmoil of excitement.

'They say Mrs Quincey's in a great stew of excitement,' Kathleen told him the following morning. 'Everyone says he's her favourite—her first born.' She sighed. 'I haven't seen him yet but they say he's ever so handsome—clever too. Good at everything. They say he's the apple of his father's eye and that he'll be rich when he dies.' She spread her arms. 'All this will be his—all them fine farms—everything.' She looked at him wistfully. 'It seems funny that folk can have so much while others have nothin' at all, doesn't it?'

Patrick frowned at her. 'Have ye no work to do, Kathleen Reardon? Have ye nothin' to do but drive a feller mad with your senseless yappin'?' He saw her lip tremble and was sorry at once for being sharp with her. 'Ah go on with ye,' he said, annoyed still more at his sudden feeling of weakness. 'Away to the kitchen with ye before they come lookin' for ye. If that tongue o' yours don't lose ye your place before you're done me name's not Patrick Reardon!'

Kathleen thrust her chin out at him defiantly. 'I'll not lose me place, so I won't! Sure I'm goin' to be a lady's maid one day, you just see if I don't!'

He stared at her. 'You! A lady's maid? And how do ye think you'll manage that? Sure ye can't even keep your own hair tidy!'

She pulled on her cap, flushing as she stuffed handfuls of bright hair under it. 'I can learn, can't I? If you can learn, so can I!'

He stared at her, the colour leaving his face. Had she somehow discovered his secret—the illicit reading lessons in the potting-shed. He strode towards her and grasped her by the shoulders, glaring down at her, his eyes black with anger.

'And what do ye mean by that, girl? Tell me, d'ye hear? Just you tell me!'

Tears sprang to her eyes as she shrank from him in fear. 'Nothin'!' Her voice trembled. 'Why I only meant that if you could learn to be a coachman one day, then surely I could learn to be a lady's maid.'

He loosened his grip on her abruptly, relieved, yet still angry with her. 'Go on back to the kitchen before ye bring trouble on the both of us,' he growled, turning away.

For a moment she hesitated, then reached out and touched his arm. 'Patrick—what's the matter with you?' she asked gently. 'Aren't you happy here? You're always so—so *angry* lately. Is it me?'

He shook his head, biting his lip, a little ashamed. 'Of course it's not you, Kathy. It's just that I—Oh!' He struck his forehead with the palm of his hand in a gesture of frustration. 'I don't want to be a servant, Kathy—even a high up one. I *hate* it. I want to be *free!*'

She looked at him perplexedly. 'But what else could the likes of us be, Patrick? We're lucky—we've a good home here, more food than we ever ate in our lives before. Isn't that bein' free?'

'No—no, it isn't!' His face creased and he threw himself down on the straw. 'You don't see, do ye, Kathy? I can't make ye understand how I feel. I want to be rich and powerful— like Mr Quincey. Not cleanin' out stables for the rest o' me life!'

Gently, she sank down beside him and stroked back the thick dark curls from his brow. 'Oh, Patrick. How could you ever be rich like the master? Why ye might as well wish to be the King himself!' She smiled at him lovingly. 'You're worth a hundred Mr Quinceys to me, Patrick,' she told him shyly. 'I love you more 'n anything else in the whole wide world.' And she put her arms round his neck and kissed him.

He put her from him gently but firmly. 'You mustn't do that any more, Kathy,' he said kindly. 'We're not children any longer and you know quite well that you're not really me sister.'

'Of course I know,' she said, shaking her head in bewilderment. 'Sure isn't *that* the very reason why I did it? It's why I said I loved ye too—cos I thought it'd make ye feel better, ye great black bear!'

The bitter feeling inside his breast softened as he looked into the naive innocence of her blue eyes and he caught her impulsively to him in a quick hug, laughing gently.

'Oh, Kathy—sweet little Kathy. What in the world would I do without ye?'

Kathleen's heart sang with joy. There was no one anywhere like her Patrick—no one!'

As Seamus had said, Charles Quincey's new mount was a highly bred bay gelding and when it arrived next day at the stables of Denmark House Patrick fell in love with the animal on sight. There was something about its restless fiery spirit that he identified with and it was soon obvious that the gelding felt the affinity too, for Patrick was the only person who proved able to quiet him. He spent most of the day settling the animal in, talking to him and crooning soft snatches of old songs as he gently groomed and cosseted him. The following afternoon Charles Quincey presented himself at the stables to take a look at his new acquisition and Patrick got his first look at the young man.

Patrick first heard voices outside the stable just as he had finished feeding the gelding and a moment later the lower half of the door was pushed open and Charles Quincey confronted him, dressed in an impeccable riding costume of the latest fashion. He was tall and broad, of the same sturdy build as his father, but he had his mother's fair colouring and pale complexion. He slapped his riding crop against his thigh, which made the horse toss his head apprehensively, and regarded the animal with satisfaction.

'You can saddle him up,' he said to Patrick. 'I'm going to try him out.'

But Patrick shook his head doubtfully. 'He's just been fed, sir. If you could just give him an hour.'

Charles Quincey turned his attention to Patrick, looking him up and down arrogantly. 'Do as you're told, damn you!' he commanded. 'Who the hell are you anyway? I've never seen you before.'

The colour rose darkly in Patrick's cheeks. 'I'm Patrick Reardon, sir,' he said quietly.

'And what position do you hold in my father's household, pray?' he asked sarcastically.

Patrick did not answer and the groom who stood by the door said, 'He's to be the new tiger, sir.'

Charles Quincey walked round Patrick, eyeing him with distaste. 'I see. So we're to have an Irish 'murphy' for our tiger next, are we? And one who presumes to tell me when I may and may not ride my own horse!' He turned from Patrick with a sneer and addressed the groom. 'Have him saddled and ready in ten minutes.' Then he turned on his heel and strode away.

The groom glanced at Patrick and reached for a saddle. 'Best to do as he says. It's better not to argue with Mr Charles.' He began to saddle the animal while Patrick stood by.

'You know as well as I do what will happen,' he said. 'You'll not be able to tighten the girth enough. The saddle'll be slippin' in no time at all.'

The groom shrugged. 'Then he'll have to find out for himself, won't he. He'll not thank you for tellin' him.'

Patrick strode out of the stable angrily, leaving the groom to his task. Mrs Quincey and her daughters were going visiting that afternoon and he was to accompany the carriage for the first time. His new livery had arrived from the tailors that morning, and in the room over the coach-house he dressed himself with his uncle's help, peering doubtfully into the cracked mirror that hung over the fireplace. The livery consisted of a dark blue coat and pale yellow breeches. A grey waistcoat and a silk hat with yellow cockade completed the outfit. Patrick hated it. The high collar and stock made him feel as though he were choking and he felt hot and itchy under the thick, unfamiliar material. Seamus, on the other hand, regarded him with great approval.

'Well, ye pay for the dressin' I'll say that for ye,' he said, slapping Patrick on the back. 'I'm sure m'lady will be well pleased with ye.'

But when she saw him, Mrs Quincey looked somewhat doubtful. She paused before setting her foot delicately on the lowered carriage step and looked at Patrick who was waiting to hand her in.

'Dear me, Reardon,' she said faintly. 'Aren't you rather *large*? I thought by the way your uncle pleaded for you that you were a starving waif!'

There was a peal of laughter from Caroline Quincey who stood with her sister behind Mrs Quincey and Patrick coloured hotly. Melissa stepped forward to lay a hand on her mother's arm.

'Never mind that now, Mama. We shall be late and that would never do.' She smiled gently at Patrick. 'I think Reardon looks most impressive and you know that the last tiger was really much too small and weak to hold the horses' heads securely. Do you not remember the time they almost bolted?'

Mrs Quincey raised her eyes heavenwards. 'Indeed I do! Perhaps you are right, my dear.' She looked again at Patrick. 'You will not grow any more, will you, Reardon? It really would be most vexing if you were to get any larger!' And with this admonishment she climbed into the carriage, followed by Melissa. Caroline, who was last to get in, pulled a face at Patrick and pinched his arm painfully.

He found the afternoon tedious and boring, with nothing to do but wait for the ladies to conclude their visits. They made three in all, one quite close by and the other two further along the river, above the High Bridge. Seamus explained to him that only barges could negotiate the part of the river above this bridge and it was certainly a quieter, more rural part of the town, the landscape made gentler by the curve of the river and the trees that grew on its banks. There was a fine old church with a tall spire and an elegant vicarage, at which the Quincey ladies made one of their calls. The other call was to Willerby Hall, an ugly red-brick mansion with many turrets where, Seamus told him, lived the Misses Fairfax who were the town's benefactresses. They ran the soup kitchen in Friar's Lane and often visited the workhouse with gifts of food and clothing. But all this was of little interest to Patrick. He longed to explore the town for himself and stood first on one foot and then on the other, occasionally sliding his finger round the tight, high collar and itching uncomfortably under the hot, close-fitting livery.

At long last the ladies came down the steps of the house accompanied by two elderly ladies whom he took to be the Misses Fairfax his uncle had spoken of. One of them stepped forward to peer shortsightedly at him.

'Is this your new tiger, dear Mrs Quincey?' she asked. 'What a splendid young creature. But isn't he very dark? Almost a blackamoor!'

49

The other lady approached Patrick and pinched his upper arm speculatively. 'An excellent specimen,' she observed heartily. 'We could do with one like him to do our fetching and carrying for us. Our poor old Hoskins is getting quite feeble.'

All the time Patrick stood like stone, staring into space and trying not to show his discomfort, while out of the corner of his eye he could see Miss Caroline Quincey grimacing at him gleefully.

By the time they arrived back at Denmark House he was in a fine temper. In the coach-house he pulled off the coat and hat, throwing them into a corner with a growled oath. Seamus spun round to glare at him angrily.

'You just pick them up at once, me lad,' he shouted. 'Spoil them and you'll find your wages docked. You're responsible for the way you look and it'd better be spick an' span or I'll know the reason why. M'lady's an eye like a hawk on her for a crease or a speck o' dust!' He strutted up to Patrick and glared at him. 'Shame on yous for an ungrateful divil. How many fine suits o' clothes like that've you ever had? Made be the finest tailor in Elvemere!'

'The devil take him then!' Patrick said vehemently. 'And the whole of the Quincey family with him!' He picked up the coat and hat and flung out of the coach-house, while Seamus shouted after him:

'Just you get changed and come and help

me with this lot! And remember to put them things away carefully. And if you're not sharp about it you'll feel the back o' me hand—big as ye are!'

Patrick swore profusely under his breath and turned the corner of the coach-house. But his foot was hardly on the bottom stair when a noise made him stop and listen. From the end stable, the one furthest from him, where the new horse was stabled, came the sound of distressed whinnying.

Throwing down the coat and hat he ran down the yard, the soles of his fine new boots ringing out on the cobblestones. As he drew near to the open stable door he heard the sound of plunging hooves accompanying the frenzied whinnies and above these noises a human voice, shrill with fury:

'Throw me, would you, you brute. Well, I'll teach you! We shall see who's master!' The words were punctuated by the vicious thwacking of his crop and as Patrick stood in the doorway he saw the new horse plunge and rear in an attempt to avoid the cruel slashes. The animal was closely tethered to a ring in the stable wall, while Charles Quincey, his pale hair dishevelled and his fine new riding clothes streaked with mud and grass stains, beat the poor creature mercilessly about the face and neck.

Rage rose in Patrick's throat, almost choking him as he stared in horror at the horse's terrified wild eyes and flaring nostrils. He sprang forward, snatching the crop from Charles Quincey's hand and flinging it into a corner.

'Jesus Christ, do you want to blind him? What in God's name do you think you're doin'?' he roared.

The young man turned a red, dirt-streaked face on him, his pale blue eyes as cold and hard as ice. 'Get out of here!' he screamed. 'And mind your own damned business, you scum!'

But he had time to say no more. Patrick launched himself through the air, landing a blow in Charles Quincey's face that sent him sprawling in the straw, then he threw himself on top of the spread-eagled figure. The two rolled over and over on the stable floor, each of them using fists, knees and elbows to punish the other. Patrick could hardly see for the blind rage that consumed him. They rolled back and forth, dangerously near the kicking hooves of the terrified horse, each of them intent only on the destruction of the other. Neither of them heard the shouts and the running feet outside.

Patrick was on top. He had the better of Charles Quincey. His hands were round the thick, white throat, squeezing it in a grip of iron, his face livid with white hot hate. Then, suddenly, hands were grasping his shoulders, hauling at him. Someone struck him a blow on the base of the neck, paralysing his arm and making him loosen his grip. He let go of the boy beneath him with a groan, allowing himself to be hauled to his feet till he hung there between the two grooms, panting, his eyes as wild as those of the horse he had defended and his black hair beaded with sweat.

When the mist before his eyes cleared he saw that the two men who stood in the doorway were his uncle and Henry Quincey, his master and the father of the boy he had almost murdered, who now lay in the straw coughing and gasping for breath. His uncle's face was a mask of horror and disbelief, but on Henry Quincey's face was a smile, a cruel, sadistic smile. He strode into the stable and looked into Patrick's face, ignoring the writhing figure of his son on the ground.

'What do you mean by it?' he demanded.

'Will ye look at the animal,' Patrick gasped. 'Will ye look at the cuts on his face and neck! He might've lost his eyes—as it is he'll be nothin' but a bundle o' nerves from now on. *He* did that!' He jerked his head towards the prone figure of Charles and spat viciously on the ground.

Seamus sprang forward in horror. 'Will ye shut yer mouth, boy. Don't ye know that this is the Master? Say ye're sorry to Mr Quincey and Mr Charles.'

But Henry Quincey waved him to be silent.

He stepped forward to examine the horse's injuries, inflicted by his son's crop. He turned to Charles.

'Get up!' he commanded.

Charles Quincey rose painfully to his feet, glaring at Patrick whose sinews stiffened under the hands of the grooms who still held him.

'The brute threw me, Father,' he said. 'I was merely disciplining him—until this lout—'

'Didn't I tell you he'd just been fed?' Patrick hissed between his teeth. 'He didn't throw you, the girth slipped. I tried to tell you it would!'

'Holy Mother o' God!' wailed Seamus from the doorway. But Henry Quincey's face was expressionless as he listened to the outburst. He walked to the corner of the stable and picked up the riding crop from where Patrick had thrown it. Holding it between both hands he stood in front of Patrick, but addressed his son.

'You're a fool, boy,' he said. 'Learn to ride properly and don't take out your temper on a valuable animal when you make a stupid mistake. *Come here!*'

The boy shambled towards his father, still clutching his bruised throat. His right eye was already swollen and darkening and a trickle of blood ran from his nose.

'If you want to vent your temper on something,' his father continued calmly, 'do it on something more dispensable—like *this!*' And without warning he raised the crop and brought it down across Patrick's face, laying his cheek open from ear to jaw.

A smile spread over Charles's face and he laughed derisively as he followed his father from the stable. As Henry Quincey passed Seamus he said sternly:

'Come and see me after dinner, Reardon. We must talk about that nephew of yours.'

## CHAPTER THREE

It was almost dark when Kathleen and Sarah crept up the wooden staircase to the room above the coach-house. Sarah carried a basket containing clean rags and a jar of salve and Kathleen, a bowl of water from the pump.

They found Patrick alone, lying on his narrow cot in the furthest corner of the room. He was facing the wall but he turned his head when he heard them enter and Kathleen let out a cry as she saw by the fire's light, the scarlet gash across his cheek. Running to the bed she knelt beside him, her eyes filling with tears.

'Oh, Patrick, your face—your poor face!' She reached out to touch the broken skin but Patrick caught her fingers.

'Don't touch it. And don't fret, Kathy. It'll be all right. Sure 'tis only a scratch.'

'It's nothing of the kind.' Sarah said briskly.

'Here, move over, Kathy, and let me see to it for him.' She uncovered the basket and took out the salve. 'Cook makes this from an old recipe of her grandmother's,' she told him. 'There's cobwebs in it and if you use it twice a day it'll help you heal nicely.' Kathleen moved aside obediently, holding Patrick's hand while he allowed Sarah to clean the dried blood from the wound.

'Everyone's talkin' about what you did,' Kathleen told him proudly. 'They're all on your side. They say Mr Charles is cruel and takes a pleasure in seein' creatures suffer. They're glad you paid him for what he did.'

Sarah shook her head. 'It's not for the likes of *us* to do the payin',' she said bitterly. 'All very well for them to talk but it won't help when you lose your place, will it?'

Kathleen stared at her and then at Patrick. 'Oh, no! Oh, Patrick, what'll you do? Who'll you work for if the Master says you're to go?'

Sarah laughed shortly. 'He'll work for no one, leastways, not round here. If Henry Quincey gives him the boot no one else in Elvemere'll give him work. His lordship'll see to that!'

'Then I'll work for meself,' Patrick said stoutly. 'Either that or leave the God-forsaken place altogether.'

Panic gripped Kathleen's heart. 'If you go you'll not leave me behind, will you?' she begged.

The frown on his brow relaxed a little as he looked at her troubled face and he squeezed her arm warmly. 'You've a good place here, Kathy,' he said gently. 'You must stay. I might take to the road, see a bit of England. On me own I could do a job here and there—live rough. It'd be no life for you. And you've said yourself, you're happy here.'

Kathleen said nothing, swallowing hard and trying to still the quaking inside her when she thought of a life without Patrick. But she forgot her own feelings when Sarah pressed the salve into his wound and she saw him bite his lip till it turned white.

'There,' Sarah said. 'It'll be better in no time now. I'll leave the jar with you and you must remember to use it every day so that you won't scar.'

He thanked her, taking the jar, then they all three turned as they heard heavy steps on the stair outside. A moment later the door opened and Seamus came in. Three faces looked expectantly at him as he took off his coat.

'Well,' said Patrick gruffly. 'Am I to go then?'

Seamus shook his head. 'No. Don't ask me how it is, lad, but ye still have your place.' He reached for his old pipe. 'Mind, I had to use every bit o' blarney in me body—and didn't I have to take a fine talkin' to meself! I'm to be responsible for you from now on. Sure you'd almost have thought I *told* you to give the lad a thrashin'!' He spat resentfully into the fire. 'Anyway—' he glared threateningly at Patrick. 'If ye kick over the traces again it'll be *me* as gets the blame—so just you be remembering that, me lad.'

Patrick gave an explosive snort and strode across the room. 'Jesus! I've a mind to go anyway. It's like bein' an animal in a cage— worse!'

'Don't be a fool,' Seamus said. 'You're lucky and you don't even know it. The Master must like somethin' about you to keep you on after what you did an' the way you spoke to him.'

'Oh yes, he likes me all right. That's why he gave me this!' Patrick fingered his cheek gingerly.

Kathleen ran forward and grasped his arm. 'Uncle Seamus is right, Patrick. Stay and swallow your pride—for my sake—*please.*'

He looked down at her imploring face for a moment, then he let out a long breath. 'All right then—I'll stay. But I'll not swallow me pride for if I tried it'd choke me!' He bent and kissed her. 'Off with you now to the house. One of us in trouble is enough, as Uncle here will tell you!'

When the two girls had gone Patrick paced restlessly back and forth over the wooden floor. He felt like a caged lion. In his heart burned a fire that would give him no peace. When Henry Quincey had struck him this afternoon he had left a mark that no salve in the world would ever eradicate.

Seamus watched him silently, sucking thoughtfully at his pipe. Secretly he admired what the lad had done even though it had been madness. True, the boy had a temper which no man in his position could afford, but he had been trying to protect a helpless creature. You couldn't get away from that.

'Tell ye what, lad,' he said at length. 'When the horses are bedded down will ye come with me to the Bell Inn for a sup of ale?'

But Patrick shook his head. 'I'd not be fit company, Uncle,' he muttered. 'I just wish—I wish—Oh!' He lifted his shoulders in a helpless gesture, unable to express the turmoil within him.

The old man nodded. 'Sure I know how you feel, lad,' he said mildly. 'Haven't I been young and full o' hot blood meself?' He took a long pull at his pipe. 'Go down now and see to the horses. Mebbe the beasts'll quiet ye. Then we'll see later.'

But when he opened the door of the end stable, the sight of the still trembling horse only fanned the flames of his anger afresh. Reaching inside his shirt he brought out the salve Sarah had left him and smoothed some of it onto the inflamed skin of the animal's face and neck. As he felt the flesh twitch with pain under his fingers he clenched his teeth tightly.

'I'll stay, but it'll only be for one reason,' he

59

said aloud. 'To pay them back for what they did this day. There'll come a day when he'll grovel on his knees to me, I swear it before God!'

The horse tossed his head, nervous at the sudden tension in Patrick's voice, and he stroked the velvet nose, crooning softly: 'There, there, me lovely. 'Tis all over for you now. He'll not hurt you again while I'm here. 'Tis only me it's all startin' for.'

In the dusk a shadow fell across the stable floor and Patrick turned to see Agnes standing in the doorway.

'You didn't come,' she said breathlessly. 'I waited but you didn't come and I wondered. I heard a rumour—Oh!' Her hand flew to her mouth as she saw the gash on his cheek. 'Then it's true! Oh, my dear.'

He shook his head impatiently. ' 'Tis nothin'. I gave someone a thrashin' for ill-treatin' a horse—and got this for me pains.'

She came further into the stable and peered at him. 'Are—are you dismissed?' she asked fearfully.

He laughed. 'Not a bit of it! Sure an' didn't his lordship beg me to stay. Seems I only did what he should have done himself! If ye ask me, I think he enjoyed himself this afternoon!'

But Agnes was not deceived. Above the bravado she heard the note of bitterness and she slid her arms around his waist and laid her head against his chest. 'Will you come for your lesson now? It may soothe you.'

But Patrick was in no mood for Agnes's restful quietness. Over the wecks he had learned his letters quickly and he felt that he could do without the daily lessons now. She had lent him some books, which he hid under his pillow and studied by the light of a candle after his uncle had gone to sleep at night. He practised his writing too and he was proud of what he had managed to achieve in a short time. But he was growing tired of Agnes and her clinging possessiveness.

'Sure it's too dark to be seein' books,' he said taking her arms from around his waist. 'I'll have to go now. Maybe I'll see you tomorrow.'

Her eyes looked up at him pleadingly. 'Promise that you'll come, Patrick—promise that you'll be there.'

'I'll be there,' he said briefly, turning away. Maybe he'd take his uncle up on that offer after all, he thought as he retraced his steps. A walk and a breath of air would do him good.

Elvemere High Street was almost as bright as day as Seamus and Patrick made their way to the Bell Inn. A full summer moon threw its reflection on to the surface of the river, and lanterns winked from the masts of boats moored in the port. On the other side of the street the windows of the fine houses were alight and their gracious occupants could be glimpsed at dinner, or some genteel entertainment. They crossed the High Bridge

61

at last, leaving the river behind them, and entered the narrow, cobbled street that widened into the market-place. Until now, Patrick had only seen the town from his position on the carriage and he was fascinated to examine, on foot, the shops, inns and buildings. Behind the market-place was a network of narrow streets leading eventually back to the river; to the warehouses and coalyards and to the great corn mill that Patrick now knew belonged to Henry Quincey. It was in the shadow of this mill that the Old Bell Inn stood, a tiny thatched hostelry where Seamus went to meet his cronies in his cherished free time.

Patrick followed him into the taproom, lowering his head to pass under the low lintel, and at once he found himself in a crowded, smoke-filled room. A hoarse voice hailed Seamus and through the haze Patrick saw a red-faced man seated at the fireside, beckoning to them. Seamus dug him in the ribs.

'That's Dick Bradshaw, the saddler,' he said with a grin. 'One o' the perks o' being a coachman, me lad, is that while there's a saddler about, ye'll never go short of a free sup o' ale!'

Patrick looked puzzled. 'Why's that, Uncle?'

Seamus chuckled. 'Why, they hope they'll get a nice fat order, don't they? And Henry Quincey has the finest stable in Elvemere.

Sure they're *all* after me!'

They elbowed their way across the room to the welcoming saddler and sat with him at a beer-stained table where he lost no time in buying them each a foaming tankard of ale and offering his tobacco pouch for Seamus's pleasure. Then he and Seamus began to talk. Patrick looked around him. The place was full of working folk like Seamus and himself, all drinking and talking with obvious enjoyment. Smoke from their pipes and from the open fire filled the room to the blackened beams above, making Patrick's eyes water. The ale made them water even more and Seamus, seeing him splutter over it, said:

'Drink up, lad. None o' your brewery stuff here. 'Tis good home-brewed ale. Nothin' to touch it in the whole o' the county. Isn't that so, Dick?'

Dick agreed, laughing heartily, and ordered more ale from a fat woman in a greasy apron who was serving at the tables. He pointed to a steaming black pot that hung on a hook over the smoky fire.

'Would you fancy a bit o' supper, Seamus?' he asked. 'Molly here makes the best stew in Lincolnshire. Don't you, me love?' He gave the woman a resounding slap on the rump which she seemed to enjoy enormously.

'Will the lad have some too?' she asked with a gap-toothed smile. And they all three looked at Patrick.

But he had no stomach for the brown mess that the woman was ladling into bowls. The ale had made his head spin and the heat and smoke made him feel smothered. He rose to his feet.

'I think I'll go for a walk, Uncle,' he said. 'I'd like to look round a bit.'

Seamus wrinkled his brow. 'Don't go gettin' yourself into any more trouble now,' he warned.

But Patrick shook his head. 'I won't. I'll see you later.'

Outside he drew a deep breath. The evening air was still and heavy with dockside smells: fish, hemp, meal and rotting timber, all spiced with the salt tang from the rising tide. To the left of the Bell Inn was a boat-builder's yard and Patrick could see the outline of the dark hulks as they stood on their stocks out of the water for repair. He kicked disconsolately at a pebble, feeling sick at heart and likening himself to one of these hulks—helpless, vulnerable, like some great beached whale. Were his strength and his sense of what was right—the only powers he possessed—always to lead him into trouble? He sighed and turned his face towards the bridge, but suddenly out of the darkness a voice hailed him:

'Hey! Young Reardon—is that you?'

And he turned to see Tom Craven, the master of the *Mary Ann*, on which he and

Kathleen had made the last leg of their journey from Ireland. His heart lifted. Here was the only man he had ever known who had treated him as an equal.

'Captain Craven! 'Tis good to see ye!'

Tom grasped his hand warmly. 'Well, well and how are you, boy? And that pretty little sister o' yours? And how do you like life on this side o' the Irish sea?'

'Ah, 'tis not so bad,' Patrick said. 'Uncle Seamus is inside if ye're wantin' to see him.'

But Tom was peering more closely now at Patrick's face; noting the damage to his cheek and the look of near despair in his dark eyes.

'I dare say Seamus has company aplenty,' he said. 'But you, boy—you look as if you could do with a bit o' cheerin' up. Will you come and take a sup with me at the Calcutta?'

'The Calcutta? What's that?' Patrick asked.

Tom laughed his big hearty laugh. 'What is it? Why a little bit o' Heaven on earth, boy—to us old salts at any rate. All shipmates there an' no better bunch o' lads anywhere.' He took Patrick's arm. 'Come and see for yourself, and as we go you can tell me how you got that nasty lookin' cut.'

The Calcutta was deep in the maze of winding streets behind the market-place, and as they made their way towards it Patrick told Tom of the events of the afternoon and felt the better for it.

Tom was sympathetic. 'Mebbe the sea's the

65

life for you, me boy,' he said. 'True, it's a hard life, but once you've your Master's ticket you've no other master but the sea itself.' He slapped Patrick on the shoulder. 'Give it a bit o' thought, boy. But not tonight. There's company, grog and wenches at the Calcutta. If the one don't make you forget your troubles the others will!'

The windows and the doorway of the Calcutta were ablaze with light and as they entered a great wave of warmth and noise seemed to hit them. Patrick felt its welcome gratefully. Although the room was no cleaner than the taproom of the Bell, the atmosphere was entirely different and the place seemed to be bulging with interesting, colourful characters all of whom greeted Patrick like an old friend. There was an old man with a wooden leg who Tom said had been a pirate in his younger days, and in one corner was a great green and red bird who could speak like a human being. Patrick had seen nothing like it in his life before, nor heard such rich, colourful speech and language. The ale, when he tried it, was more palatable than that at the Bell, and Patrick found that almost before he knew it he had downed three tankards full, bought for him by the generous customers and friends of Tom's. His spirits lifted and he began to feel happier.

The food and drink were served by several pretty girls and there was one in particular who took Patrick's fancy. She had an abundance of fair curls peeping out from under her frilled mob-cap and the low cut neck of her print dress revealed smooth white mounds which his fingers itched to touch. Noticing his partiality for the girl, Tom called her over.

'Hey, Tabby! Here's a lad a-sighin' for love of you! Come an' give him a smile.'

The girl giggled and sidled up to them. Tom nudged Patrick.

'Go on then—put your arm round her and give her a squeeze. That's what a pretty waist is made for, ain't it, Tabby, me love?' He winked broadly at the girl, who giggled again and perched herself on Patrick's knee. She slid her arm around his neck and the men laughed to see Patrick's colour rise in his cheeks. Seeing Tabby at closer range he noted now that she was not as young as he had first thought—perhaps in her late twenties. It did nothing to dampen his ardour, however, but rather increased it. He smiled and did as Tom had suggested, giving her waist a squeeze. Tom tossed the girl a coin.

'Be good to him, Tabby. Take him upstairs for half an hour. He's had a bad time and he deserves it.'

Tabby caught the coin deftly and put it safely away in the top of her stocking, revealing a plump thigh to Patrick's speechless gaze. Inside his chest his heartbeat quickened and the blood began to sing in his ears. Suddenly bold, he caught the girl to him, kissing her and closing his hand over one of the firm round breasts. She stroked his cheek.

'Poor love,' she said caressingly. 'Someone *has* been treating you rough. Will you come upstairs and let me make it better for you?'

' 'Tis not 'is face as wants seein' to!' a raucous voice called out, and a chorus of laughs, whistles and cat-calls went up.

But Patrick was past caring. He held the girl's hand tightly as she led him through the crowd to the foot of a wooden stairway at the back of the room. More ribald remarks were called out, which Tabby answered pertly, pulling at Patrick's arm as he stumbled up the stairs behind her.

At the top she drew him into a room and closed the door, shutting out both noise and light. To begin with Patrick could see nothing, then his eyes accustomed themselves to the light and he saw that Tabby was undressing. She had already stepped out of her skirt and thrown aside the mob-cap, letting her fair curls tumble down her back. Now she was loosening her bodice. His stomach lurched as he saw in the dim light from the dormer window that she wore nothing beneath the dress. Inside him something seemed to erupt. It was almost akin to the rage that had overwhelmed him when he had witnessed the beating of the horse this afternoon. He lunged forward, grabbing the

68

girl by the waist and tearing the loosened bodice from her.

'Here! Steady on! What's the hurry?' she cried, stumbling backwards, but no more words were possible as Patrick's mouth covered hers demandingly. She had expected him to be awkward and fumbling, for she could see that he was only a boy, for all his size. She had even been prepared to tell him what to do as she had with so many other lads, but Patrick surprised her. Throwing her on to the bed he took her violently, like some hungry animal devouring its prey. It had been a long time since she had encountered such virility. At last he rolled away from her, spent and sobered and she reached out to bury her fingers in his damp curls.

'Well,' she said appreciatively, 'aren't you a clever boy, then? I bet you never knew you had it in you, eh? A proper tiger you are and no mistake. More man than a dozen o' them big-mouths downstairs put together!' She rolled over to kiss him lingeringly. 'Will you come and see Tabby again then, love?'

Patrick nodded and closed his eyes. Suddenly nothing seemed to matter any more. Inside himself he felt elated, complete, assured. All those vows he had made to himself—that had seemed so wild and impotent—now seemed totally real and possible. Yes, one day he would be as good as Henry Quincey—*better*! Refreshed, he opened his eyes and looked up at Tabby, grinning.

'Come and see you again? I'll do better than that—I'll see you again *now!*' And he rolled her on to her back with renewed delight.

It was very late when Patrick crept up the stairs to the room above the coach-house, but Seamus was awake and waiting for him, his candle still burning.

'Where in the name o' the Holy Mother have ye been, boy? I've been nearly out o' me mind!'

'It's all right, Uncle,' Patrick assured him. 'I met Captain Craven and he took me to the Calcutta.'

Seamus raised the candle to peer at him. 'Are ye drunk, lad?'

Patrick shook his head. 'I am not.'

Seamus grunted and lay back on his bed. 'Sure I don't hold wi' that Calcutta. 'Tis nothin' more'n a whore-house if ye ask me!' A sudden thought made him sit up in bed and raise the candle again to look at Patrick. He had been puzzled by the lad's docile manner and sobriety, but now . . .

'Ah, is *that* it then?' he asked. 'Is it a *man* they've been makin' of ye?' he chuckled. 'Well anyhow, it seems to have done ye a power o' good whatever it was!'

\*         \*         \*

Kathleen and Sarah lay side by side in the little

70

room over the laundry. It was a hot night, too hot for sleep, and Kathleen's head was full of troubled thoughts. Since that day when the terrible thing had happened to Patrick a change had come over him. She and Sarah had managed to clean the dirt from his new livery and the place on his cheek had healed well enough, helped by Cook's cobweb salve, so it was nothing to do with either of those things. But there was something about his manner that puzzled her. It was as though somehow, overnight, he had become completely grown up. He was now a man—a strange, silent man with something inside, driving him. It was funny, because although she now felt she knew him less and feared him more, her love for him was stronger than ever, and that was why she was so disturbed by the tale Sarah had come to her with this evening.

She turned her head to look at the mound in the other bed.

'Sarah,' she whispered. 'Sarah—are ye still awake?'

There was a rustle as the other girl turned over. 'Mmm, I can't sleep. It's much too hot. But we must try, Kathy, or we'll never get through the work tomorrow. Shut your eyes now.'

'I can't,' Kathleen complained. 'And 'tis not just the heat. Are you sure it's right—about Patrick and Miss Dale?'

Sarah groaned. 'I *told* you—Fred, the

gardener's boy, said he *saw* them—goin' into that old pottin'-shed behind the glasshouse.'

'But why would they go there? What would they be doin'? I just don't see—' she broke off as she heard Sarah's smothered giggle.

'Don't be such a loony, what do you think they was doin'?' she spluttered. 'What else would a lad and lass go hidin' away for?'

Kathleen's face burned in the darkness. She couldn't believe it—she couldn't! Since she had been at Denmark House Sarah had acquainted her with the facts of life. She knew well enough what the girl was hinting at. But Patrick and Miss Dale, Master Paul's governess! The two seemed so unlikely together.

'Sarah Smith, I think you've a mind like a midden!' she said hotly.

Sarah sniffed and tossed her head as she threw herself on to her other side in a huff. 'Well, don't believe me then,' she said. 'Find out for yourself and I hope you like what you find! That brother o' yourn is no different from other lads! Don't kid yourself that he is—'cos he isn't!'

All next morning Kathleen thought about it. The same thoughts went round and round in her head like a dog in a treadmill coming to neither end nor conclusion. She was unaware that what she suffered was the oldest emotion in the world—jealousy. All she knew was that it hurt unbearably, making her touchy and irritable, and when Patrick came to the kitchen

72

after luncheon to perform his daily task of carrying away the kitchen refuse she followed him outside, determined to tackle him.

'Now, Patrick Reardon!' she said, hands on hips. 'Just you tell me what is it that you and Miss High and Mighty Dale get up to in that potting-shed of an evening!'

He caught his breath in surprise. 'Who's been talkin'?'

'Never you mind,' she snapped. 'So it's true then?'

He frowned at her blackly. 'Mind your own business, Kathleen Reardon and keep your nose out o' things that don't concern ye!' He picked up the buckets. 'An ye can tell whoever's been gossipin' to do the same,' he flung over his shoulder at her.

Angry tears filled her eyes. She would find out—she would! That Miss Dale! And her the daughter of a man of the church! Well, that was Protestants for you!

Patrick's face was like thunder as he buried the rubbish in the pit at the bottom of the kitchen garden. Truth to tell, he had been having trouble with Agnes. It would be bad luck indeed if anyone were to discover their secret meetings now, just when he had decided to end them. He knew that all he required now to perfect his reading and writing was plenty of practice. He had no need of Agnes's teaching any longer. It had never been his intention to become a scholar. He knew his limitations—

73

but he also knew that he would never attain his ambitions if he remained illiterate. Agnes, however, had other ideas: she kept urging him to allow her to teach him other things—history and geography. Blindly infatuated as she was and deeply ashamed of the unladylike urges within her, she had managed to persuade herself that she had his education and welfare at heart. She saw herself almost as some kind of missionary, choosing to forget as quickly as she could the way his nearness affected her when they were alone together in the close confines of the potting-shed and the way his kisses made her feel like melting wax.

And so the daily meetings continued, with Agnes now the pursuer and Patrick the unwilling quarry. But Kathleen's words had greatly disturbed him and by the time he set out to meet Agnes that evening he had decided to tell her once and for all that they must not meet again. The fact that they had been seen and there was talk must surely make her see the danger.

He was not prepared, however, for her tears and protestations. As they sat together in the dimness of the potting-shed he stared helplessly at her as the unexpected torrent was released.

'How can you say so calmly that we must not meet again after—after all we have been to each other?' she sobbed. 'Do you care nothing for me now?'

Patrick was perplexed. There had been nothing between them but a few kisses, so why was she so upset? 'Of course I care for you,' he said awkwardly. 'I'm grateful for what you've done for me—but folk are talkin'. We've been seen. I wouldn't like you to lose your place.'

'I don't care. I love you, Patrick!' She looked up at him, her eyes filled with pain. 'We could run away together—we could be married.' She threw her arms around his neck. 'Oh, Patrick—*please* don't speak again of parting! I can't bear it!'

He put his arm round her trembling body, holding her uneasily. It was going to be harder than he thought to shake her off.

Charles Quincey had excused himself early from the dinner table on the pretext of having some studying to do. Something was afoot in the servants' quarters and he was determined to find out more about it. He had overheard two of the grooms talking this morning. It was something to do with that prim little ghost of a governess and young Reardon, the young swine who had knocked him down in the stable on the first day of the holidays. He owed him a sharp lesson and this could be just the opportunity he was waiting for.

He stood silently on the landing, listening to make sure none of the servants were about, then, as quietly as he could, he crept down the back stairs. At the bottom of these was a stone flagged passage which led to the kitchen and scullery. A door at the far end gave on to a yard. In summer this door was open all the time. As he stood in the passage wondering what to do next, he heard voices coming from the scullery where two of the maids seemed to be washing up. He crept closer to listen as one of them was raised slightly.

'Oh all right—you can go if you're no more'n a minute. You know as well as I do it'll be me as gets the blame if Cook finds you gone!'

'I'll be quick,' came the reply. It was the Irish girl, Reardon's sister. 'Sure you'll hardly notice I'm gone. I just want to find him—make sure he's not doin' anything that'll get him into trouble again. Didn't he almost lose his place once already?'

Sarah snorted impatiently. 'Then *go*—and don't waste time standin' there yappin'. But mind—don't blame me if you don't like what you find!'

There was the sound of scurrying feet and the girls' excited mumblings and Charles slipped quickly behind the door as the Irish girl came out into the passage. He gave her a moment and then slipped out and followed her into the yard. He was just in time to see her heading for the kitchen garden and his heart lifted gleefully. They were playing right into his hands.

Kathleen tripped along almost at a run, through the herb garden, closest to the house, across the vegetable patch and through the fruit garden where Charles almost lost sight of her among the tall raspberry canes and currant bushes. Finally she disappeared behind the glasshouse where Hobson, the gardener, grew the figs and nectarines that were his mother's special delight.

Stealthily he crept round the corner of the building and saw the girl standing near the door of a wooden shed as though summoning up all her courage. His heart quickened as he saw her reach out her hand and lift the latch. A moment later she had thrown the door open to reveal the lout Reardon and his brother's governess clasped in each other's arms. He stepped forward triumphantly, pushing the speechless skivvy aside roughly.

'A pretty sight!' he laughed derisively. 'I swear I've seen no funnier in my life!' He stood there in the doorway, his feet planted firmly apart and his head thrown back, guffawing loudly. 'I wonder what my mother would say,' he speculated, 'if she knew that her precious baby were being instructed by a harlot who allows herself to be pawed by the lower servants when her charge is in bed?'

Patrick sprang to his feet in an instant and lunged at the grinning Charles, bellowing with rage, but before he could land a blow Kathleen leapt forward with a cry of alarm, grabbing his arm and hanging on to it desperately.

'Don't hit him again, Patrick—*please*!' she

77

begged, while Agnes stood back among the shadows, white-faced and shaking. She only just managed to evade the blow intended for Charles's face and he staggered back a little, his face colouring angrily.

'She's right. I do not advise you to try that again, Reardon,' he warned. 'You will learn that you have a worthy opponent in me. There are more subtle ways to punish than with the fists, as you shall see.' He turned his attention to Agnes. 'You had better get back to the house, Miss Dale,' he advised. 'There may be a way to save your situation. It is my belief that this lout has led you astray and I shall do what I can to help you.'

She stepped forward, eyeing him fearfully, then gave one last pleading look at Patrick, who stood clenching and unclenching his fists in an agony of self-control. Charles watched them with obvious amusement.

'You may consider yourself fortunate that I have delivered you from the hands of this scum, Miss Dale,' he continued. 'Heaven only knows what fate may have overtaken you but for my intervention.' His lip curled as he took in her crumpled dress and the wisps of hair escaping from her neat chignon. 'I advise you to go to your room at once before you are seen,' he said pointedly. 'Other members of my family may not be as understanding as I.'

Deeply humiliated, Agnes turned and walked away, her head bowed, glancing just once more at Patrick from under her lowered lashes. Charles Quincey turned his attention for the first time to Kathleen.

'So this is your sister, Reardon,' he said, pinching her cheek painfully. 'Well, let me tell you that if you do not toe the line in the future *she* shall be the one to suffer!' He looked Patrick up and down with hate gleaming in his pale eyes. 'Or are you such a lout that you'd let your womenfolk do the suffering for you?' he said contemptuously.

Patrick let out a low growl and Kathleen saw the sinews in his arms tighten. There was a white line of fury around his mouth and she gave a small startled cry:

'Patrick—No!'

Charles Quincey grabbed her arm and twisted it behind her back, smiling with sadistic pleasure at her shrill cry of pain.

'Come one step nearer, Reardon, and your sister's arm will snap like a twig. Do not make the mistake of thinking you can get the better of me. I can bring you to your knees in a moment if I choose!' He put his foot into the small of Kathleen's back and sent her cannoning into Patrick's arms whilst he strode off arrogantly towards the house.

Kathleen clung sobbing to Patrick. 'Oh—I knew there'd be trouble—I *knew* it! What's to become of us? Oh Mary, Mother o' God, save us!'

But Patrick shook her roughly. 'Stop that

will ye! Why in the name o' God couldn't ye mind your own business like I told ye to? It was *you* led him here. Why couldn't ye be told?'

She stared up at him with brimming eyes. 'Me? But I didn't mean any harm. I was worried. You nearly lost your place that other time and—'

'And just what did ye think I was doin' to lose me place this time?' he demanded angrily.

She flushed hotly and looked away. 'I thought—well, that you and Miss Dale—well that you—'

He shook her again. 'You thought what he said was true, didn't ye? Well, I'll show ye something!'

He went into the shed and came out holding the books that Agnes had left behind. 'Here—' he said thrusting them under her nose. 'This is the terrible sin that we were committin'! She was teachin' me to read an' write!'

Kathleen stared at the books and then back at Patrick. 'To read and write—*you*?'

'Yes. She's been teachin' me for a long time and now I can do it, Kathy. I can write me own name properly instead o' puttin' a cross like when we was bonded. Don't ye see what it means, Kathy? I don't have to let folk treat me like dirt now. I'm goin' to be somebody some day, just like I told ye!'

But Kathleen looked at his shining eyes with some misgivings. Patrick being Patrick she

80

could only see his newly acquired knowledge leading him into more trouble.

It was two days later, when he was mucking out the stables that Patrick heard the deep lugubrious voice of Mr Simpson, the butler, in the yard outside, giving instructions to Seamus. It was rare for Mr Simpson to come to the stables and Patrick stopped work and edged closer to the door to hear what was being said.

'The carrier's cart leaves the market-place at noon,' Simpson was saying. 'The mistress has asked me to arrange for someone to take Miss Dale's box along. The young lady will make her own way there.'

When he was sure the butler had gone Patrick emerged and confronted his uncle. 'What was that about?' he asked. 'Where is Miss Dale goin'?'

Seamus lifted his shoulders disinterestedly. 'Seems Master Paul's governess is leavin',' he said. 'Goin' back to her father at Malfrey Chapel, or wherever it is.'

'I've finished mucking out,' Patrick said quickly. 'I'll take the box if you like.'

Seamus peered at him suspiciously. 'I hope the young lady's leavin's nothin' to do wi' you, lad.'

Patrick shook his head. 'Nothin' whatever! How would it be?'

Seamus shrugged and ambled off to the coach-house where he was waxing the fine coachwork of the carriage in which he took

81

such great pride. Let them all get on with it. It was none of his business anyway.

Patrick quickly finished the task in hand, washed himself at the pump and by eleven thirty was ready and waiting with the handcart at the back door when the boot-boy staggered out with the heavy box on his back. Agnes followed behind, red-eyed, dressed in a plaid travelling mantle and a small black straw bonnet. No one said a word as the box was loaded on to the handcart but once out of sight of the house Patrick stopped and turned to her.

'What's happened?' he asked. 'Why are you goin' home?'

She walked on, her face pale and her lips set in a tight line.

'Please—' she whispered. 'Do not stop here. We are conspicuous.' But when they reached the market-place and stood waiting for the carter's arrival he coaxed the story from her.

'I am sent home in disgrace,' she told him, her voice almost inaudible.

'But why?' Patrick asked. 'You must tell me. Is it on my account?'

She shook her head. 'It was that night—when Mr Charles discovered us. He came to my room and said that he wanted to help me. He said that if I—did for him what I had done for you he would say nothing about his discovery. I told him that I had been teaching you to read and write and that I thought he

82

was already quite proficient at these skills.' She bit her lip. 'He flew into a temper and seemed to think that I was mocking him. He tried to—to force his will on me and when I resisted he went away, threatening me quite dreadfully.' She took a deep breath in an effort to compose herself. 'Yesterday morning Mrs Quincey sent for me. She said that it had come to her notice that I had been sneaking out to meet a man in secret. She could not have a person of light morals in charge of her small son, therefore I was to leave at once.'

The blood pounded in Patrick's head. 'Agnes—I'm sorry,' he said. 'Charles Quincey is no better than a gutter rat to do this to you. But why did he not tell about me?'

Agnes sighed. 'Poor Patrick. I fear he may have worse torments in store for you. Perhaps, on reflection, I am the fortunate one. At least I have my home and family to go to. I shall tell my father the truth and I know he will believe me and forgive my foolishness.'

Patrick nodded thoughtfully. 'I've a mind to leave too—to go away.'

But she shook her head. 'You cannot break your bond until the year is up. If you do they will find you and put you in prison. You must consider your sister as well as yourself.' She touched his arm. 'Anyway, Mr Charles will be going back to school before long, then life may be easier for you.'

Patrick knew she was right. He watched her

trying to conserve her frail dignity alongside the carrier on his cart as it rumbled over the cobblestones of the market-place. And he remembered Charles Quincey's words about punishing him through his womenfolk. Well at least Agnes was safe. But what about Kathleen? The thought turned his blood to ice as he trundled the empty cart back to Denmark House. If anyone laid a hand on her he would kill them! That he would.

His mind was in a turmoil that night as he lay on his bed. The injustice of what had happened was bad enough. But the thought of what Agnes had said troubled him still more. Finally he got up and went across the river to the Calcutta, hoping to find more affable company there to divert his mind.

He found Tom Craven in the taproom and told him the whole story of his relationship with Agnes and its outcome. To his surprise, Tom threw back his sandy head and laughed.

'I'm sorry for the lass,' he said at last. 'But there's no denying that that young swine Quincey has done you something of a favour!' Patrick shook his head and the captain went on: 'Didn't you say yourself that the lass was gettin' a might too fond o' you? Well, you don't have to worry any more. Quincey saved you the trouble!'

For a moment Patrick stared at him. Until now he had been feeling guilty about Agnes, but now, all at once he saw the simple truth of what

Tom was saying and he began to laugh too. In the midst of their laughter Tom nudged him and nodded to where Tabby could be seen across the room, elbowing her way eagerly towards them and swinging her hips provocatively.

'If you take my advice you'll cheer up and forget all about it m'lad,' he advised, slapping Patrick on the back. 'Take life's troubles and pleasures as they come.' He winked broadly. 'An' if I'm not mistaken there's pleasure in the offing!'

# Part Two
# The Quinceys

# CHAPTER FOUR

Henry Quincey sat in his study, a bottle of port and a glass before him on the desk. He had left instructions for his son, Charles, to come to him here on his return from his office in York Place. He had been home now for twenty minutes and the insolent young pup was keeping him waiting. It proved to him that the decision he had made regarding the boy's future was the right one, though he did not expect Charles to share his view.

He poured himself another glass of the rich dark beverage and sat back to relish it. The boy was spoilt. His mother had always doted on him and he guessed it was because he took after her side of the family, not only in his fair skin and hair, but in the arrogant manner with which he seemed to have been born. The Graves family had inherited their wealth and had always taken it for granted. Henry gave a short bark of laughter. Huh! Look where it had got them! He had always known that old Sir Edward had despised him for his yeoman background and had hated the working businessman he had become, but he had been more than glad to give him his only daughter when he heard what Henry's yearly income amounted to!

As his thoughts turned to his wife, Amelia,

Henry's mouth twisted. She was a good mother and ran his house with style and elegance. He had to admit that she had kept her side of the bargain in that, but in other matters she was no more joy to him than a block of wood—less, for a block of wood could be fashioned into something of beauty. Under his hands Amelia froze into solid ice. She had done what she considered her 'duty' and provided him with two fine sons and daughters, but since the birth of young Paul her bedroom door had been firmly locked against him. He shook his big sandy head, thinking of his daughters and wondering if they would offer their future husbands as cold a bed, for he supposed their mother would have instilled into them the notion that to be virginal in spirit was the only way to repair the violation done by marriage. Would they have believed it? There was no way of knowing what went on inside a woman's head—behind the serene smiles, the nodding ringlets and the innocent eyes peeping over the top of a fan. So many promises remained unmet—eyes and bodies that looked so soft and yielding proved hard as steel as often as not. Caroline had his spirit. She'd be a handful. He chuckled to himself. Melissa, on the other hand, had grown into a gentle, restful young woman. Dull? He wondered. Ah well, it would surely depend on the husband he chose for her and he thought he had just the one. But for the moment it was Charles with whom he was concerned.

A bold tap on the door preceded Charles's entrance. Henry looked up as his son came into the room. He was a good-looking young man, though not in a way Henry admired. The arched eyebrows and flared nostrils gave him a foppish look, while the well moulded lips seemed to belie the weak chin. Charles had celebrated his nineteenth birthday last August and in Henry's view it was high time he began to learn what real life and work were all about.

Charles looked at his father with the familiar lazy insolence. 'You wanted to speak to me, Father?'

Henry looked him up and down with undisguised irritation. 'Yes—and when I said "on my return from the office" I meant just that—not half an hour after!'

Charles smiled unconcernedly. 'I'm sorry. I did not know you had returned.'

'Nonsense!' Henry snapped. 'I sent Simpson to tell you—and you know it very well, sir. When I give an order in my own house, I expect it to be obeyed. Sit down, boy!'

Charles sat down, looking sulky and affronted. His father pushed the port bottle towards him. 'Have a drink, lad.'

But Charles wrinkled his slim nose. 'I thank you, Father, but no. I am sure that if you had asked him, Simpson would have decanted it for you.'

Henry's face turned a dull red. The damned

boy was even beginning to talk like his mother! 'I dare say you're right,' he said coldly. 'If I asked him he'd do it because I bloody well pay him—but I'm not asking him because I don't choose to!' He rose and walked round the desk to stand before his son, broad-shouldered and thick-necked as a bull, his grey-green eyes flashing. 'Just remember too, will you, that I pay you also—and while we're on the subject I'll tell you why I sent for you. I've decided it's high time you came into the business.'

Charles stiffened in his chair. 'What do you mean?' His face had turned pink and Henry noted the change of colour with satisfaction.

'I mean, lad, that you're to leave that fancy school of yours and come home. You'll go through the business till you find the job that suits you best and start being some use in the world!'

Charles was on his feet now, his pale skin flushed and his fine brows drawn together. 'But—I'm to go up to Cambridge next autumn, Father—I can't—'

'No such word as can't, lad,' Henry said firmly. 'I managed with a few years at Elvemere Grammar School myself; you've had a sight better education than I ever had and I did well enough. Besides, Cambridge is for intellectuals—men who want to become professors—teachers and the like. You're to be none of them. Your future is here and it's time you stopped wasting time and got on with it.'

As though the matter was at an end, Henry turned his back and poured another glass of port, raising it till the light from the lamp on his desk made the liquid sparkle like rubies. He contemplated it appreciatively, then downed it at one draught.

'Please, Father—I beg you to reconsider.'

Henry turned as though surprised to see his son still there. 'I've told you, boy—it's done,' he said lightly. 'I've made up my mind. I sent in your notice to Flixby College and your place at Cambridge is already cancelled. There's nothing more to be said. You'll leave at the end of next term.'

Angry tears filled Charles's eyes as he faced his father. 'I hate the business,' he shouted. 'I won't work in it—I tell you I *won't*!'

'Oh yes you will, sir!' Henry informed him. 'That business has done you proud ever since you were born. It's educated, clothed and fed you. I've made it flourish and grow and you'll carry it on after I'm gone—do you hear me?' His voice vibrated the air till the fire-irons rattled, and Charles glared at him across the desk, his face scarlet and perspiring. He opened his mouth, then shut it again hopelessly. Then he turned and flung out of the room.

Henry let out a sigh. His face relaxed and he chuckled to himself. That would show the young pup who was master! Thought he was going to live out his life as a useless idle gentleman, did he? Well, he'd learn! He pulled the bell-rope and sat down comfortably at his desk. A moment later the door opened softly and Simpson entered on noiseless feet. As he did so he carefully averted his eyes from the port bottle which stood in a ring of its own contents on the leather desk-top.

'Sir?'

Henry looked at him, the averted glance had not escaped his notice, in fact he derived a certain pleasure from it. 'Send the girl in to mend the fire,' he said. 'Oh, and you can tell Miss Melissa to come to me here at once.' He might as well get it all over in one go, he told himself, then they could all enjoy their Christmas.

While he waited he got up and went to the window, opening one of the shutters to look down on the view below. Down there lay the port and the town. Lights twinkled in windows and in the rigging of the ships, moving gently on their moorings. A light powdering of snow lay over everything, highlighting the buildings in the moonlight. Across the river he could see the bulk of Quincey's mill and far away to his left, beyond the High Bridge, he could just make out the long low sheds of the rope walk. Already he owned a good section of the town's commerce and he nursed a secret dream deep in his heart: one day Elvemere would belong to him—all of it. Maybe the new young Queen would bestow a knighthood on him and when it happened he'd have no one to thank for it all but himself.

A noise behind him made him spin round, awakened from his reverie. A maid had come in and was putting coal on to the dying fire. He looked more closely at her. This was a girl he had not seen before, small and pretty with copper-coloured hair, fiery where the glow of the fire touched it.

'Who are you?' he demanded.

She stood up, smoothing her apron. 'I'm Kathleen Reardon, sir.'

He frowned. 'Where's Stevens?'

'If you please, sir, she's poorly with a bad cold—so—so I've come instead.'

He pursed his lips. 'Reardon—the same name as my coachman. Of course, you're a relative of his—niece, is it?' She nodded and he frowned again. 'And sister to that young limb of Satan of a nephew of his?'

'Step-sister—if ye please, sir,' she corrected.

He raised an eyebrow. 'Step-sister? Well, let's hope you take after your uncle in matters of subservience and not him!'

She blushed. 'Will that be all, sir?'

He walked across the room, the port glass still in his hand, and looked down at her with interest. 'How old are you, Kathleen?'

'Nearly sixteen, sir.' She felt her face grow hot under his gaze. It was the first time she had been this close to the Master and she found his proximity awesome. Towering over her he seemed enormous and although he wore fashionable, well cut clothes there was an earthiness about him, a feeling of the open air which nothing could quite dispel. He had a large head, made leonine by his abundant tawny hair and whiskers. His face was ruddy and his eyes were like grey-green fire; alert and perceptive, accustomed as they were to assessing people.

'Sixteen, eh? And how long have you been with us now?' he asked.

She considered for a moment. 'It'll be two years come next March, sir.'

He nodded. 'Happy, are you?' She nodded eagerly and he smiled. When Henry Quincey smiled it was like the sun bursting forth from behind a cloud. It was one of his greatest weapons and he knew it. He was not a patient man but he was possessed of a certain charm and he knew instinctively when to use it. 'Ah— and what of that step-brother of yours, eh?'

The smile faded from Kathy's face. Patrick's rebellious ways were a constant source of anxiety to her. Only last week he had been rude to Miss Caroline and had received another lecture from Uncle Seamus. One of these days she was sure they'd lose their places because of it, because she'd not stay if Patrick went. She bit her lip and gazed up in fear at this giant of a man.

'He's—happy enough—thank ye, sir.'

He laughed. 'I don't think that is quite true, Kathleen. I think the lad is restless—tired of

96

being a stable-lad maybe and wanting something more exciting to do.'

She stared speechlessly at him. How would he know so much about Patrick? He must take more notice of the servants than they realised—but then, of course, he did see Patrick several times every day. She shook her head vigorously.

'Oh no, sir—he's real *contented*—really he is!'

He threw back his head and laughed again. 'If he is it's the most sullen show of contentment I've ever seen. Indeed, if he hadn't such a way with the horses I'd—' He broke off and looked at her shrewdly, his eyes narrowing slightly. 'You think a lot of your step-brother, don't you? You'd like to see him get on?'

Her eyes lit up. 'Oh I *would*, sir. He's real clever—with other things as well as the horses. He can read, sir!' she told him proudly.

His eyebrows shot up. 'Read, eh? Well I'll—' He turned, hearing a rustle in the doorway. Melissa stood there.

'Simpson said you wished to speak to me, Papa,' she said quietly.

Henry nodded briskly. 'I do. Come in, m'dear and sit down.' He looked at Kathy. 'That'll be all now m'girl. Be off with you.'

Kathy hurried out with a shy half-smile at Melissa, who smiled in return and then looked at her father.

'She is a very good girl. Not experienced in above-stairs work as yet, but she does her best. I hope you were not taking her to task, Papa.'

'Nothing of the sort,' Henry said. 'I was simply taking an interest in her. I think you know that I leave the servants to you and your mother.'

Melissa cleared her throat and looked at her father expectantly. 'What was it you wished to speak to me about, Papa?'

'Ah yes.' Henry sat down at his desk and folded his arms upon it, leaning towards her confidentially. 'It may or may not surprise you to know that I have had an offer of marriage for you.' He was gratified to see her cheeks colour. At least the girl had some feeling in her. He smiled. 'Do I need to tell you the name of the young man who made the offer?'

She raised her eyes to his hopefully. 'Was it—was it John?'

He nodded, smiling. 'It was indeed. I take it you would find him to your liking?' He smiled at her shy whispered "Yes, Papa". 'I thought you would. I have told him that I have no objection to the match. After all, the merging of the Quincey family with the Gages could be beneficial to future generations.' He reached across the desk and covered her small white hand with his large brown one—strong as a farmer's yet soft as a gentleman's. 'You must be sure to give us some bonny grandsons, eh, Melly?'

He had not used the pet name for her since she had left Miss White's Academy two years ago and his use of it now embarrassed her slightly. He took the reason for her blush to be on account of his mention of future grandsons and he added quietly: 'While we're on the subject, you mustn't listen to all your mother has to say on the more intimate side of marriage, Melly. Your only real 'duty' is to bring him joy—and that means to his bed as well as the rest of his house.'

Scarlet-faced she rose quickly, snatching her hand from his, her eyes bright with humiliation. 'If that is all, Papa, I have a great deal to do to help Mama.'

He sighed and poured the last trickle of port into his glass. 'Yes—yes, all right, you run along. The Gages are to dine with us, as you know, on Boxing Evening. I expect John will speak to you then.'

As the door closed on Melissa's outraged back he gave an explosive snort. Blast all well-bred women and their damned mealy-mouthed ways! Give him an honest-to-God country lass any day!

Safe in her room, Melissa leaned against the door and drew a long breath. It had happened! He was going to ask her—he really was! Oh, John. For as long as she could remember she had loved him; and since he had returned from college, so tall and handsome with his brown hair and laughing blue eyes, her feeling for

99

him had deepened even more. Now it seemed that, miraculously, he returned her love. He was to ask her—the day after tomorrow! How would she contain herself until then?

Then a thought occurred to her—what would her Mama say? Melissa knew it was not the kind of marriage her mother had in mind for her at all. She had cherished the hope of taking her elder daughter to London next year and persuading her Great-Aunt Graves to present her at court. She often spoke of how she would have been presented herself if Grandpapa had not faced ruin at the time. She had also hinted that she might then have made a more 'suitable' marriage herself.

But Melissa was far too happy to let any of this cloud her thoughts for long. If Papa said that she was to marry John, then that would be the end of the matter, whether Mama liked it or not. For the present it should be her secret which she would hug to herself in delight.

At dinner that evening the expressions round the table were varied. Charles sulked openly, whilst next to him his sister, Caroline, fizzed with Christmas excitement. Young Paul, newly home from school and delighted at being allowed down for dinner with the adults, chattered to his mother about life at school, whilst Melissa was starry-eyed and preoccupied.

Amelia Quincey looked round at their faces and then at her husband's. It was obvious that he had been imbibing again before dinner; a habit that she abhorred. It was equally obvious that something was afoot. Neither Charles nor Melissa were themselves and she knew that both of them had been closeted with their father earlier. She was determined to discover what had passed between them before the evening was out. As soon as the dessert plates had been removed she rose from the table and inclined her head towards Paul.

'Run along now, my darling. Nurse will be waiting for you. Caroline, dear, perhaps you will take him up.'

Caroline rose obediently and reached for her younger brother's hand, but his face puckered as he snatched it away.

'I don't have to be *taken*. I'm nine now. And I don't need Nurse any more either!' he said petulantly.

'You do as your mother tells you, boy,' Henry Quincey growled. 'Or you'll spend Christmas Day in your room, sir!'

'I don't like Nurse any more,' Paul said fearlessly. 'She won't talk to me or play with me—she hasn't got any teeth. She smells too —' he wrinkled his small nose. 'She smells—of trifle!'

Henry threw back his head and roared with laughter. 'Trifle, eh? That's a good one!'

Amelia threw him a disapproving, reproachful look and frowned hard at her small son who stood confidently smiling now at the success of his last remark.

'Really, Paul! It is not at all clever or funny to make game of people in a lower station to ourselves. Nurse is getting old now and you must show her the proper respect.'

'Rubbish!' Henry contradicted cheerfully. 'She drinks like a fish and always has done. She should have been pensioned off years ago. Send her home before she sets the house on fire.' He grinned at Paul. 'Go with your sister now, lad. And do as your mother says.' He glanced at Amelia. 'Are you and the girls going to take your coffee in the drawing-room? Charles and I have matters to discuss.'

Amelia did not answer, but with a withering look she swept out of the room, followed by Melissa.

In the drawing-room Melissa glanced at her mother and moved towards the piano. 'You seem a little overwrought, Mama. Would you like me to play for you?'

But Amelia shook her head. 'No. Sit down, Melissa. I wish to speak to you before Caroline returns. Your Papa sent for you earlier this evening, I believe. What was it he wanted to say to you?'

Melissa sat down and folded her hands in her lap, trying to appear composed. 'He—he wished to tell me that John Gage had asked for my hand, Mama,' she said. 'And that I could expect a proposal shortly.'

Amelia's mouth twisted bitterly. 'And no doubt he gave the young man his blessing.'

Melissa nodded. 'I believe so.'

Amelia leaned forward. 'You do not have to accept, child, just because your Papa wishes it. You know the plans I had in mind for you?'

Melissa bit her lip and lowered her eyes. 'It is all right, Mama. I am very happy. I love John.'

Her mother's eyes flashed angrily. 'You are aware of course why your father is so in favour of the match?' she observed tartly. 'The well at the brewery is showing signs of running dry. George Gage, John's father, has perfected a new filter plant. It is your father's dearest wish to get his hands on it!'

But Melissa's eyes were dreamy. 'I am only glad that I can be of help to Papa too by marrying John,' she said, then, seeing her mother's distressed look, she added gently: 'You may rest assured, Mama, that I would never marry a man whom I could not love.'

'Love!' Amelia snapped. 'What do you know of love? It is not as you would believe, child. Once you are married to a man you have nothing—you *are* nothing, even your own body does not belong to you any more!' She shuddered delicately. 'All that one may hope for in marriage is the respect of others, gained by one's position. Money is important, of course, but not when it is acquired by such people as George Gage.'

'I believe he is a good and kind man, Mama,' Melissa put in. 'And that he has educated his children at the best of schools.'

Amelia sniffed. '*Breeding*, child! No money can buy that and no school can teach it. You have it through my side of the family. It will grieve me sorely to see it thrown away.'

At that moment the door opened and Caroline came in. Her face was flushed with excitement.

'Guess what?' she said gleefully. 'I've just passed Charles on the stairs and he was so angry! He says Papa is making him leave college and has cancelled his place at Cambridge!' She stared at the two shocked faces, well satisfied with the impact she was making. 'He is to go into Quincey's at Easter!' she concluded triumphantly.

A faint cry of horror came from Amelia's lips:

'Oh, my son, my poor darling!' She rose to her feet, a wisp of lace handkerchief to her trembling lips. 'I must go to him at once!'

\*      \*      \*

'What's done is done and there's an end to it, madam!' Henry's voice thundered as he glared at his wife across the bedroom they no longer shared. For the past hour she had been haranguing him. He had known she would, of course, but it was late and there was a limit to the indulgence a man could show his wife.

'Get to bed now, for God's sake, woman.

It's all in their best interests. You must allow me to know best in these matters.'

'In *your* best interests, you mean,' she returned venomously. 'For the good of the business—of Quincey's!'

He had been sitting wearily on the edge of the bed, but as she spat the word 'Quincey's' at him he rose angrily.

'Why do you always speak the name with such contempt?' he demanded, his face darkening with fury. 'Where would you have been without it, I'd like to know? Your father was quick enough to unload you on to me when he saw me making good—when he realised that all he'd ever leave you was a pocketful of debts! Who'd have had you if I hadn't, eh?' He tossed his shaggy head back and looked at her disdainfully. 'I'll tell you, shall I? No one! You'd have been lucky to have found yourself a place as a governess! So don't let me hear you speak of Quincey's in that tone again!'

She turned from him, shrinking a little at his formidable anger. He crossed the room to lay a hand on her arm.

'Listen, Amelia,' he said, more gently now. 'Melissa is happy. She loves young Gage as much as he loves her. It'll be a good match and a profitable one. As for Charles—have you seen the reports from that school of his? I did give them to you to read. He's never going to amount to anything in the field of learning.

Quincey's will be his one day. It's his inheritance, damn it! Surely it's not asking too much that he should take an interest in it?'

Amelia gave a resigned sigh and removed herself from the direct line of Henry's port-laden breath. 'There is no need to swear, Henry,' she said faintly. 'Nor to shout. I am not deaf!'

'Then will you please accept my decisions and not interfere?' he said.

She drew her mouth into a tight line. 'I suppose I have no choice.'

He glanced at her with dislike. 'No—I don't suppose you have,' he said harshly.

She turned to go but he suddenly remembered something and put out a hand to stop her.

'Oh—by the way, about young Paul. He's right about Nurse. I'll pack the old body off after Christmas. An old woman is no company for a healthy growing lad. There's that young Irish girl, Reardon's niece. She seems a lively young thing. She could act as nurse to him while he's at home in the holidays.'

Amelia wrinkled her nose. 'But she's only a scullery maid. She has no knowledge of children.'

'She's Irish, isn't she? Seems to me the Irish know of little else!' he said. 'Besides, Paul's not a baby any longer—it's not likely that we'll be having any more, is it?' he asked pointedly.

A dull flush spread from Amelia's neck up into her cheeks. 'No—that is extremely unlikely,' she muttered.

He nodded. 'Right. That's settled then. You'd better see Mrs Brown about it as soon as may be. Nurse has that little cottage I gave her when the boy went to school. I'll see that she doesn't want for anything. She's done us good service for the past twenty years.'

Amelia's face was sour. 'Hardly—if what you said at dinner is true. Will she not merely spend the money on drink?'

He shrugged. 'And what if she does? That'll be her look-out, won't it?' He took a step closer to her. 'Some resort to drink as the only comfort they can get.' He grasped her arm and held it firmly, looking tauntingly into her eyes. 'Come on, Amelia,' he said. 'It's Christmas— will you not make me a warm bed for once?'

She gave a small outraged shriek and wrenched her arm away, opening the door and whisking through it in a flurry of skirts. As he stood just inside the threshold he could hear her feet running along the corridor and he laughed bitterly.

'That's it, go on—run!' he said aloud. 'You flatter yourself if you think I'd chase you— damned frigid woman that you are! I wouldn't mind if you ever had been a pleasure to me— but you never were—not once!'

He began to undress, throwing his clothes angrily in all directions. Christmas, he told himself bitterly, ought to be more rewarding than this!

The servants' hall was gay with evergreens and the fire burned brightly as they all sat round, their chairs in a semicircle. Christmas Day was over as far as the work was concerned and now they could all get down to the serious business of enjoying themselves. Henry Quincey had provided his annual contribution of three bottles of his second best hock, and Cook had proudly brought out the cake and mince pies she had made. Sarah was busy roasting chestnuts on the bars of the grate.

Kathy looked around her with delight. This was her second Christmas at Denmark House. Last year she had been overcome with the grandness of it all but this year it all seemed better than ever. Poor Stevens' illness had made it necessary for her to help upstairs and her eyes had never stopped popping with the splendour of the decorations: the swags of evergreen that adorned the staircase and every room; the preparations and the atmosphere of excitement that pervaded everything. When she had been chosen to help above, Sarah had at first been jealous, which had spoilt things a little, but Kathy had managed to jolly her out of it and now tonight, the entire staff of Denmark House were together, from Mrs Brown, the housekeeper, right down to the boot-boy. Patrick and Uncle Seamus were also included and sat, shining with cleanliness, gently perspiring in the unaccustomed heat, talking and laughing with the rest of the company.

Simpson looked round, counting heads as he poured the wine ceremoniously and asked suddenly where Nurse was. Mrs Brown shifted uncomfortably in her chair.

'I went up to her room to ask her down,' she said. 'But she was—er—indisposed.'

Parkes, the lady's maid, wrinkled her nose. 'I expect you mean drunk,' she said outspokenly. 'If you ask me I think it's a disgrace to put a child in the hands of that disgusting old creature!'

Her old enemy, Stevens, looked up from her chair nearest the fire, where she sat, swathed in shawls. 'Don't speak of poor old Nurse like that!' she said. 'She's been at Denmark House longer than any of us. Why she even brought Mr Charles into the world. Surely she's entitled to a little respect in her old age.'

'Now, now, we'll have no arguments on Christmas night,' Mrs Brown interrupted. 'As a matter of fact Mrs Quincey told me this morning that after the holiday Nurse is to be pensioned off for good. Young Master Paul doesn't really need a nurse any more now and the mistress has asked me to spare one of the maids to care for him during the school holidays in future.'

At this piece of news a buzz of surprised conversation went round the room and Parkes said loudly: 'I sincerely hope that *I* shall not be expected to look after the little brat. He was spoilt enough before he went away, but I declare that school has made him even worse. Besides, I have enough to do now, with three ladies to attend to.'

Stevens glared at her, her red nose glowing in the firelight. 'I suppose you think that *I* haven't enough to do!' she said indignantly.

'Please—*please!*' Mrs Brown silenced them with a fiery flash of her spectacles. 'We are here to enjoy ourselves. I did not intend to mention it until tomorrow but as the matter seems to be causing such a disturbance I will tell you now that the mistress has asked for Kathleen to carry out these duties. The rest of you need not concern yourselves.'

All eyes swivelled to stare at Kathy, whose cheeks flamed with embarrassment and surprise.

'Me?' she asked incredulously. 'But—what'll I have to do?'

'You will be acquainted with your duties in good time,' Mrs Brown said dismissively. 'And now let that be an end to it.'

The wine helped to relax the tension and as the cake and pies were passed round everyone complimented Cook, declaring, as they did every year, that this was the best cake yet. Then Seamus brought out his old fiddle and the dancing began. They danced all the old favourites: Sir Roger DeCoverly, Black Nag and the rest, then Seamus struck up an Irish

110

jig.

'Come on, Kathy and Patrick,' he called. 'Show 'em how to do a real dance!'

Patrick stood up and took Kathy solemnly by the hand. At first they were a little shy and stiff, but the music of Seamus's old fiddle soon infected their feet and bodies. Faster and faster they danced, cheeks pink and eyes sparkling. Seamus sawed away, his nimble old fingers flying over the strings while the others watched, clapping to the rhythm. One by one they rose to join in till finally they were all dancing—all, that is, except Simpson and Mrs Brown, who sat in black-clad splendour, smiling indulgently in the firelight. Tomorrow the household would be back to normal. The discipline and formality of the servants' hierarchy would reign once more. But tonight it was Christmas, the one night in the year when they were all equal. Let there be jollity.

At last, hot and exhausted, they stopped dancing and dropped into chairs, red-faced and laughing. Cook brought in mugs of ale from the pantry amid cheers and they all fell silent as they refreshed themselves.

Kathy touched Patrick's hand. 'It's almost as good as the Christmases when we were little,' she said, smiling. But he shook his head.

'We were free then,' he said with a hint of bitterness in his voice.

She looked at his profile for a moment, wondering despairingly how she could help.

Since they had come to Elvemere she had been so happy. After the poverty and near-starvation they had endured after their father's death, Denmark House seemed like Heaven to her. To have clean clothes to wear, three good meals a day and pleasant company—honest work for which one was paid—Kathy felt it was all she could ever ask of life. But with Patrick it was different. Why must he always kick against authority? Every time Mr Charles came home there was some kind of trouble between them. It was as though they were sworn enemies. Lately it had been Miss Caroline too. She had always taken a delight in teasing Patrick, but lately the teasing had taken a cruel turn and he had begun to retaliate dangerously. Sometimes Kathy wondered how it would all end.

She sighed and entwined her fingers in his. 'Tell me what it is that's troublin' ye,' she begged. 'Let me try and help.'

He shook his head, pulling at the collar of his shirt. 'It's hot in here. I feel as if I could choke. Let's go outside for a breath of air.'

They got up and left, unnoticed amid the chatter, went through the passage and out of the door into the yard. She looked up at him.

'Where will we go?'

'The rose garden,' he told her.

She gasped. 'But we're not allowed.'

He laughed. 'Who'll know? They're all too busy with their own pleasures. Come—' He took her hand and they began to walk—

112

through the gate, across the kitchen garden to the arch in the high yew hedge that led to the rose garden. The light of the full moon on the snow made everything appear sharply etched, brighter than day in a ghostly, ethereal way. Kathy shivered and Patrick turned to look at her.

'Is it cold ye are?'

But she shook her head. 'It's just the beauty of it. Oh, we're lucky to live in a place like this, Patrick. We *are*—don't you think so?'

He sighed, drawing her inside the arbour where he sat with Agnes Dale on the day when she had read him *The Indian Serenade*. They sat silently, side by side on the bench, and he looked down at her, wondering how to make her understand.

'I'm not like you, Kathy,' he said uneasily. 'I can't be content as you are. I want to be free— I'll always want it.' He looked at her. 'I've made up me mind—when spring comes—I'm leavin'.'

She stared at him, her eyes wide. 'Oh, Patrick—no!'

He found her hand and squeezed it. 'I must, Kathy. I love the horses and I'm good with them. I can get another job—maybe on a farm or livery stables—somewhere where I don't have to be bonded.'

She shook her head, her eyes round with anxiety. 'You—you wouldn't break your bond here, would ye, Patrick? If ye do that they put

113

ye in prison—sometimes they flog ye!'

He put his arm round her reassuringly. 'I'd not do that. I've told ye—I'll wait till spring. Then I'll try me luck at the hirin' fair.'

Her chin went up. 'Then so will I!' she said resolutely.

He shook his head. 'No, Kathy—no! You must stay here. You like it. You're happy.'

Tears welled up in the huge blue eyes. 'Not without you. I wouldn't be happy with you gone.'

His arm tightened about her shoulders, tenderness making his throat thicken. 'Don't ye see, Kathy darlin'—if I go by meself I can do a man's work—live as rough as I have to. One day I mean to make me fortune—but if I had you with me—'

'You wouldn't be as free as ye want to?' she finished for him.

Reluctantly he nodded. 'At first—don't ye see? I'll come back for ye when I've made good and I'll make a lady of ye,' he promised fervently. 'As fine a lady as any ye've seen— finer!'

She swallowed hard. 'Promise—promise me, Patrick.'

He looked into her eyes. 'I promise ye faithfully, Kathy. By all the holy saints I promise ye.'

She gulped back her tears. 'Oh, Patrick—I love ye,' she whispered. 'I love ye so much it hurts me.' She reached up to put her arms

114

around his neck, then she pressed her lips to his. They had kissed many times before, as children who are brought up together do, but suddenly to Patrick it was as though a mist had cleared—as though the truth shone out as sharply as the moonlight as their bodies touched and their lips made contact.

His arms tightened round her and in his heart there was a sudden pain. The fierce protectiveness he had always felt towards her was now mingled with something else. Kathy was a grown woman now. Her thin, childish body had rounded and blossomed and as he held her in his arms he was shocked at the sudden stirring of desire that leapt within him.

Appalled at the sudden involuntary surge he tried to put her from him, but she clung to him. Deep inside, a womanly instinct told her that, strong though he was, she could enslave him at this moment with the touch of one finger, if she chose to.

'Patrick,' she whispered softly, her warm, sweet breath caressing his cheek. 'Don't leave me—don't ever leave me. Sure I'd die without ye.'

It was enough. His arms straining her to him, he kissed her hungrily—her mouth, her throat, her closed eyelids. His fingers pulled the pins from her hair till it came tumbling down in a thick bronze curtain. Before he had time to think he was unfastening her bodice with trembling fingers. Then suddenly his eyes met hers and he stopped, stricken and ashamed.

'Oh—Mother o' God, I'm sorry, Kathy! Oh my God, forgive me!' He got to his feet and turned away, his hands to his face.

Without a word she got up and went to him, putting her hands on his shoulders and making him turn. 'Don't say that, Patrick. Don't be sorry,' she said softly.

He looked down at her, his eyes hurt and bewildered. 'But you're—you're me *sister*, Kathy. It's wrong—a mortal sin.'

'No, no—not your blood sister,' she said soothingly. 'We'd different parents, love. T'was only that we were brought up in the same house—that me Da married your mother. Sure you know that as well as I do meself.'

He nodded slowly. 'I suppose you're right—it just feels wrong.'

She smiled her little secret smile and reached up to wind her arms around his neck. 'Not to me, it doesn't. I've always loved ye this way, Patrick. You're all the world to me and ye always were.'

He enclosed her with his arms again, gently and thoughtfully this time and yet with complete surrender. How could he go now? he asked himself. How could he leave Kathy? This strange, new, beautiful Kathy? And how was it that she had known so long of this love that had only just been revealed to him? It was all very bewildering, just when he thought he saw the path ahead so clearly. He found her lips again and sighed resignedly—all thoughts of freedom melting from his mind like spring snow. His senses still reeling he felt her clasped hands between his shoulder blades and their soft strength seemed to him like velvet-covered chains.

## CHAPTER FIVE

Simpson inserted the tall red candles in the silver candelabra and set them, one on each side of the floral centrepiece Miss Melissa had created specially for the occasion: spicy-scented chrysanthemums, Christmas roses and holly. The handmade lace tablecloth was like a tracery of snowflakes on the polished mahogany, and the silver gleamed richly. He stood back, viewing his work with satisfaction as he turned to Stevens.

'You have made a very nice job of the table, Stevens. You can tell the others to stand by now. I'm about to announce that dinner is served.'

Stevens nodded, her cheeks flushed with excitement. Somehow word had filtered through and everyone below stairs knew that tonight Miss Melissa's life was to take a dramatic turn. It was as though they all waited with bated breath, just as Melissa did herself.

In the drawing-room the Quinceys and the Gages sat stiffly, somewhat ill at ease with one another, mainly because Amelia's disapproval pervaded the atmosphere like a noxious fog, hanging pall-like over the gathering. George Gage and her husband, Henry, may have been friends since boyhood but she herself had no ties with the family, neither did she desire any.

She glanced at Harriet Gage, overdressed and plump, her faded wax-doll prettiness rapidly blurring into coarseness. Her daughter, Christabel, took after her with her pouting baby-face and affected lisp. Her pale hair was dressed in an elaborate ringleted style and she wore what Amelia considered a great deal too much jewellery for a young girl. Her dress too was immodestly décolleté and her large brown, cow-like eyes followed Charles disconcertingly wherever he went. Inside Amelia's breast irritation rankled. *One* Gage in the family was more than enough! She sincerely hoped that her son would not be inflamed by the sight of so much bosom. She knew only too well the weakness of the male sex in such matters and she supposed that even her own darling Charles would not be proof against natural male sinfulness when it was thrust under his nose in this vulgar manner!

'The shops are really most divine! Have you seen them, Mrs Quincey?' Harriet Gage was talking animatedly about a recent visit to London, when she and her daughter had

118

accompanied her husband on a business trip. Amelia looked at her and smothered a yawn.

'Oh yes,' she said lightly. 'I used to visit London regularly as a young girl—to stay with my aunt, Lady Elizabeth Graves. One tires of it after a time.'

'Oh, I don't think I should *ever* tire of it!' put in Christabel, in what Amelia considered a very forward manner. 'The opera and the parties and balls! Oh, I could live there for ever!'

Amelia looked at her haughtily. 'If one knows the *right* people it can be amusing, I suppose,' she conceded.

'We were invited to a musical evening at the home of Lady Broome,' Mrs Gage said with satisfaction. 'George met Sir Hilary Broome at a luncheon connected with the Chamber of Commerce.' She sighed. 'Of course the conversation everywhere one went was about the dear Queen's forthcoming wedding. Isn't it romantic? They say that dear Victoria is *quite* in love with her Prince.'

Amelia stiffened. Really! 'dear Victoria' indeed! Anyone would think that the wretched woman knew the Queen personally!

'Lady Broome is inviting some friends to stay at her London house so that they may see the bridal procession go past,' Christabel announced. 'There is to be a dinner party afterwards—and fireworks. She hinted that an invitation might be sent to us!'

'Now, now, Christabel. How many times have I told you not to count your chickens before they are hatched?' said her mother reprovingly.

It was at this moment that Simpson announced that dinner was served. Amelia was deeply grateful. These two women seemed to bring out the worst in her and she felt sure that even her iron control would have snapped in another minute. Really, the thought of this woman and her odious daughter being received in a noble household! It was too ridiculous. They must surely have imagined the whole thing!

Presiding over her dinner table she felt more in control of the situation. Thank Heaven for a good cook! On the menu was mock turtle soup, at which Cook excelled, followed by sole à la Colbert; roast pheasants; turkey; sirloin of beef and baked ham; Christmas pudding and mince pies followed by Flame pudding and Apples à la Portugaise. Let Harriet Gage better that! With satisfaction she noticed that the greedy little eyes lit up as the food was served. At least it kept the wretched woman quiet!

Melissa lifted her eyes to look at John, seated opposite. It was strange; they had known each other for so long and had always been completely at ease with one another, yet tonight she felt shy and a little apprehensive, almost as though he were a stranger. His eyes met hers across the table and he smiled reassuringly, making the blood rush to her cheeks. If only dinner were over and they could speak to each other alone. Papa had promiscd her that he would arrange it. She stared down at the food on her plate, wondering how to make a convincing pretence at eating it.

The ladies had been in the drawing-room for almost half an hour when Henry Quincey made his appearance. Harriet Gage was still scoring points off Amelia, whilst Christabel and Caroline exchanged a conversation that was liberally peppered with barbed remarks. Melissa sat in a corner, nervous and edgy, irritated by the rigidity of convention and yet glad to hide her confusion in it. When the door opened and Henry stood there, mellow from his port, a cigar between his fingers, her heart almost leapt out of hcr breast.

'Melissa, my love,' he said, smiling indulgently. 'I believe John would like to speak to you. You'll find him in the conservatory.'

She rose shakily to her feet, feeling sure that her legs would not bear her weight. She looked around at the faces turned up to hers—her mother's, closed and expressionless, her sister, Caroline's, grinning wickedly, Mrs Gage's, smiling encouragement and Christabel's, openly envious.

'Will—will you excuse me, please?' she muttered and left the room with as much dignity as she could manage.

In the hall her father closed the door and patted her shoulder. 'Off you go then, Melly,' he said thickly. 'And don't make it difficult for the lad.' And with these words of advice he turned to walk back to the dining-room.

When she went in he was standing with his back to her, looking out over the snow-covered, moonlit lawn, a tall, slim figure in his well-cut evening clothes. He turned at the soft rustle of her gown and smiled, holding out both of his hands to her.

'Melissa.'

She went to him and put her hands into his. 'John—Papa said that you wanted to speak to me.'

He nodded. 'I spoke to your Papa a few days ago. I believe he has told you?'

'Yes—he did.' She lowered her eyes. Suddenly he laughed and she looked up at him in surprise.

'Oh, Melly—dearest. How formal we are!' He drew her towards him. 'There is so much to say and so few words to say it with. But I think you already know that I love you and want you to be my wife. Will you say "yes"?'

She laughed with him, the tension within her suddenly released. 'Yes, John—yes!'

He sat down on the small stone bench by the window, drawing her down beside him. 'There— that's over. What a relief!' He looked into her eyes, suddenly serious. 'You *do* want

122

to marry me, don't you, Melly? I mean, you're not just saying yes because your Papa wants you to?'

She smiled at him gently, pressing his fingers. 'I do want to, John. I love you—I believe I always have.'

He slid his arms around her and kissed her gently on the lips. It was the first time they had kissed and it was almost like meeting for the first time. The children they had been to each other were gone and in their places were two young adults made suddenly acutely aware of each other; for the first time alive to a new and delicious sensation. John pulled her closer and kissed her again, harder and more searchingly this time and when he released her she was trembling, a little shaken by his intensity.

'Please—' she whispered breathlessly. 'We must not—not until we are wed.'

But he laughed gently and held her close. 'It is only a kiss, sweetheart.' He looked down at her. 'You are so dear. Your little heart flutters like a bird. I can feel it beating its wings.' His lips found hers again, this time more gently and she relaxed in his arms.

'Oh, John,' she whispered. 'I love you so.'

Next morning the whole house was buzzing with the news. Miss Melissa was to be married at Easter. It was clear that she was deliriously happy. One had only to look at her pink cheeks and starry eyes. It was also clear that her father was happy; never had he been in such a good mood. Other members of the family had their own views, it was observed. Mr Charles was unconcerned, being preoccupied with his own, less fortunate circumstances. Mrs Quincey was tight-lipped and irritable whilst Miss Caroline seemed to have a younger sister's natural curiosity.

Sitting on Melissa's bed, she watched her sister going through her wardrobe and listened to her talking about the proposed honeymoon which was to be spent at a small house the Gages had recently bought on the Norfolk coast. Eventually, she asked the question she had longed to ask since last night when the happy pair had made their announcement.

'Melly—did he kiss you? What was it like?' She threw herself back against the pillows, her hands locked behind her head as she gazed dreamily at the ceiling. 'Did he swear his undying love and clasp you to his pounding heart?'

Melissa turned to stare at her young sister. 'Caroline! Whatever have you been reading?'

Caroline giggled. 'Some of the girls at school have novels. Oh, come on, Melly, you can tell me. What did he *do*?' She sat up, her eyes sparkling and eager.

'John is a gentleman,' Melissa told her reprovingly. 'He did nothing except ask me to marry him—nothing improper, that is.'

Caroline pulled a face. 'How boring. But he must have *kissed* you—of course he did, didn't he?'

Melissa turned back to the wardrobe and resumed her inspection, but Caroline had seen the warm flush that crept up her sister's neck and she nodded with satisfaction.

'Well, I hope that when someone proposes to me he'll do more than just kiss me,' she said reflectively. 'I want to bring men to their knees—to drive them wild with desire for me!'

'Caroline!' Melissa's eyes were round with shock. 'You had better not let Mama hear you talking like that!'

The younger girl laughed. 'As if I would! I do believe Mama would like it if there were no men in the world at all. I don't think there is one that she likes—except her darling Charles, of course. Did you see the way that awful Christabel was setting her cap at him last night?' Her hand went suddenly to her mouth as a thought occurred to her. 'Oh—do you realise that when you are married to John she'll be related to us? Horrible thought!'

Melissa smiled. 'Quite right. And she'll be an even closer relative if Charles decides to make her his wife!'

This thought was too much for Caroline and she gave a snort of unladylike amusement: 'Pshaw! I would have thought that even Charles could do better than that! He's furious with Papa, you know—swears to have his revenge on him for depriving him of his education.' She sighed, looking thoughtful.

125

'Melly—do you think Charles is the passionate type? One cannot see one's own brother as a man somehow.' When her sister refrained from replying she pursued the question even further: 'Is John the passionate type?'

'I am sure he is not,' Melissa said firmly.

Caroline sighed. 'Oh—what a pity. I shall have to be sure that the man I marry *is*. Any other kind must be so dull!' And for a moment she fell silent, thinking of dark, flashing eyes and black curling hair; of broad shoulders and the capable brown hands that held her pony's head for her as she mounted. 'Melly—' she said in a low voice. 'Don't you think that Reardon is terribly handsome?'

Melissa met her sister's gaze through the mirror as she held a blue dress against herself. 'Reardon?' she repeated vaguely. 'Do you mean Reardon the coachman or Reardon the stable-lad?'

Caroline pulled a face. 'Melly! You're not listening. I mean Reardon the stable-lad, of course—Patrick. He's handsome, don't you think so?'

'I hadn't noticed,' Melissa said lightly. 'He's just a servant.'

The younger girl shook her head. 'He is also a *man*. Haven't you looked at him lately? He makes shivers go up and down my spine when he gets that angry look in his black eyes.' She gave a little shudder, folding her arms around herself, and Melissa looked at her curiously.

'Is that why you tease him so—to see his eyes grow angry?'

Caroline shrugged. 'I suppose so. I like to see how far I can push him.'

'That is most unfair,' her sister chided her. 'One day you will go too far. For you it is mere amusement, but for Reardon it could mean the loss of his place.'

'I wonder what he would do?' Caroline reflected, her eyes half closed.

Melissa shrugged, putting the dress she was holding back into the wardrobe. 'Go into the navy perhaps—or maybe the army—the cavalry.'

'No, silly! I meant I wonder what he would do to *me!*' Caroline bit her lip tightly, catching her breath as she contemplated the prospect. 'Would he *beat* me like he beat Charles that time, do you think?'

\*     \*     \*

'So I'm to start tomorrow. Won't it be grand?' Kathy sat in Seamus's chair in the room above the coach-house. As usual her mob-cap was flung aside and the mass of unruly bronze hair hung in confusion about her shoulders. Patrick regarded her affectionately.

'You're comin' up in the world, to be sure,' he told her. 'But be sure and don't forget that it'll be back to the kitchen with ye when young Master Paul goes back to school.'

'I know, I know,' she assured him. 'But at least I'll get to sleep in the big house while the worst of the winter's on. That room over the laundry's freezin'. Stevens told me there's fires burnin' up there on the nursery floor day an' night!'

Patrick smiled and bent to kiss her. 'I'm glad,' he said softly. 'If it's what you want and you're happy, I'm glad.'

She stood up and put her arms round his neck. He was well over six feet tall now and she had to stand on tiptoe to do it. 'Maybe one day we could both hold high positions in this house,' she told him. 'Or even bigger ones with the real gentry.'

He smiled indulgently at her and said nothing. He had given up worrying her with his own dreams; for the moment he was content to let things ride. His chance would come one day. He knew it deep in his bones, and when it did he would grasp it with both hands. In the two years he had been at Denmark House he had defied Mrs Quincey's request not to grow. He was now a veritable young giant; and as strong as a lion. He was no longer 'tiger', having outgrown both position and livery long ago; but he had such a knack with the horses that he had made himself irreplacable in the stables. So much so that Seamus often wondered what he had done before the lad's arrival. He seemed to have an almost uncanny rapport with the animals and knew how to heal and soothe them by some inbred instinct which, Seamus privately told himself, undoubtedly came from his gipsy blood. He had a fiery temper too, though, for the gentle forbearance he held for animals seldom extended to human beings. One day, Seamus often mused, it would lead him into trouble—maybe serious trouble. Across his left cheek Patrick still carried the faint white scar which Henry Quincey had inflicted with his son's riding crop. Every time he shaved, Patrick saw it, though now it was partly hidden by the thick sideburns he wore. Even so, he never saw it without making a silent vow: One day he would make Henry Quincey pay for it!

He put his arms round Kathy's waist and kissed her deeply. 'Ye'd better go now, darlin'. Seamus'll be up for his supper soon.'

But she nestled her head against his chest, savouring his warm embrace and longing for the day when they would be together all the time and not have to snatch hurried moments like this. She raised her face to look into his eyes.

'Kiss me again—please, Patrick.'

He bent his head once more to hers, fighting down the feeling she aroused in him. Not for Kathy the lusty pleasures he enjoyed with Tabby at the Calcutta. One day, when they could be married, he would learn to harness his desire and love her as tenderly as she deserved. Till then he must slake his restlessness elsewhere. But, God! It was unbearably hard to let her go when she clung to him so sweetly. He held her close, cradling her head against his cheek with one hand.

'Go now, darlin',' he whispered huskily. 'You must go!'

A slight noise made them both start and spring guiltily apart. Sarah stood in the doorway, a shawl wrapped round her plump shoulders and her nose red from the cold.

'You're wanted in the kitchen, Kathy,' she said sharply. 'I know you've got a better job now, but it don't start until tomorrow, remember?'

'She only came up to give me the news. She was just leavin',' Patrick said.

'So I *saw*,' Sarah said pointedly, staring coldly at him.

As they went silently across the yard, Kathy tried to take Sarah's hand but she pulled it away.

'Oh, what's the matter, Sarah?' she asked. 'Nothin's been the same with us since Christmas.'

'Nothin's the matter,' Sarah said sulkily.

'Yes there is.' Kathy stopped walking and confronted her. 'You're jealous, Sarah Smith— because it was I was picked for work upstairs and now because I'm to take care of Master Paul. I can't help it if I'm asked, now can I?'

Sarah reddened and turned away. 'You're ridin' for a fall, Kathleen Reardon, you mark my words! Kissin' your brother like that too! You're a wicked girl—that's what you are!'

Kathy's cheeks flamed. 'I'm not! He's not me *real* brother. You know that! Haven't I told ye a hundred times?' She gave Sarah a push. 'You're jealous—because you wish it was you kissin' him! That's all it is.'

This was a lot nearer the truth than Sarah cared for and she reached out and grabbed a handful of Kathy's hair, tugging it viciously, her face dark red with fury.

'Bitch!' she said venomously. 'Irish bitch! You'll have somethin' *bad* happen to you before you're done—you just see if you don't!'

She turned and ran the rest of the way across the yard with Kathy staring after her, stunned into immobility. What had come over her—placid, kind-hearted Sarah who had been her best friend? The way she had looked at her just now—as though she hated her! And the thing she had said: 'somethin' bad will happen to you'. Kathy shuddered. She had heard tell of curses and of the 'evil eye' and as she stood there watching Sarah's flying apron strings disappearing round the corner she felt as though she had just been a victim of it.

The winter began in earnest on the following day. Snow fell steadily all day in a silent white swirling fury and by nightfall the whole county was in the grip of the worst frost for many years. The river froze and during the weeks that followed much of the town's trade

131

came to a virtual standstill. Ships and boats already in the port were iced in and their crews were forced to look for alternative employment, of which there was little on shore.

At Denmark House the gardeners were idle and Henry Quincey set them to work, rolling the snow on the lawn till it was hard and firmly impacted. Then they watered it lightly to form a thin surface of ice. On this manufactured skating rink the family and their friends whiled away the hours with pleasure while the town waited for its enforced hibernation to end. Kathy was quick to learn and she and Paul spent their mornings playing on the ice, the sound of their laughter echoing like bells on the crisp, brittle air and their breath floating like vapour feathers. Paul had taken to Kathy from the first moment he saw her. He loved her childish sense of fun and her pretty face with its huge, sparkling blue eyes. Although he was not an easy child she had no trouble getting him to bend to her will. She had an instinctive talent for making mundane things seem like a game, and for Paul the holidays had never flown so fast or so pleasantly.

Sometimes they would visit Patrick at the stables for the boy had long admired the big young man with the strong brown arms, who had such talent with the horses. He had promised Paul that when the thaw came he would take him riding again and make an

132

expert horseman of him.

They were halcyon days for Kathy. It was like living her childhood over again, though she had not enjoyed the first one half as much.

Almost best of all was the comfortable, warm room she had to sleep in. Sometimes she thought of Sarah, shivering alone in the little room above the laundry and she would experience a little pang of guilt, but not for long. After all, her elevation was only temporary. When Master Paul returned to school she would have to go back to sharing a room with Sarah and she couldn't quite forget the things Sarah had said to her in her jealous rage.

It was one afternoon during the first week in February that Henry Quincey came upon his son and Kathy playing at snowballs in the park. Sheltered by a thicket of evergreens, he watched them for a while, noticing the new, fresh colour in his small son's cheeks and the sparkle in his eyes. Gone was the sulky, spoilt look he had worn, gone too was the petulant tone of voice. When he spoke now—called out and laughed with Kathy, his voice was full of carefree exuberance. Henry looked at the girl. On that first evening in the study, he had recognised a potential sensuality, a glowing warmth. There was a refreshing frankness about her, none of the inhibitions the higher-born women had. It wasn't the first time he had watched her in secret since Christmas Eve and now, as his eyes followed her movements, he noted again with pleasure the curve and colour of her cheeks, the confusion of tumbled hair and the swell of her young breasts as she lifted her arm to throw a handful of snow. His stomach muscles tightened. How old had she told him she was? Sixteen? His eyes glazed with lustful imaginings. She was a peasant—an Irish peasant. In two or three years she would probably be fat and overblown, but now, in the full flower of her youth, she was lovely, luscious as a ripe peach.

He stepped out from his cover and his small son ran towards him shouting gleefully. Kathy had her back towards them and, not having seen Henry, she turned and hurled a snowball in the child's direction with a yell of triumph. A moment later she clapped her hand to her mouth as it hit Henry Quincey hard in the middle of his chest. He brushed the snow from his coat, laughing, and, taking Paul by the hand, he walked towards the transfixed and blushing Kathy.

'I was just about to ask if I might join in the game,' he said. 'But it seems I have already joined!'

Kathy bit her lip. 'I'm terrible sorry, sir. I didn't see ye there.'

Henry looked down at her, enjoying her confusion. 'Well, well,' he said to Paul. 'Kathy says she is sorry, but I think she should be punished, don't you?'

The boy caught his father's teasing mood and he jumped up and down excitedly. 'Yes, Papa—yes!'

Henry looked over his son's head into the girl's eyes. Wide, blue, innocent—yet with a woman's instinctive wisdom in them. 'What shall we do with her?' he asked, his heart quickening at the thought of what he would *like* to do with her.

Paul considered for a moment, then pointed excitedly. 'Let's throw her in the drift, Papa,' he shouted. 'Over there in the hollow, the snow's ever so deep!'

They advanced on her, father and son, and she backed away with a little stifled cry, a thrill of delicious fear tingling her spine. Paul made a leap, cat-like and caught at her skirt, throwing his arms about her waist.

'I've got her, Papa!'

'You take her feet,' Henry said to the boy. He put his hands under her arms and felt the satisfying firmness of her breasts beneath his fingers as together they lifted and swung her.

'One—Two—Three—Throw!'

Kathy found herself flying briefly through the crisp air to land with a soft thud in the deep snow. It almost covered her, coming up on either side of her like an icy grave. Paul and his father laughed heartily, then she saw Henry's ruddy face bending over her. He extended a hand.

'Can you get up?'

She took the hand he offered and he pulled her to her feet. Snow clung to her hair and eyelashes and coated the back of her dress. She shook herself like a small animal and Henry handed her her shawl which she had hung over the branch of a nearby tree.

'Here—better put this on before you catch cold.' He draped it over her shoulders, his fingers lingering on the warm skin of her neck. She smiled shyly up at him.

'Thank ye, sir. We must go now. It must be time for Master Paul's tea.'

'May I come and play with you again?' he asked, looking meaningfully into her eyes.

She blushed. 'I'm sure Master Paul would like that, sir.'

'And you, Kathy—would *you* like it?'

She bit her lip, suddenly aware that his question had a mysterious, deeper meaning. 'W—why, yes, sir,' she whispered, lowering her eyes in confusion. 'I—I think so.'

He patted her cheek. 'Away with you then,' he said jovially. 'Or you'll find yourself in trouble with Cook and that will never do.'

In the servants' hall the talk was all of the young Queen's wedding and of the one which was to take place soon at Denmark House. Of the two, Miss Melissa's was by far the most interesting, their having a first-hand part to play in it. There was to be a reception here at the house and Cook was already in a flutter about the mountain of food she would have to prepare. Extra staff was to be engaged for the occasion and the dressmaker was to take up temporary residence in the house during the week preceding the wedding.

None of the other servants had shown Sarah's hostility to Kathy and after Paul had gone to bed each evening she would come down and sit with the others for a while before going to bed herself. Sometimes she would creep out to the stable-yard to spend a few precious minutes with Patrick, though when she did this she always felt Sarah's accusing eyes on her when she returned.

That evening, as the talk turned to weddings once more she fell to dreaming of the day she and Patrick would wed. She saw herself dressed in a gown just like the one being made for Miss Melissa—of blue silk shot with lilac, like a delphinium, with a cream straw bonnet lined with the same material. She would float down the aisle to Patrick like a piece of gossamer and he would be waiting, tall and handsome in a fine tail-coat and a cravat with a diamond pin like the one the master wore. The clock on the high mantel-shelf wheezed and struck nine, bringing her thoughts back to the present with a jerk. The candles were being lit and the lower servants were preparing to retire for the night. She stood up quickly to join them and jogged Sarah's arm as she did so.

'Who d'you think you're pushin'—Miss

High and Mighty?' Sarah glared at her.

Quick tears filled Kathy's eyes. 'I'm sorry. I didn't mean to.' She touched Sarah's arm. 'Oh, Sarah, please don't be so nasty to me. I'll be back in me old job soon—and in me old room along with you.'

Sarah shrugged and pulled a sour face. 'And what am I supposed to do about that then—dance for joy?' She pushed Kathy out of the way and left the room hurriedly.

The nursery was at the back of the house on the second floor, divided from the servants' bedrooms by a heavy door at the top of the back stairs. There were five rooms altogether: day nursery, night nursery, schoolroom and two bedrooms, one for the nurse and one for the governess. At present Kathy and Paul had the suite of rooms to themselves. Kathy looked into the night nursery at the sleeping Paul. Putting her candle down gently, she drew the covers up round his shoulders and brushed back a lock of hair from his forehead, then, taking up her candle again, she closed the door and went to her own room.

She undressed and slid into bed, luxuriating in the warmth of the room. It was warm enough to sleep without her nightgown and this she did, for that way they would last longer. She stretched her limbs deliciously between the cool sheets. Up here they were made of fine linen and felt so smooth after the coarse calico ones she shared with Sarah in the room over the laundry. Soon all this luxury would be over. There were only two weeks left of the holidays. Would she miss it all very much? she wondered, then decided that she would go without a great deal to have Sarah nice to her again.

She had no notion of how long she had been asleep when the noise woke her. She opened her eyes to see the door opening and the next moment she gasped in amazement to see Henry Quincey standing there. He wore a silk dressing-gown and in his hand he carried a lighted candle, which he placed carefully on the table by the bed.

Her first thought was that something must be wrong. Perhaps the house was on fire— perhaps Master Paul was ill! But if so why had she not heard him call? Alarmed, she sat up, holding the sheet against her. Henry held a finger to his lips.

'Shh. Don't make a noise. We don't want to wake the child.'

'W-what is it?' she whispered. 'What's wrong?'

He smiled. 'Nothing's wrong, Kathy. I'm here, that's all. You knew I'd come, didn't you?'

She frowned and shook her head. 'No, sir— no, I didn't know.'

He stood by the bed, towering over her. 'Oh, come now. I saw the way you looked this afternoon—and when I asked you, you said "yes".'

So that was what he had meant! She had puzzled over the way he had looked and spoken to her this afternoon. Kathy's heart was beating fast as she looked round desperately for a way of escape. But he had read the look in her eyes and quickly moved to the door, locking it and dropping the key into his pocket.

'Come now, Kathy,' he said soothingly. 'You're not going to disappoint me, are you? I hope you remember who I am?'

She shook her head. 'Please—no, don't—I didn't mean what you thought—' She broke off, her eyes wide with fear as a half sob escaped her lips. He leaned across her, his eyes hardening.

'Be quiet! Don't make a sound,' he commanded between clenched teeth. 'If you do it'll be the worse for you. Do you want to find yourselves out in the cold tomorrow—you and that brother of yours?'

'Not Patrick—please don't do anything to Patrick,' she begged.

His eyes glinted with triumph. Of course, she would do anything to save that brother of hers, he should have remembered. He snatched the sheet from her fingers and threw it back, his eyes glowing as they feasted themselves on her nakedness.

'Listen,' he said thickly. 'There's only one reason why you got this job and this room and

140

I believe you know it. This is no time to start playing the innocent.' He sat on the edge of the bed and grasped her shoulders. 'Co-operate, Kathy, and everything will be all right for you and your step-brother. I'm not a man to be refused. I've a talent for making people wish they'd never been born. Do you doubt that?' His eyes burned into hers and his fingers bit deeply into the flesh of her shoulders. She shook her head dumbly. He nodded, his eyes narrowing. 'Very well, we'll have no more nonsense then.' He threw off the dressing-gown and lay down beside her.

It took every once of control she possessed to bite back the scream that rose in her throat but she kept thinking of Patrick and the day Henry Quincey had laid his cheek open with the riding crop. His large soft hands moved over her body, relentlessly exploring, and his mouth crushed hers stiflingly, his breath heavy with alcohol. In the candle-light his eyes were glazed and bloodshot. She closed her eyes and bit her lip till she tasted blood. He took her swiftly, his long abstinence making him too eager to prolong his pleasure, but even when he rolled away from her with a groan he did not let her go, but held her round the waist with a grip of iron.

She shed no tears, but lay numb with shock, staring into the dancing shadows the candle flame threw onto the ceiling. He turned to her, his breath still rasping.

'I'll come to you again,' he whispered. 'It'll be better next time. Don't worry, Kathy. I'll make you like it in the end.' His mouth crushed hers again before he got up and put on the dressing-gown. He lifted the candle and took one last look at her as she lay there, too shocked even to pull up the covers.

'Go to sleep now, Kathy,' he said quietly. 'I'll come to you again soon. Next time will be better for you, you'll see.'

As the door closed softly behind him she rolled onto her side and drew her knees up to her chin, the tears scalding her cheeks. 'Oh, Holy Mother, help me—help me,' she whispered over and over again. She could not get the sight of Henry Quincey's lustful face and the feel of his hands on her body to leave her mind, but when she closed her eyes all she saw was Sarah's face, twisted with jealousy. 'You'll have somethin' *bad* happen to you before you're done—you just see if you don't!' The words echoed in her head—echoed and re-echoed. She was cursed. There was no hope for her—none at all!

# CHAPTER SIX

April came to Elvemere that year in a blaze of glory. Once the winter snow had melted it was as though nature determined to redeem herself. Everyone's heart seemed lifted by the sudden arrival of spring and at Denmark House energy was renewed as preparations for the wedding progressed. Everyone had their part to play and not least among them was Patrick.

It was his job to groom the horses for the occasion, especially the pair of greys selected to draw the wedding carriage. He was kept busy from morning till night, taking horses to the farrier—unthinkable that any Quincey horse should cast a shoe on the great day!— grooming, braiding, polishing harnesses and administering doses, whilst Seamus directed the refurbishing of the carriages.

In the kitchen, Cook was like an angry wasp, buzzing here, there and everywhere, scolding, red-faced, growing more and more bad-tempered as the day drew nearer.

Kathy was once more in charge of Paul, home again for the Easter holidays after the short spring term. She had, in fact, never moved out of her room on the nursery floor. Henry Quincey had managed to persuade his wife that she should stay there and maintain the rooms in good order during term-time in addition to her other tasks in the kitchen. His nocturnal visits to her had become a twice-weekly ritual, one that Kathy dreaded. Sometimes he would stay for over an hour, submitting her to humiliation of both mind and body. The only way she could endure it was to shut her mind completely from what was happening to her and, afterwards, refuse to think about the next time. This attitude of mind wrought a change in her which some were quick to notice. She grew quiet and withdrawn—or, as Sarah chose to see it— secretive and sly.

She rarely saw Patrick now, avoiding him as much as possible, unable to meet his eyes. She felt that he must see in her the degradation she was forced to suffer. She knew that she could never marry him now, sullied as she was, her body spoiled and misused. She saw her future as a desert, bleak and arid, stretching before her without relief. Things could only get worse. Her only pleasure was in the boy, Paul, and in Miss Melissa who often sought the peace of the nursery when the wedding preparations grew too much for her. Kathy now rarely spent her evenings in the servants' hall, making the excuse that she had sewing to do upstairs and when Melissa discovered that she sat alone in the schoolroom most evenings, she often joined her there.

One evening she picked up a nightgown of

her young brother's that Kathy had been mending and studied it thoughtfully.

'You sew very well, Kathy,' she said, looking up at the small bronze head bent over the needle. 'How would you like to come with me and be my maid when I am married?'

Kathy lifted her head slowly to gaze at Melissa in disbelief. 'Come with you, Miss Melissa?' The work dropped into her lap as she thought of all it would mean—delivery from Henry Quincey and his increasing demands—escape from the eyes of the other servants, especially Sarah—from Patrick and the pain and guilt she felt each time she looked at him. Tears came into her eyes. 'Oh, Miss Melissa—if only I could!'

Melissa was moved by the tears, attributing them entirely to gratitude. 'Well, I see no reason why you should not,' she said. 'You are wasted here, spending your time as you do between kitchen and nursery, which is for most of the time empty. Any other girl could take your place. Mr Gage and I will have only the minimum of servants to begin with, so you would have a variety of tasks to do, but later I should like you to concentrate on serving me personally. Would you like that?'

'Oh—I've always wanted to be a lady's maid,' Kathy said wistfully.

Melissa smiled. 'Good. I shall speak to Mama about it tomorrow.' She looked at Kathy and hesitated before she spoke again:

'Is anything troubling you, Kathy? You seem sad somehow. Not as happy as you once were. If anything is wrong I would like to think that you would tell me about it.'

Kathy looked longingly into the gentle grey eyes. If only she could unburden herself—ask for help. But to tell Miss Melissa about the sort of man her own father was—of what took place late at night up here in the room next door. If Miss Melissa knew what she had done—even though she could not help herself—Kathy was sure she would not want her within a mile of her fine new home. She shook her head.

'I'm all right, Miss—thank ye.'

Melissa reached out and touched her hand. 'I expect you must feel homesick at times.'

Kathy grasped the suggestion like a dying man clutching at a straw. 'Yes, Miss. I do—a little,' she said gratefully.

\*　　　\*　　　\*

Charles was in the blackest of moods. His last term at school had dragged and he had felt out of things. It was to him as though he had already left and although he hated the thought of entering his father's business he was not unwilling to say goodbye to Flixby when the time came. In fact he felt, at the moment, that he belonged nowhere. Even his mother, usually so lovingly sympathetic, seemed too busy with his sister's wedding to lend an ear to his complaints. Deprived as he was of the chance to mould his own career, he nursed a deep and bitter resentment towards his father. He shared with Patrick a sense of injustice and a desire to repay the wrong Henry Quincey had done, though neither of them realised it.

It was a beautiful morning, clear and sparkling and he stood in the middle of the empty stable-yard, slapping his crop impatiently against his thigh and shouting:

'Hallo there! Where the devil are you all?'

The door of the room above the coach-house opened and Seamus appeared, his brown face flustered and his sparse grey hair awry. He ran down the steps, pulling on his coat as he came.

'I'm sorry, Mr Charles,' he muttered breathlessly. 'Were ye wantin' somethin'?'

'Well of course oim wantin' somethin'!' Charles mimicked Seamus's accent. 'I'm not standing here shouting to exercise my lungs damn it!' He looked round. 'Where's that lout of a nephew of yours?'

'He's out exercisin' the horses, sir,' Seamus told him. 'Those that don't get ridden regular like. What with the weddin' an' all, the young ladies haven't been out much lately. Was there somethin' I can get you?'

Charles snorted explosively. 'Well of course there is, man! What do you think I want—a pound and a half of potatoes? I want my mount of course. See that he's saddled up at once!'

Seamus scratched his head. 'There are no grooms, sir. 'Tis too early.'

'Then bloody well get on with it yourself, you old fool!' Charles roared. 'I won't be kept waiting another minute!'

Seamus scuttled to the end stable to get Jason, Charles's bay gelding. He smarted with resentment. Even the Master himself had never spoken to him like that. He felt that even though he was a servant, his age and position should command a little respect at least. He had his dignity like any other creature and it wasn't his job to saddle horses.

He led the gelding out into the yard and went to fetch a saddle from the tackroom. Jason rolled his eyes and tossed his head apprehensively when he saw Charles standing there. The animal had never forgotten the thrashing he had received at the hands of this man and he had hated and feared him ever since. He pawed the ground restlessly as he was saddled, and when Charles mounted he reared and waltzed, tossing his mane and whinnying. Charles reined him in viciously and kicked at the animal's flanks till he brought his head round, and urged him out through the gate that led to the park.

As he closed the gate after them, Seamus sighed and shook his head. By the time they got back Patrick would have another sick horse on his hands—and with the wedding only days away too!

Patrick had been riding since dawn. He loved this time of day, especially in spring when the grass was beaded with fresh dew and the sky was a high blue arc. The first primroses and violets were out under the trees and hedges, and he dismounted from Meg, Miss Melissa's mare, to rest her and to gather a bunch of the sweet, delicate flowers for Kathy. Perhaps she would come today. He sighed. There was something very much amiss with Kathy lately. She hardly ever found time to come out to the stables now as she used to, and when she did she was uneasy and strange with him. He lay awake at night, puzzling over it and asking himself if it could be because of anything he had done or said. He could hardly believe it was. They had known each other so long—all of their lives almost. Surely it was not possible for them to misunderstand each other?

As he gathered the fragile blooms his thoughts were all of Kathy; the violets were just the colour of her eyes and the primrose petals had the same softness as her skin. If only he had the money he could marry her and they could go away from here—have their own home—a little farm, maybe some land and animals of their own.

'So this is the way you exercise the horses! What in God's name are you doing, man?

149

Have you gone soft in the head or have you found yourself another governess?'

Patrick straightened up, dropping the handful of flowers he had gathered, a dull flush darkening his cheeks.

Charles towered over him, still astride his mount. The wind had dishevelled his hair, and his pale face was flushed with exertion. But it was Jason, the gelding, which drew Patrick's attention. The animal's flanks heaved with exhaustion and his usually glossy coat was dull and flecked with sweat. His mane was tangled and stringy and the foam that dripped from his mouth was stained with blood. Patrick's stomach lurched and he leapt forward to grasp the bridle.

'What have you done to him?' he demanded angrily.

Charles made a swipe at him with his crop. 'Mind your own business, lout—get back to your flower picking!'

But Patrick was staring now at a four-inch gash on the horse's hind leg. 'You've lamed him, by God! Get down!' His dark eyes flashed at Charles. 'Christ! Why do you treat him like this? What has the poor beast ever done to you?'

Charles lashed out again with his crop and at the same time kicked viciously at Patrick's head. He felt unsure of himself out here with no one to see what might happen and he didn't like the look in Patrick's eyes. He remembered only too well the feel of those large hands around his throat and he wasn't anxious for a repeat of the experience.

'Get away from me!' he cried shrilly, kicking out again. He kicked at Jason's sides, but the horse was too exhausted to move and just stood there enduring the punishment, his head low and his ears laid back.

Patrick gripped the end of the riding crop as it swished towards him for the third time. The palms of his hands were leathery from hard work and he barely felt the sting of its impact. Gripping it hard, he pulled and the next moment Charles toppled out of the saddle with a yell and lay sprawling on the grass at his feet, his eyes rolling with fear as he looked up.

Patrick longed to throw himself down on top of him—to choke the life out of his miserable, cruel body. His stoutly booted foot itched to kick in the white cowardly face staring up at him, but he restrained himself. His love for Kathy and the past two years of service and discipline had taught him to think twice before such rash action, though it was still far from easy for him. He stood there, the crop still in his hand, glaring down while Charles Quincey edged away on his backside and scrambled to his feet.

Once up he made a dash for the mare. Patrick shouted: 'Leave her! You'll mount no animal that's in my charge!'

But Charles had already thrown himself

151

across the saddle and before Patrick could reach him he was astride and moving on the rested mare.

'You'll pay for this morning's work, Reardon!' he flung over his shoulder, brave now that he was out of reach. 'I'll see that you do.'

Patrick swore under his breath and turned his attention to the gelding, leading him gently to a nearby stream to drink. He took off the neckerchief he wore and soaked it in the cool water to bathe and bind the animal's leg, all the while speaking softly and encouragingly to him, then he began to lead him home, walking at a gentle pace. As he went he heard the church clock strike six and he sighed. He'd be all behind with his work this day.

They were waiting for him as he led Jason into the stable-yard: Charles Quincey and his father, with the grooms standing silently by, their faces troubled and curious. As soon as he saw Patrick, Charles shouted triumphantly:

'There! What did I tell you? Look at my mount! I knew he'd be in a sorry state, the way he was riding him!' He pointed at Patrick who stood staring disbelievingly from one to the other.

'Why were you not exercising your own horse?' his father asked.

'Because *he'd* taken him—Reardon! He's always had a fancy for that horse—because he was mine, I suppose,' Charles lied. 'He'd gone before I got here. So I took Meg instead. When I saw him he was putting Jason at a hedge all of six feet high. Look at the gash he's got!' He turned to his father. 'The creature's fit for nothing but dog-meat now. His wind is broken. Just look at him—ruined!'

Henry Quincey stepped forward to look at the horse, his face dark with anger. He looked at Patrick, his eyes shrewd. He was a rough, impertinent fellow, but he had a way with horses. It was unlike him to treat them like this—unless . . .

'Well—what have you to say for yourself'?' he asked. 'Did you do this out of spite? If so, by God I'll—'

'Wait!'

They all turned to see Seamus coming down the coach-house steps, his wrinkled face twitching with concern.

'I was here, sir,' he said firmly. 'It was Mr Charles took that horse out. Didn't I saddle him up meself? Patrick was already out on Miss Melissa's mare!' He stood on the bottom step and looked his master in the eye. 'I'm not one to speak out of turn, sir, but I can't stand by and see an injustice done, so I can't!'

Henry Quincey nodded briefly. Seamus was his oldest and most trusted servant. He knew he would not lie to save himself, let alone this lad. Anyway, he had suspected the truth of the matter already. He turned to his son, his

153

colour deepening.

'Get inside, sir!'

Charles blanched. 'Are—are you going to take the word of a servant against mine?' he asked, his voice rising.

'I said, get inside,' Henry repeated. 'Or do you wish me to tell you what I think of you out here?'

Charles turned and flung away, his mouth twisted with fury as he gave Patrick a last bitter glance.

'Better do what you can for the animal,' Henry Quincey told Patrick brusquely. 'Then take him to the knacker. Get on with it.' He turned and walked towards the house.

Charles was waiting for his father in the study. He knew better than to defy him and go straight to his room as he would have liked. Henry came in and closed the door behind him quietly. It was still early morning and he had no wish to create a disturbance at this hour.

'What in God's name got into you?' he growled. 'You've had that horse no time at all and you've ruined the animal—why?'

Charles lifted his chin defiantly. 'It's my horse. I shall ride him any way I wish.'

'No you will not, sir!' Henry brought his fist down hard on the desk. 'That kind of behaviour is an example to no one. You have let yourself down—and if you are to be in charge of men at Quincey's—' He broke off as Charles turned away with a sneer. 'Oh, I know

154

it doesn't suit you,' he said. 'But let me tell you this—you'll be fit for nothing else, m'lad. If there wasn't Quincey's for you to step into you'd be lucky to get into the army or the church! I'm what I am today through hard work and by God I'll see that you make the best of your opportunities too!' His face was purple as he stepped closer to his son, clapping a hand on to his shoulder and turning him to look into his eyes. 'Another thing, boy—don't *ever* lie in the way you did this morning. Young fool! You might have known damned well you'd be found out. What do you think they're doing out there now?' He flung out his arm. 'Laughing at you, that's what. Laughing at *my son*! From old man Reardon down to the "tiger". Laughing at you for the idiot you are. By Christ, I'd be laughing too if you were anyone else—and if you hadn't just cost me a good horse.' He shook his head. 'You've a hell of a lot to learn.' He opened a drawer in his desk and took out a ledger, thrusting it at Charles. 'Here—you can take this and study it. Maybe it'll keep you out of mischief for a while. It's the mill accounts. See if you can think up a more efficient method of book-keeping. Learn how to handle people and horses without half killing them—and for God's sake learn how to tell a lie folk can't see through like glass!'

They stared at each other for a moment with undisguised dislike, Charles clutching the ledger to his chest as though to protect himself. Then Henry shouted exasperatedly:

'Oh—get out of my sight before I clout you one—you great nelly, you!'

Charles got out, his heart torn with impotent rage. Once in his room he flung himself face down on his bed and wallowed in a welter of tears. Self-pity, fury and a longing for revenge churned within him. 'Just you wait!' he muttered. 'I'll get you *all* in the end. I'll kill you—*kill you!*'

But Henry Quincey had been wrong about at least one thing that morning: there was no laughter in the stable-yard. Once Jason was in his stable he collapsed and nothing Patrick could do would get him on to his feet again. It was as if the animal had given up—lost the will to live.

Patrick was busy all day long, but he kept returning to the end stable to talk to the horse which had always been his special favourite; to coax him and sing to him—fondle his ears and the scars on his face that he owed to his master. By the time evening came the sound of Jason's laboured breathing filled the yard. Patrick was frantic. He begged Seamus to help him improvise a sling with which to haul the dying horse to his feet, but the old man shook his head sadly.

'Ah, sure, what's the use, boy? If you get him well you've only to take him to Arthur Adams to be put down. The Master would never keep

156

a crippled horse in his stable. Why not let him go peaceful-like in his own stable?'

So Patrick sat all night with Jason, stroking the velvet nose and the silky mane he had always taken such pride in. Softly singing the old songs he knew so well, till at last in the early hours the horse quietly died with his head in Patrick's lap. There in the stable, with only a lantern for light, he looked down at the still animal and wept the first tears of his life. They were bitter and painful and he promised himself there and then that no Quincey would ever make him shed more. He would kill first!

Charles had studied the ledger all afternoon and evening. He had refused to come out of his room for the rest of the day, fearing that the other members of the family should see the ravages of weeping on his face. But he had become extremely bored and had at last turned to the ledger in sheer desperation. To his surprise he had soon become fascinated by it, especially when he saw that he could indeed think of a more efficient method of book-keeping. He would show his father that he was not such a dolt after all. The remark about the army and the church still rankled.

It was well after midnight when he decided to seek his father out. He was so inflamed with his new ideas that he felt they would not keep until morning and he knew that although his father retired when the rest of the family did, he often worked in his room until the small hours. He would show his father that if he had to go into the business he would at least prove his worth.

The house was dark and he took his candle with him along the corridor to his father's room which was at the top of the main staircase, but just as he reached the end of the corridor and was about to come out on to the wide, square landing, the flame guttered and went out in a sudden draught. Charles swore softly, but almost immediately he saw the reason. In the moonlight coming in through the venetian window over the stairs he saw that the door of his father's room had opened and Henry stood on the threshold, a candle in his hand. Charles stepped back into the shadows to watch as his father stood listening for a moment, his face lit by the candle flame which he protected with his hand. Then, satisfied that no one was stirring he made his way along the opposite corridor and disappeared from sight.

Charles stood for a moment, speculating the reason for his father's stealth. It was almost as though he were about to do something secret and underhand. It took Charles a moment only to decide to follow.

At the end of the corridor a door stood open, the door that gave on to the back stairs. He hesitated. Why should his father have gone this way? Puzzled, he began to ascend the stairs, his slippered feet making no noise. At the top he paused. To the left were the servants' rooms, to the right the heavy door to the nursery was ajar. Slowly a suspicion crept into Charles's mind. He pushed the door open and slipped into the corridor, standing quietly in the darkness beyond. Facing him at the far end of the passage was the nurse's room. He remembered it well from his own nursery days. He crept closer and as he did so he heard the rhythmic squeaking of the bed-springs and the low rumbling of his father's voice as he indulged himself in his twice-weekly lust.

His heart beating fast, Charles applied his eye to the keyhole and saw that his suspicions were confirmed. At the sight he saw, illuminated by the single candle on the bedside table, he wanted to shout with triumphant laughter. His father, writhing naked with the Irish maidservant—and by the look of resigned forbearance on the girl's face it had been going on for some time! Oh, it was rich—rich! Now it would be *he* who held the whip hand—*he* who called the tune. He would make his father eat the words he had spoken this morning. Eat them till he choked! Unheard, he turned and made his way back to his room, turning his back on the sounds of his father's pleasure and looking forward gleefully to the morrow, when he would make him pay for them.

\*　　　\*　　　\*

Patrick stirred in the straw and opened his eyes. The first pale light was peeping through the cracks in the door and he stood up, shaking the stiffness from his limbs. He looked across to where Jason lay, motionless and dead, and he felt again the anger and desperation he had known last night. He had always felt a strange affinity with the horse. They had come to Denmark House at the same time and had shared the same enemies and the same friends. Jason had been cut down in his prime on the selfish whim of an arrogant man—not even a strong man either, but a gutless, feelingless lump who had no more courage than to take out his spite on a dumb, innocent animal. Patrick swore that he should suffer for it. If it took him the rest of his life, he—Patrick Reardon—would make him!

He washed at the pump and went round to the kitchen door to see if there was a brew of tea going. Sarah was always about at this time, though he knew that at present Kathy would be above with the young fellow. Sarah always had a smile and a cup of tea for him in the early morning and he had never needed either more than he did today.

She looked up when she saw him standing in the doorway. 'Mornin', Patrick. How's the poor horse?'

'Dead,' he said briefly. 'Would there be a cup of tea, Sarah?'

160

She looked at the stubble on his face and the bits of straw clinging to his clothes. 'Have you been up all night in the stable?' she asked.

He shrugged. 'I have—but no matter.'

She poured him a mug of strong tea from the pot on the hob and beckoned to him. 'Come and sit a minute. You look done in. Will you eat a bit o' bacon if I fry it for you?'

He nodded, managing a smile, and she began to busy herself with the big iron pan. For a while he watched her in silence, then he asked: 'Sarah—do you know if there's anything wrong with Kathy?'

She coloured guiltily and said without turning: 'Wrong—no, not that I know of.'

He shook his head. 'There's somethin'. I thought maybe she'd have told you, you bein' her best friend.'

'Not now, she isn't,' Sarah said. 'Not since she was put up in the world!'

Patrick looked at her sharply. 'Then there is somethin'—tell me.'

Sarah shrugged. 'It's nothin' more than she feels she's too good for the likes of us now, if you ask me,' she said petulantly. 'If I were you, Patrick, I wouldn't worry. There's better fish in the sea than ever came out of it—specially for a good-lookin' feller like you.'

But Patrick wasn't listening to her flattery. He frowned. 'Kathy wouldn't change like that—not Kathy.'

Sarah put the plate down in front of him.

161

'Don't you believe it,' she said. 'I've seen it happen before—folk who seemed nice turning high an' mighty when a better chance comes along.'

Patrick ate his bacon thoughtfully. He had no doubt that what Sarah said was true, but not in Kathy's case. She would never do that. Hadn't she begged him to stay at Denmark House? Hadn't she said she loved him and that she always had? No—there had to be more.

'Sarah,' he said slowly. 'Will you see what you can find out? You're inside and you see and hear more than I do. Will you—for me?'

She looked at him for a long moment. She would have done anything to be in his favour. She thought him the most handsome young man she had ever set eyes on and she would have given the soul out of her body to be in Kathy's shoes. She smiled softly at him.

'I'll see—there's a lot to be done what with the weddin' an' all. Mebbe after—though I'm no sneak, mind!'

\*         \*         \*

Charles walked quietly down the stairs, the heavy ledger under his arm. It was only seven thirty but he knew his father would be in his study, preparing work for the coming day. He smiled to himself, remembering what he had seen through the keyhole up there on the

162

nursery floor last night. Now they would see who called the tune! He tapped politely on the door and Henry called to come in. He entered and laid the ledger on the desk, the reminiscent smile lingering on his lips.

Henry looked up. 'Good-morning, Charles. I see you've got your humour back again. What brings you down so early? Have you finished looking at the accounts then?'

Charles nodded. 'Yes, Father. I think I could devise a better method than the one employed. I have made some notes on a sheet of paper. It is here.' He opened the ledger to reveal the paper covered in his large, scrawling handwriting. Henry studied it for a moment, his eyebrows lifting slightly.

'Mmm—' he said at length. 'Well, I'm glad to see that you're taking an interest, lad. Maybe we'll even give your idea a try—maybe next year.'

Charles smiled blandly. 'I will take charge of the mill accounts immediately, Father,' he said quietly. 'With an office of my own—and my name on the door!'

Henry looked up, amused. 'I'm afraid it'll be a long time before you're up to that, boy. Though I'm glad to see that you've ambitions in the right direction.'

'Not ambitions, Father—*intentions*!' Charles said through clenched teeth. 'That is if you wish to retain your good name in this town— *and* this house!'

Henry Quincey rose to his feet, his eyes narrowing as he stared intently at his son, his colour deepening.

'What the devil are you talking about?' he asked, his voice ominously low.

But Charles was undisturbed. He was enjoying himself. 'I wanted to talk to you about my ideas last night,' he explained. 'But you weren't in your room. I saw you leave it, in fact. I was curious, so I followed and saw you—entertaining yourself with the Irish girl—Paul's nurse.' He cleared his throat delicately, enjoying the spectacle of his father's bulging eyes and purple cheeks. 'I take it you would not wish the matter to reach Mama's ears?'

Henry's chest heaved as he took a deep breath. He rocked slightly on his heels, then walked round the desk to face his son squarely.

'I suggest you go and tell your mother at once,' he said.

Charles stared at him, the triumphant smile vanishing from his face as his eyes goggled wildly. 'T—tell her? But I thought—I thought—' He spluttered and gasped as his father's hand shot out and grabbed him by the collar.

'You *thought*! This time you thought too damned much! Listen to me, boy—' He thrust his face close to Charles's perspiring one. 'I will not be blackmailed in my own house by my own son—d'you hear me?' His voice rose to a roar. 'If I want to amuse myself with a servant girl I'll do so. I pay them, don't I? I pay you too and don't you *ever* forget it!' He let go of his pallid son abruptly and turned away.

'You—you are unfaithful to Mama,' Charles spluttered.

Henry turned, a grim smile on his lips. 'All right—I've told you what to do about it. Tell her, if you're so concerned, I'm sure it must be just what she wants to hear on the eve of her daughter's wedding. Tell her and see where it gets you! Can you support her? Can you support yourself?'

'You're a—a monster!' Charles accused shrilly, perilously close to tears.

Henry walked towards his son again and regarded him thoughtfully for a moment. 'Be at the mill promptly on Monday morning,' he ordered. 'And don't come dressed like that. The work you'll be doing will be dirty work— the sort you seem to prefer!'

Choked with defeat, Charles turned to go, but Henry wasn't finished.

'Just a minute—'

Charles turned and as he did so the back of his father's hand caught him a ringing blow on the side of his head.

His ear singing, he lost his balance and staggered heavily against the wall. Henry eyed him with distaste.

'You never learn, do you, lad?' he said coldly.

Outside the door Sarah stood transfixed, the Master's early morning tea-tray in her hands.

Her heart was hammering fast. She had promised to find out what she could but she had never dreamed that such information would be hers so soon—or so surprisingly!

So *that* was it? Kathy had been letting the Master have his way with her! She would never have thought her that sort, but you could never tell—and didn't they say that the Irish were a loose-livin' lot? No wonder she'd got herself a better job and had been moved into the house to sleep. It all fitted now! She'd have something to tell Patrick now all right. Kathy had bigger fish than him to fry these days. By God she had!

She stood back as the door flew open and Mr Charles came stumbling through it, his hand to his head. Through the open door she saw Henry Quincey, seated again at his desk, his face flushed and triumphant. She stepped over the threshold and cleared her throat.

'A-hem—Please sir, here's your tea,' she said demurely.

# Part Three
# The Gages

# CHAPTER SEVEN

Melissa opened her eyes as a sunbeam, playing through a chink in the curtain, danced on her lids. She gazed dreamily up at the ceiling. It was her wedding day; the day she had thought would never come was here at last. Throwing back the covers she sprang lightly out of bed and ran to draw back the heavy curtains. The sun streamed in. She clasped her hands. It was going to be a beautiful day. All would be well. Everyone knew that it was a good omen for the sun to shine on your wedding day. Not that she needed any omen, loving John as dearly as she did.

The door of the room flew open and Caroline looked round it, her face wreathed in smiles.

'What did I tell you? I knew it would be a fine day! Oh Melly, aren't you excited?' She bounced into the room and pirouetted joyfully.

Melissa sat on the bed, her knees drawn up and her arms clasped around them, her grey eyes dreamy. 'Oh, yes. We shall be so happy, Caroline, I know we shall. Oh, I'm so lucky.' She looked wistfully at her younger sister. 'But I shall miss you.'

Caroline laughed gaily. 'Oh poo, what nonsense! You will have far too much to think of. Besides, you will be but half a mile away. I

169

shall visit you often, never fear.' She hugged her sister. 'Oh what fun, Melly, to have a house of your very own!'

Melissa and John were to live at Holbrook Lodge, a small house given to them as a wedding present by John's father. It was only a stone's throw from Willerby Hall and stood on the wooded stretch of the river above the bridge.

'The Misses Fairfax will be including you in their "good works" programme,' Caroline said teasingly. 'Before you know it you will find yourself dishing out gruel at the soup kitchen on Wednesdays and Fridays!'

The girls laughed together but a moment later Parkes came into the room and began to move about with brisk efficiency, laying out brushes, combs and underwear.

'Your breakfast will be up directly,' she said to Melissa. She eyed Caroline disapprovingly. 'And you had better go down for yours now, Miss Caroline, or you'll never be dressed in time.'

The wedding was to take place at noon and everyone in the kitchen was bustling. Cook wanted all the trays out of the way as soon as possible so that she could begin on the preparation of the wedding breakfast. It was to be held in the library, a recent addition to the house, opening off the morning-room. It ran the whole depth of the house, one wall lined with books and the facing one hung with

Henry Quincey's fine collection of pictures, some of which he had purchased from the estate of his late father-in-law. Tall glazed doors at the garden end led on to the terrace and it was hoped that if the day were fine, the guests would be able to spill out into the sunshine.

In the stable Patrick had finished the grooming and was about to go across to the coach-house to see if Seamus needed his help when he heard a soft rustle and turned to see Kathy standing just inside the stable door. She drew in her breath.

'Oh, Patrick, they look beautiful!' Her eyes glowed softly as she looked at the greys standing proudly like something from a fairy-tale, their manes and tails brushed into spun silver and their coats gleaming with health.

'I think they'll do.' He moved to her quickly and drew her into the shelter of the stable where no one could see. Taking her in his arms he kissed her hungrily. 'Ah, Kathy, where've ye been? I've missed ye. Is anything wrong?' He looked into her eyes and saw them fill with tears. 'Darlin' what is it?'

She swallowed hard. 'I—I've come to—to say goodbye,' she said painfully.

He stared down at her. 'What d'ye mean, goodbye? Where're ye goin'?'

She bit her lip. 'I'm to go to Miss Melissa's new house today—after the weddin's over—to help get it ready for when they come back from their honeymoon. Then I'm to stay on as her maid.'

He shook his head, frowning. 'You're to leave Denmark House?'

She grasped his arms. 'I shan't be far away—only a bit above the bridge. I'll come and see ye—often,' she told him breathlessly.

He pulled her close to him. 'Oh, Kathy—I'll miss ye so. Why didn't ye tell me?' As he looked down at her an idea formed in his mind.

'Kathy,' he said excitedly. 'D'ye think they'd be needin' anyone for their own stable? If we were both there, we could be married!'

But to his surprise she pulled away from him and turned her head. 'No—they've all the servants they need for now.'

He grasped her shoulders and bent to look into her eyes. 'Kathy—what is it? You *do* still love me, don't ye? You do still want us to be married one day like we said?'

She bit her lower lip hard to still its trembling and her eyes slid away from his intense look. 'One day—maybe.'

He frowned. 'You don't sound very sure. There's somethin' wrong with ye, isn't there? I've known it for some time. Ah, come on, Kathy—ye can tell me what it is, surely?'

'Patrick! Where are ye?' Seamus's voice calling urgently across the yard broke the tension between them and Kathy slipped from his grasp.

'I'll have to go,' she muttered and ran lightly

across the cobbled yard, calling a brief greeting to Seamus as she went. Patrick emerged from the stable just in time to see her slip through the gate and he stood staring after her in bewilderment, his heart heavy.

All the servants were assembled in the hall to see Melissa and her father leave for the church and when she appeared at the top of the stairs a gasp of delight and admiration went up. She looked beautiful; tall, slender and graceful in her dress of delphinium blue trimmed with ivory lace. On her head she wore a light straw bonnet, lined with blue and trimmed with orange blossom and sprigs of lilac and in her hands she carried a posy of the same flowers encircled with lace. Henry eyed his daughter proudly as he waited for her at the foot of the stairs.

'You're a picture, Melissa,' he said, holding out his hand to her. 'A daughter fit for a king!'

Parkes and the dressmaker fluttered round her, rearranging the folds of her gown as Simpson stepped forward to open the door. Outside the gates stood the wedding carriage with its immaculate pair of greys and Seamus seated behind them, dignified and splendid in his new livery and tall shining hat. Stevens, as representative of the staff, stepped forward and gave Melissa a bunch of white heather tied with a blue ribbon.

'From us all, Miss Melissa,' she said, dropping a curtsy. 'With our best wishes for your happiness.'

Melissa smiled radiantly and tucked the heather into her posy.

'Thank you—thank you all.' And on her father's arm she went down the steps to the waiting carriage.

As the door closed a buzz of excited conversation began.

'I don't care what anyone says. I still think lilac's unlucky,' Cook said lugubriously.

Parkes sighed. 'I do think I might have been allowed to go to the church.' She began to go upstairs, a disgruntled pout on her lips.

Simpson and Mrs Brown hustled the rest of them down the kitchen stairs, remarking that there was still plenty of work to be done before family and guests arrived for the wedding breakfast.

In her corner by the wall, Kathy's face was wet with tears. Today she had seen Miss Melissa's dream come true—and her own shattered. Although he didn't know it she had said goodbye to Patrick for ever. She knew this was the way it must be. He deserved better than the wretch she had become. She would devote the rest of her life to Miss Melissa—or Mrs Gage as she soon would be. That should be her life's work. But oh—would her heart ever stop aching for Patrick? It felt as though it must break in two.

'Come along Kathleen! What are you dreaming about? I'm sure that Cook can do with all the hands she can get.' Mrs Brown shook her arm and Kathy stirred herself and felt in her apron pocket for a handkerchief.

'Sorry—yes, of course, I'm going this minute.' She scurried down the stairs while the housekeeper looked after her, shaking her head. Silly sentimental child. But then it was said that these Celtic races were all alike.

St Mary's Church was full to overflowing with the cream of Elvemere society. The Misses Fairfax were there, wearing last year's summer bonnets. Dr Maybury, his new young wife and his handsome son, Robert. The Muxworths and their family of six daughters, sitting beside the Revd Clutterbuck's wife and two young sons. George and Harriet Gage sat in their front pew, gazing solemnly at the backs of their son John and his groomsman.

The mellow sound of the organ and the scent of flowers drifted out through the open door to reach Amelia as she waited anxiously in the porch. With her stood Caroline and Christabel, the bridesmaids, delightfully pretty in gowns of pale pink and bonnets trimmed with rosebuds. Amelia twitched nervously at the skirt of her lavender silk gown and Caroline admonished her gently for the second time:

'Oh, Mama, do go into church now and take your seat. Melissa and Papa will be here at any minute. You must not let them find you out here still!'

175

But it was not her daughter's arrival that concerned Amelia. Charles had been missing since last night. All day yesterday he had been silent and morose and when she had gone to his room early this morning it was to find that his bed had not been slept in.

'Where can he be?' she muttered distractedly under her breath. She had no intention of letting anyone know that anything was amiss, especially any member of the Gage family. It was extremely humiliating though. In the absence of her husband, Charles was to have escorted her to church. It was unthinkable that she should walk to her pew alone!

At that moment Rupert Clutterbuck, the rector's young son put in an appearance. He was a fresh-faced, pleasant youth of seventeen and he looked uncertainly at Amelia, clearing his throat.

'Ahem—Mama sent me to enquire if you were unwell, Mrs Quincey,' he said, blushing furiously. 'She—er—instructed me to ask if there is anything I can do for you.'

Before Amelia could reply, Caroline interjected: 'Oh, how very kind of you, Mr Clutterbuck. Perhaps you would be so kind as to escort Mama to her pew. My brother seems to be unavoidably detained.'

'Why, of course.' Rupert blushed more deeply than ever as Caroline rewarded him with her dazzling smile. He gallantly offered his arm to Amelia. 'It would be an honour if you would allow me, Mrs Quincey.'

Caroline sighed with relief as her mother meekly took the proffered arm and disappeared into the church just as the wedding carriage came into view at the top of the church's elm-lined drive. Seamus drew the greys to a smooth halt at the door and Henry helped his daughter to alight. The bridal party assembled in the porch—the signal was given to the organist who struck up the first rousing chords of the wedding march—the ceremony had begun.

\*      \*      \*

At Denmark House the reception was in full swing when Kathy crept up the back stairs to put together her few possessions in preparation for leaving. Mrs Brown had advised her to slip away whilst the family and guests were occupied, so that she might leave the house unseen and walk the half mile to Holbrook Lodge. She had lectured her on how fortunate she was to have been offered such a good place after such a short time in service and said that she hoped Kathy appreciated the fact. Kathy had taken her leave of the other members of the staff briefly, most of them being too busy to say more than a cursory farewell. Only Sarah had more to say to her. She looked Kathy up and down with open distaste.

'So you're off then? Leavin' the clearin' up

to others—as usual.' She tossed back her head with a sneer. 'But bein' *in favour*, you wouldn't expect to soil your hands too much, would you?'

Kathy shook her head miserably. 'Mrs Brown told me to go now,' she said quietly.

Sarah gave her a sour look. 'Maybe she thinks the same as me—good riddance to bad rubbish!' And she turned her back in contempt.

With a heavy heart Kathy climbed the back stairs to the nursery, hoping for a last glimpse of Paul. She had said goodbye to him earlier when she helped him to dress for the wedding. He had hugged her fiercely.

'I'll miss you, Kathy,' he said, kissing her cheek. 'But I've asked Melly if I can stay with her next holidays so that we can be together.'

Her thoughts were of the boy as she reached the top of the stairs and pushed the door open, but as she did so a sound caught her attention. Her heart lifted. She had thought that Paul would be enjoying himself downstairs. He must have come up to say a last goodbye to her after all. She opened the door of his room but it was empty, so she went along the corridor to her own room.

She saw him as soon as she opened the door. He lay sprawled across her bed. His clothes were stained and crumpled, his eyes wild and bloodshot and his face was covered in a thick fair stubble. When he saw her he sat up and threw out his arms.

'So here you are! I thought you'd never come. I've been waiting here hours for you!'

Bewildered, she shook her head. 'What is it, Mr Charles, sir? I was just going to leave for Miss Melissa's new house—oh—I mean Mrs Gage's.'

He laughed drunkenly. 'My illustrious sister can wait.' He rolled off the bed and stood swaying in front of her. 'It seems that you are in great demand with various members of this family,' he said slurring his words. 'So I decided that I really must see for myself what it is about you that is so bewitching.' He made a sudden grab at her, grasping her arm and drawing her to him. 'Mmm—pretty little thing, aren't you?'

She shook her arm free. 'Please, Mr Charles,' her heart was beating fast. 'They'll be lookin' for ye—please go downstairs.'

He rocked unsteadily, glowering at her. 'You don't fancy me, eh? Rather have someone else, would you? Come on, Kathy. I know what you are—what you do. I've seen!' He made a lunge at her, throwing his whole weight against her. She fell backwards, clutching at his shoulders for support, a cry escaping her lips. They fell together on to the bed in a sprawling heap, Charles landing heavily on top of her. She cried out as his weight crushed the breath from her body, but he growled at her to be quiet, pressing his

179

hand over her mouth whilst the other pulled her skirt up above her thighs. Horror overwhelmed her. Not again—not another of the Quincey men. 'Oh God spare me,' she prayed desperately as she struggled helplessly. Suddenly, above the sound of Charles's ragged breathing a sound came to her.

'Kathy! Kathy, where are you? I've come to say goodbye. We are—' Melissa's light, clear voice stopped abruptly as she appeared in the doorway. Her brother leapt up from the bed and stood sheepishly shuffling his feet, while Kathy, flushed and dishevelled, adjusted her clothes.

'Charles! What are you doing here?' Melissa demanded. 'Where have you been? Poor Mama has been quite out of her mind with worry!' She surveyed the state of his clothing with distaste and stepped towards him, sniffing suspiciously. 'I believe you have been drinking!' She looked at Kathy. 'Did he hurt you? Are you all right?' Kathy nodded and she turned again to her brother. 'I think you had better go to your room and stay there,' she told him. 'Mama has made the excuse that you are indisposed so you will not be missed. Please do not let her see you like this, I am disgusted that you should behave so on my wedding day.'

He stumbled past her to the door and turned. 'I'll tell you something, sister, *dear,*' he said sarcastically. 'I don't give a damn whether

180

you're disgusted or not. But I can assure you that there are a great many more things in this house that would offend your fastidious senses. Maybe it's a good thing you are leaving it.' He glanced at Kathy. 'And taking that little slut with you!' And with that he lurched out into the corridor.

As they heard the door at the end of the passage close, Melissa sat down beside Kathy on the bed, taking her hand.

'Are you sure he did not hurt you, Kathy?' she asked anxiously. 'I am so sorry. I don't know what I can say to excuse him except that things are not easy for him at present. He has allowed his disappointment to get the better of him, I am sure he would not have behaved so had he not been under the influence of strong liquor.'

Kathy made a great effort and smiled at her mistress.

'Sure I'm all right, miss, thank ye. He didn't hurt me at all. It was only frightened, I was. I didn't expect to find him here. Now I must pack me things and go—and so must you, I think.'

Melissa smiled, relieved. 'I wish you were coming with me now, Kathy. It will be so pleasant by the sea. But we are to have servants who come in daily.'

Kathy nodded. 'I know, miss. That's as it should be with you only just married an' all.'

Melissa blushed, her eyes dreamy as she

181

thought of the days and nights ahead, alone with her new husband. 'You must try to remember to call me Mrs Gage and madam now, Kathy,' she said gently. 'Though I shall always be Miss Melissa to you when we are alone, shall I not?' She bent and touched her cheek lightly to Kathy's, then she was gone in a flurry of silk and a cloud of sweet perfume.

Kathy rose with a sigh and put together her few belongings. Fifteen minutes later she was walking away from Denmark House towards the High Bridge; leaving behind her the laughing guests, the Quincey family, Sarah, Uncle Seamus—and Patrick—Patrick. Her feet dragged as she walked and she wondered how it could be possible to live out the days and the weeks without him.

\*       \*       \*

That evening in the servants' hall the staff of Denmark House had their own celebration of Miss Melissa's wedding. Above stairs the guests had all departed and the family, apart from Charles, had gone to dine with the Gages. The hired extra help had stayed on to help with the marathon of washing-up and now they too had left. Henry Quincey had given Simpson three bottles of wine that the staff might drink the health of his daughter and her new husband.

Unlike Christmas, it was a quiet occasion.

182

As with all weddings there was a feeling of anti-climax once the bride and groom had departed and exhaustion had reduced most of the servants to a state of limpness. It was pleasant, however, to sit round and talk of the day, now behind them, to make their own comments and judgements and to speculate on whose turn it would be next to wed.

Patrick sat stiffly in his corner. He didn't care for the taste of the wine and the fragment of wedding cake had not been enough to feed a fly. All day he had felt a strange numbness, unable to believe that Kathy had really gone—that he wouldn't see her again unless he made a special journey. Ever since he could remember she had always been there, under the same roof, sharing things with him. She had said she would come and visit him, but there had been an odd remoteness about her voice when she said it. As for their future—the marriage he had hoped for—she seemed reluctant even to speak of it. He put down his glass, catching Seamus's eye.

'I'll be away to bed the horses now,' he said. 'Then I'll go up meself. Good-night.'

Seamus frowned. The lad had not been himself all day.

'Can ye manage, lad?' he asked. 'Shall I come and help ye?' But Patrick shook his head. He wanted no company this night but his own. 'I'll manage fine on me own,' he said. 'You stay and enjoy yourself, Uncle. It's been a long day.'

Outside he breathed deeply of the spring dusk. How did people manage to stay inside all of their lives? One hour in a stuffy room was as much as he could bear. He walked round to the stables and bedded the pair of greys first, talking to them encouragingly as he did so. He was just fastening the door of their stable when a sudden noise made him start. He peered into the half light.

'Who's there?'

Sarah stepped out of the shadows. 'It's only me. I thought you might like some company, Patrick.'

He shook his head. 'I've work to do. Why don't you go back inside and enjoy yourself with the others?'

She moved forward, blocking his way. 'They're all old—my idea of a good time is different from theirs.' She sidled up to him. 'I'd rather be with you, Patrick.'

'Sure I'm not good company tonight,' he said abruptly.

'Because of her—because Kathy's gone and left you?' she said sharply. 'She's not worth it, Patrick. I told you—there's more fish in the sea.'

He turned and went into the next stable without answering, intent on his task, hoping she would go away. She stood in the doorway, watching him for a while, then she moved to him again and put her hand on his shoulder.

'Forget her, Patrick. Why don't you let me comfort you? I want to. I've always liked you. Don't you like me at all?'

He looked down at her impatiently. 'Of course I like you, Sarah, but—'

She stopped his words by reaching up and pulling his head down, fastening her lips on his, at the same time pressing her body close to his. Shocked and repelled, he disentangled her arms from around his neck and thrust her from him.

'Sarah! Will ye stop it! For Christ's sake go away and leave me in peace.'

In the half light he saw her flush hotly. 'Oh! So I'm not good enough for you. Is that it? Well I'll tell you something now. You asked me to find out why she was cooling off you and I found out. She's no better than she should be, that one. I'd not do what she done! Not if it was the richest man on earth!'

He turned to look sharply at her. 'What do you mean?'

She nodded triumphantly. 'I thought that'd make you sit up and take notice! You've always wanted to get on, haven't you? An' I reckon you've always told her that too—well *she* found a quick way to do it. *You* got no part in her future now, I can tell you!'

His hands shot out and grabbed her by the shoulders.

'What are you talkin' about, woman? Speak up! Tell me the truth and stop talkin' in

185

riddles.'

Her eyes blazed up into his. 'Kathy was clever. She knew how to get a better place. She's been lettin' the Master have his way with her these past six months or more—so there Mr High and Mighty Reardon!'

His stomach lurched as his fingers bit deeply into the flesh of her shoulders. 'What do you mean—have his way with her?' He began to shake her. 'Come out with it and tell me what you mean—*tell me*!'

Her heart thudded with fear now as she looked up into his eyes. They glowed like hot coals and the fingers that held her fast were like iron bands. She swallowed.

'You know what I mean—he's been goin' to her room at night—*havin'* her—' she shook her head. 'There's a word for it but I'll not soil me lips with it.'

He started as though she had doused him with cold water, then he fastened his hands around her throat, his face a mask of pain. 'Christ! It's not true!' he growled deep in his chest. 'You *dare* to come and tell me a tale like that about Kathy! If I hear that ye've said it to anyone else I'll kill ye—d'ye hear—*kill ye*!' He let go of her abruptly and she fell back against the wall, choking and rubbing her bruised throat.

'You're *mad*!' she coughed hoarsely. 'All of you Reardons—wicked and mad!'

He lunged at her again and she gave a shrill

186

squeal and fled through the open door. As he stood there he heard her feet running across the yard, then the squeak and clang of the gate. He turned towards the quiet horse behind him, pressing his face against its warm flank.

'Oh, Jesus,' he moaned. 'Oh, Jesus let it not be true.'

From the servants' hall came the thin sound of Seamus's old fiddle and the voices of the others, raised in song. It seemed they had regained some of their energy and were enjoying themselves in the time-honoured way. By the sound of them they would not be ready for retiring for many an hour. Patrick opened the door of the pantry quietly and took a mug down from the row of hooks on the shelf, filling it from the tapped barrel of ale. He drained it at one gulp and refilled it immediately. Maybe if he had enough he would sleep, able to blot out the thoughts that Sarah's words had evoked. It couldn't be true. Sarah was a spiteful bitch. She had once been Kathy's best friend but she had been jealous of her for some time past now. All the same— Kathy had been behaving oddly of late. But they were pledged to each other. If the thing Sarah described had happened it must have been rape—but if so why hadn't Kathy come to him for help? She knew he would have killed for her if he had to.

He drank mug after mug of ale until his

head swam, then staggered uncertainly out again into the stone-flagged passage. The singing still filled the air and he found himself joining in with the words as he groped his way towards the door. He had just reached it when the door to the servants' hall opened and he heard Cook's voice call:

'I'll get some ale. I'm sure we're all thirsty as fishes!'

He slipped out into the darkness, keeping close to the wall, hoping to lose himself and his unendurable thoughts among the shadows.

\*　　\*　　\*

Charles was sober now and sat in his room, washed, shaved and dressed in fresh clothes. He remembered little of last night except that he had begun it in an alehouse and ended it—he thought—in a brothel somewhere along the riverside. He deeply resented the fact that he remembered nothing of it and was disappointed now at having missed his sister's wedding to which he had looked forward. Above all, he resented his father—the cause of it all. Sitting there in his room he went over the scene in his father's study again. It seemed that Henry Quincey was invincible. Nothing could touch him. He could do as he pleased with and to whom he liked and suffer no recrimination whilst he—Charles—was deprived of everything he valued—education, respect, even dignity.

He fumed. By God he would make his father pay some day. Suddenly he thought of Reardon, his old enemy. He owed him a blow and by Heaven he had the very weapon with which to deliver it. Why had he not thought of it before?

He came out of his room on to the quiet landing. The house was empty. He remembered now, the rest of the family had been invited out for the evening, to dinner at the Gages. He smiled to himself. At least he had been spared the simperings of the frightful Christabel. His stomach rumbled loudly in the silence and he was reminded that he had eaten nothing all day. He thought of the copious food that must have been consumed at the wedding breakfast and swore under his breath.

In the dining-room he tugged at the bell-pull, but it was some time before Simpson appeared. The man looked surprised at being summoned and not a little affronted.

'You rang, Mr Charles?' he said, his eyebrows raised.

Charles looked up from his father's chair at the head of the table. His feet rested on its polished surface and he looked arrogantly into Simpson's disapproving face as he recrossed his ankles.

'I believe I did—some time ago. I had almost forgotten! I'll have something to eat,' he said. 'And be quick about it this time!'

Simpson nodded. 'Will something cold be acceptable, sir? Cook was told that dinner would not be required tonight.'

Charles swung his feet to the ground, a ripe remark on his lips, then he thought better of it. Simpson might complain to his father and it seemed he would take any servant's word against his.

'Oh, all right, I suppose something cold will have to do then,' he said grudgingly. 'I suppose you're all drinking yourselves stupid downstairs, celebrating my sister's marriage.'

Simpson inclined his head slightly. 'We have toasted the health of Mr and Mrs Gage, sir—with the Master's permission, of course.'

Charles laughed. 'Of course. And the Reardons—are they there too?'

Again Simpson nodded. 'Reardon senior is below, sir. His nephew retired early, after bedding the horses for the night.'

A slow smile spread over Charles's face. 'See that a tray is sent up to my room directly, Simpson,' he said. 'I shall be stepping out for half an hour. I will eat on my return.'

To reach the stables, Charles went out on to the terrace and through the garden door. He passed the window of the servants' hall and heard their raucous singing with satisfaction. Reardon would be alone in his quarters. So much the better.

Reaching the stable-yard he stood and listened. There was no sound. Obviously the lout was upstairs in the room above the coach-house. His foot was on the bottom step when he heard a sound coming from the empty stable at the end. The one vacated by his own horse, Jason. Running silently across the yard he listened at the door and heard mumblings as Patrick turned in the straw, talking in his sleep. Charles pushed open the top half of the door and peered in. As his eyes accustomed themselves to the gloom he saw Patrick lying in the straw, knees drawn up, arms across his chest. He smiled sadistically. He was going to enjoy this.

Opening the bottom half of the door he strode across to where Patrick lay and gave him a kick in the ribs.

'Hey—Reardon!' he shouted. 'Stir yourself, lazy swine. I want to talk to you!'

Patrick roused himself and sat up, rubbing his eyes. 'What? What is it?'

'It is I—Charles Quincey. And I've come to tell you something I think you should know. About that slut of a sister of yours!'

Patrick was awake instantly. He scrambled to his feet and faced the pale eyes that glinted at him maliciously through the gloom.

'What is it?' he repeated, the ale still misting his brain, making him feel heavy and stupid.

'It's time you knew a few things about her,' Charles said loudly. 'For instance, did you know that she was a whore?'

Patrick blinked with shock as the word hit him like a bullet. His fists clenched automatically and his eyes opened wide.

'You—you dare to say that!' He lunged forward but his limbs seemed heavy and out of control. Charles sidestepped neatly and he stumbled and fell headlong into the straw. Charles stood over him, head thrown back and legs planted firmly apart.

'I'll say it again as you seem somewhat the worse for ale,' he said. 'Your sister's a whore— a dirty little slut! I've seen her cavortings with my own eyes. She'll let any man have his way with her if the rewards are right. Why, I'd have had her myself this very afternoon had we not been interrupted! I swear I've never seen a wench so eager—panting like a bitch on heat!'

Patrick gave a roar of fury and made a grab at Charles's leg but again he stepped aside, laughing. 'You're drunk, Reardon,' he taunted. 'An Irish drunkard with a dirty trollop for a sister. Nice servants we have at Denmark House, I must say!'

On his feet, Patrick lurched towards him again, but Charles was ready. He delivered an almighty punch to Patrick's solar plexus, doubling him up, then, as his head came down he received a cracking blow to the jaw. As Patrick collapsed once more into the straw Charles strode to the door and turned to regard his handiwork with satisfaction. Then, with a loud derisive laugh he walked away, rubbing his skinned knuckles and looking forward with relish to the supper that awaited him.

Patrick sat up painfully, his head ringing and his stomach churning. He drew up his knees and bent forward, his head between them. God in Heaven, that was the second time he had heard it. Could it be true? Kathy! Oh God, Kathy! He struggled to his feet and stood leaning against the door-jamb, sweat trickling down his face. He clutched at the door as the yard swam about him, then he staggered to the grating in the middle of the yard and leaned forward, vomiting violently until he thought he would eject the whole of his inside.

At Holbrook Lodge, Kathy lay in the neat little room under the eaves, her eyes wide and sleepless and her mind numb with misery. This was the first time in all of her life that she could remember being parted from Patrick. She liked the house well enough, pretty and smart as it was with the latest fabrics and furnishings. The staff consisted of herself, a cook and a boy for the rough work, but the house was small and the three of them would not be overworked. She turned over, thankful that she need no longer fear the sound of stealthy footfalls in the corridor outside her door; the rough pawing of her body and the torture that followed. Henry Quincey's promise to 'make her like it' had not materialised. In fact she could not make herself believe that such an act could ever bring pleasure to any woman. If she and Patrick had married would it have been the same between them? Could she have come to loathe her darling Patrick for the same reason? She could not believe it. It must have been different. Ah well, now she would never know and as she could never marry Patrick she would marry no one, but serve Miss Melissa all of her days.

She closed her eyes and saw Patrick's face wearing the hurt, bewildered look it had worn this morning when she had said good-bye. The vision made her heart contract until she cried out with the pain. She thrust her fist into her mouth and felt the hot tears scald her cheeks and trickle between her fingers.

'Patrick—' she sobbed. 'Oh, Patrick, forgive me—forgive me!'

*       *       *

In the room above the coach-house Seamus held his candle over the bed and looked down at the figure sprawling on it. It was not like Patrick to fall abed like that, still wearing his clothes and boots. He sniffed. The rank odour of vomit rose to his nostrils and peering more closely he saw that the lad's good shirt, worn especially for the occasion, was stained and filthy. Then he noticed the angry bruise darkening on Patrick's jaw and suddenly everything fell into place. He remembered hearing Simpson say that Mr Charles had asked where Patrick was. He had obviously been looking to settle their latest quarrel over the horse. The old man sighed and shook his head. He had grown fond of the lad, even though he was not of his own blood. But there was that about him that boded ill. It was almost as though there was some terrible curse upon him. Trouble seemed to walk with him like a shadow.

Patrick stirred and opened his eyes to look up into the face, made grotesque and distorted by the candle's flickering.

'I'm leavin' here tomorrow, Uncle,' he said flatly. 'I'm leavin' for good. I can't abide Denmark House or the Quinceys any longer. I'm done this time—done.'

Seamus sat down on the edge of the bed frowning. The lad's tone troubled him. It wasn't like him to give up—to be so defeated. 'Ah, sure you'll feel better in the mornin', boy,' he said. 'It's been a long day. Get some sleep now.'

Patrick sat up and looked into Seamus's eyes. 'Did you hear—did anyone say anything—about Kathy, Uncle?'

The old man shook his head. 'Only that she's gone to be Miss Melissa's maid.' He patted Patrick's shoulder. 'She's done well for herself, lad. Ah she's grown up a grand little lass. She'll not be far away, don't fret.'

195

Patrick sighed with relief. Sarah had not spread her vile gossip after all then. 'I'll go to the hirin' fair tomorrow,' he said. 'An' try me luck.'

'There're worse places than this—far worse,' Seamus warned. 'You'd best mind you don't jump out o' the fryin' pan into the fire, lad. If it was me now, I'd say nothin' till I saw the way the land lay. If you found nothin' to your likin' you could always come back then.'

Patrick nodded, but his thoughts were of Sarah—of Charles Quincey and the poisonous accusations they had both made against Kathy. Should he try to see her—to ask for an explanation? He shrank from the idea. How could he ask her such a thing? No, she had said she would visit him. When she came he would know. If she never came—well that would tell a story in itself. He turned on the pillow so that his uncle should not see the pain in his eyes.

Undressing, Seamus watched him with concern. As he blew out the candle he heard the church clock strike midnight.

'Ah well,' he mumbled under his breath. 'So that's Miss Melissa's weddin' day done with—an' I hope it's brought her more happiness than some I could name!'

# CHAPTER EIGHT

Elvemere market-place on fair-day was a transformation, full of new and fascinating sights and sounds and smells absent on every other day of the year. As he mingled with the crowd, Patrick felt his heavy spirits lifted a little by the bustling atmosphere. This morning he had been paid his annual wage and he had added it to the other money he kept in the linen bag under the pallet where he slept. He had spent hardly any of it. His food and clothing were provided, and on the rare occasions he had visited the Calcutta, Tom Craven or one of the other captains he had become acquainted with had bought his ale.

Now, with the money-bag inside his shirt, bumping reassuringly against his chest, he wandered round looking with wonder at all that the fair had to offer. Never before had he seen so many diverse articles for sale in one place: pots and pans, combs and ribbons, stools and chairs. There was a sweetmeat stall and a knife-grinder—and a man who pulled teeth for a penny a go. Patrick grinned at the noises coming from inside the tent and at the small boy banging a drum almost as big as himself, the dual purpose of which was to advertise his master's skill and to drown the sounds of suffering coming from within.

Outside another tent a man loudly proclaimed that the fattest woman on earth was to be seen inside, whilst at another a two-headed cow was cheerfully advertised with tempting, gaudy pictures on a placard.

But Patrick was not to be parted from his money by such trivialities. He would have better uses for it when the time came, though he was still hazy about what that chance might be.

The hiring fair was in Bridge Street, leading off the main market-place. There men and women stood and waited, eager to find employment early in the day so that they might enjoy the fair in comfort for the rest of the holiday. Patrick surveyed them with interest. Each of them wore some symbol of their trade or skill. The shepherds carried crooks, while the carters and wagoners wore a piece of whipcord around their hats. Thatchers sported fragments of woven straw pinned to their smocks.

On the other side of the street the prospective employers walked up and down. They seemed to be mostly farmers, and Patrick approached one or two, but he found that they all wanted bonded hands and preferred married men whose wives and children would provide them with cheap labour. For some time Patrick talked to a thatcher who told him that he travelled from place to place and could ask good wages for his skilled craft. He was looking for an apprentice, but would pay no wages but food and shelter for a year.

At last Patrick turned away in despair. In spite of his longing to wander he found quite suddenly that he could not bring himself to leave Elvemere. As long as there was the least possibility that Kathy might need him—come to him—still want his love, then he had to be where she could find him.

He walked back to the market-place, to the stalls and sideshows, looked at this and that, watched the people dressed in their Sunday best and was wondering what to do next when the sound of a posthorn attracted his attention. He followed its direction and found a crowd gathering round a platform decked out in red and white striped canvas. A showman was making some sort of claim and Patrick elbowed his way through the crowd to hear what it was. He wore a flashy tailcoat and top hat and as Patrick came within earshot he heard the man extolling the power and strength of someone he called Sambo the Iron Man. His offer was: 'Five golden sovereigns for any man who can beat him in ten rounds or under!'

It was then that Patrick noticed that the platform had ropes around it and he began to understand. At that moment the man blew another blast on his horn and a gasp went up from the crowd as a figure emerged from a tent at the back. He was huge and his skin was as shiny and black as ebony. He must have been well over six feet tall and his hair was a cap of tightly frizzled wool. He smiled, showing strong, white teeth and flexed his mighty shoulders, making the biceps bulge and ripple. Some of the women screamed and giggled with delight. The man in the tailcoat held up one of the powerful arms.

'Ladies and gents—I present the mighty Sambo—the Iron Man. Who'll fight him for a shillin'? If you stays on yer feet for the ten rounds yer gets yer shillin' back. If yer *beats* the Iron Man yer takes five golden sovereigns 'ome to the wife tonight!'

A man in front of Patrick began to push his way forward but his wife dragged him back.

'A broken 'ead's all you'll git!' she yelled at him. 'An' much good you are wi' a sound 'un!'

The crowd roared with laughter as the man's face reddened and the showman called out again:

'Oh, come on, gents all! I was told that Elvemere was full o' well set up lads but I don't see 'em. Where are they, eh?'

'I'll fight him!' Patrick heard himself shout.

The crowd fell silent as all eyes turned towards him. The man in the tailcoat leaned forward and extended a hand.

' 'Ere's a sport at last! An' a fine-lookin' chap too, if I may say so. Come right up 'ere, good sir.'

The crowd parted for Patrick as he stepped

forward and made his way up the wooden
steps at the side of the platform. Reaching
inside his shirt he took out the money-bag and
extracted a shilling. The showman watched
him with interest.

'A man o' means if ever I saw one!' He
winked at the crowd as he took Patrick's
shilling from him, eyeing the bag with greed.
But Patrick wasn't listening. He was sizing up
the Negro with fascination. He had never seen
a black man at close quarters before and he
was intrigued by the colour and texture of his
skin and the shape of the features.

'If you'd like ter take orf yer shirt and boots,
sir—' the showman was saying. 'Sambo 'ere
always fights barefoot.'

Suddenly Patrick was aware of a problem:
what to do with the money-bag nestling inside
his shirt. Where could he put it for safety? The
showman had already seen it and passed a
comment. It would surely be stolen if he laid it
down anywhere.

'All yer things'll be quite safe with me,' the
showman said, reading the expression of
uncertainty on his face. He grinned, showing
broken and discoloured teeth and Patrick felt
more apprehensive than ever. He couldn't
back out now—and yet if he lost his money—

'You can give them to me, fellow.' A well-
dressed man stepped forward from the crowd,
smiling. 'I shall stand here where you can see
me and hold your things for you. If you give

them to that rogue the chances are he'll have sold your boots before the first round is over!'

The crowd laughed while the showman grimaced good-naturedly, addressing the crowd again:

'As you'll see, gents all, the good Dr Nichols is with us again—to see as 'ow Sambo don't murder no one!' He nudged Patrick. 'You can give yer togs and yer cash to the doctor, mate. Straightest bloke in Lincolnshire 'e is—more's the bleedin' pity!'

Amid more laughter Patrick stripped off his shirt, then his boots, pressing the money-bag into the toe of one of them. Then he handed the bundle to the doctor, who smiled at him encouragingly.

'Good luck, my good fellow.'

Almost before Patrick had time to draw breath the showman struck a gong and the Negro was upon him, raining blows to his head and body. Patrick staggered backwards and his gall rose as the breath was battered from his chest and the already bruised skin of his jaw split painfully. Suddenly his vision cleared; this black mountain of a man epitomised all that had ever angered him, from his step-father's enemies to Henry Quincey and his hated son, Charles. Inside his head he saw pictures framed in blood and fire: the beautiful horse, Jason being cruelly beaten—Kathy being raped and abused—Sarah's face as she spilled out her malice, her mouth twisted and her eyes small points of pale light.

He gave a mighty roar and with all his gathered fury and frustration he hurled himself at the Negro, delivering a mighty blow to the centre of the face that was, momentarily, Sarah's. Then he followed it with one for Henry Quincey and another for Charles.

The Negro staggered back, unprepared for such an onslaught and Patrick seized the opportunity he saw opening up before him. Lowering his head he rammed it into the great hard belly. Sambo grunted and his head jerked forward. Patrick got in two more blows to the face, while behind him he was dimly aware of the crowd's excitement. Instructions were shouted at him—encouragement—but he was blind and deaf to all except his grim determination to finish his opponent.

He struck out, connecting whenever he could. He took plenty of punishment himself, but soon he was no longer aware of the pain and the blood which stung his eyes and trickled thick and salty into his mouth. His eyes focused on the Negro's face as another blow sent his head snapping back. Both eyes were rapidly closing and his thick lower lip was split in two places. Patrick went in for the kill. Dimly, through the red, roaring mist inside his head he heard the gong being repeatedly struck but it meant nothing to him. His fists were like pistons, ramming rhythmically at the Negro's body and head—till suddenly there was nothing in front of him to hit any more. He stopped and looked around him dazedly. The crowd was cheering deafeningly and he peered out at them. Then he saw the dark body crumpled on the floor at his feet.

Someone was holding up his arm and proclaiming him winner. He dimly registered that it was the man who they called Dr Nichols. Now the showman was arguing: ' 'E never stopped when I sounded the gong. T'ain't fair!'

'But you didn't sound your gong when you thought that Sambo was winning!' Dr Nichols protested. 'Come on, pay up you rogue. He's a game and plucky lad and he won fair and square—didn't he?' This last was addressed to the crowd who roared their agreement. One or two of the men began to call out ugly threats and at last the showman grudgingly gave in.

'Oh all right—all bleedin' right! 'Ere's yer boodle—five shiners.' He counted the coins into the doctor's hand and Patrick was helped down from the platform amid cheers and whistles.

The doctor handed him his shirt and boots and he began to drag them on painfully. 'Can you walk?' the doctor asked him. He nodded, but stumbled a little as the doctor took his arm.

'Better come along with me. My surgery's in Friar's Lane, not far from here. I'll soon have you to rights.'

Friar's Lane was a narrow alley opening off the market-place between Thomas's, the undertaker, and Meredith's the ironmonger. From there it wound its way gently downhill to where the House of Correction stood like a grim sentinel at the bottom. It was the habitat of the poor, with its second-hand clothes shops, tumble-down cottages and pawnbrokers. It was here that the soup kitchen operated twice weekly, run by the Misses Fairfax and it was next door to this place of charity that Dr Nichols had his surgery, in the front room of a cottage for which he paid a rent of sixpence a week.

He took a key from his waistcoat pocket and opened the door, motioning to Patrick to enter. The stone-flagged floor was scrubbed clean and in the centre of the room stood a deal table and two chairs. This was all the furniture the room contained except for a cupboard on the wall and a shelf which held a bowl and a pitcher of water. The doctor opened the cupboard and took out a clean cloth and a small brown bottle. He poured some water into the bowl and told Patrick to be seated while he examined the battered face and torn knuckles, then he looked into his mouth and gently probed his body to see if there were any broken ribs. At length he straightened up and smiled at Patrick.

'You're a very lucky young man. Only superficial injuries. You should have seen some of the poor creatures I have treated after a bout with the Iron Man. That is the reason I always attend.' He soaked the cloth in the water and began to bathe Patrick's face, scrutinising it with interest as he did so. The Irish accent had already attracted his interest but the swarthy skin and black curling hair, the dark eyes and high-bridged nose didn't go with it somehow.

'You're Irish,' he observed. 'From what part?'

Patrick winced slightly as the tincture of iodine from the small brown bottle was pressed into a cut on his cheek. 'County Limerick,' he answered.

The doctor nodded with a smile. 'I thought I'd placed the accent. I know it well. I had an Irish mother.'

Patrick looked up at the man with renewed interest. It was puzzling. He was a doctor, yet his clothes were shabby and well-worn. He spoke and conducted himself like a gentleman and yet by these surroundings he was not rich. He would be about thirty, Patrick guessed. He had a strong face and would stand no nonsense as he had proved today at the boxing booth; yet his blue eyes were kind and compassionate and his hands with their capable square palms and long fingers were sensitive and gentle as a woman's.

'D'ye often go to the old country?' he asked.

The doctor smiled. 'Not so often since my

mother died. How long have you been in Elvemere—er—I do not believe you told me your name.'

'Patrick Reardon, sir—an' I've been here two years. I work at Denmark House, in the stables. Me uncle, Seamus Reardon, is coachman there.'

The doctor put away the bowl and the tincture of iodine and took another, larger bottle from the cupboard with two glasses. 'That explains how you come to be here,' he said. 'Elvemere is not the easiest place to arrive at from Ireland. You won't find many compatriots hereabouts.' He poured two tots of brandy and handed one to Patrick. 'Here, drink that. It'll buck you up. You took a fair beating from the black fellow.' He sat down on the other chair and sipped from his own glass. 'So you work at Denmark House—for Henry Quincey? And do you like it there?'

Patrick sighed. 'I like the horses. 'Tis the finest stable in the town. But to tell you the truth, sir, I want to be free. I'm sick o' bein' a bondman. I want to be me own master.'

He spoke with such vehemence that the doctor looked up in surprise, raising his eyebrows. 'I see that you feel strongly on the subject. Could that be the reason why you took on the Negro today?'

Patrick considered. He had not wholly understood his impulsive reaction to the challenge. He might easily have lost a shilling

207

of his precious savings. Maybe the doctor was right; maybe he had to fight the Negro to prove to himself his own worth. He nodded slowly.

'I think it was, sir.'

The doctor shook his head. 'Please don't keep calling me "sir", my name is Jonathan Nichols.' He studied Patrick intently. 'Is there no other job you might try, Patrick? Have you no other skills beside your work with horses?'

'I have not,' Patrick admitted, 'though I *can* read.'

Jonathan Nichols looked up. 'And how did you manage that?'

'I—learned. A-a friend taught me.'

With a sudden gasp, the doctor reached into his pocket and withdrew something. 'Here—I almost forgot that I still had your prize money.' He put the five shining coins on the table and watched as Patrick took them up eagerly and added them to the rest of the money in the linen bag. Patrick noticed the doctor's look and stopped.

'Oh—I was forgettin'—what do I owe ye, doctor?'

Jonathan laughed. 'Get away with you. I'm not on duty now. I did what I did as a friend. After all, it is fair-day.'

Patrick smiled. 'Thank ye sir, I'm very much obliged to ye.' He looked around. 'You wouldn't be wantin' a strong man to help, would ye?' he asked hopefully.

Jonathan shook his head regretfully. 'I'm afraid I can't afford one, Patrick. I have to be my own servant. You see I treat only the poor. They pay me what they can—which isn't much—sometimes nothing at all, but I turn no one away. I do this because the poor souls have no one else to look after them and I have to make my living from my wits.' Patrick looked puzzled and Jonathan laughed.

'Let me explain. When my father died he left me a little money. I make it work for me.' He nodded towards Patrick's money-bag lying on the table. 'You should do the same, you are obviously not a spendthrift.'

Patrick leaned forward, frowning in concentration, his interest aroused. 'And how would I be makin' it work for me, doctor?' he asked.

'Well, to begin with, have you ever thought of depositing your money in a bank?'

Patrick's hand moved instinctively to the bag and he shook his head. 'That'd be like givin' it to someone else. I mightn't get it back.'

Jonathan pursed his lips. 'That is so, though unlikely when you choose the right bank. But all investments have that risk attached. There is the interest though and that is where the benefit lies.'

'Interest—what would that be?'

'When you lend your money to the bank it adds a little to it each year, so that when you wish to withdraw it you have more than when you started.'

Patrick's face cleared, lighting with interest and Jonathan continued: 'Or, of course, one can purchase shares in a company. The most popular at the moment are railway shares. Did you know that there is talk of bringing the railway to Elvemere? Yes, you could do a lot worse than invest in the railway.'

'An' would I be gettin' the interest with that too, doctor?' Patrick asked eagerly.

Jonathan nodded. 'You would indeed, except that instead of a fixed rate such as the bank would give you, your interest would depend on the profits made by the company.'

Patrick thought hard. He had heard the seamen in the Calcutta talking of the railways. If there were one running through Elvemere it would make a great difference. He thought of Henry Quincey and his fleet of river barges— surely they would not be needed any more. There could be a decline in some of his other ventures too. The thought made his heart quicken and he pushed the bag towards Jonathan.

'Can you buy the shares for me, doctor?'

Jonathan was taken aback. He had taken the lad's silence as uncertainty—even bewilderment—but now he saw that the opposite was the case. He chewed his lip thoughtfully.

'You must not be too trusting, Patrick. I

might be a rogue, waiting to steal your money and cheat you.'

Patrick laughed. 'Not you, doctor. I think I know better than that. I want you to do it—if you will.'

Jonathan frowned. 'I really think you should take more time to think about it, Patrick. After all, as you yourself have already said, it is all in the nature of a gamble.'

But Patrick had made up his mind. There was no shaking him. He had seen a way of striking the first blow at Henry Quincey, a blow that would hurt him far more than any physical one could. He pushed the bag of money firmly into Jonathan's hand.

'I've done all the thinkin' I need to,' he said decisively. 'I want ye to buy the railway shares for me—please.'

Jonathan sighed. 'So be it then. But keep a little back. Let me use only your winnings. You may need the rest. You said you were looking for work.'

'No!' Patrick held up his hand. 'I've changed me mind. I'll stay where I am. It'll be different now. Me luck has changed. I can feel it.' Not for anything would he leave Denmark House now. He would stay and watch Henry Quincey's downfall, relishing every failure as it came. Happy to be an onlooker.

Jonathan looked at the excitement gleaming in the boy's eyes with vague unease. 'Well, if you're sure.' He took the bag and put it safely away in his own pocket. 'I will see that you get the share certificates when I have completed the transaction.' He hesitated, then took out the bag and extracted a florin from it, passing it to Patrick across the table. 'Here, at least take this. You must have something to spend on fair-day. Celebrate your induction into the world of business.'

Patrick had no idea what he meant but he picked up the coin with a grin. ' 'Tis a bargain, doctor. Sure I'll do as ye say.'

And the two shook hands on the deal.

The taproom at the Calcutta was packed with revellers in various stages of inebriation. Patrick looked around them. He could see no familiar faces today. He made his way to the counter where he bought himself a mug of ale and then elbowed his way to a corner where he could see a vacant place on one of the benches under the window. Two men were already seated there and they eyed him as he sat down.

'Good-day,' one of them greeted him. He nodded acknowledgement and took a deep thirsty draught of his ale.

The men looked at each other and then again at Patrick.

'Are you off one o' the ships in the port, lad?' one of them asked.

Patrick looked at them properly for the first time. The one who had spoken was thin, with mean, shifty eyes, the other was heavily built with a bushy beard.

'No,' he answered guardedly. 'I work across the river—My work is with horses.'

'Horses, eh?' The thin man nodded approvingly. 'Good with them, are you?'

Patrick shrugged. 'I reckon I am.'

The man put his hand in his pocket. 'I like you, lad,' he said. 'Here—have another drink. Get it yourself, will you? I've got a bad leg.' He placed a shilling carefully on the table in front of Patrick who shook his head. He didn't know why but the men made him feel uneasy.

'Thank ye all the same, sir, but I'm only here to look for a friend.'

It was true enough. He had hoped to see Tom Craven. He knew the *Mary Ann* was due in any day now. He had also looked forward to spending some time with Tabby. His eyes raked the smoke-filled room for her now and caught sight of her coming down the stairs. He shouted and waved his arm. And when he looked back to the table he saw that the shilling had been removed. He waved again and called a greeting to Tabby as he saw her pushing her way towards him through the crowd and as she reached him he said:

'Get me a plate o' somethin' hot, Tabby, love. Sure me belly's as empty as a barrel.' He raised the mug of ale to his lips but to his surprise Tabby sprang forward and dashed it from his hand. It crashed to the ground, sending its contents splashing over the other occupants of the bench.

Patrick sprang to his feet. 'What in God's name are you doin', woman?'

But Tabby was busy grovelling in the sawdust on the floor. After a moment she stood up again, her face red and her eyes blazing. She threw something in the face of the thin man.

'There! Take it back you sneakin' pig!'

Patrick saw that the object she had thrown was the shilling the man had offered him. It bounced off the man's collar and landed on the table in front of him.

'Pick it up an' sling your 'ook!' Tabby screamed. 'Trick a poor innocent lad into bein' took for a soldier would you? Well not at the Calcutta you don't! Get out, the pair o' you. You'll get no more ale 'ere!'

The men rose and pushed past her with a shrug and Patrick turned to her, still puzzled. She shook her head at him.

'You—you're not fit to be out, are you? Gone like a lamb to the slaughter, you'd have done if I hadn't seen in time. They was recruitin' sergeants. They put the Queen's shillin' in your ale. One sip and you'd have been theirs.' She clicked her tongue. 'You look as if you've been in the wars again too. I don't know about you, I'm sure.'

He let out a long breath. 'Recruitin' sergeants? Phew, thanks, Tabby. I reckon this is me lucky day.' He grinned and pulled her close to him. 'Have ye time for a bit of a

214

cuddle upstairs then?'

She touched his bruised face. 'Well lookin' like that no one else'll fancy you, will they? Good job I know you.'

He bent his head and gave her a resounding kiss on the mouth and she giggled.

'You wouldn't let nothin' stop you, would you, Paddy Reardon? Oh, come on up then.'

In the little room under the eaves Patrick took his time over his lovemaking with Tabby. Her firm, plump body felt good under his hands and her little moans of pleasure made him feel confident and manly again. As he entered her and felt her eager response he made a sudden decision and when they lay together afterwards, relaxed and sleepy, he turned to her with a question.

'Tabby—will ye marry me?' To him at that moment it seemed the perfect solution. Kathy had gone—he might never see her again. It would be good to have Tabby to tell his troubles to—to warm his heart and satisfy his body. She would be the perfect consolation.

She turned her tousled head in the crook of his arm to look up at him. 'Oh Paddy—don't be daft!'

He frowned. 'But I mean it. We get on well, don't we? You like me—and what I do to you.' He ran a hand up the length of her body, cupping it round one breast and smiling down at her. But she shook her head again, looking a little wistfully at his long, well made body; the dark golden skin and flashing eyes. He was a fine young man, the finest she had ever known—and such a lover. If only . . .

'I'm a good ten years older than you, love,' she told him. 'And what would I do with a husband? Haven't I got all the husbands I need? Anyway you'd soon get tired of bein' married to a whore.'

He stopped caressing her and looked into her eyes. 'Whore? What do you mean?'

She laughed. 'I suppose there are nicer words for it, but there's no use pretendin' is there?' She saw the expression on his face and the smile left her eyes. 'Oh come on, Paddy, you knew that was what I was—you must 'ave. Why else do you think the landlord lets me bring you up 'ere?'

He sat up, his muscles tensing in anger. 'But—I never paid you anything,' he spluttered.

She knelt up and put her hands on his shoulders. 'No, but the others do, love. I always let you do it for nothing because I've always 'ad a soft spot for you—me bein' your first woman an' all.' She began to pull her petticoat over her head. 'Don't take on, love. We can always 'ave a bit o' fun any time you like. Specially if you come when we're not busy.'

Anger and resentment rose up hotly in Patrick's chest. Women! Christ, were they all the same? Did they all use their power and

216

their bodies to bring men to their knees? Was *that* what they were all about? Well let it be so then!

With a savage cry he tore the petticoat from her and pushed her back on the bed, throwing himself on top of her. He crushed his mouth to hers, oblivious of the bruises and the cut on his lip which opened again against her teeth. He thrust himself into her brutally and mercilessly, his energy and potency seemingly inexhaustible till at last he gave a loud cry of triumph and rolled away from her. He began to drag on his clothes, ignoring the curled, weeping figure on the bed. Finally he put his hand into his pocket and drew out two pennies, throwing them on to the bare floor by the bed where they bounced and rang out their insulting reproach.

'There's your payment, whore! Thanks— you've seen the last o' me!' And he strode out of the door and down the stairs.

Ten minutes later he stood by the bridge watching the still water of the river. Now, with his temper cooled, he felt sick and disgusted with himself. He shouldn't have let his temper get the better of him, especially when Tabby had saved him from the recruiting sergeants. But wasn't he sorely provoked? He felt foolish to think he'd been taken in by Tabby these two years. In a way he supposed he had known that he wasn't the only one she gave her favours to—but to hear her say it like that! He could bite out his tongue now for asking her to marry him! But the girl couldn't help what she was any more than he could.

He turned and retraced his steps. He must make his peace with Tabby or he'd not rest tonight. As he went into the Calcutta again the atmosphere almost choked him. The smoke and fumes of tobacco, wood and charred food mingled with the odour of unwashed bodies. Patrick grimaced. Give him the open air and horses any day. As his eyes became accustomed to the smoke-filled atmosphere he saw Tabby across the room, laughing with a burly sailor. He made his way across to her as she began to ascend the staircase.

'Tabby—I'm sorry. I shouldn't . . .' His voice tailed off in mid-sentence as she turned halfway up the stairs and looked him full in the eyes with the force of her anger burning like flame. She threw back her head, hands on hips.

'What's the matter, sonny—didn't you get your money's worth?' She reached into the bosom of her dress and pulled out the two pennies he had thrown at her, holding them up for all to see.

'Here's what 'is Lordship 'ere give me,' she called in a loud, ringing voice. 'Tuppence! then 'e 'as the bleedin' cheek to ask me to marry 'im!'

A great roar of laughter went up as all eyes turned on Patrick, shrinking in their midst.

218

The next moment the pennies landed at his feet.

'There—take 'em back, son!' Tabby shrieked. ' 'An come back when you've learned 'ow to do it proper!'

*     *     *

Seamus stirred on his bed and looked up as Patrick came into the room over the coach-house.

'So you're back after all, boy?' he said quietly.

Patrick nodded. 'I am that, Uncle. I've a mind to give it another year.'

Seamus blinked at his nephew in the candle-light. He noted the discoloured eyes and the dried blood on his lip—the broken skin on the knuckles as the lad unbuttoned his shirt. He'd been scrappin' again then? Ah well, if it helped to cool his temper. He wondered briefly who the recipient had been this time, but his wonderings were overshadowed by his relief at having the lad back with him again. He grinned and pulled the blanket up round his skinny shoulders.

'G'night then, boy.'

'Night, Uncle.' Patrick slid into his bed gratefully. His whole body ached with the day's abuse of it. He ached inwardly too. The roars of laughter and the humiliation Tabby had heaped on him at the Calcutta rankled sorely.

219

It would be many a long day before he could show his face in there again, yet he knew that he had deserved it. He had learned one thing from the incident: a thing done—a decision made—could not be gone back on. In future he must not be so hasty. His thoughts turned to his new friend, Dr Jonathan Nichols and the big step he had taken, giving him all his money to invest. Had that been a hasty decision? No—something deep inside him told him not. Fate had thrown him in that man's path this day and a deep instinct told him he had taken an important step into the future.

## CHAPTER NINE

Kathy leaned weakly against the wall and wiped the cold sweat from her brow with the back of her hand. The vinegar had made her vomit violently—she supposed that was what was meant to happen. Guilt overcame her once again as she tipped the five pennies out of the empty mug and clasped them in her hand. It had been stealing. What if someone had seen her take them from the church collection plate? She must put them back as soon as she could. She waited, cold in spite of the warmth of the July morning. She had swallowed the infusion—how long before it took effect, and what would happen to her when it did? Oh God, if only it would all be over.

It was quite a stroke of luck that Peg Mawby, Harriet Gage's cook, had a sister who was a midwife. She came to see her sister every Tuesday afternoon when Kathy would make tea for them. The conversation was always about the latest births and it had been from the information Kathy had gleaned from these overheard conversations that she had first realised that she herself might be pregnant. She had also gathered that there were at least two ways in which this condition might be 'cured'. One was to drink vinegar in which pennies from the church collection had been soaked; the second was to hold the hand of a dead man for two minutes by the clock. She had chosen the former, pushing the thought of the alternative to the back of her mind. It had been bad enough taking the pennies, holding a dead man's hand would be worse. Where would she find a dead man, anyway?

Tears began to trickle down her cheeks.

'Oh, Holy Mother of God,' she whispered desperately. What she was trying to do was a mortal sin, she knew, but she had no choice. Surely the Holy Mother would realise the trouble she was in and have mercy on her.

But in spite of its vile taste and her stomach's violent rejection of it, the vinegar produced no results. As she went about her work Kathy was filled with despair. If only she

221

could see Patrick. She was sick with longing for the sight of him and the strength of his arms around her. It was three months now since she had left Denmark House but it seemed more like three years. There was something wrong with Miss Melissa too. In spite of her fine new home and her handsome, adoring husband she seemed downcast and preoccupied. It was as though the light had gone out of her and it troubled Kathy. More than once she had mentioned it to Peg Mawby but the cook had been scathing:

'She wants ten young 'uns about her skirts like I've had,' she said with a snort. 'All yellin' their heads off for bread—and a man as can't work for the rheumatics and the ague, then she'd 'ave summat to be un'appy about—'ceptin' she wouldn't 'ave time to be!'

But Kathy couldn't agree with the comparison. Misery was misery, however it was caused. And the likes of Miss Melissa weren't born to the same kind anyway. But although she felt for her mistress and longed to help her, she could not presume to ask what troubled her.

As Caroline had predicted, the Misses Fairfax had lost no time in recruiting Melissa into their little army of charitable ladies and on the day following she was to take her first turn at the soup kitchen. She asked Kathy to accompany her.

'Mrs Gage will also be there,' she said,

222

referring to her mother-in-law. 'And she will be taking her cook, Bessie. You will be able to make yourself useful to her, I have no doubt.'

But the following morning, as she stood over the vast pot of turnip soup, Kathy was so nauseous that she almost fainted. Melissa was most concerned. She had ordered Kathy out into the fresh air where she was to stay until she felt better. When she returned she found Bessie less sympathetic. She had resented the implication that any soup she had cooked had caused nausea and now she cast a shrewd eye over Kathy.

'Often suffer from a weak stomach, do you?' she asked pointedly.

Kathy bit her lip. 'No—not often.'

The woman sniffed. 'Only gets you in the mornin's, eh?' When Kathy did not answer she went on, still stirring the pot: 'If you don't know what ails you the free doctor's here today, bein' market day. He's about three doors up.' She jerked her thumb over her shoulder. 'On the other 'and, there's a woman I know down Fish Lane—'

'Thank ye—mebbe I'll see the doctor,' Kathy said. She recognised the challenge in Bessie's words but she had no intention of confiding in her, she would ask charity of no one either. The church collection pennies were in her skirt pocket still. She would offer them to the doctor. Perhaps he could help her.

Friar's Lane was milling with people going

223

to and from the market-place. Kathy asked a passer-by and was directed to the cottage with the doctor's sign in the window. Two people still waited outside, a woman holding a sickly baby and a grey-faced man who leaned against the wall coughing. Kathy took up her position and waited.

At last her turn came and she went into the tiny scrubbed room. The doctor looked up at her with a smile and she was surprised to see that he was quite young, with a pleasant, open face and curling brown hair.

'Please sit down.' He indicated a chair opposite his table. 'And pray do not look so afraid. I shall not eat you. Now, what ails you, child?'

Kathy lowered her eyes and bit her trembling lip to keep it still. 'Please sir,' she whispered. 'I—I get terrible sick in—in the mornings. I think—I think I'm going to have a baby—sir.'

Jonathan Nichols looked up at her. 'How old are you, child?'

'Sixteen, sir.'

'Don't call me "sir". My name is Dr Nichols. Will you tell me yours?'

'Kathleen, doctor. Kathleen Reardon.'

'Well, Kathleen, there could well be another reason for your sickness. Are you married?'

She hung her head. 'No, doctor.'

He nodded. 'And the lad in question—would he be willing to marry you if what you

224

fear is so?'

She looked up at him, her eyes wide and fearful. 'Oh, no, doctor. It wouldn't be possible and anyway I—I wouldn't want it. No one must know. I—I have to do something.'

He sighed. It was a very old story, as old as the world. 'Well, first we must ascertain if what you suspect is, in fact, true.'

After asking more questions he made a brief examination and shook his head at what he found. The girl was at least three and a half months pregnant and he was well able to hazard a guess at the circumstances. She was clearly not an immoral girl and he had not missed the fear in her eyes when he had mentioned the father of her child. It would be a case of intimidation and rape. He saw many such amongst the servant class. He poured water into the basin on the corner table and began to wash his hands thoughtfully.

'What is your work, Kathleen?' he asked.

'I've a new place, doctor,' she told him. 'I work for Mrs John Gage. I'm her maid.' She fastened the last of her buttons and looked at him with pleading eyes. 'Oh, please, doctor, is there anything I can do to stop it? I don't want to lose me place and go to the workhouse. I've tried the pennies in vinegar and I don't know where to find a dead man—' she broke off as he turned to shake his head at her, frowning.

'Those things can do nothing but harm to you, child.' Some of the noxious methods the fens people employed in the vain hope of maintaining good health appalled him. 'You must face the fact that God has sent you this burden, Kathleen,' he said kindly. 'I am very much afraid that there is nothing you can do but to bear it.' He looked into her stunned face with compassion. 'Have you a kind mistress?' She nodded dumbly. 'Then why not tell her. Throw yourself upon her mercy. I am afraid that is the best—the only—advice I can give you. As for the sickness, you will find it will soon pass now.'

Kathy turned unsteadily towards the door. 'Thank you, doctor. Mebbe I'll do as ye say.' She put her hand into her skirt pocket and drew out the pennies, holding them out to him. 'This is all I've got, doctor. I hope it's enough for your trouble.'

Stepping forward he closed her fingers over the coppers and shook his head. 'Keep them, Kathleen. I only wish I could do more for you.'

Her hand was on the door handle when he suddenly asked:

'Have you a brother here in Elvemere?'

She turned to look at him in surprise. 'Why yes, doctor. I have to be sure. His name's Patrick Reardon—only he's me step-brother.'

Jonathan nodded. 'I thought so. I recently made his acquaintance. Will you remember me to him when next you see him? Tell him I have that which I promised to get for him.'

'I don't see him any more, doctor,' she said

sadly. 'Not now that we're at different places.'

'But you visit him surely—and he you?'

She shook her head. 'If he knew about the way I am—' she looked up at him with fear in her eyes again. 'You wouldn't tell him, would ye, doctor?'

He rose and came to her, patting her shoulder. 'You can be sure that your secret is safe with me, Kathleen. But you need all the friends and family you have at this time. You cannot hope to keep your condition secret for long. Patrick is a good fellow, he would surely help you. If you take my advice you will tell him as soon as possible.'

What he suggested was out of the question but Kathy nodded, thanking him again. Out in the narrow street she felt strangely cheered. Although the doctor had offered her no solution he had been kind and it had been a relief to unburden herself to another human being. If it was, as he had said, God's will that she should bear the child she carried, then somehow she must find the strength to face it through.

Back at the soup kitchen she worked extra hard to make up for the time she had taken off. Bessie was more than willing to take advantage of her eagerness, standing over her as she scrubbed the stone-flagged floor to make sure she did it properly.

'You go and see that Doctor Nichols then, did you?' she asked. 'Give you some physic, did he?'

Kathy pushed a strand of hair out of her eyes with the back of her hand, nodding noncommittally. Bessie snorted.

'Told you you'd be worse before you was better, I'll be bound!'

But Kathy refused to be drawn.

When it was time to go home Melissa insisted that she travel in the carriage with her. As Kathy leaned back against the cushions with a sigh of relief she looked anxiously at her.

'You are not at all yourself, Kathy. How long have you been feeling like this?'

Kathy remembered Doctor Nichols' advice to 'throw herself upon her mistress's mercy' and took a deep breath. 'Not long, Miss Melissa. It's—I'm—' Her breath caught as the words froze in her throat. 'Oh—I can't say it—I can't tell ye!'

Taken aback, Melissa looked at the girl's bent head and heaving shoulders in distress. 'Oh, come now, Kathy. It surely cannot be as bad as you think. You must certainly tell me what it is at once. I cannot bear to see you so upset.'

The kind words only made Kathy weep all the harder, making words impossible, and when Melissa looked out of the window and saw that they were almost at Holbrook Lodge she reached out to pat Kathy's knee.

'We will go straight to my room and talk there,' she said kindly. 'Do dry your tears.'

When they had reached the haven of Melissa's boudoir Kathy looked fearfully at her mistress. How to begin? When she knew the truth Miss Melissa would surely be repelled and disgusted with her. Not only that but she would ask questions to which Kathy could not give the answers. She would assume the worst. In her anxiety to get her ordeal over and done with she blurted her confession in a single sentence almost as soon as the door had closed.

'Oh, Miss Melissa—I'm going to have a baby!'

Melissa spun round to stare at her and for what seemed an eternity the two looked into each other's eyes, too stunned to speak. It was Kathy who broke the silence at last with a small, stifled sob. Melissa went to her.

'Are you sure of this, Kathy?' she asked quietly.

Kathy nodded. 'I went to see Dr Nichols in Friar's Lane. It's true enough. Oh, miss, I've done what I thought would stop it—but it hasn't. Oh, miss—' She stuffed her fist into her mouth. 'What am I to do? Will I have to go?'

Melissa looked at her with troubled eyes. 'Please try to stop crying, Kathy,' she begged. 'You will make yourself ill. You may rest assured that I shall not turn you out into the street. We shall think of some plan. Will you tell me the name of the father?'

But Kathy shook her head. 'I can't. Don't ask me, Miss Melissa, for I can *never* tell ye!'

Melissa was slightly taken aback at the girl's vehemence until she suddenly remembered something. On her wedding day had she not caught Charles, her brother, molesting Kathy in her room? Hot anger filled her. Why had men such vile instincts? Why must women be their victims, powerless against the humiliation and sufferings heaped upon them? She took both of Kathy's hands in hers and looked into her eyes.

'Only tell me this, Kathy. Were you the unwilling victim of an attack upon your person?' Kathy nodded, her head low with shame and Melissa pressed her fingers. 'I thought as much,' she said, almost to herself. 'How long before the child is born, Kathy?'

'I think it'll be about Christmas time, miss.'

Melissa nodded, brows drawn together. 'You must give me time to consider—to decide on what is the best course. Go downstairs now and do not distress yourself any more. We shall find some solution.'

When she had gone, Melissa lay down on her bed. She felt sickly herself. The throng of people at the soup kitchen, jostling each other in their hunger—their unwashed bodies in the July heat. The atmosphere had been suffocating. She was grateful that she had remembered to take her vinaigrette. And now, this news about Kathy. It was certainly a problem she would rather not have had, beset as she was with other cares.

Marriage had been a sad disappointment to her. Not only a disappointment but a shock. Even after three months she could hardly believe that the sweet, gentle young man she had believed herself to be so in love with could have brought her to such humiliation. Who would have thought that such a serene, composed exterior could hide such baseness?

On returning from her honeymoon she had confessed to her mama that she had been right when she had remarked that after marriage a woman's body was not her own. Amelia had simply smiled smugly.

'You cannot say that I failed in my duty, child. I tried to warn you. God in Heaven above knows what I myself have had to suffer. But you would not listen and now you must endure it until your family is complete, just as I did.'

Melissa had been appalled. How could she endure it? And yet she must if it was one of the duties of marriage. Why had no one told her—warned her of what would be expected of her? She closed her eyes as her head throbbed painfully. She was going to have one of her headaches again. Thinking of her relationship with John always brought it on. All she could hope for was that her children would come quickly so that she could be spared before too many years had passed.

Suddenly her eyes flew open. A way to help Kathy *and* herself had come into her mind like the answer to a prayer.

*     *     *

'And then, at the end of the summer, say in September when your condition becomes obvious, we will go to the cottage by the sea and stay there until the child is born.'

Kathy stared at her mistress. She was shocked at the idea that had just been presented to her. It was certainly a solution to her problem, it was true. But such a deception! Would it be right? Mr John had been so kind to her. It seemed wrong to deceive him like this. Slowly she shook her head.

'Oh Miss Melissa. It seems—it seems so—so wicked!' she whispered.

Melissa crossed the room and took her shoulders, looking down into her eyes directly.

'You can believe me, Kathy, when I tell you that I have good reason for doing this. It is not wicked and you must not think of it as such. I believe that I know the identity of your child's father and, being who he is, the child will be kin to me—my flesh and blood, so it is only right that I should take it. Am I not right?'

Kathy raised her eyes in wonder. How could Miss Melissa have found out? 'Yes,' she whispered. Melissa went on:

'In employing this slight deception we can avoid disgrace for everyone concerned. Do you not agree?'

Kathy nodded, hope rising joyfully in her breast. It seemed she was to be forgiven after all. 'But the Master, Miss Melissa?' she enquired, chewing her lip.

'You may safely leave that with me,' Melissa told her. 'What do you say, Kathy? Do you agree?'

'Yes—if you think it'd be best.'

Melissa drew a long breath. 'Very well. It shall be arranged. Have no more fear, Kathy. All will be well.' She left the little room on the top floor, closing the door behind her firmly and standing on the landing to recover her breath. Her heart was beating like a drum. It was half achieved. Kathy had agreed, now she had only John to face. She said a silent prayer as she went down the stairs to the drawing-room.

John looked up as she came into the room and his heart gave the familiar twist of pain. She was so lovely, yet so remote. He had longed so much for the day when she would belong to him, yet she was no more his now than she had been a year ago before their betrothal. He had always found her innocence delightful and endearing but that was before he realised that it concealed a repulsion of all intimate contact between man and wife. Her attitude was driving a wedge between them. They were fast becoming strangers and he was at a loss to know what to do about it. He smiled as she sat down and took up her embroidery.

'You are pale, my love. I hope your morning with the Fairfax ladies did not tire you?'

She shook her head. 'No, though it was rather a harrowing experience. I have the greatest admiration for the Misses Fairfax, working as closely as they do with the poor.'

He smiled wryly. 'They must surely have assured themselves a comfortable place in Heaven.'

She looked up at him sharply, her grey eyes flashing. 'I dare say you think them odd because they have not married. For myself, I think their lives well used.'

He crossed the room to sit beside her and slipped an arm round her shoulders. 'Oh, Melly, please don't be so sharp—so distant with me. Why can we not be easy together as we were before our marriage?'

She edged away from him. 'Everything has changed, John. You know in what way.'

He dropped his arm to his side with a sigh. 'Oh, Melly, will you never forgive me for being a man? If I had only known that you were so— so unprepared. Can we not talk—so that you become used to the idea?'

'It is hardly a subject for the drawing-room, John. Please let us drop it and speak of more pleasant things. Your mother was looking very well today—'

He grasped her hands. 'Melly, I *love* you! Can't you see what your coldness is doing to me?'

Melissa looked into his eyes and her heart contracted. For a moment she saw the old John, the dashing, gallant John who had been content with kisses, who had never allowed her a glimpse of the physical urges that now seemed to possess him. She wished as fervently as he did that things between them could be the same as before. She put her hand on his shoulder.

'Oh John, dear, I *do* love you,' she said softly. 'If only you knew how much.'

His arm slid round her slender waist and drew her close. 'But if that is true how can you remain so cold?' She felt the rapid beating of his heart as he kissed her. 'Will you not give me another chance, darling? I promise you I will be gentle.'

But she pushed him firmly from her, the familiar panic rising in her breast. 'John—wait. I have something to tell you.'

He looked at her. 'What is it, dear?'

She swallowed. 'I—I have reason to believe that I—that we are to have a child.'

He stared at her. 'Melly! Are you sure?'

'Quite sure.' Her eyes avoided his.

He took both of her hands. 'Have you consulted Dr Maybury?'

She shook her head. 'There is no need. I am in good health.'

'Nevertheless, you should not take chances. I will ask him to call tomorrow.'

'No!' She stood up, her face crimson. 'Please do not fuss, John. It is all quite natural. There is no need for Dr Maybury to call. If I feel the need of him I will tell you. I have Kathy to take care of me.'

'And me, love—and me.' He took her in his arms again, kissing her tenderly. 'May I not come to you tonight, darling?'

She looked at him with outraged eyes. 'Surely it is out of the question now, John? You must see that!' She backed away from him as his arms dropped to his sides. 'Good-night,' she said. 'I think I will go to bed now. I have a headache.'

He reached for her hand. 'But you said just now that you were in good health. We should be closer now, surely?'

Her voice trembled as she turned to him. 'That will come later, perhaps—after the birth. Good-night, John.'

As the door closed behind her he sat down again, lowering his head into his hands despairingly. God! How could he make her understand? How could he endure it? He thought of the coming child and tried to console himself with the anticipation of fatherhood, then his head snapped upwards as a thought suddenly struck him: Melissa could not be pregnant! It surely was not possible. Their marriage had never been fully consummated. On the few occasions that she had permitted him to share her bed, Melissa had been so overcome with fear—so inhibited that it had been impossible, so how could it be so? Was she lying simply to hold him at bay? Surely she would not use such an excuse. A suspicion that had nagged at him for weeks came to the fore once again: was there someone else in Melissa's life—someone perhaps with whom marriage had been impossible? It would certainly explain her coldness towards him. He had been away at college for three years, after all; they had seen very little of each other since they had grown up. Her father had been very eager for their marriage on business grounds. Had Melissa complied out of duty to him?

Angrily he rose and poured himself a glass of whisky, downing it at a gulp and refilling it at once. The thought of Melissa loving someone else was like acid eating into his heart. He didn't want to think about it. If only she had told him the truth he would have tried to help her forget. He would forgive her anything if only she would try to be a true wife to him, but this—this deadlock between them was impossible to bear.

'Oh God help me,' he muttered, pressing the cool glass against his forehead.

The drawing-room door opened to admit Kathy. 'Mr Charles Quincey to see you, sir,' she said, bobbing her bronze head.

Charles swaggered in, pinching Kathy's cheek when he saw that his sister was not present. He was dressed in his finest clothes, his blond hair sleek and well brushed and his cheeks flushed. He came forward to slap his brother-in-law on the shoulder.

'Drinking alone, John? A most unhealthy habit! And why the glum face?'

John sighed. 'Melissa has retired early. I confess I was feeling rather downcast.'

Charles laughed loudly. 'Marriage beginning to pall, eh? Well, I can't say I'm surprised. Personally, I never could understand what you saw in that sanctimonious sister of mine!'

John coloured hotly. 'Melissa is a wonderful girl. If you hadn't been indulging yourself too freely, Charles, I'd take you to task for insulting my wife in her own house!'

Unperturbed, Charles threw himself full length into a chair, pulling a wry face and waving a hand airily.

'Come off it, John. If you had to work all day in that God-awful stinking mill you'd take a drink or two when you got home—if only to take away the smell of corn meal and unwashed peasants! God, I could puke as soon as I enter the place. Stop being so bloody pompous and give me a glass of whatever that is you're drinking.'

Reluctantly, John poured him a whisky and Charles cocked an eyebrow at him as he took the glass.

'By the way, what *is* wrong with Melissa tonight? It's not like her to take to her bed this

238

early.'

John shrugged. 'She has been helping the Misses Fairfax at the soup kitchen. She is tired.'

Charles looked round the elegant room. If she had little else, at least his sister had good taste. He admired the gilded overmantel and the two fine paintings flanking it, the comfortable chairs and *chaise-longue;* the fine soft carpet and the brightly polished steel fender. Over by the window was Melissa's piano, a generous wedding gift from Great-Aunt Graves in London. The whole effect was gracious and charming. He raised his glass.

'Here's to your happy home, old fellow. I must say, your father is a damned sight more generous than mine! It must be nice to have your own establishment to come home to—and a postion of trust in the family business.'

John drained his glass and looked thoughtfully at his brother-in-law. 'It's all I ever wanted. I believe I can say without boasting that I have earned it.'

Charles pulled a face. 'I confess you do sound a trifle pious. Some people are damned easily pleased, I suppose. My father never gave me the chance to find out what I wanted. Straight into Quincey's, whether I liked it or not!' He drained his glass and looked up at John with a bitter expression. 'I'll bet that little swine Paul gets everything his way.' He held out his glass for a refill. 'Still, Mama tries to make it up to me in her own way, God bless her. She's managed to persuade Great-Aunt Graves to subsidise the paltry wage Father pays me.'

But John wasn't listening to Charles's complaints. His thoughts were still with Melissa and her earlier announcement. He longed to know the truth of the matter. The whisky decanter was almost empty now and his consumption of it had released his natural reticence. He sat down in the chair opposite Charles and looked at him thoughtfully.

'Charles—about Melissa. While I was away at college did she have any other admirers?'

Charles looked surprised. 'Not that I know of. Not that Melissa would have confided in me if there had been. We've never been close. I believe there was some popinjay of a music master—but that was only schoolgirl's fancy, I am sure.' He grinned mischievously. 'Why old fellow? Is she giving you a hard time?'

John slumped in his chair disconsolately. 'I—I have reason to believe that she does not care for me as she should,' he said painfully.

Charles threw his head back and laughed. 'I take it from your discomfort that you are speaking of affairs of the bedchamber. I've heard the same complaints before from other newly married fellows. You really are very naive, Johnnie, old chap. *Nice* women are not for such things. They are brought up to abhor them. I am led to believe that most married men find that kind of satisfaction among the lower orders.' He chuckled lewdly. 'Now that little servant-girl of yours—Kathy, isn't it? She's good for a tumble. Why not?'

But John got up and walked restlessly to the window. 'I *want* no one but Melissa. I love her,' he said vehemently.

Charles grinned indulgently. 'Very commendable of you, but what you have to understand is that ladies of breeding find that kind of thing indelicate. It offends them deeply. Believe me, your only chance of happiness is to look for your fun elsewhere.' He got up and joined John at the window where he stood looking gloomily out into the gathering dusk. 'Look, why not come and spend the evening with me? There's a company of travelling players at the Town Hall. I have one of their playbills here.' He drew a gaudily-coloured paper from his pocket and held it out to John who read that Mr and Mrs Edmund Delaney and company would present a programme of plays for the entertainment of ladies and gentlemen at the Town Hall, Elvemere for one week, commencing 10th July. Having read it he looked at Charles. It would be good to get away from the house for a while and forget his worries.

'All right, I'll come,' he said, picking up the depleted decanter and holding it up to the failing light. 'But let's finish the whisky before we go.'

241

Charles laughed and held out his glass. 'That's more like it, Johnnie. Here's to a happy evening!'

*　　*　　*

The large assembly room at the Town Hall was crowded to bursting point. At the far end a stage had been erected with red plush curtains in front. Chairs and benches had been set out in rows for the audience, who now waited for the play to begin with ill-concealed impatience. John and Charles managed to find seats in the front row and Charles nudged John, leaning over to shout into his ear above the din:

'I understand that the company have taken a private room next door at the White Hart for use as a green-room. Shall we take a look afterwards?'

John nodded. He would have liked to ask what a green-room was and what they would do there, but he felt thick-headed from the whisky and the heat of the room and unequal to the effort of making himself heard above the noise.

At last the curtains parted and the play began. Fuddled as he was, John had difficulty in following the plot but it seemed to be about a young woman masquerading as a man. She was dazzlingly beautiful, with dark flashing eyes and an abundance of black curls and how

242

anyone could possibly mistake her for a man seemed ludicrous to John. The scanty costume she wore revealed shapely legs and thighs and the curves of her voluptuous figure were anything but masculine. If Charles shared his view he certainly did not allow it to spoil his enjoyment of the play, and in the interval he turned to John, his eyes gleaming.

'Isn't she adorable, eh, Johnnie?'

John turned glazed eyes towards him. 'Who?'

'Who? Why, the girl who's playing Viola, of course! Sophia Wood is her name. I mean to make her acquaintance after the show. What do you say?'

John blinked. 'How do you mean to do that?'

Charles shook his head exasperatedly. 'At the green-room, of course! Isn't that what it's for, you idiot?' John opened his mouth to speak but Charles held up his hand. 'Shh. The second act is beginning.' And he leaned forward eagerly, determined not to miss one word or movement of the lovely Sophia Wood.

As they came out into the market-square later John gulped gratefully at the cool night air. The dulling effects of the whisky had diminished now, leaving him with a dry mouth and an aching head. He would just as soon have gone home to his bed, but Charles grasped his arm firmly.

'Come along, old fellow, round to the back.

The best part of the evening is about to begin.'
He jabbed an elbow into John's ribs. 'Who
knows—we might even find an obliging wench
who will alleviate your frustrations!' And
laughing gaily he pulled John after him down
the cobbled alley which led to the rear
entrance of the White Hart Inn.

The alley opened out into a yard at the end.
It was flooded with light from a window which
gave on to it and through the dimpled panes
John saw that the room was full of people
laughing and talking loudly. Some of them
were instantly recognisable from their costumes,
as players, and Charles tightened his grip on
John's arm.

'In we go, Johnnie—and do try to look more
cheerful. You look as though you're going to a
funeral!' He pushed the door open and
propelled John before him into the crowded
room.

It was very hot and the air was heavy with
the odour of mutton pies and ale, making
John's stomach heave. They were greeted by a
stout, florid man who still wore the costume
of Sir Toby, and Charles immediately fell
into conversation with him, flattering him
outrageously and making sure the man knew
that he came from a family of some influence
in the town. John soon gathered that the man
was Edmund Delaney, the actor-manager of
the company.

Charles lost no time in extolling the beauty

and talent of Sophia Wood and was in full flow on this subject when Delaney looked towards the door and announced in his deep, resonant voice:

'Ah! Here is the lady herself. She is m'niece, y'know, sir. I will try to attract her attention.'

All heads turned to look towards the doorway in which Sophia stood framed. She had changed out of the boy's costume she had worn in the play and was now attired in a stunning gown of ruby silk trimmed with black lace. She carried a black lace fan and her abundant hair cascaded about her creamy shoulders in a mass of glossy ringlets. One glance at Charles confirmed for John that he was completely captivated.

Edmund Delaney was quick to notice his stunned expression too. He laughed and slapped him on the back.

'She walks in beauty like the night, eh, dear boy? I'll warrant you'd like to meet her, what?'

Transfixed, Charles nodded, his eyes still riveted on Sophia's face as she came unhurriedly towards them across the room, her dark eyes bold and provocative, well aware of Charles's hungry eyes as she paused to exchange a word with this one and that. Fluttering her fan and laughing gaily she passed through the crowd, her red lips parted to reveal small, perfect white teeth. At last she was at her uncle's side, smiling up into his face, dark eyes sparkling. Picking up her hand he kissed the fingers in a flamboyant gesture.

'Ah m'dear gel, here is a gentleman who is afire with admiration for ye. May I present Mr Charles Quincey. One of Elvemere's foremost businessmen—m'niece, Sophia, star of m'company.' He handed Sophia's hand to Charles who took it eagerly and raised it to his lips.

'It is sheer delight to make your acquaintance,' he mumbled, while John stood by bemused. Never had he seen his brother-in-law so smitten and confused. His skin was flushed and the hand that held Sophia's trembled like a boy's. They moved away together and John started as a pert voice spoke at his elbow:

'You look lost, sir. Are you looking for someone?'

He looked down to see a girl standing at his side. He vaguely remembered her face from the small part she had taken in the play and he smiled politely, shaking his head.

'No. I came with my brother-in-law but he is—ah—otherwise engaged. I think it is time I went home.'

The girl took his arm, her plump cheeks dimpling into a smile. 'Oh pray do not leave so soon, sir, before I have even learned your name. Tell me, did you enjoy the play?'

She drew him across the room to where a table was laden with food and drink. 'Allow me to tempt you, sir. I am told that playgoing gives

246

a gentleman an appetite.' She nudged John and gave a peal of laughter which he found oddly infectious. He allowed her to press a glass of wine into his hand. 'Now will you tell me your name, sir?' she asked. 'Mine is Rosemary.'

'J—John,' he responded, running a finger round the inside of his collar. The room really was unbearably hot and stuffy. Rosemary refilled his glass and he drained it thirstily.

'Poor John, you look so hot,' she said soothingly. 'Would you like to go where it is cooler and perhaps take off your coat for a while?'

He nodded eagerly. 'Thank you—if you could show me to such a place.'

She gave another peal of laughter and filled his glass again. 'Drink this first. This wine is very refreshing. I'm sure you will find it quenches your thirst.'

She led him out of the room and through a dim passage; up a flight of stairs and along a corridor, then she paused to take a key from the bosom of her dress. Standing in the doorway, John saw a comfortable room with a low ceiling. It contained a large four-poster bed and the window was open, letting in a cool breeze. Rosemary pulled him inside and bolted the door, then, reaching up, she wound her arms around his neck and kissed him soundly on the mouth.

'That's better, isn't it, Johnnie,' she said

softly, helping him off with his coat.

He allowed the sleeves to slide from his arms, closing his eyes and swaying slightly as the cool air caressed his face. It was so deliciously fresh in this room after the heat downstairs and he thought of the soft bed longingly. When the girl pulled him towards it he went willingly, smiling as he collapsed on to the coverlet. He was dimly aware of Rosemary undressing and climbing, naked, on to the bed beside him, but to him it might all have been part of a dream. A moment later he sank into oblivion and nothing Rosemary could do could stir him.

When he awoke, John could not, at first, make out where he was, then he turned and saw Rosemary's tousled head asleep beside him and everything came back to him with a jolt. He was consumed by shame. What had taken place between them was a hazy blur. Slowly, he got up and found his coat, smoothing his rumpled hair. Then, with one eye on the sleeping girl, he slid back the bolt and let himself out of the room.

He was well clear of the inn before he felt for his pocket-watch to see what the time was. He found it was gone and so too was the money he had taken out with him. So that was it: the girl had simply intended to rob him all along. He closed his eyes, wrinkling up his face in fury at his own stupidity. He should never have allowed Charles to persuade him to go to that place. How foolish and naive of him to be duped like that! Why had he not seen through the girl's ruse?

As he reached the High Bridge he heard the church clock strike one and he leaned over the stone parapet to watch the black silken water flowing beneath. Towards Denmark House the tall houses and the ships in the port were etched against the night sky. In the other direction—the direction of Holbrook Lodge, the trees on the riverbank whispered softly, stirred by the night breeze. He thought of Melissa and his heart contracted. Could it be that she had suffered as he was doing now— had loved impossibly? He squared his shoulders and made a resolution. There must be no more secrets between them. He would make her tell him the truth. He would confess tonight's folly to her as illustration of his trust and understanding. Somehow—somehow he would earn her love even if it took years, for he knew now without any doubt that the love of his own dear Melissa was the only love he would ever want.

*       *       *

Awakened by the urgent tapping on her bedroom door, Melissa sat up in bed, her heart pounding in her throat.

'What—what is it?'

'Let me in, Melissa.' John's voice came to

her, muffled through the thickness of the wood.

'No—I cannot—it is late.' Her voice shook as she grasped the covers to her.

'Please. It is urgent. I *must* talk to you.'

She hesitated. He sounded distressed. He *was* her husband. She must let him in. Slipping out of bed she padded to the door and unlocked it. John came quickly inside, closing the door and leaning against it.

'Melissa—dearest—' he began, but she began to back away from him.

'No—*no!*'

He shook his head. 'Please, for God's sake listen to me, Melissa. I will not move from this spot. I will not touch you—only listen.'

She nodded, biting her lip nervously. 'Very well—I am listening.'

He swallowed hard, his mouth suddenly dry. It was so difficult to know where to begin. 'I have been out—to the play with your brother, Charles,' he said breathlessly. 'I foolishly allowed him to persuade me to mingle with the actors afterwards at the White Hart Inn. One of them—a girl—invited me to her room.' He shook his head. 'I had taken too much to drink or I would not have behaved so. Indeed I fell asleep as soon as I got there and afterwards, on the way home, I found that she had robbed me of my watch and money.' He took a small step towards her. 'The point I am trying to make is that I would never have gone there at all if—' he broke off as she turned from him, tears starting from her eyes.

'If I had been a dutiful wife to you. Is that what you are trying to say?' she asked brokenly.

'No, no, Melissa. I don't mean that at all!' He crossed the room and took her trembling shoulders, turning her towards him. 'I want you to know that I have guessed why it is that you cannot love me—you loved elsewhere and were deceived.' He looked earnestly into her eyes. 'If it is so confide in me, love. Tell me and I will be your comfort—because I *love* you, Melissa.'

She stared at him incredulously. 'What are you saying, John?'

He took her two cold hands in his and held them against his chest. 'I know that there is no child,' he said gently. 'There cannot be because we have never loved in the way that would have made it possible. Now do you see?'

She pulled her hands from his and turned away, covering her burning face with her hands. 'And you thought that I lied to you because—because I loved someone else?'

He lifted his shoulders, staring perplexed at her bowed head. 'What else could I think?'

'Oh, John.' She spun round to face him, tears streaming down her cheeks. 'You make me ashamed. It is true—I have deceived you, though not in the way you think. There has never been anyone except you. I have never—

*could* never love anyone else. Can you ever forgive me for the pain I have caused you?'

There was a silence as they stood looking at each other. It hung between them like a delicate strand of silk until John broke it by whispering her name. He stepped forward, taking her in his arms.

'Oh, Melly, why are you so afraid? Why can you not trust me? Am I such a monster that you must lie to keep me at bay?'

She clung to him, shaking her head, incapable of words as a surge of love for him consumed her. His fingers loosened the thick braid of hair till it fell about her shoulders, then he took her face between his hands and gently kissed her lips, knowing that the tremor that shook her body this time was no shudder of revulsion. Very gently he unfastened the neck of her nightgown and eased it over her shoulders. As it slipped softly to the floor she held out her arms to him.

'Love me, John,' she whispered. 'Please love me—now.'

Later, as she lay contentedly in the circle of his arms, Melissa told John about Kathy and the child she carried; of the wild, improbable plan she had devised to pass it off as her own. John smoothed the hair back from her brow and kissed her tenderly.

'My sweet, I know that you are fond of the girl, but you must surely see that it would not be right for us to take on her unfortunate

252

offspring. There will be children of our own. It would not be fair to them.'

She looked up at him. 'But you don't understand, John; the child will be of my own blood. I have not yet told you the whole of the story. On our wedding day, just before we left Denmark House, I went up to the nursery to say goodbye to Kathy. I found Charles in her room. He was very much the worse for drink and he was molesting her. Today, when I implied that Charles was the father of her child, Kathy did not deny it.'

John groaned. Charles! The fellow had much to answer for. 'Even so, love, I do not think it would be wise. We will think of some other solution. Rest assured, we shall not allow Kathy or the child to suffer. It may be possible to find her a husband. In fact I believe I might know the very man.'

Melissa kissed her husband's cheek. What a wonderful husband he was. And how foolish she had been to fear his lovemaking. Now she and John were truly one and could never be parted except by death.

'I love you, John,' she whispered as he drew her closer. He kissed her and a moment later they both slept, his arms still round her and her hair spread across his chest like a loving mantle.

# Part Four
# Sophia

# CHAPTER TEN

'Is it true that the mistress fainted when she read Mr Charles's letter?' Sarah asked, round-eyed.

The staff of Denmark House sat round the breakfast table, their undivided attention on Stevens whose face was smug with importance. She had just come down from serving breakfast and had just confirmed for them that the rumour that Charles Quincey had eloped some time during the night, was, in fact, true. They had all waited with bated breath for Mr Simpson to retire to his pantry and now that he had, all heads inclined eagerly towards the parlour maid.

'Can you imagine Mrs Quincey *fainting*?' she said in reply to Sarah's question. 'Put out, she certainly was, but faint—never! She blamed the Master, of course. After young Master Paul went upstairs I heard them at it hammer and tongs! He says it's all her fault and she says it's his. You should've heard them!'

'Well, I'm glad he's gone—for Patrick's sake,' Sarah said stoutly. 'Always gave poor Patrick a bad time, did Mr Charles. Not that he couldn't stand up for himself when he chose,' she added proudly. 'It's just that he controls himself better these days.' Since the night she had told Patrick about Kathy and he had half throttled her he had been quieter, treating her with an indifference she had misinterpreted as contrition.

Cook, who sat opposite, reached across and prodded her arm sharply. 'Pass the bread, girl and give over day-dreamin'. If you ask me, I think it's terrible. I don't know what folks is comin' to and that's straight—a well-bred young man like Mr Charles, runnin' off with a common actress and one he hadn't known above a few days! It's an outrage, that's what it is!'

'And poor Miss Christabel Gage so sweet on him, too,' Parkes put in. 'A marriage between the two of them would have joined up the two families a real treat.' She shook her head. 'Such a pity.'

'I've heard it said she's very beautiful.' All eyes turned again on Sarah, who continued: 'Jet black hair and dark eyes, Sophia Wood her name is. Polly Laws who works in the kitchen at the White Hart told me. I think it's lovely!'

'You would, bein' daft!' Cook sniffed. 'You got black hair and dark eyes on the brain, you 'ave, m'girl, and you'd better get your mind back on your work while you've still got the chance!'

Sarah sighed and rose to begin clearing the table. What did any of them know about it? They were all *old*!

Upstairs in the dining-room Amelia

258

Quincey sat in her chair, her breakfast plate untouched on the table before her whilst her fingers twisted restlessly together in her lap. Henry Quincey paced the room like a caged tiger. Today's irritating development was the last straw in a series of harassments. He was being pestered to sell some of his farm land for railway development and he was holding out against strong opposition. A railway in Elvemere would do nothing that he could envisage to further his interests—in fact some of his businesses, flourishing now, would go to the wall. Of course, George Gage was all for it. His small engineering works would benefit a hundredfold. Further up the river at Bannford they had stuck out and the railway company had been forced to make a detour. Henry had cherished great hopes that the same would happen here; that he would have enough influence to bring it about. It seemed he had hoped falsely, however. Some of the greedy beggars couldn't wait to have those great noisy monsters roaring across the countryside, poisoning the air and taking the bread out of decent folks' mouths. No doubt the fools had been infected by the 'railway mania' and had tied up all their money in the company. Well, why should *he* pull their chestnuts out of the fire for them? Personally, Henry felt that it was high time the Government intervened.

'I don't think you have heard a single word I have said, Henry!' Amelia's shrill voice cut in on his thoughts jarringly. He spun round on her, his face red and angry.

'It's like I said, Amelia. If you'd not spoilt the lad—made such a fool of him, he'd have settled down well enough. Anyway, he's only sowing his wild oats, as they say. Leave him be, he'll be home soon enough when the money runs out. Perhaps now you can see the sense of keeping him short.'

'In his letter he says that he intends to marry this creature, though,' Amelia pointed out. 'I do wish you would go after them, Henry, and bring him back before he does something foolish.'

'And how the devil would I find them—answer me that, madam?' Henry spluttered exasperatedly. 'And who is supposed to attend to my business while I am away, pray? Are *you*?'

Amelia winced. 'Do please keep your voice down. The servants have enough to gossip about already. Charles has stated his intention of going to London. It would not be difficult to find him, surely?'

'London's a big place. It could take months. I've told you, he'll be back.'

'You could trace him through Mr Jarvis, Aunt Graves's solicitor,' Amelia said patiently.

Henry glared at her. 'Jarvis? Why should he go there?'

She swallowed hard. 'Because when the money he has taken with him runs out, as you put it, that is where he will replenish it.'

He stared at her, his eyes narrowing. 'Now wait a minute—if you think I'm going to send money up there for him—pay his wages when he isn't here to earn them—'

'No—no,' she waved a hand at him. 'He will go to Mr Jarvis to claim the allowance Aunt Graves pays to him—and has ever since he entered the business.' She bit her lip as she watched his complexion change from red to purple, then to white. 'It—it is only the money that would come to him in the event of her death, Henry,' she stammered. 'She wished him to have it now.'

'She wished? *You* did, you mean—you and *him*! You let him talk you into persuading the old woman!' Henry grasped the back of a chair, trying to control his urge to seize his wife and shake her. 'Well, I hope you're satisfied. Maybe now you can see what thanks you get. Can't you see what you've done? You can resign yourself to the fact that you've lost your precious son, madam, for I'll not waste a minute of my time looking for him. For all I care he can rot in Hell with his fancy woman and good riddance! Young Paul can have Quincey's instead!'

So immersed had they been in their argument that neither of them had heard the front doorbell ring, nor Simpson's quiet entry, and when he uttered a discreet cough they both spun round, Henry's face bristling with florid rage, whilst Amelia was deathly pale.

'Well—what do you want, man?' Henry thundered.

Simpson bowed his head respectfully. 'I am sorry to disturb you, sir—madam, but a—person has called to see you—a Mr Edmund Delaney. I tried to dissuade him but he is most adamant. He says it has to do with his niece and that the matter is of the utmost urgency.'

Henry glanced at Amelia. 'Delaney—is that the name of the—er—?'

'I think it would be better to see the man,' she said quickly.

'Right—put him in the study, Simpson. I'll be in directly,' Henry said purposefully. Then, to Amelia: 'You stay here, madam. This is none of your affair. This is to be between man and man.'

She bit her lip. 'Remember that there is nothing to be gained by losing your temper, Henry. Hear the man out, I beg you. I have no doubt that he wishes for the safe return of his niece. If the interview were to be handled properly, the outcome could be of advantage to us all.'

'I'll handle it my way,' said Henry stubbornly. 'And I advise you to attend to your household duties, madam, and leave the resolving of this matter to me.' And so saying he left the room, slamming the door behind him with a crash that set the breakfast dishes rattling.

Edmund Delaney stood before the fireplace in the study; a portly, flamboyant figure in his outdated cut-away coat and gaudy cravat. His plaid pantaloons were skin tight and stretched across his corpulent stomach alarmingly, and his bald pate shone as though it had been polished with beeswax. The face beneath it was fringed with white curling whiskers. Henry was slightly taken aback by the man's appearance. Most of the local businessmen of his acquaintance dressed soberly. He had never before had dealings with showmen or entertainers and he instinctively mistrusted the man on sight.

'Mr Delaney?' he enquired guardedly.

The man nodded amiably and extended a plump, white hand. 'Edmund Delaney, at your service, sir. Have I the honour of addressing Mr Henry Quincey?'

'You have,' Henry told him abruptly. He took out his pocket-watch and looked at it. 'I was due at my office ten minutes ago. You will appreciate that I am a very busy man, so if you'll be so good as to state your business.'

Delaney cleared his throat irritably, though his benign expression remained firmly glued to his face. 'Indeed I will, sir. It appears that your son has eloped with my niece, Sophia.'

'So I understand,' Henry snapped. 'I take it that you have come here to enquire as to their whereabouts. Well I can save you time by telling you that I am as wise as you are.'

Delaney shook his head. 'A bad business, Mr Quincey. A bad business indeed. To think of that innocent young girl being lured away from the bosom of her family—from her livelihood—by the promises of a young man of the world like himself. I sincerely trust that he will wed her, sir. Her poor aunt is most distraught.'

Henry cleared his throat. 'I dare say no more so than the boy's mother,' he said coldly. 'I agree that it is, as you say, a bad business, but I fear there is nothing to be done about it. Let them get on with it, I say. Let them stew in their own juice!'

Delaney assumed an expression of horror and took a step backwards. 'It is all very well for you, sir,' he protested. 'This sort of thing cannot harm a young man's reputation—but my poor innocent Sophia—!'

'Your poor innocent Sophia didn't *have* to go!' Henry barked. 'She'll have gone willingly enough if I'm any judge, no doubt thinking she was on to a good thing! I dare say she was glad enough to give up the life of a wandering vagabond!'

Delaney's face turned the colour of putty and his small eyes bulged as he stared at Henry. 'Wandering vagabond!' he boomed, his resonant voice vibrating with emotion. 'I will excuse that term, sir, putting it down to your obvious ignorance of our profession. Mine is a company of actors and actresses of the highest

264

accomplishment and I must further press the point that your son has depleted that company, sir, robbed me of my leading lady. I shall be forced to end my season here in Elvemere, losing two nights' takings!'

Henry sighed wearily. 'So that's what it was all about—money! I might have known.' He tapped his pocket. 'All right—may as well come right out with it. How much?'

Delaney smiled ingratiatingly, feigning surprise. 'Oh—well—how very good of you, sir—uncommon good—'

'I said how much?' Henry said impatiently. 'Never mind the flannel. I've already told you I'm late.'

'Well, let's see. Two nights—we've played to capacity houses—I would think—shall we say—ten pounds, sir?'

Henry pushed the notes into his hand and picked up the man's top hat which rested on the corner of his desk. Pushing it into Delaney's hand he opened the door. 'If that is all, I'll show you out,' he said with an air of finality.

Delaney shuffled out into the hall, stuffing the notes into his pocket as he went. Henry opened the front door and turned to him.

'I'll bid you good day, Delaney. And if you ever dare to come back here bleating about your slut of a niece I'll have you kicked down the steps. In fact I'll do it myself. So be warned!' And so saying he slammed the door on the astonished Delaney's back.

*       *       *

The unusual sound of merriment came from the tackroom as Seamus and Patrick ate their lunch of bread and cheese. Sarah had sneaked out to join them and to bring them the latest gossip, though it was no longer news to them. Seamus had been waiting outside the front door with the brougham to take Henry Quincey to his office when the unfortunate Delaney had been ejected and his account of the scene had the young people rolling with mirth.

'The cheek o' the feller!' he said indignantly. 'To be walkin' right up to the front door and ringin' the bell as bold as brass! A disgrace to a good Irish name if ye ask me. 'Tis no wonder he left with a flea in his ear.'

'I don't see why,' Sarah rejoindered. 'If his niece was good enough for Mr Charles, why shouldn't he? Stevens said the Master had to pay him to keep his mouth shut. I wonder if Mr Charles'll marry her and bring her back here?'

'Only time'll tell,' Seamus said, shaking his head. 'But I reckon I know one person who'll shed no tears if he stays away.' He glanced at Patrick who gave an answering grin.

In the three months that had passed since the hiring fair Charles Quincey had lost no

266

opportunity of taking out his frustrations and dissatisfaction on Patrick. Many a time he could willingly have killed his master's son, but Patrick had made himself a promise: one day he would see the Quinceys eat dirt. In order to do that he would have to remain at Denmark House—and he would have to stay out of trouble. He had made this hope his whole reason for living and he would let nothing spoil it.

Seamus swallowed the last of his tea and pulled himself stiffly to his feet, wiping his mouth with the back of his gnarled hand. 'Ah well, better get on I suppose. Thank ye for bringing us our scoff, Sarah, lass.' He trotted out of the door on his short, bandy legs to resume his work in the coach-house. Patrick made to follow him.

'Patrick—wait a minute—' Sarah put a hand on his arm. 'It's good to hear you laugh,' she said shyly. 'I'm glad Mr Charles has gone—for your sake. He made your life a misery. There's some that say as you've lost your spirit, but I know that ain't true.'

He shrugged. 'No use making more trouble for yourself. He didn't worry me anyway.'

'I know. You're too big a man to be bothered by the likes of him.' She sidled up to him, smiling. 'You could've thrashed him with one hand tied behind your back, couldn't you? I know you would've too if it hadn't been for losin' your place. He knew it too and he took advantage of it, the toad!'

He moved away from her uneasily. 'I've me work to do, Sarah. And Cook'll be lookin' for you, won't she?'

She shrugged. 'Let 'er go an' boil 'er head! I'd do anything for you, Patrick. If—if there was ever anything you wanted, you would ask me, wouldn't you?'

He backed towards the door as he saw her reach out her arms to him. The girl was always hanging round. She made him uneasy. He had asked Seamus not to leave them alone together but the old man was always forgetting. He put out a hand for the door-jamb and saw Sarah's face change as she looked past him at the doorway. Turning he saw Caroline Quincey standing there dressed in her newest riding habit.

'So this is where you are, Reardon,' she said crisply. 'What are you doing here, Sarah?'

The girl's face coloured. 'I came to get the basket and tea-can, miss,' she said.

'Then get about your business, girl, and allow Reardon to do his work. I shall have to speak to Cook about you if I find you loitering out here again.'

As Sarah scuttled past her, red-faced, she smiled at Patrick. 'As it is such a beautiful afternoon, I thought I would ride,' she said. 'And I would like you to accompany me, Reardon.'

Patrick shook his head. 'I'm afraid I can't be

spared, miss.'

She frowned. 'Nonsense, of course you can. I have already asked Seamus and he agrees that my brother's horse needs exercise.' She struck his arm with her riding crop. 'Come along, Patrick, don't be so stiff-necked. You know you'd rather be riding on an afternoon like this than polishing harnesses!'

Without another word he walked past her into the yard and presently reappeared with the two horses. As they neared the paddock she gave him a sidelong glance.

'You're very morose today. I take it you are not missing my brother, Charles!' She laughed. 'Surely you should be happy today, Patrick. He hardly made life pleasant for you, did he?'

Patrick shrugged. 'It makes no difference to me, miss. Sure 'tis none of my business.'

She raised an eyebrow. 'Tell me, Patrick, do you view us all with the same indifference?' When he failed to answer she urged her horse forward impatiently, obliging Patrick to follow, and for the next ten minutes they rode hard over the meadows, jumping hedges and ditches, till at last she reined her mount in the shade of some trees and slid from the saddle, her cheeks pink and her hair escaping in blonde tendrils from under her veil.

'We shall rest here,' she commanded, pulling off her hat and throwing it on to the grass. 'Will you walk a little with me?'

Patrick dismounted and secured both horses

to a sturdy branch, then he followed Caroline as she wandered towards a stream that flowed through the meadow. As he drew level with her she asked:

'Were you surprised to hear that my brother had eloped with an actress? Didn't you think it romantic?'

His expression did not alter. 'Like I said before, miss: it's none o' my business.'

She turned to him. 'Nevertheless, you must have your opinion. I am perfectly well aware that the servants' hall has been buzzing with gossip. You may tell me what you think, Patrick. I shall not carry tales.'

'What I think can't matter to you, Miss Caroline,' he said.

'But it does,' she insisted. 'You have to admit, it is romantic.'

He shrugged. 'I'm not sure that I know the meanin' of that word.'

She threw herself down on the grass. 'How dull and boring you are today. And it's so hot.' She looked up at him. 'Oh, for goodness' sake sit down. There's no one to see us.'

Reluctantly, he lowered himself on to the grass beside her and she stole a glance at him. His shirt was open at the neck, showing his golden skin and the thick black hair that grew on his chest. His face was bronzed by the sun and summer air, and his hair was as glossy as jet. A delicious shiver of excitement went through her as she looked at the strong brown hands and she reached out a finger to stroke the back of one of them.

'I have heard it said that you are very fond of your step-sister, Patrick. Do you not miss her?' she asked quietly, and saw his colour deepen as he answered:

'She chose to go her own way.'

Caroline looked at him speculatively. She had heard rumours about Kathy, servants' gossip. She wondered if he had heard it too. 'You don't visit her when you have time off, then—nor she you?' He shook his head, tugging at the grass and she went on: 'I could give her a message from you if you wished, I usually see her when I visit my sister. Shall I ask her if she wants to see you?'

'No!' He turned to her angrily, his eyes dark, and she felt a shiver of excitement run through her veins again.

'Very well. It was only an idea. How angry you look, Patrick.' She caught her breath as she looked at him. The barely suppressed passion in him fascinated her as it always had. More than ever she wanted to goad him, to see that passion erupt and watch its splendour explode like a firework. She imagined the huge, powerful hands holding her and pictured herself melting in submission. Quivering with delight she leaned closer and said softly:

'Wouldn't you like to kiss me, Patrick? You may if you wish.'

He looked at her in astonishment. Her blue

271

eyes gazed boldly into his, laughing, teasing, whilst with the tip of her finger she traced the outline of his jaw. Why, she was no better than Tabby at the Calcutta! he told himself. Was it possible that she was offering herself to him in the same way? Were *all* women alike? For a moment he was tempted to kiss the soft pink mouth so eagerly offered, then he remembered his promise to himself and he thought of what would happen if anyone found out. She wasn't worth it. Rapidly, he scrambled to his feet.

'The horses will be chilled, miss. We'd best be getting back.'

She got up and brushed her skirt peevishly. 'Chilled—on a day like this?'

'We rode hard, miss, hard enough to make 'em sweat.' He strode back to where they had tethered the horses, Caroline following at a run to keep pace with him, her temper rising to match her disappointment.

'How very *coarse* you are, Reardon,' she taunted. 'You look like a gipsy, did you know that?'

He untied the reins of her mount and turned to her. 'Me father was a gipsy, miss, or so I'm told.' He looked at her blandly. 'Will I help ye up?'

She put her foot into his cupped hands and swung herself into the saddle, kicking out as she did so to strike his shoulder a vicious blow with the toe of her boot. 'I always thought that

272

gipsies had more spirit,' she said, her eyes like ice. 'You're just a lout, Reardon—a coarse, ugly lout!'

He looked back at her passively. 'Just as ye say, miss.'

'Ohh!' She jerked the head of her mount round and urged it towards home. Patrick followed, but when she leaned forward and urged the mare to a gallop he let her go.

'I hope ye break your lovely neck—*Miss Caroline*,' he muttered under his breath.

When he reached the stable-yard he found Seamus unsaddling the mare and Caroline nowhere in sight. The old man looked at him in surprise.

'Where've ye been, lad—and what did ye do? Miss Caroline was in a fine temper.'

'Well she might be,' Patrick said darkly. 'Next time she comes askin' for me to take her riding tell her I'm too busy—send someone else with her.'

Seamus watched him as he strode away, leading his mount back to the stable. What was up now? he wondered, scratching his grizzled head. It seemed that trouble waited for Patrick round every corner.

Since he had ceased to visit the Calcutta, Patrick had begun to frequent the Bell Inn on his time off. He soon grew to know many of the regular customers there, who were, for the most part, servants like himself, though Dr Nichols occasionally looked in as well as one

273

or two of the ships' captains. For weeks now the conversation had been centred on the Great Eastern Railway, which, it now seemed certain, was coming to Elvemere. The prospect of its advent was viewed with mixed feelings. The innkeepers and ostlers feared that they would lose money when travellers no longer needed to make an overnight stop. The White Hart would bear the greatest loss, being the town's coaching inn. Some businessmen prophesied that the river and roads would fall into disrepair with the loss of turnpike tolls and the dues that vessels paid to the General Works Trust. Older men said gloomily that there was sure to be a rise in law-breaking when the felons hanging from crossroads gibbets would no longer be seen by travellers, whilst country cottagers feared that they would never again regulate their day by the cheerful blast of the post-horn.

As Patrick sat in his corner, listening to it all, he had only one thought: how to get more money to invest in more railway shares. In his view it could not fail to open a whole new life for people like himself. He saw it as the golden gate of freedom, just waiting to be opened. Under his mattress in the room over the coach-house rested the parchment wallet containing his precious share certificates. When Jonathan Nichols had handed them to him he had promised himself that he would add to them before the year was out and he felt sure that if he kept his ears and eyes open for long enough a way to do this would become known to him.

One night Tom Craven came in, hailing him from across the smoke-filled room, his big round face smiling and ruddy as ever.

'Well, well, if it isn't young Reardon, though I hardly knew you, you've grown so big!' Tom slapped him on the back heartily. 'What'll you have then, lad?'

Although Patrick protested he soon found Tom returning to the corner with two foaming pint pots.

'It's months since I last clapped eyes on you, lad,' Tom beamed. 'Do you not go to the Calcutta any more?'

Patrick shook his head. 'I like it better here,' he said evasively.

Tom took a deep draught of his ale and leaned back. 'Well now, how are you—and how's that pretty little sister of yours? The wife and I often talk about you two and old Seamus. Are you all well?'

Patrick nodded. 'Well enough, thank ye, Tom, though Kathy's got a new place now, so I don't see much of her.'

Tom looked closely at him. 'And what of you, lad—are you happy at Denmark House? You're lookin' a bit down in the mouth.'

Patrick leaned forward, suddenly eager to share his ambitions with someone. 'Tom—you know how I've always hated bein' bonded—

275

well, I'm hopin' soon to be me own master!'

Tom thrust out his lower lip, looking suitably impressed. 'How's that then, lad?'

Patrick lowered his voice. 'I've been savin' me wages and buyin' railway shares. I won some money fightin' a feller at the hirin' fair too. It all went into the railway.'

This time Tom was truly astonished. Most young fellows he knew would have blued the money on ale. He pushed his cap on to the back of his head and his mouth dropped open in surprise.

'Railway, is it? And how did you come to drop on that idea?'

Patrick told him all about the fight at the fair and the way Dr Nichols had befriended him, advising him on the investment of his winnings. When he had finished Tom leaned back, his red face glowing.

'Well, blow me down! Are you reckonin' on taking up the fight business then, lad?'

'No, but I would like to find some way to make extra money,' Patrick said.

Tom leaned forward, glancing round to see if anyone were listening. 'Could you handle a cargo if I was to get you one?'

Patrick frowned. 'A cargo—what do ye mean?'

'A *cargo*,' he whispered hoarsely. 'Mainly baccy and tea, I gets. You'd be surprised how many on the river do it. You could find your own customers and charge your own price,

276

then we'd share the profit. What d'you say, eh?'

Patrick stared at him in amazement. He'd never had the least idea that Tom Craven was a smuggler.

'What about the Customs Officers?' he whispered. 'Don't they come aboard and search?'

Tom laughed. 'Why bless you, lad o' course they does. They never finds nothin' though 'cause I've got a special hidin' place, see.' He winked broadly and tapped the side of his nose. 'My Meg has pockets sewn into the inside of her petticoat. All the stuff's hidden in them, under her skirts. That's one place they're not goin' to look. Well, would you, lad? My Meg's got a heart as big as a bucket but a face as'd freeze the whiskers off your chin!' He slapped his knee and laughed heartily, choking over his ale. 'Well, what do you say, lad?' he asked when he had recovered his breath. But Patrick shook his head. He'd do nothing risky. His future was too precious to take chances with, though, as he told Tom, he would have given a lot to have seen Meg Craven stand her ground with the Customs men, her skirts stiffened with contraband!

Finding the company somewhat tame, Tom soon left for the Calcutta, disappointed when Patrick would not join him, and he had hardly left when Jonathan Nichols's friendly face appeared in the doorway. Seeing Patrick, he made his way towards him and sat down. He brought the news of a rise in the value of the shares and Patrick found himself telling Jonathan of his wish to make more money to invest. Jonathan was thoughtful for a while.

'I have a piece of land you might tend,' he said at last. 'That is if you think you could find the time. You might grow vegetables and sell them.'

Patrick looked up, his eyes shining. 'Ah, doctor, sure that'd be grand. I could pay ye some of the money I made back in rent.'

But Jonathan shook his head. 'Just tend the herbs that are growing there for me. I use them in the salves and physics I make, that will be all the rent I ask. They don't take up much room. You'd be doing me a favour. Is it a bargain?' He held out his hand and Patrick shook it warmly.

'It is indeed, sir. It is indeed!'

\*       \*       \*

Kathy stood in the middle of the drawing-room carpet, her hands clenched into tight fists and her lips pressed together to stop her face from crumpling. She had never quite believed that it could actually happen—that Miss Melissa would take her child and bring it up as her own. From the beginning it had seemed too good to be true. But all the same, disappointment and apprehension overwhelmed

278

her as she stood trying to think of something to say to the suggestion that Melissa had just presented her with. She took a deep breath and moistened her lips.

'A husband, you say, Miss. But who? I don't know of anyone who'd have me the way I am.'

Melissa nodded. 'I was coming to that, Kathy. There is a man who once worked for my father-in-law, Mr Gage—at his works, you understand. Will Harrap is his name. A few years ago he was involved in an accident at the works which unfortunately left him crippled. Since then he has worked as a carpenter in his own home, which is a cottage in Mill Row. Lately his mother has died and he has no one to care for him or the cottage. He is considerably older than you, Kathy, but I do feel that you could be of great comfort and help to one another.' She looked searchingly at Kathy. 'What do you say—will you meet him?'

Kathy bit her lip. What would Patrick say? By rights she supposed she should ask him first, being the head of the family. Hadn't he promised her Da on his deathbed to look after her? But all that was past. How could she ask him? The mess she was in had changed everything. She swallowed and asked timidly:

'What—what if I don't take to him, Miss Melissa?'

Melissa's brow clouded. She felt bad about going back on her promise to take the child, but it had been made on impulse and she saw

279

now that John was right. If only Charles had not run off with this actress woman she would have made him face his responsibility himself. As it was, John's suggestion of Will Harrap as a possible husband for Kathy seemed the ideal solution.

'I'm afraid you must put the future of the child first now, Kathy,' she said gently. 'You have that to consider before your own feelings. If you marry Mr Harrap you will have a home of your own. Since his disablement Mr Gage lets him live rent-free at the cottage. And from all that I hear he is a kind and gentle man. I am sure he will be good to you and the child.'

There was a silence as Kathy stared at the carpet. She knew she had no choice. Miss Melissa wouldn't want to send her to the workhouse but that's what it would come down to in the end, for she'd not be able to do her work properly once she grew heavy with the child. Slowly, she nodded her head.

'I—I'll meet Mr Harrap then, Miss Melissa—if you think it'd be best.'

Melissa gave a sigh of relief. 'I'm sure it is, Kathy. I shall have to engage a new maid, of course, when you leave. But I would be most happy if you would continue to sew for me. It would give you an extra income and a little independence. Would you like that?'

Kathy's sad face brightened a little. 'Oh, miss, I would! It'd be as though I hadn't lost me place altogether.'

Melissa smiled. 'That is so. You shall come to the house once a week and bring the baby so that I can see how he is progressing. I shall look forward to it.'

The first meeting between Kathy and Will Harrap was arranged for the following Sunday. John invited him to call on Kathy at Holbrook Lodge at half-past five in the evening, in time to take her to evening service at the 'Iron Church' which was the name the locals had given to the tin-roofed Wesleyan Chapel in St Mary's Street. At five twenty-five Kathy was ready and waiting nervously, wearing her best dress of dark green plaid and a bonnet which Melissa had given her especially for the occasion. Her bright hair was drawn back into a modest chignon, making her eyes appear enormous in her pale face.

Although she was waiting for it, the discreet tap on the back door made her start and she opened it with trembling fingers to find Will Harrap waiting patiently for admission.

He was a short, thick-set man and it was difficult to guess at his age, though the grey hair and lined face certainly put him at more than forty. He was dressed, like Kathy, in his Sunday best and would have looked very smart if it hadn't been for his right leg which was misshapen and visibly shorter than the left. Under his right arm was a home-made crutch with which he supported himself, the top padded with a piece of carpet.

'Would you be Miss Kathleen Reardon?' he asked shyly. When he smiled the wide mouth opened slightly, revealing large, sound teeth, which Kathy found oddly reassuring. His brown eyes too were as clear as a child's. Kathy relaxed a little and held the door wide for him to enter.

'I would—will you please to come in.'

He pulled off his cap and looked around uncertainly. 'Is it all right—with Mrs Gage, I mean?'

She nodded. 'Oh yes. She told me I was to ask you to take a cup of tea before we set out. I have it all made and ready.'

He swung himself over the threshold on his crutch and sat on the chair that Kathy pulled out from the table for him. She poured two cups of tea from the enamel pot on the hob and sat down opposite him at the table. Suddenly she was tongue-tied and awkward. The situation was so unreal to her. Was this man *really* to be her husband? The idea was so dismaying that she felt a flush creeping slowly up her neck. It was all so different to what she—and Patrick—had planned for their lives. The thought of Patrick made her heart break. If only none of that with Mr Quincey had ever happened. If only she could wake and find the whole thing a bad dream.

'Might as well come straight to the point,' Will was saying. 'Mr John Gage said as how you was looking for a husband to take care o' you. Well, I'm lookin' for a wife. There's not many as'd take on a feller like me, crippled and ugly like,' he grinned apologetically. 'Knockin' on a bit too as you'll have noticed. But I can still do a fair day's work and I'll be good to you. I've a nice cottage too. Ma always took a pride in it. You can come and look if you've a mind.'

Kathy looked into her teacup. 'You know about—about the child?'

He nodded. 'Mr John's told me all about that. Never you fear that I'll cast it up in your face, for that ain't my way. It'll be good to have a little'n about the place. Oh, I know that there's some as'd give a bad name to such as you, but I want you to know that I ain't one o' them. I know as there's folks in this world that'll take advantage of them as can't defend themselves. Mr John says as you're a good lass and that's good enough for me—'specially now as I've seen you for meself.'

Kathy looked up at him, a lump in her throat. 'You're very kind, sir,' she whispered. 'I'm much obliged to you. I—I'll try hard to be a good wife, so I will.'

He smiled and pulled himself upright, tucking the crutch under his arm and holding out his hand to her. 'That's settled then, except that I'd like you to call me Will. I ain't no "sir" an' never will be. Shall we go?'

She took her shawl from the hook behind the pantry door and threw it round her shoulders while he looked on approvingly.

'I'll be right proud to be seen with you at chapel tonight, Kathleen,' he said. 'Bonny as a robin, you are.'

She opened the back door for him, blushing at the unexpected compliment. She'd been punished for what she'd done but she was beginning to think things might not be so hard for her after all. If she could make this poor man's life a little easier, maybe the Holy Mother would pray for her forgiveness. As for Patrick—all she could hope for was that he would never know of her shame. She must try to forget the love they had known—and hope that he would forget it too.

*       *       *

'I see your Kathy's walkin' out then!'

Patrick turned to look at Sarah, the curry-comb poised in his hand. 'What do you want with me this time?' he asked irritably. 'Why can't ye leave a feller to get on with his work in peace?' He turned back to the horse he was grooming.

But Sarah was used to his moods. She came into the stable, a smile on her lips. She had done everything she could think of to make Patrick like her, all in vain. Maybe she would get more reaction out of him by making him angry, and today she had the perfect weapon for it.

284

'Don't you want to hear about that step-sister o' yours then?' she taunted. 'Well, I can't say as I blame you for goin' off her after what she done. The bloke she's got now is a cripple and an old man at that. I don't know how she could, I'm sure I don't.' She saw with satisfaction that the back of his neck had reddened. Encouraged, she stepped closer. 'Seems she's not particular who she has nowadays.' She reached out to touch the rippling muscles on his forearm. 'I reckon she must've been mad to take up with anyone else when she could've had you, Patrick.'

He shook her hand off roughly. 'I'll not tell ye again—will ye go away and leave me alone, girl,' he growled.

She laughed. 'An' what if I don't? What'll you do, eh?'

He turned to face her. 'I'll come and tell Cook, that's what. I don't care if you lose your place. It'd be a relief to me to be rid of you, so it would!'

Her face flushed hotly with anger. 'Who do you think you are, Patrick Reardon?' she spat. 'There's Miss Caroline out here all hours. You don't tell her to sling her hook, do you? Is it her you fancy your chances with? Thinkin' to follow in Kathy's footsteps, are you?'

One of his large, powerful hands shot out and grabbed her shoulder. 'Shut your vile mouth this instant, girl, or I'll shut it for ye! *You*—you're not fit to lick my Kathy's boots, you're not!'

'*Your* Kathy, is she?' she flung back at him. 'Well not for much longer, she ain't—if she ever was!'

'What are you saying—what do ye *mean?*' he shook her.

'The banns've been read twice—*that's* what I mean,' she shrieked triumphantly. 'After next Sunday she'll be marryin' Will Harrap—hoppy leg an' all—and good luck to them, I say. Lord knows she ain't missin' much in you. Good looks ain't everything. A real nasty temper, you got!' She rubbed her shoulder as he let her go. 'Get you in real trouble, one of these days, you see if it don't.'

He laid down the curry-comb and looked at her menacingly but she laughed shrilly as she skipped out of his way, almost colliding with Seamus as he came in through the door. He glared at her, his walnut face black as a thunder cloud.

'Will ye be off to your work this minute, girl, or will I be tellin' Mrs Brown herself the nuisance ye are? When I passed the kitchen door a minute ago I heard Cook yellin' fit to wake the dead. Now, will ye be off with ye?'

As the girl slunk past him he looked at Patrick, pushing his cap to the back of his head and pursing his lips reproachfully. In answer Patrick lifted his shoulders in a helpless gesture.

'Sure t'was none o' my doin', Uncle. She'll

give me no peace. The girl's drivin' me mad—an' so's the other one too, damn her.'

Seamus nodded sympathetically. He knew the lad had done his best to stay out of trouble since he had made the decision to remain at Denmark House and he had to admit that it wasn't made easy for him. That lass Sarah had been making a real nuisance of herself lately. If it didn't stop soon he would have to have a word with Cook about her. But Miss Caroline—ah, she was another kettle of fish entirely. What did the likes of her want with Patrick, he wondered. Why wouldn't she leave him be? It was beyond him. But then women always had been a puzzlement to him anyway. Stepping forward, he patted Patrick's shoulder.

'Hold up, lad. If you keep your temper they'll soon stop their shenanigans and give up. They enjoy seein' ye rise to the bait, d'ye see?'

Patrick sighed and shook his head despondently. He gave a final stroke to the horse he had been grooming and turned to Seamus, his eyes troubled. 'Have ye—have ye heard any talk about Kathy, Uncle?' he asked.

Seamus frowned. He knew there was gossip among the other servants but he'd closed his ears to it. For one thing, he knew the little lass was good. He'd stake his life on it. And for another, he knew that if she had done anything wrong she'd not be in Miss Melissa's household this minute.

'Jealousy, lad,' he said. 'All jealousy. Take no heed. Sarah's been green with envy ever since Kathy was given the job of Nurse to Master Paul. 'Tis nothing but talk.'

'But she just said that Kathy was to be married,' Patrick insisted. 'She said the banns had been called twice. The man's a cripple called Will Harrap. D'ye know him?'

Seamus did know him. He was a good enough fellow, but old enough to be Kathy's father. Besides that he was a staunch chapel man and went regularly to the 'Iron Church'. Seamus felt uneasy as he looked at Patrick's anguished face. Kathy'd surely never set foot in the 'Iron Church'. It'd be a mortal sin.

Patrick made a decisive move towards the door. 'I must find out, Uncle. I must get at the truth, once and for all.'

'No!' Seamus moved swiftly to bar his way. 'Do nothin' hasty, lad.' He knew only too well that in his present mood Patrick would only find trouble for himself. 'Leave it to me,' he said persuasively. 'I'll find out what's goin' on. Sure I'm after taking the mistress and Miss Caroline to Holbrook Lodge this afternoon. I'll have a word with Kathy herself if I get the chance.'

But when Seamus returned with the carriage that afternoon, one look at his face told Patrick that his worst fears were confirmed. When he had seen to the horses he made for the quarters over the coach-house where Seamus had retreated.

The old man sat in his shirt-sleeves before the fire, waiting for the kettle to boil. As Patrick came in he was lighting his pipe and he looked up over the flame of the lighted spill, his eyes clouded.

'Well?' Patrick stood over him.

'Sit down, lad,' Seamus said wearily. 'I managed to speak to Kathy and it's true enough. She's to marry Will Harrap and the wedding's to be next week. More than that I couldn't get out o' her.' He shook his head. 'I'm sorry, lad.'

Patrick turned away angrily, striking his forehead with the palm of his hand. 'But *why*, Uncle? Where's the sense of it? Did she not think of askin' *me*?'

Seamus sighed. 'It's as I told ye, lad, I could get nothin' from her but the bare truth. All I know is that she's her mind made up an' nothin'll change it.' He shook his head. 'Ah, mebbe it isn't so bad at that. He's a good enough feller an' she'll be well looked after, that's somethin' isn't it?'

A flood of words rose in Patrick's throat but they choked him before he could utter them. He would have married Kathy if she had only come to him. Surely she knew how much she was hurting him by doing this! Didn't she know that he would have forgiven her anything if she'd only asked? If only he knew the real truth about her and Henry Quincey. If only she hadn't turned away from him. They *belonged* together. His fists clenched and he screwed up his eyes in an effort to blot out the pain. God! It was like having a limb torn from his body. Christ! How could he bear it?

He ate no supper that night and he refused Seamus's suggestion that he should take himself off to the Bell Inn for solace. At eight sharp the carriage was ready to take the Quincey family out to dine but before he went Seamus cast an anxious glance at his nephew.

'After ye've bedded the horses, why don't ye get an early night, lad?' he suggested. 'Sure ye look done.'

Patrick nodded abstractedly. 'I'm all right, Uncle. Yes, mebbe I'll do as ye say.'

It was a fine, mellow evening and settling the horses for the night, talking to them and feeling the familiarity of their response gave Patrick some comfort. He had settled the last of them and was just securing the stable door, when out of the corner of his eye he caught a movement among the dusky shadows by the coach-house. He thought he saw someone run lightly up the wooden staircase to the room above and he wiped his hands on his breeches, his lips setting in a determined line. If that was Sarah again he'd have done with her once and for all. This time she'd be sorry!

He strode up the stairs and flung the door wide. But it was not Sarah who stood before the fireplace in the twilit room, but Caroline,

290

her blonde hair loose around her shoulders. She wore a pale blue house-gown and her lips curved in a smile at his surprise.

'Well, Patrick—aren't you pleased to see me?'

He looked around him helplessly. 'What do you want here? I thought you'd gone out with the others.'

She walked slowly towards him. 'I told them I had a headache, Patrick,' she purred. 'I thought it too good an opportunity to miss, to spend a little time with you while Seamus is out of the way.' She looked up at him, her head on one side. 'I do think you might say something nice to me.'

'You'll have to go,' he said flatly.

'Oh! I don't call *that* nice.' She was standing close to him now, looking up at him, pink lips pouting provocatively. He caught the sweet scent of her and his nostrils flared. He turned towards the door but she slipped swiftly round him to stand in front of it, holding out her arms.

'Don't run away from me, Patrick. I want to talk to you. I've been thinking and I believe I know why it is that you're so stiff and cold towards me. You think I want to make trouble for you—to make you do something rash just for the fun of it. Well it's not true. It's simply that I find you attractive—more attractive than the insipid milksops who are always being thrown my way. Don't you believe that?'

He stared down at her. 'What do you want, Miss Caroline?' he asked hoarsely.

She smiled seductively. 'Don't you know, Patrick? If you don't, then you're not the man I took you for!' She moved a step closer, putting her two hands against his chest, but he snatched at her wrists and pushed her roughly back. A mixture of emotions raged inside him. He still ached for Kathy; still longed for her with all his heart and soul—but his mind and his body wanted this girl and he resented her for it. God, how he resented her!

'Whore!' he growled at her. 'Get out of here. Do what ye like—get me thrown out if it pleases ye. You're no better than that brother o' yours with your fancy words and your money and position. It's in the gutter ye should be, be rights—the lot o' ye!'

She threw her head back and laughed, her eyes sparkling. 'That's more like it, Patrick—go on, tell me more. You're so splendid and exciting when you lose that temper of yours!'

He stared at her, the flushed cheeks and parted lips aroused him but in the back of his brain a warning bell rang. Seamus had been right when he said that they 'enjoyed seeing him rise to the bait'. He knew that he was playing into her hands. Chewing his lip he turned away.

'I'll say no more—just go. Leave me alone.' He moved to the fireplace and there was a long silence. He thought she had slipped away,

292

but when he turned to look she was still standing there by the door, head thrown back, eyes gleaming.

'I was at my sister's house this afternoon,' she said quietly. 'I saw Kathy—and heard some news about her.'

He sighed wearily. 'Ye can save your breath. I know—she's gettin' married.'

She began to cross the room to him. 'Ah—but do you know the reason, Patrick? Surely you wondered why your step-sister would agree to wed an elderly cripple, eh?'

He shrugged, trying not to wince as she twisted the knife in the wound. 'I don't know—I don't know.'

'My sister confided the truth in me, Patrick, though she did not tell Mama. Would you like me to tell you?' She stepped up close, raising her face to whisper: 'It's because she had no choice. It was either that or the workhouse. She's going to have a child, Patrick—and she won't say who the father is.' She smiled up at him. 'I wonder if *you* know?'

Behind his half closed eyes a million stars seemed to explode. 'It's not true,' he said between clenched teeth. But in his heart he knew that it was—just as certainly as he knew who the father must be. The idea of it sickened him, making his head swim and his stomach churn. He made for the door, but again Caroline quickly barred the way.

'So now who do you call "whore", Patrick?

293

Tell me that!' she flung at him.

Frustration and fury welled up inside him like a boiling cauldron. If she wouldn't get out of his way she could take what was coming to her—damn her! Grasping her by the shoulders he jerked her roughly to him.

'*You're* the whore—you're one because you choose to be. That's the worst kind! My Kathy had no choice. She was taken against her will—used like an animal—by an animal!' He shook her hard. 'And would ye like to know the *name* o' that animal? You say you wonder if I know who the father o' the child is—well I do—and his name's Quincey—Henry Quincey! He's rotten through and through—like all of the Quinceys and I hope he rots in Hell, God damn him!' He glared down at her, his eyes blazing and the sinews in his neck knotted like rope. 'He took what was mine and now I'll take what's his—devil take him!' He grasped the material of her sleeves in his hands and with one mighty wrench he tore the dress from her shoulders. She gave a shrill squeal but before she had time to move he had picked her up and tossed her doll-like on to the bed, throwing himself on top of her and forcing her legs apart with his knee.

'Make a sound and I'll choke the life out o' ye,' he hissed at her, his hands tightly round her throat. 'This is what ye've been askin' for—now ye're goin' to get it!'

He made no attempt to be gentle with her,

his anger and bitterness demanding that he inflict pain. He relished her gasps and feeble struggles as he overpowered her with sheer brute strength. A thin scream issued from her throat as he entered her, then she lay still and silent beneath him, her eyes wide as she stared up at him.

It was over quite quickly and as he rolled away from her his groan was not one of pleasure but of revulsion and disgust, both with himself and her. She lay still. He waited for her to get up and leave but there was no move from the still figure that lay against his back. Fear stirred in him. Had he squeezed her throat too tight? Had he killed her? He rolled over to look at her face in the half light. Her eyes were huge and luminous as they looked into his and her lips began to move as she whispered:

'Oh, Patrick—I never would have believed it. You're wonderful! I'll be your slave, Patrick—anything you like. Now you're truly mine!' She threw herself across his chest, grasping his shoulders as she kissed his cheeks and eyelids, finally fastening her lips hungrily on his mouth. 'Do anything you like with me, Patrick,' she whispered between kisses.

Wearily he thrust her from him. 'You got what ye came for. Now will ye go and leave me in peace? I want no more o' ye.'

She looked at him. 'Was it really true—about Papa?' She sat up, making no attempt to

295

cover her nakedness.

He nodded. 'It's true enough. I suppose he thought he was entitled to do as he wanted with his servants. It seems that none o' ye think of us as human beings anyway.'

She smiled and picked up one of his hands, placing it over one breast. 'It's an interesting thought, except that now I'm *your* servant. Isn't that fun?' She threw back her head. 'Oh—when I think of the times we shall have together!'

'No!' He snatched his hand away as though her body burned it. 'No—I'll have no more!'

She smiled calmly. 'Oh, but that's where you're wrong. Deny me, Patrick and I shall tell Mama what you have told me about Papa being the father of Kathy's child. If she were to find out she'd see to it that Kathy left Elvemere and never came back. Do you want that?'

He sprang up. 'I'd marry Kathy meself!'

'Then you'd both be in trouble,' she told him. 'How long do you think you'd last if I were to tell them what you did to me just now?' She turned her shoulder towards him and traced with her fingers the dark marks of his fingers. 'They *hang* men for rape, Patrick!' She laughed cruelly at the look of blank astonishment on his face. 'Kathy would hate to see you dangling from a gibbet—and so would I. What a waste it would be.' She pulled the tattered remains of her gown around her and

296

stood by the door, looking at him with triumphant amusement.

'You've never won a battle against a Quincey yet, Patrick. We always win, so why not just give up? After all—all I want is to give you pleasure.'

He listened to her footsteps going down the stairs, his heart cold within him. Once more he had allowed himself to fall victim to his own overruling emotions. But he'd beat the Quinceys yet for all the sufferings they'd caused him. Beat them or die in the attempt!

## CHAPTER ELEVEN

Amelia folded the letter with triumphant satisfaction. At last she had engineered the return of her favourite child and his new bride. It had been quite simple really; so simple that she had been surprised not to have thought of it at once. Enlisting the help of Great-Aunt Graves she had had Charles's allowance discontinued. Without it the couple could no longer afford to live in London. She had sent a letter addressed to Charles to the office of the solicitor who dealt with his allowance, with instruction for it to be given to him when he called. The result was in her hands at this moment: a contrite letter from her son, saying that he hoped all was forgiven and that he intended bringing his bride, Sophia, home to Denmark House this very week.

Henry looked up and noticed the smug look on his wife's face across the breakfast table. When she smiled it usually meant that she had scored over him in some way, nothing much else amused her. His brows came together apprehensively.

'What are you smiling at, madam?'

She looked up. 'Charles is coming home. I know you will be pleased to see him. Would you care to read his letter?'

He waved away the proffered sheet of paper with an angry snort. 'No, I would not! So he's coming back, is he? With his tail between his legs, no doubt. That harlot left him, has she?'

Amelia smiled calmly. 'No. She is coming with him.'

He stared at her incredulously. 'You mean to tell me that you will receive a woman of that sort as your daughter-in-law? You surprise me, madam!'

She sighed patiently. 'It will be but a matter of time once she is here. When Charles sees how ill at ease she is in his own environment he will at last realise how unsuitable she is as his wife. Besides, this house could be a most uncomfortable place in which to live under—certain circumstances,' she added pointedly. 'I am confident that in time the young woman will respond to a little monetary persuasion as readily as her dreadful uncle did.'

Henry's eyes narrowed. God save him from the devious female mind! At least she was right about one thing though: Amelia knew how to make life uncomfortable, he'd grant her that!

'And in the meantime I'm to keep the pair of them, I suppose,' he said.

Amelia frowned. 'Charles can go back to his work at the mill as before. After all, it is his inheritance.'

'His work at the mill?' Henry repeated with a mirthless laugh. 'And what else is that but keeping him, I'd like to know? That lad couldn't do an honest day's work if his life depended on it!'

But Amelia wasn't listening, her mind was too concerned with domestic plans. 'They are expected the day after tomorrow,' she said, glancing again at the letter. 'I shall have to speak to Mrs Brown about preparing a room for them. Charles's old room will be quite unsuitable.'

Henry rose from the table. 'Well, I'll leave you to it. For myself, I intend to see as little of them as possible. Perhaps it would be as well if they had two rooms and kept to themselves. If I come into contact with that son of mine too much he'll be in danger of having his head knocked off his shoulders!'

Amelia shuddered as her husband left the room gustily, slamming the door behind him. If only he would at least try to acquire a little gentility. Sometimes he behaved and spoke like a common peasant! She sighed resignedly. There seemed little hope of changing him now. With an air of resolve she rose from the table. There was much to do and plan if she were to have her son back again. There was no time to be lost.

*         *         *

Charles had dozed fitfully on the journey from London. It was hot and the coach was airless. They had tried opening the windows but had been so abominably choked by flying dust that they had been obliged to close them again. Opening one eye he glanced across at Sophia, sitting opposite. At first she had surprised and delighted him with her boldness, her flamboyant beauty and bounteous generosity. Never had he known so warm a pair of arms, so gay and infectious a laugh or so thrilling a body, but a month of marriage had already taken the edge off his enthusiasm. He had begun to suspect that he would not be able to satisfy her cravings for much longer. Everywhere they went she was admired, both for her beauty and her sparkling personality. Every man who set eyes on her wanted her— he read it in their eyes. At first he had enjoyed it, confident of her devotion to him, but lately he had viewed the lustful glances with more than a hint of insecurity.

300

Sophia's extravagance shocked him too. She wanted everything she saw and would never appear in the same gown twice. He had begun to wonder if her craving for material things was the key to her eagerness to marry him. But he told himself that once back in Elvemere everything would be different. There would not be the temptations, either of the flesh, or materially. She would live in a grand house—secretly he hoped that Amelia would bring her into line—and no Elvemere man would cast covetous glances at a Quincey woman.

Feeling his eyes on her Sophia returned his look. 'How much longer have we to endure this torture?' she asked peevishly. She had not wanted to leave London, especially to return to the flat, dull countryside of Lincolnshire. The little she had seen of them had led her to suspect that its inhabitants were just as dull. On first meeting, she had been under the impression that Charles had wealth of his own. Now it seemed that various members of his tedious family held the purse-strings. It was all very trying.

'Not much longer. We are almost there now,' Charles said looking out of the window. On his right the river flowed, its surface gently ruffled by the early October breeze. Through the golden leaves of the trees he could see Holbrook Lodge. He pointed.

'Look dearest—there is my sister's house.'

She glanced out briefly, smothering a yawn.

'Really?' she said, wondering how the daughter of such a rich, influential man could bear to live in anything so poky. She could barely conceal her excitement and curiosity, however, when the post-chaise they had hired at the White Hart drew up outside the gates of Denmark House. Charles handed her down and together they went up the steps. Charles instructed Simpson to take care of their luggage and they passed into the hall where Stevens, eyes goggling with curiosity, was waiting to take their outdoor things.

'Is my Mother at home?' Charles asked, as yet unsure of their welcome.

Stevens nodded. 'Madam is in the drawing-room, sir, if you would care to go in.'

He hesitated, looking at Sophia who said irritably: 'Well, what are we waiting for? This *is* your house, isn't it?'

'Of course.' He flushed and offered her his arm. 'Will you come with me, dearest?'

She glanced at the door through which Stevens had vanished. 'Shouldn't that girl have announced us?'

He smiled indulgently. 'Hardly in our own home, my love.'

It was Sophia's turn to colour. 'Well, of course, I knew that—I just thought that as you had been away—'

He dropped a kiss on her forehead. 'Don't worry. Mama will soon teach you the ways and manners necessary to—'

She slapped his arm hard. 'Pray do not patronise me, Charles. And do let us go in. I am tired of loitering here in the hall like a sewing woman!'

As they entered Amelia rose from her chair and held out her arms. 'Charles! Oh, my dearest boy, how glad I am to have you home again!' She embraced him, then held him at arm's length looking him over critically. 'Oh, but how thin you have grown! My poor boy. Is there no good food in London?'

Charles pulled a wry face. 'I am quite well, Mama, except for the fact that Great-Aunt Graves has cut off my allowance.'

'I have been informed and it pained me to hear of it,' she said hypocritically. 'But I am confident that she will relent when she hears that you have returned to the bosom of your family.' Sophia cleared her throat loudly and Amelia looked up. 'But how remiss you are, Charles. Pray present your charming bride to me.' She added in an undertone: 'I take it that you are in fact married?'

Charles smiled. 'Indeed, the knot has been tied these many weeks,' he said somewhat inaccurately. 'Mama—may I present Sophia?'

The two women eyed each other with thinly veiled hostility. Amelia took in the bold, dark eyes and full, sensuous lips; the sumptuous hair and—in her view—vulgarly elaborate gown. She had always suspected her son of excesses, but this! She held out a limp, white hand, a brittle smile on her lips.

'Welcome to Denmark House, my dear. You must be fatigued by your journey. I will ring for Stevens to show you to your room.'

Sophia smiled back, missing none of the crackling fire smouldering beneath the cool words and icy glance. She saw the same kind of hostility in most of the women she met, especially the married ones. There was little doubt that Amelia Quincey intended to make short work of her, but she had reckoned without Sophia's determination, which was almost as strong as her desire for position and wealth.

'Thank you, you are very kind.' She inclined her head, demurely lowering her lashes, then she put a hand on her husband's arm. 'Are you coming too, dearest?'

He looked from mother to wife and back again. He would dearly have liked to stay and talk to Mama. He wanted to ask her what his chances were of securing a more fitting position at the mill and of his father's view of his elopement. But he knew from the look on Sophia's face that she would sulk if he did not accompany her.

'Very well, my love,' he said meekly.

'If you will return here I will order tea in half an hour,' Amelia said stiffly. 'I am sure you will agree that it is essential for us to talk, Charles.'

He nodded. 'Exactly so, Mama—so we

shall—so—' But it was at that moment that Stevens entered in answer to Amelia's ring, cutting him off in confused mid-sentence.

Upstairs in the largest guest-room Sophia looked around her, pulling her mouth down at the corners.

'If we are to stay here for long there will certainly have to be some changes,' she said. 'Those curtains are so old-fashioned—and the *bed!*'

Charles looked at the offending piece of furniture. 'I see nothing wrong with it. It is comfortable enough, I believe, and there is room for two.'

Sophia shrugged. 'It may be well enough for the purpose for which it is intended and that is about all one can say of it!' She unfastened her dress and stepped out of it, then turned her back to Charles. 'Will you unlace my stays, darling?'

He looked uneasily at her smiling reflection in the mirror. 'Aren't you going to change? Mama said tea in half an hour.'

She pouted at him. 'Don't you want to make love first? There is plenty of time. It seems such an age since last night.' She saw his hesitation through the mirror and her eyes narrowed. 'What is it? Have you developed inhibitions or can it be that you are tiring of me already?'

'Of course not—you know that is not true.'

'Then what are you waiting for? We are

305

wasting time.' She fumbled impatiently with the laces herself, throwing the stays onto a chair and stripping off the rest of her underwear.

But even Sophia's warm, naked body in his arms could not arouse Charles at that moment. So great was his anxiety about the immediate future and so uneasy was he under his parents' roof that he was completely unable to comply with his wife's wishes. She was furious with him.

'Am I suddenly so unattractive?' she asked, turning away to dress again. 'You had better beware, Charles Quincey. There are many who do not find me so. I did not know I had married a weakling!'

He pulled her to him and kissed her ardently. 'Believe me, darling, it is only that I am anxious about our future. Once this evening is over I shall be as passionate as ever—I promise.'

She looked coolly into his eyes. 'I hope you are right, though I cannot see why you should be so fearful. You are the heir to the Quincey estates, aren't you?'

He nodded. 'Of course—but you have not yet met my father. He is a hard man. He and I have never been good friends, in fact I believe that on occasions we have hated each other.'

She smiled, scenting a challenge. 'Then we shall have to work doubly hard on him, my love,' she said. 'We shall have to show him that marriage has had a good influence on you.' She took his face between her hands and kissed him. 'Have no fear, I intend to twist your father round my little finger—even though your dear Mama hated me on sight!'

He looked shocked. 'Surely not. I thought she was most civil to you.'

She laughed. 'Exactly! Now come and help me choose a gown—one that you think she will approve of—if I possess such a garment!'

Ten minutes later they made their entry once more into the drawing-room, where Amelia waited with the tea-kettle boiling on its little spirit stove. Sophia wore a dress of deep violet blue in which she looked breathtakingly beautiful. Over tea the three made polite small talk while Amelia tried in vain to hide her rising irritation at Sophia's refusal to take her many hints that she wished to speak privately with her son. Her attempts were finally thwarted completely by the arrival of Henry who had returned early from his office.

He came into the room with his accustomed lack of ceremony and, ignoring his wife completely, spoke directly to his errant son:

'So you've come home at last then, sir! Well, what have you to say for yourself, eh? I warn you, it'd better be good. What you've done will take a deal of living down, I can tell you!'

But before a pink-faced Charles could reply, Sophia stepped forward. 'I can assure you, Mr Quincey, that Charles is deeply sorry for any distress he may have caused—as indeed I am myself. I only hope and pray that I shall be able to help him to make good any rift that we have caused in your family harmony. If you could only understand the depth of our feeling for one another—the wild impulse that prompted us to take what we now know was an unpardonable action.' She linked her hand through Charles's arm and smiled adoringly up at him. 'Dear Charles can be very impetuous and very persuasive as you must know,' she said coyly.

Henry cleared his throat noisily. He was completely disarmed. Never had he seen such dazzling beauty combined with such eloquence and spirit. He would never have given his son the credit for such good taste. However, he had no intention of allowing himself to be beguiled.

'I thank you, but I would prefer my son to speak for himself. I take it that you are his wife, by the way, as he has not had the courtesy to present you.'

'I have hardly been given the chance, sir,' Charles protested, red-faced. He took Sophia's hand formally. 'Father, this is Sophia—my wife,' he added lamely.

Henry took the long white fingers and, as Sophia obviously expected it, raised them to his lips.

'Well, I am pleased to make your acquaintance at last m'dear,' he said gruffly. 'I can see that you have your husband's interests at heart. That is as it should be and I am sure we shall be able to work out some plan that will be to our mutual benefit.'

Looking on, Amelia seethed with annoyance. Henry thought himself so shrewd and clever, so hard-headed and far-thinking, yet already he was allowing this woman to take him in with her soft words and her flauntings. The plan was intended to rid Charles of the creature, yet here was Henry actually encouraging her!

Henry looked at Charles. 'You can have your old job back at the mill—starting tomorrow. That suit you?'

Charles's mouth dropped open. 'My *old* job? I had thought you might offer me something better—something a little more dignified, Father. After all, I am now a married man.'

'Don't you think you're rather putting the cart before the horse?' Henry laughed shortly: 'Huh! You should have known that a young gentleman has no right to ask the hand of a lady until he is confident that he can support her. As you have chosen to do things in this upside-down manner then you must carry it through!' He walked to the fireplace and turned to survey them all. 'You need have no fear, I shall see that you're promoted as soon as you've earned it.' He turned his attention to Amelia for the first time. 'I shall go up to change now, madam, and I shall see you anon.'

As he reached the door he turned. 'Oh—when Caroline comes in you can tell her I wish to speak to her before dinner in my study.'

As the door closed behind him the three faces gazed at it, each occupied with their own thoughts. In Charles's heart the old hate for his Father was renewed. He had taken great delight in humiliating him just now in front of Sophia. And now, more than ever before he was forced to endure it. Not for the first time he questioned the wisdom of his hasty marriage.

Sophia was intrigued. She had seen right away that Henry was ten times the man his son was. He was truly the head of the family and it would take all the wiles of her repertoire to break him down. Before she met him she had visualised him as a challenge, now she looked forward to the conquest of that challenge as eagerly as she would have tackled a difficult new role in the theatre.

As for Amelia, her emotions were in a turmoil. How *dare* Henry humiliate his own son before this woman? It seemed he was never satisfied unless he were bringing some poor unfortunate to their knees and Charles had always been the favourite butt for his worst barbs. His mention of Caroline had troubled her too. He had recently been threatening to procure a husband for her youngest daughter and the young man he had his eye on was, in her view, even more

310

unsuitable than John Gage had been for Melissa. He was the pale-faced young curate from St Mary's, Victor Jellings. She and Henry had had some disquieting discussions about the girl over the past few weeks. Henry feared that she was too high-spirited—that it was time she was 'wedded and bedded' as he so vulgarly put it. She would not have admitted it to him, of course, but she had also been slightly disturbed by the girl's demeanour of late. She had taken to riding a great deal. It was hardly ladylike, Amelia considered, to ride more than twice a week. Besides, it was so bad for the complexion. Then there was something about the girl's manner, a kind of suppressed excitement. She was inclined to agree that marriage would quieten her but though Henry's choice appalled her she knew from bitter experience that nothing she could do would change his mind once it was made up.

\*  \*  \*

Caroline came in through the back entrance and stood for a moment with her back against the door while she regained her breath. Her heart was beating fast from her hard ride back from the meadows and her whole body still glowed from her latest encounter with Patrick. The fact that he disliked her, yet found her irresistible excited her immensely. She never tired of the cat-and-mouse game she played with him. So deep was she in her thoughts that she did not hear Stevens come out into the passage, and when the parlour maid spoke she started.

'Oh, Miss Caroline. The Mistress said to tell you that you're to make haste and dress for dinner. The Master wants to see you in his study when you're ready. Time's getting on, you'll have to hurry.'

Annoyed at being taken unawares, Caroline pushed rudely past Stevens and went up the back stairs, not wishing anyone to see her flushed cheeks and dishevelled hair. Half an hour later she presented herself obediently in her father's study, looking demure and composed in her cream silk dinner dress.

He looked up as she came in. Damn it, the girl looked as though butter wouldn't melt in her mouth, yet he could have sworn differently. She was the only one of his children who favoured him in temperament and he knew her moods because they matched his own. If he hadn't known how carefully she was watched he would have sworn that the girl had a lover. There was a new knowing look in her eyes and it made him uneasy. As was his habit he came straight to the point:

'Ah, Caroline, there you are at last, then. I wanted to speak to you about a very important matter. I have found a husband for you. There—what do you say to that?'

Her eyes opened wide. 'A husband, Papa—

but who?'

He smiled. 'I would have thought you might have guessed. It's young Mr Jellings from St Mary's. He is very well connected and an amiable young man. He—'

'The *curate!*' Caroline cried, shrilly interrupting him. 'That—that stupid idiot? He can't string two words together without stammering over them—and he has clammy hands!' She stamped her foot. 'I won't marry him—I won't!'

Henry rose to his feet to glare at his younger daughter across the desk. 'You will do as you are told, miss!' he thundered. 'It is my belief that you are doing yourself no good, kicking your heels round here all day. Since your sister was married and you left Miss White's you have had no direction and I know quite well that the devil finds work for idle hands!' His eyes seemed to look right through her and she took an involuntary step backwards. It was almost as though he knew! 'You will wed Mr Jellings as soon as it can be arranged,' he continued. 'He has already spoken for you and I am to give him my answer before the week is out.'

Caroline swallowed, her heart beating rapidly. 'Mama mentioned my going to France, to a finishing school,' she said, grasping at straws.

Henry shook his head. 'As I remember it, you made a great fuss and said you didn't wish to leave Elvemere. Anyway, with this new railway coming there may not be money for such fripperies. No, it shall be settled. I shall ask Mr Jellings to dine with us on Friday evening and I shall give him my permission to speak to you.' He resumed his seat as though the interview was at an end, but Caroline did not leave. Hands clenched into tight fists, she stood her ground.

'What—what if I refuse him?' she said, her voice quivering.

He silenced her with a look. 'I don't think you will,' he said in strong, measured tones. 'I strongly advise you to go away and think about it.' His face softened as he saw the familiar lift of her chin. 'Caroline,' he said quietly. 'It is sometimes necessary to compromise in this life. The Quinceys are looked up to in Elvemere. We have a duty—an example to set. But it need not spoil life for you if you go about it the right way. Do you understand what I mean?'

Her lips curved slightly as she looked at him. Was he saying what she thought he was saying? Could it be possible? Then she remembered what Patrick had told her about her father and the girl, Kathy. She nodded and turned to go, her cheeks pink. As she reached the door he said: 'By the way, your brother and his new wife have arrived. I'm sure you will appreciate the need for tact at dinner—if only for your mother's sake.'

She took herself up to her room to await dinner. She had plenty to think about, but she drew some small comfort from the anticipation of making life uncomfortable for her new sister-in-law. It would seem she had things all her own way. She had taken what she wanted without caring what anyone thought. Caroline meant to see that she paid for it now!

Dinner that night was a nerve-racking affair. Charles sulked openly, while Sophia sparkled with wit and charm, seeming quite impervious to the resentment of her new female in-laws and concentrating on Henry, who was the only person at the table eating his food with obvious enjoyment. After dessert he invited Charles to take port with him and when his offer was spurned he took himself off alone, whilst Amelia, Caroline and Sophia repaired to the drawing-room for coffee.

It was only when they were seated in comfort that Caroline felt free to fire the first of her arrows.

'I understand that you are an actress, Sophia,' she said sweetly. 'I find that fascinating. What a strange and unusual life you must have led, travelling from place to place. You must find it very odd to be actually living in a house!'

Sophia looked at her with cold eyes. 'When I was with my uncle's company we stayed only at the best hostelries,' she said haughtily.

'I see.' Caroline's eyes were round and innocent. 'Perhaps in that case we should have offered you a mug of ale instead of coffee,' she said arching her eyebrows.

'You really must forgive my daughter,' Amelia put in. 'Here in Elvemere we live very quietly. We are unfamiliar with the world of— er—entertainers.'

Sophia smiled, her dark eyes flashing fire. 'Of course, I was prepared. Charles warned me that the people of Lincolnshire are totally ignorant of cultural matters.' She rose to her feet, noting with satisfaction the dull flush which crept up Amelia's neck. 'I hope you will forgive me, I am tired after the journey and I should like to go to bed.' And she swept from the room with a rustle of her flame-coloured taffeta, leaving mother and daughter staring at each other.

Upstairs she found Charles lying fully dressed on the bed, his face a mask of gloom. She frowned at him impatiently, shaking her slim shoulders.

'What's the matter with you? Why did you come up here and leave me to face those two vultures alone. Surely you can see that I need your support. I had to pretend to be tired in order to escape.'

He opened his eyes and looked at her disinterestedly. 'I'm sure you exaggerate. I have yet to see you at a loss for words. Anyway, they were polite enough to you at dinner.'

She looked at him through the dressing-table mirror. 'Yes, while your father was there. Once he had left the room they were like a pair of cats with a juicy mouse—all teeth and claws!' She patted her hair. 'However, they shall not have the better of me—with or without your help. Now that I have their measure I think they will find they have their match in me.' She went over to the bed and looked down at him. 'But I thought you would be talking to your father. Surely you are not going to accept his offer without a fight? You must surely be a laughing stock. Henry Quincey's son and heir doing a job that any dolt could do! He means you to fight. He is testing you. Can you not see that?'

Charles sighed wearily. 'You may think you know him, but you don't. He will only humiliate me in some other way if I defy him in this.'

She looked at him with contempt. 'So you are going to let it lie at that? And how are we to live, pray, on the pittance he will pay you? Are we to stay here under this roof where we are despised? Where is the fine new house you promised me?'

He groaned and rolled over to bury his face in the pillow. 'Hold your tongue, Sophia. You are fast turning into a scold. It isn't ideal for you, I know, but what do you think it is like for me? You can have no idea what it is like to work in that stinking mill all day!'

She grasped his shoulder and shook it. 'Then fight him, you fool! Stand up to him. He'll respect you for it.'

317

But he shook his head. 'You don't know him, Sophia—you don't know him.'

She stood back, regarding him for a moment. 'Maybe not, but I intend to,' she said, half to herself.

Downstairs in the hall, she stood for a moment outside the door of the study, then she raised her hand and tapped on it smartly. From within Henry's voice called gruffly:

'Come in!'

She opened the door and slipped quickly inside, grateful that she had been able to do so unobserved. It was already clear to her that in this house it was advisable to play one's cards close to the chest and Sophia would have been the first to admit that it was a method of play that appealed to her strongly.

Henry swung round in his chair to see who had entered and his eyes registered surprise when he saw her standing by the door.

'Oh! Come in, come in, m'dear. Have a chair. Is there something I can do for you?'

With just the right amount of hesitation she crossed the room and sat in the chair he indicated, dropping her eyes demurely from his gaze as she did so.

His eyes swept over her. Devilish handsome woman. Older than Charles by several years if he was any judge. Those eyes! He recalled Delaney's description of her: 'That innocent young girl.' If she was innocent he'd eat his hat! Damned attractive though. He reached

318

for the tantalus on his desk and fingered the sherry decanter.

'Can I offer you a glass of sherry wine, m'dear?'

She shook her head. 'I thank you, no. I am rather distressed, Mr Quincey.' She raised her eyes to his, giving him the full benefit of their lustrous beauty. 'I am very much afraid that I may have caused a rift between you and Charles—that you may be punishing him for marrying me. And I know he would not quarrel with you for fear of making me feel worse. He is so anxious to make good at Quincey's and to please you, sir. I am sure you have no idea of his respect and admiration for you, but I am afraid that this menial work to which you have condemned him will quite break his spirit.' She bit her lip. 'I am quite distraught to think it is I who have spoilt the relationship you once shared.'

He looked up at her. The passionate dark eyes were melting and limpid now, full of wifely concern. He was taken completely off guard. 'My dear, pray do not distress yourself,' he said, his voice unusually soft and gentle. 'I cannot deny that going off the way he did caused me a great deal of anxiety. It was my intention to teach him a lesson. But I did not intend that lesson to extend to you.' He reached across the desk to pat her hand. 'Let me be honest with you, m'dear. My wife has always spoilt Charles more than was good for

319

him. If he is to enter the world of commerce he must be hardened. It is right that he should know what hardship is. He has always had things far too easy—always been under the impression that he had only to reach out and take.' He smiled at her. 'Which I imagine was his attitude in winning you!'

She smiled back at him. 'I sincerely hope that I was not too much of a shock for you, sir.'

He shook his head. 'Quite the contrary, m'dear. If I may say so I think my son is a very lucky man—a very lucky man indeed!' Their eyes held for a second, then Henry cleared his throat. 'Pray do not call me sir, m'dear. It sounds so very formal.'

She raised her brows a fraction. 'Do you wish me to call you "Papa"?'

Henry flushed. He felt far from fatherly at this moment. Again he cleared his throat. 'Ahem—I hardly think—' He leaned forward and lowered his voice conspiratorially. 'How about calling me Henry, eh? I have a feeling that you and I are going to be good friends.'

She smiled. 'I should be honoured—though I take it you mean me to use your Christian name only when we are alone. I feel that other members of your family will not feel that I have earned the privilege.' The long black lashes swept downwards again. 'But to go back to Charles and our position: I was hoping some day to have a little home of my own. Since my parents died I have known no settled home and it has long been a dream of mine.'

Henry picked up one of her long white hands and stroked it gently. 'And so you shall m'dear. As I said, I have no wish that you should suffer. If there is anything you want— anything at all—you must come and ask. You will not find me a mean man.'

She stood up and walked round the desk to him purposefully, then, with a good imitation of girlish guile, she bent and kissed his cheek. 'Thank you, Henry,' she breathed. 'I am indeed fortunate to have found such a generous father-in-law. I felt from the first that we should understand each other. I hope one day to repay you for your kindness.'

He looked up at the lovely face so close to his own and it was with difficulty that he resisted the impulse to pull her on to his lap. Instead he smiled benignly. 'Nonsense— nothing to repay. Off you go now and pray do not trouble that pretty head of yours any further.'

As the door closed behind her he sighed. What a woman! And what the devil had she seen in that weak-kneed son of his? Except youth, of course. But Henry had a reason other than admiration for making an ally of Sophia. It seemed to him that she would make a good accomplice. There was a shrewdness about her. She was the onlooker who saw most of the game and he had a strong suspicion that she enjoyed a conspiracy—especially if the rewards were right.

\*       \*       \*

Patrick lay on his bed halfway between sleep and waking. Every bone in his body ached. Ever since he had taken on the piece of land Jonathan Nichols had offered him he had worked on it at every opportunity. He had been lucky in that it had already been sown with vegetables in the spring, but, as Jonathan had explained, the old man who used to tend it had died leaving the seedlings and weeds to tangle themselves into a wilderness. Patrick had worked hard, managing to save some of the young plants from being choked, and as the vegetables came to maturity he had harvested and sold them round the cottage doors whenever Seamus could spare him. The old man warned him to keep to the other side of the town, for if the secret of Patrick's venture got out he would be punished for it, even though he more than made up for the time away from Denmark House.

It was during one of his selling expeditions that he had come unexpectedly face to face with Kathy again. Knocking on the door of a cottage in Mill Row late one October afternoon he had found himself looking into her eyes for the first time in six months. For a full minute they stared at each other, then she said in a whisper:

'Come inside, Patrick—please.'

She held the door wide and he stepped into the spotless kitchen, then he turned to look at her properly for the first time. She was heavy with the child now, but more beautiful than ever. There was a new maturity in her eyes, the girl he had once known was gone for ever and it wrenched at his heart to realise that she would never come back. He longed to take her in his arms and hold her close, instead he said in a tight voice:

'How are ye, Kathy?'

'I'm fine.' She looked up at him. 'You knew—about the child and about me marrying Will?'

He nodded, his eyes dark with pain. 'I know what happened—I know who it was brought you to it—devil take him!'

She felt her cheeks burn and her eyes dropped from his. She would have liked to ask how he knew—who had told him, but she could not bring herself to discuss it with him. After a moment he asked:

'Where is he—your husband, I mean?'

She looked up. 'Will? He's gone to buy wood. Every so often he goes with the carrier's cart to a timber yard at Bannford.' She blinked rapidly, trying to prevent the tears from falling but it was no use. 'Oh, Patrick!' she choked. 'I've missed ye so. What did they tell ye about me? Why didn't ye come to me? Were ye too ashamed?'

His eyes burning, he grasped her to him, closing his arms round the frail shoulders. 'Don't! Don't cry, Kathy darlin'. Sure I know it was none o' your doin'. But I didn't know the truth of it till it was too late.' He looked down at her. 'Is he good to ye—this Will?'

She nodded, sniffing back the tears. 'Oh, he is, Patrick. He's given me a home and a name for the child. He's kind and good and I'm grateful to him.'

He looked at her searchingly. 'Are ye after sayin' that ye love him, Kathy?' he asked thickly.

She looked up into his anguished brown eyes and thought her heart would break. 'Oh, Patrick,' she said, her voice breaking on a sob. 'I have a husband that isn't you and a child that isn't yours. I feel like I'm torn up in little pieces but there'll only ever be one man for me, God forgive me!'

He kissed her then and held her shaking body close to him. 'Why didn't ye tell me when he started on ye, Kathy?' he asked fiercely. 'We could've gone away somewhere together— somehow we'd have managed. *Why* didn't ye tell me?'

'I was afraid—afraid for you, for both of us. He threatened to hurt ye again. I didn't realise what might happen. It seems silly now but it didn't come into me mind that I might get like this.'

There was nothing to be done about it. They both knew as they stood there, clinging hopelessly to each other, that the die was cast—their future already set in the mould. Nothing either of them could do or say would alter it. After a moment Kathy broke away from him and, wiping her eyes on a corner of her apron, she looked up at him, her lip trembling.

'Will ye have a cup o' tea? I've a pot made.'

He shook his head and lifted the sack of vegetables from the floor where he'd dropped it. 'Here—have a cabbage and some potatoes. I've some fine turnips and carrots too. I'll not charge ye anything, Kathy. Have some to make broth, ye must keep up your strength.' He opened the sack and heaped a generous selection on to the table. 'There. I grew 'em all meself.' He looked at her uncertainly. 'I'll have to be goin' now. Will I tell Uncle Seamus I've seen ye?'

'Oh, yes please. Give him my love,' she said. 'Tell him I'm sorry I couldn't tell him the truth that day when I saw him at Miss Melissa's. It was just that I was too ashamed.' Her blue eyes held his for a long moment. 'Will ye come again, Patrick? *Please* come. It won't matter if Will's here. He knows about you and he'd like to meet you. He's a good man and we manage fine. I go to Miss Melissa's every week for the sewin' an' she pays me well—' She stopped talking abruptly as Patrick grasped her in his arms again.

'Oh, Kathy love,' he moaned. 'Oh, my God!'

She held him tightly. 'Is—is it all right for you at Denmark House now?' she asked him. 'Are they treatin' you right?' She searched his eyes fearfully. 'Ye are keepin' out o' trouble, aren't ye?'

He nodded. 'Don't worry about me.' He looked down. 'When will it—when will the child be born?'

'Christmas,' she answered, trying to smile. 'Sure isn't it a good time for it to happen?' But his eyes were full of fear as they looked into hers.

'Will it hurt? Will there be a woman to help ye?'

She nodded. 'I'll be fine—you'll see. I'll get word to ye—somehow.'

And so he had left her. That had been two weeks ago but ever since he had known no peace. Every time he closed his eyes he saw her small pointed face with those huge blue eyes so full of longing and regret and he wondered how he could have stayed away from her so long. How could he have felt bitter towards her. She had been a helpless victim and he knew now how that felt. Wasn't he himself in the same position at this moment?

He spent almost every waking hour avoiding Caroline Quincey. She was like a festering thorn in his flesh—taunting, tempting, leading him to the very edge and then, as often as not, leaving him unsatisfied. He hated her as much as he hated her father—and lately he had

326

begun to fear her too, for it was clear that the game she was playing would bore her some day. And when Caroline Quincey was bored she was also dangerous. Lately she had become more and more reckless. Taking risks fascinated her but he knew only too well what would happen to him if they were discovered, especially now that she was betrothed.

But Patrick was not the only person to be bewildered by Caroline's behaviour. Henry was baffled by his daughter's apparent change of heart. When young Jellings had proposed she had accepted him without demur. He had been prepared for a stormy passage on that Friday evening and had been astonished when the young man had come to him afterwards, flushed and quivering with pleasure, to tell him that his suit was accepted. Questioning her he could get no satisfaction either. She stood demurely on the other side of his desk, eyes modestly downcast, answering his questions in monosyllables.

Finally he decided that the time was ripe for enlisting Sophia's help. Since his return to work at the mill, Charles had become increasingly touchy and irritable. When he came home in the evenings he drank too much and, as often as not, took himself off after dinner to some entertainment he had found elsewhere. He seemed to have quite lost interest in Sophia, seeing her no doubt as the cause of his present predicament. Life with her female in-laws could not be particularly pleasant either. Neither of them lost an opportunity of making her feel small—often before the servants, who would have treated her with the same disrespect had she not—to Henry's secret amusement—put them firmly in their places. Though she was well able to hold her own, Henry could see that the situation was beginning to weigh on her heavily.

It was one evening when she had come downstairs early for dinner that Henry called her into the study. He opened the door as she was passing and beckoned her in, looking round to make sure no one saw before closing the door and inviting her to take a chair. He seated himself opposite and poured two glasses of sherry, pushing one across the desk towards her, his face thoughtful.

'My dear—I wonder if I might ask you a small favour?' he began. She smiled a little guardedly.

'I would be delighted to help in any way—if I am able—Henry.'

It was the first time they had spoken alone since that first evening, therefore the first time she had used his Christian name. The thrust of pleasure it brought him relaxed his face into a smile.

'Thank you, Sophia.' He cleared his throat and tried to get his mind back on to the problem in hand. 'It has to do with Caroline,' he told her. 'As you know, she has just become betrothed to Mr Jellings.'

She nodded, trying hard to keep from smiling. It was a situation she had found extremely amusing. Headstrong, spirited Caroline and that pale, perspiring young curate. It was quite clear that Amelia disapproved of the match too—therefore, why? As though he read her thoughts, Henry went on:

'He is very well connected. He has an uncle who is a bishop and a cousin who is married to a Member of Parliament.'

She looked up at him innocently. 'Then what, may I ask, is the problem?'

He sighed and shifted uncomfortably in his chair. 'That's just it, m'dear. Can't put a finger on it. She didn't like the prospect of marrying him when I first suggested it—yet she accepted the fellow as meekly as a lamb when he proposed.' He shook his head. 'I've a feeling there's something wrong somewhere.'

Sophia moistened her lips. 'I hope you will forgive me for asking, Henry, but why did you choose Mr Jellings? Caroline is young and, I am sure, a good match for any young man.'

He nodded. 'Quite so. I take your point. I thought young Jellings would be a steadying influence. It has seemed to me that the child was too—too high-spirited for her own good. She seemed old for her years—' He fumbled for words. 'Precocious.'

She looked straight into his eyes. 'You feared she might take a lover and ruin her chances of a good marriage?'

Her bold words and the look which accompanied them quite took his breath away. He was at the same time shocked and intrigued. She had hit the nail on the head, of course, and he nodded somewhat reluctantly.

'Well—er—'

'Surely it is her mother you should be consulting,' Sophia went on. 'I am sorry to say that Caroline and I are not the best of friends. I am certainly not in her confidence and I fear that any attempt to help in this matter would be taken as interference.'

'I don't think you quite understand, m'dear.' Henry leaned towards her earnestly. 'I am not asking you to *speak* to Caroline about this. What I had in mind was that you might—shall we say, keep an eye on her, so to speak.'

Sophia raised her eyebrows slightly. 'You mean that you think she is seeing someone and you want me to watch her and try to find out who it is?' she said baldly.

Henry spluttered over his sherry. Really! The girl was very direct. However, when he looked at her he thought he detected a glint of interest in her eyes. Encouraged, he went on:

'Not to put too fine a point on it—yes—in a most subtle and discreet way, of course.'

'Naturally.' She smiled at him. 'As a matter of fact, Henry, I have been meaning to have a talk with you. Charles is very unhappy at the mill and he seems to have quite forgotten the

330

home he promised me. His unhappiness is making him squander all the money he earns. Do you not think he might be given a better position?' She looked at him through the half-lowered lashes and Henry felt his pulse quicken.

'Is the young fool neglecting you?' he asked thickly.

She sighed and lifted her shoulders. 'I must admit that our marriage does seem to have lost some of its sparkle,' she said forlornly.

He leaned across the desk and covered her hand with his own. 'He must be mad,' he said softly. 'Believe me, m'dear, if you help me in this—for the sake of the child's future and her good name, you understand—I shall see that you are amply rewarded. Is it a bargain?'

Beneath the lowered lashes her eyes shone. 'Indeed, I believe it is, Henry. Leave the matter with me and I will do my best for you.'

He saw her out into the still empty hall, contriving as she passed him to touch the warm, bare flesh of her shoulder with his fingertips. The nearness of her, her vibrant presence made him tingle with excitement. No woman had ever aroused him as much. But he realised that she was not easily won; she had a mind which matched his own and he admired—and desired her for it.

# CHAPTER TWELVE

Amelia was pleased with herself. She had devised a plan which, it seemed, would solve many problems at one blow. There were just four weeks to go till Christmas; the time was right for a visit to Great-Aunt Graves in London. Whilst there, she and Caroline could shop for clothes and material for the wedding, which had been planned for Easter. No doubt Aunt Graves would wish to make her own contribution, being too old and infirm to travel to Elvemere for the ceremony. But the main object of the exercise was to re-introduce Charles into his aunt's affections.

Over the past months she had watched his dissatisfaction with Sophia grow and when she considered the time was ripe she had called him to her room one night for a talk. He looked tired, his eyes were puffy and dark-circled. She knew of course that he drank too much, but she put it down firmly to his unhappiness in marriage.

When he had seated himself comfortably before the fire in her boudoir she began:

'My dear boy, I have asked you to come here because I cannot bear to see you looking so ill. You cannot deceive me. I know the reason all too well. I fear that you have made a grave mistake in choosing Sophia for your wife. Am I not right?'

He leaned back, closing his eyes. A month ago he would not have admitted it to anyone, but now he was ready to agree. The fact was, Sophia was more than he could handle. She wanted too much—too much of everything. In his present position her material wants were impossible to meet and her sexual appetite, which at first he had found so exciting, now simply repelled him. As he had once told John, nice women were not supposed to enjoy sex and the fact that Sophia so obviously did, led him to believe that he was not the first lover she had had. She was five years his senior— five years that she admitted to. She could have had a dozen other men in her life. Slowly he nodded in answer to his mother's question.

'I am afraid you are right, Mama. I was a fool to act as I did. I wish now with all my heart that I had asked for your advice.'

She pressed his shoulder warmly and crossed to sit opposite him. 'You were not ready for marriage. Your father was right in that, at least. But do not worry, all may not yet be lost, my dear. I have had a letter from Great-Aunt Graves in which she indicates that if you were to have the marriage dissolved she would be willing to re-establish you as her heir and resume your allowance.'

He sighed. 'But how could this be done, Mama?'

She smiled. 'Her solicitor, Mr Jarvis, is a

clever man. I have no doubt that he will know of a way to have the marriage annulled. Remember that you were under age at the time. I feel confident that something can be arranged. Now, listen carefully. I am planning to take Caroline to London next week to shop for her trousseau and for Christmas. You shall accompany us. What do you say?'

His face brightened—then fell again. 'But what about Sophia? She will expect to come too, especially when she knows we are to go to London.'

Amelia sighed and shook her head. 'I am afraid you will have to assert your position as a husband, Charles. I wish to help you, but I cannot be expected to do everything for you!'

He nodded reluctantly. 'And Father—what of him?'

Her lips set in a thin line. 'You may leave your father to me. I shall simply tell him that I wish you to come as our escort and protector. As he will not wish to accompany us himself he can hardly object. You had better begin on your packing. We shall be away for a week at least.'

\*     \*     \*

Since his betrothal to Caroline had become official, the Revd Victor Jellings had been a regular visitor at Denmark House. He was a tall, willowy young man with pale skin and hair. His eyes were a curious light green, like pond-water, and blinked through steel-rimmed spectacles with an air of short-sighted meekness and innocence. However, Victor's outward appearance hid a determined spirit that few—including Caroline—would have guessed at. Once safely wed to her he had resolved to be master in his own house, but for the present he was content to let her think what most people thought: that he was as meek as the proverbial lamb—malleable material for a budding matriarch. Badly needing her considerable dowry to augment his meagre stipend, he was too diplomatic to do otherwise.

Sophia watched them together with interest. Caroline treated her fiancé with ill-concealed contempt and it became clearer every day that Henry had been right: Caroline had a lover. What was more, she intended to keep him, her marriage to Victor providing a convenient respectable front behind which she would continue to do as she liked. Who was he though? That was a puzzle. The girl never left the house without a chaperon—except to go riding. A suspicion crept into Sophia's mind, one which, the more she thought about it, the more likely it became. It was one wet afternoon as they sat sewing in the drawing-room that she tentatively brought the subject up.

'A pity it is such a wet afternoon, Caroline,'

she said sweetly. 'You must be missing your daily ride.'

Caroline looked up at her sharply. 'Not really,' she said lightly. 'My pony needs daily exercise, it is true. But I am quite content to let ·one of the grooms do it for me occasionally.'

Sophia lowered her eyes to her work. One of the grooms. Could it be possible? Not being fond of riding herself she had had little to do with the stables since she came to Denmark House, but she would certainly investigate. Caroline looked across at her speculatively. Had Charles told her yet of the proposed visit to London? She knew he had been putting it off. She smiled inwardly. The smug smile would soon be wiped from that face when she knew she was to be left behind! She watched out of the corner of her eye as Sophia's needle went in and out. Perhaps she should help her brother by breaking the news for him. The idea excited her and she looked up, her eyes bright and hard as crystal.

'How will you amuse yourself when we are away in London next week?' she asked casually, and although her own eyes were on her needle she noticed that Sophia stopped working abruptly. She felt the dark eyes on her as Sophia's voice asked crisply:

'In London—you and your mother?'

'Charles, too,' Caroline said innocently. 'We are all three to visit Great-Aunt Graves. But

336

surely Charles has told you?'

'No, he has not.' Sophia's tone was dry and brittle.

Caroline's eyes grew round, and she bit her lip. 'Oh dear! I do hope that I have not spoken out of turn—though of course you would have to know, wouldn't you—eventually? It seems that our aunt is anxious to see us with Christmas and my wedding being so near. I am sure that one day you too will be welcome— once the poor old lady has had time to recover from the shock of your runaway marriage. I am afraid she was very upset by it, Charles being her favourite nephew.'

Sophia smiled, containing the fury that burned within her. 'Of course. Naturally, she will approve of your betrothal to Mr Jellings.'

Caroline returned the smile unblinkingly, though a slight flush painted her cheeks. 'Naturally. I believe we are to stay in London for a week, but the time will no doubt pass quickly for you. If you ask him I am sure Papa will put the carriage at your disposal and you can pay some calls and do your Christmas shopping.'

'How very kind,' Sophia smiled mildly, longing at the same time to grasp the blonde ringlets and pull till they came out in her hands. Let the little bitch smile while she still had the chance, she told herself. She would have the last laugh yet!

Later, in their room as they changed for

dinner, she confronted Charles with the news Caroline had given her and found him unrepentant.

'It is essential that I go alone to make my peace with my aunt,' he told her. 'She may resume my allowance if I show her that I am sorry for offending her. Your presence would only aggravate matters. Surely you appreciate that?'

'I see it only too well,' she told him, her dark eyes flashing dangerously. 'What I see is that I am to be swept under the carpet like some unfortunate mistake, whilst you resume your former life as though you were still single! If I had known before, Charles, that you were so immature I would have thought twice before marrying you!'

He rounded on her. 'I too would have "thought twice" as you put it, if I had known then what I know now!'

'What do you mean?' she demanded. He turned away from her contemptuously but she grasped his arm. 'What do you mean? Tell me at once!'

Her voice had risen and he took her by the shoulders, shaking her roughly.

'Be quiet! Do you want the whole house to hear? Since you ask, I'll tell you what I mean: you are the kind of woman a man should keep as a mistress, Sophia—not marry. If I had been older—as old as you, for instance—I might have realised that. I would also have seen that you were after money and position.'

'Huh!' She threw back her head and stared at him coldly. 'If *that* were so I was certainly in for a disappointment wasn't I, Charles?' She took a step towards him. 'And whilst we're on the subject of disappointments I'll tell you something else: had I known that you were incapable of satisfying a real woman—that your tastes lay elsewhere—with members of your own sex for instance, I would not have come within ten yards of you!'

Anger blazed in his eyes as he stared at her. 'How dare you say that to me? Can I help it if you disgust me? I cannot make love to a woman with so little restraint. It is as I told you—I don't want a whore for a wife!'

She gasped as though he had thrown cold water in her face. Her first instinct was to fly at him—to claw his face. But something stopped her. Deep down inside her a small voice told her that things could yet go her way. She needed time—time to think, to assess the situation and make plans. She turned from him and began to take off her jewellery.

'I shall not be coming down to dinner,' she told him coolly. 'You may tell your Mama that I have a headache. I am going to bed.'

He looked at her for a long moment. 'Very well,' he said at last. 'When I come up I shall not disturb you. I shall sleep in the dressing-room.'

She shrugged. 'As you please.'

He looked at her again. Her mention of a headache had brought him an unnerving thought. If she were to become pregnant he would never be rid of her. 'I shall sleep in the dressing-room from now on,' he told her.

She laughed derisively. 'You need have no fear for your virtue on my account, Charles. The mere sight of you without your clothes makes my flesh crawl!'

\*     \*     \*

The last of the horses had been exercised and Patrick was rubbing down Bonny, Caroline's mare. It had rained for three days running and he had been grateful for the respite it had given him from Caroline's company. He knew, however, that it could not last and he was right. He had just finished and was throwing a blanket over the mare's steaming back when a sudden dimming of the light told him that someone was standing in the doorway. Turning, he saw that it was Caroline and his heart gave the familiar plunge.

She came in, closing the lower half of the door behind her and smiling lazily at him.

'Well, have you missed me, Patrick?' she asked, sidling up to him. He ignored the question. 'Do ye want to ride? 'Tis a very soft day. I've exercised your mare, so there's no need.'

'Of course I don't want to ride. I want to

talk to you,' she snapped. 'We'll go up to the hay-loft. Come along.' She took his hand and pulled him towards the ladder leading up into the loft opening. Reluctantly, he followed. By now he knew better than to thwart her.

Once they were alone in the dim warmth of the hay-loft she looked at him with the familiar glint in her eyes.

'I am going away, Patrick—tomorrow, to London. We shall be there for a whole week, so we must make the most of this afternoon. Mama has gone out and Sophia is lying down with another of her headaches, so we shall not be disturbed.' She wound her arms around his neck. 'Well—aren't you going to kiss me, Patrick?'

He bent his head to brush her lips with his own. He knew it was useless to try to stand out against her. She was perfectly capable of carrying out her threat to accuse him of rape, but besides that she had the power to arouse him against his strongest will. His firmest resolve melted when she pressed herself against him as she did now. He hated her for it and he hated himself too.

She sank into the hay, pulling him down with her. 'What will you do when I am married?' she asked teasingly.

He looked at her with narrowed eyes. He had heard about the Revd Victor Jellings and his meekness of manner and wondered at the unlikely match Henry Quincey had made for

341

his daughter. Yet strangely, she seemed satisfied with the prospect.

She stroked his cheek with a fingertip, laughing gently. 'I hope you didn't think I was about to desert you, Patrick,' she said. 'You do see what it will mean, don't you? No more sneaking out to meet in corners like this. I shall take you with me just as my sister Melissa took your step-sister, Kathy. And when Victor is out of the house we shall have it to ourselves!'

He stared at her, appalled. 'But—surely that could not be? All I know is horses—I could not do any other work.'

She laughed. 'Oh yes you can, Patrick. You do very well in the work for which I need you! Much better, I am sure, than poor Victor. Oh, Patrick, you would die of laughing if you saw him trying to kiss me! His lips are as cold and wet as his hands! Oh yes, I shall need you more than ever after I am married. You shall be bonded to me. How shall you like that?' Her eyes sparkled and she began to unfasten her dress. 'We have all afternoon,' she said, pulling at his shirt. 'All afternoon and three days to make up for, not to mention all the days I shall be away!' As she fastened her lips on his, his heart sank. If what she planned came to pass he would be more than merely bonded, he would be enslaved for life. Day by day he feared discovery, for he knew that if it came, Caroline would do nothing to help him but would safeguard her own name. He wished with all his heart that she would grow tired of him but it seemed unlikely. Even now as the warmth of her naked flesh touched him he felt the familiar irresistible urge taking him over and within minutes he was making love to her with all the savagery she craved. Her body twisted and turned under him, her tumbled hair mingling with the hay as she uttered abandoned moans of ecstasy.

It was almost four o'clock and beginning to grow dark when they descended the ladder. Caroline's hair was dishevelled and full of bits of straw, but her eyes sparkled and her cheeks were flushed. At the foot of the ladder she turned her face to his.

'I'll never let you go, Patrick,' she said fervently. 'No one ever had a more exciting lover. Oh, I can't wait to be married and my own mistress! You shall look so handsome in the smart livery I shall order for you!'

He watched her run across the yard, his heart heavy with despair. The 'smart livery' she had spoken of reminded him of the days when he had first come to Elvemere as 'tiger'. He hated being dressed up like some poor pathetic performing animal. Surely there *must* be some way he could escape!

As he turned he caught a movement in the shadows and he stiffened. God in Heaven! Had someone heard them? Was he discovered after all?

'Please don't worry. You have nothing to fear from me.' It was a woman's voice and as she stepped forward into the light he saw that it was Charles Quincey's wife who stood facing him; a tall, handsome woman with eyes and hair as dark as his own. She stepped forward and laid a hand on his arm.

'It's Patrick, isn't it?' He nodded. 'Well!' She smiled. 'Miss Caroline certainly has you in a cleft stick, hasn't she?'

His heart plummeted. So she *had* heard after all. He flushed a dull red. 'You—heard then, ma'am?' he muttered.

'Don't look so stricken. I mean you no harm,' she told him. 'In fact I think I might be able to help you. Do you want to be rid of her, or are you happy with things as they are?'

The directness of her question shocked him, yet at the same time hope flooded into him like a breath of fresh air.

'It—it's not possible for me to get free, ma'am,' he said. 'Ye see, I'm a bondman. I've no choice but to go where I'm told. If I was to run away I'd be brought back and put in prison. Besides, Miss Caroline has said that she'd say things against me that could get me hanged.'

She drew in her breath sharply. 'I see. A nice family we've got ourselves into, you and I, eh, Patrick?' She stepped closer to get a better look at him. It seemed a pity that such a magnificent creature should be brought to this.

344

But she thought she saw a way of helping Patrick—and herself at the same time.

'If I were able to give you a sum of money, could you go away from here?' she asked. 'Lie low till the hue and cry died down?'

His heart leapt, then he remembered Kathy. It was almost her time. He couldn't go away from Elvemere until he was sure she was safe and well. 'I suppose I could stay out o' sight, ma'am,' he said slowly. 'But money—I don't know. If I was to be caught with money on me I'd be hanged for stealing it—that's sure.'

'But you can't escape without money, Patrick. You'll have to take that chance,' she told him. 'The best thing would be for you to get right away and stay away. Otherwise I couldn't be responsible for the consequences. What do you say?'

He nodded eagerly. Surely for money he could get someone to hide him—buy their silence. He could lie low until the spring when his bond time would be up. Work would soon be starting on the new railway. Maybe he could lose himself among the gangs of navvies he had heard about. He'd heard tell that a good many of them came from the old country. Hope filled his breast until he could almost have wept and on impulse he reached out and took her hand.

'Oh ma'am—if ye could do this for me it'd be like savin' me life,' he said, his voice thick with emotion.

'Then I shall certainly try, Patrick,' she told him gravely. 'I can make no promises but I have great hopes.' She patted his hand. 'I'll see you again soon. In the meantime, not a word to anyone, you understand?'

It was darkening fast as she made her way across the yard and up to her room. She was well satisfied with the afternoon's work. She would have her revenge on Charles and his hateful mother and sister. It would be she who came out on top. If it were the last thing she did she would see them all in Hell!

On the morning that Amelia, her son and daughter departed for London, Sophia stayed in her room. From the window she saw their boxes being loaded, then watched them all get into the carriage. A little later, Henry left for his office in the brougham driven by Patrick. She felt a little desolate, alone in a house full of hostile servants—hostile, with the exception of Patrick. He had good reason to be grateful to her, or would have, if her plan went as she hoped it would. But even if all went well he would still be in danger unless he kept well out of sight. If he had known just how *much* danger he might not have agreed to co-operate so readily!

As she idled away the day her resentment against the Quincey family grew: Amelia with her long aristocratic nose and her cold, disapproving looks; Charles, his weakness belying his good looks, and Caroline! Was *she* the perfect well-bred girl? If she was, then Sophia preferred an honest tavern harlot any day!

She heard Henry return from his office at five and at six thirty Parkes knocked and entered, her thin face pinched with disapproval.

'The Master says I'm to ask if you need me, madam,' she said, her voice sharp with resentment. 'And he'd be obliged if you'd dine with him at seven as usual.'

Sophia's first impulse was to refuse, then she changed her mind. Amelia had never offered her the use of her maid and Charles could not afford to employ one for her. Why should she not avail herself of the woman's services? After all, she had no one else to serve at present. As for dining with Henry, it was the perfect opportunity to put her proposition to him.

She kept Parkes busy, choosing the most elegant of her dresses, a deep rose silk with an overdress of black lace, which Parkes considered vulgar. Sophia saw this and insisted on having it pressed, then she decided that she would have her hair dressed in a new way, entailing masses of curls and ringlets and although Parkes seethed with indignation she could do no less than her best. When Sophia joined Henry later in the drawing-room, his eyes told her that the effort had been worthwhile.

'Good-evening, m'dear,' he said, getting to

his feet and coming to meet her. 'May I say how very charming you look this evening? I am flattered to think you have gone to so much trouble for me.'

She inclined her head graciously. 'Thank you for sending Parkes to me, Henry. I felt I must justify your kindness.'

'Not at all.' He smiled. 'It is flattering that you should wish to please your father-in-law.'

She raised her eyes to his in the direct way he admired so much. 'On the contrary, it is a pleasure to dress for one so appreciative.'

At that point the conversation was interrupted by Simpson who had come to announce that dinner was served, but later, when he and Stevens had withdrawn. Henry brought up the subject of the task he had set her.

'I hesitate to ask, m'dear, but I have been wondering if you have managed to find out any more about the matter we were discussing the other day.'

She looked up, a frown temporarily clouding her smooth brow. 'I am afraid I have, Henry,' she said. 'I have rather disturbing news and I had hoped not to spoil your dinner with it.'

He put down his knife and fork. 'I see. Better get it over with in that case. I don't believe in putting off unpleasantness.'

She took a deep breath. 'Very well. I am afraid it is as you feared. Caroline does indeed have a lover. I have spoken to the man—

though of course Caroline does not know of this. I have to tell you that he will not be shaken off so easily either. When I told him the affair must stop he threatened to go to Mr Jellings and tell all.'

Henry blanched. 'By God! Tell me who the fellow is and I'll have the hide off him!'

But Sophia shook her head. 'I was not able to learn his name, but I do know that he would willingly elope with Caroline unless some attractive alternative is offered.' She looked at him. 'I must also tell you that I believe that she would willingly go with him—and even more so were there to be an angry confrontation.'

He shook his head. 'And I suppose this "attractive alternative" you speak of is money?' She nodded and he asked baldly: 'How much?'

She looked up, trying to assess what it might be worth to him. It would need to be a sizeable sum, for she intended to split the money with Patrick, her own share enabling her to rejoin her uncle's company. By the time Charles returned from London she meant to be far away from Elvemere. She moistened her lips. 'I believe that two hundred pounds might persuade him to leave the town,' she said calmly.

Henry choked over his wine, set down the glass and looked at her with heightened colour. 'Two hundred? I should damned well think it would! Can't you get him to take less?'

She sighed. 'I thought you would want him

349

to have enough to go abroad, which is what I suggested,' she said. 'I'm afraid I more than half promised him that amount on our next meeting. It is not an occupation I enjoy and I am not anxious to prolong the negotiations.'

At once he was contrite. 'Of course not, m'dear. Please forgive me. I was overwrought or I should not have spoken to you like that. If you tell me the time and place of your meeting with the fellow I will handle the rest of the affair myself. I had no business to ask you to do it in the first place.'

'I am afraid that would be most unwise,' she said quickly. 'If he thought I had betrayed him, he would have no hesitation in going back on his word. I am sure of it. I think you must allow me to finish what I have started.'

'Very well, if you insist.' He leaned forward, chewing his lip. 'Tell me, m'dear—if it is not too indelicate—do you know how far the—er—alliance has advanced between them?'

She lowered her eyes. 'It is not my habit to tell tales, Henry—let me just say that if Caroline were my daughter I would get her to the altar without delay.'

His colour deepened again. 'My God—the swine! If I could get my hands on him I'd—'

'I think you should give him the money and be sure that he has gone by the time she returns from London,' she interrupted. 'Even if you were to do as your anger urges you, you could not undo what has already been done.'

350

His shoulders slumped. 'Of course, you're right. I've no choice and it's not worth getting worked up about.' He looked at her with a wry smile. 'Were you very disappointed, m'dear, at not going to London with them?'

She smiled a little wistfully. 'How could I be when I have such an attentive father-in-law to keep me company?'

He felt his pulse quicken. 'No doubt you'll be wondering about that promotion we talked of—for Charles,' he said.

'No—in fact I'd almost forgotten.' She sighed. 'I am sorry to say that Charles cares very little for any efforts I might make on his behalf. He prefers to improve himself in his own way and in this I am a hindrance.'

Henry's face assumed a disgusted look. 'I suppose he's gone to creep round that old woman again, eh?'

She nodded. 'I am afraid he regrets our marriage and wishes he had not been so hasty.'

'This is often the way of it with young men like Charles.' Henry clicked his tongue sympathetically. 'If only I could have advised you, m'dear. I know that son of mine only too well. He's immature and spoiled. That was why I insisted on making him work hard—thought it might make a man of him.' He looked at her thoughtfully. 'What can I do to make up to you, Sophia—both for your disappointment and for the service you have done me?'

The way his eyes moved over her did not

escape her notice and suddenly a new plan began to take root in her mind. She looked at him with eyes brimming with longing—a trick she had learned as an actress. 'There is nothing, Henry,' she said, a slight break in her voice. 'You have been kind to me—the only person in this house to have made me feel welcome. It is enough in itself.'

He felt his heart swell. 'Oh, my dear, have you been so unhappy here?'

She gave a shuddering sigh. 'How can I tell you? You cannot know the loneliness of a loveless marriage.'

'I can. Believe me when I tell you that I can indeed,' he said fervently. He would have risen to come to her, but at that moment Simpson entered the room to enquire where they would take coffee.

'What the devil do you want, man?—Yes we'll both take coffee and you can tell Stevens to put the tray in the drawing-room. Mrs Charles will pour,' Henry said irritably.

Later, as they drank their coffee before a blazing fire, Henry began to hint to Sophia that his own marriage was less than idyllic. He sat beside her on the sofa and took her hand.

'I can't tell you, m'dear, how comforting it is to talk to someone as beautiful and sympathetic as yourself. Might I say that I hope you and Charles will resolve your difficulties? Would it help, do you think, if I bought you a little house of your own?'

She lifted her shoulders and sighed. 'I would say this to no one but you, Henry, but it has occurred to me that Charles may be thinking of ways to be rid of me. Perhaps it would be better and happier for all concerned if I returned to my uncle and aunt.'

Henry clasped the hand he held tightly. 'Oh no, you must not speak of such a terrible thing. As long as I am Master of this house you shall be welcome here.'

She turned the full force of her dark, dramatic eyes on him. 'Thank you, Henry. You are so good to me, indeed I could wish that your son were more like you.'

The lustrous eyes held his for a long moment, their effect on him was almost hypnotic. Slowly, he moved closer, his free arm sliding round her waist, then, cradling her cheek with his hand, he kissed her, lightly at first, then as her lips responded to his, more urgently, till his whole body trembled with desire. Together they sank back against the cushions of the sofa and Sophia's eyes closed as his lips caressed her eyelids and throat. His hand stroked the smooth skin of her neck and shoulders and she felt the rapid beat of his heart as his body pressed close to hers.

'Please—I beg you—' she gasped breathlessly. 'This is madness. I—we are not free to behave so—however much we might both desire it. I must go to my room.' She got to her feet and stood before the mirror, smoothing her disarranged hair and pressing her fingers to her flushed cheeks. In an instant he was beside her.

'Forgive me, Sophia,' he said huskily. 'But don't tell me it was all on my side.' He took her shoulders and turned her to face him. 'What you say is true: we are both shackled by marriage, but it cannot prevent us from feeling, can it? We are both human and warm-blooded. We have our needs and recognise them. Are we to suppress those needs?'

She bit her lip and lowered her eyes from his, shaking her head. 'Surely—we must.'

His fingers bit deeply into the flesh of her shoulders as he held her, bending her back so that she was forced to raise her eyes to his. 'I have never met a woman like you, Sophia,' he said thickly. 'I do not mean to let you go now that I have found you. I want you and I mean to have you. Both our partners have cast us off. We can hurt no one. Oh, Sophia, say yes.' He drew her close again and kissed her passionately again and again till she pushed him firmly from her and turned away, her hand to her mouth.

'You—must give me time to consider,' she said breathlessly. 'I did not expect this. My thoughts are in turmoil.'

'Of course, so are mine.' He seized her hands and pressed them to his lips. 'But I do know one thing for sure, Sophia—that I love you and I mean you to be mine.'

She looked into his eyes. 'Are you asking me to be your mistress, Henry?'

'I'd do anything in the world to make you happy,' he said. 'You can ask whatever you like.' He took a step towards her but she held up her hands.

'Please, Henry—I must have time to think.'

He looked at her hungrily. 'When will you give me an answer?'

'Soon—I don't know when, but soon.'

'But—you feel as I do?' He was like a boy in his eagerness.

She nodded, eyes downcast. 'Yes, Henry. I cannot deny it. I do.'

Upstairs in her room a little later she sat before the dressing-table mirror, regarding her reflection. She had meant it when she had told Henry that what had happened between them had been unexpected. It was true that she had felt an under-current between them since their first meeting but she had never expected it to burst to the surface with such effusiveness. In the palm of her hand she held the power to rule Henry Quincey and to have her revenge on his family. Alternatively, on the dressing-table lay the two hundred pounds which Henry had taken from his safe and given to her before she retired. So what should she do? Use her half of the money and make her escape—or become Henry's mistress?

Far into the small hours she lay awake thinking. The idea of returning to the life of a travelling player seemed tawdry and unattractive to her now. On the other hand, life in Elvemere as Henry Quincey's mistress—hidden away like a caged bird, looked down on by society—did not appeal to her much either. No, Sophia decided that she must have more than that. She needed security and respect and somehow she would have them—and Henry too. Finally she fell asleep without having made a decision. There was plenty of time, she told herself. Henry's ardour would be the better for keeping and she had found in the past that problems had a way of resolving themselves, given time and patience. She would sleep on it and see what the morning brought.

During the days that followed Sophia kept to her room, making the excuse that she had a cold. The two hundred pounds rested safely at the back of her handkerchief drawer and she could not make up her mind. Should she perhaps take *all* of it and go to London to try her fortune in the theatre there? It was a gamble, to be sure, but no worse a gamble than taking a chance on Henry's becoming tired of her and casting her off. But as the week drew to its close the solution to her problem presented itself to her.

On Friday morning, after Henry had left Denmark House for his office, she ventured downstairs to the morning-room where she rang for Stevens and ordered a light breakfast.

She had just started to eat it when there was a tap on the door and Mrs Brown, the housekeeper, entered. In her black bombazine she looked even more hostile than the other servants, though she spoke respectfully enough:

'I hope you will forgive me for interrupting your breakfast, madam,' she began. 'But a letter has just come. It was brought to me by a passenger on yesterday's London coach and it is from Mrs Quincey.'

Sophia looked up. 'I hope there is nothing wrong?'

The housekeeper shook her head. 'No. It is just to inform me that they—that is the Mistress and Miss Caroline, will be home tomorrow instead of on Monday. It appears that the Mistress has suffered a slight cold and in any case she wishes to prepare for young Master Paul's return from school at the end of next week.'

'And my husband will not be returning with them?' Sophia asked, piqued that she should receive the news from a housekeeper.

'Not at present it seems.' The woman folded her hands, her eyes glinting smugly behind the spectacles. 'Are there any instructions you wish to give—madam?'

The slight emphasis on the 'madam' was unmistakable and Sophia seethed inwardly. 'No, except to have fires lit in the bedrooms and you had better tell Cook that there will be four for dinner tomorrow.'

The housekeeper looked affronted. 'Naturally those things would have been attended to as a matter of course,' she said stiffly. 'Is there anything else?'

The idea, when it hit her, struck Sophia like a flash of lightning. She hardly heard Mrs Brown's acid tones as the plan unfolded in her mind like the pages of a book. She smiled her most dazzling smile at the housekeeper.

'Just one thing: I think we will not tell Mr Quincey of the change of plan,' she said. 'We will keep it as a surprise. Do you agree?'

Mrs Brown's eyes blinked behind the spectacles uncomprehendingly. 'Just as you say, madam. It is not my place to agree or disagree.'

Later that morning Sophia went out to the stables, making sure she was not observed. She found Patrick in the tackroom and gave him the package containing the notes.

'There is a hundred pounds in there,' she whispered, pushing it into his hands. 'And if you take my advice you'll go at once. She's due home tomorrow and it would be better if she found you gone.'

He stared at her, stunned, then looked at the package in his hands.

*A hundred pounds*! He'd never seen so much money in his life. How had she managed to get it for him? Immediately he was on his guard, fearful and suspicious.

'Is—is it all right, ma'am?' he asked. 'I mean—it isn't—?'

'Stolen—is that what you're trying to say?' Sophia's direct brown eyes looked straight into his. 'No. It was given freely on condition that you take yourself off. Oh, don't worry,' she added quickly. 'No one knows who you are. But once you disappear from here it will become obvious very quickly.' She looked at him. 'Have you anywhere to go? I daresay my uncle could do with a strong young man like you. His company will be in Oxfordshire now.'

But Patrick shook his head. The *Mary Ann* was in port. Tom Craven would take him aboard, he knew that. First he would see Kathy and Jonathan Nichols, with whom he would leave his windfall, then he would leave Elvemere altogether—at least for a while. 'I'll be all right, ma'am,' he said. 'Sure I have me own plans. Thank ye for helpin' me. I'm in your debt. If there's anythin'—' A sudden noise outside made him break off and Sophia shook her head.

'Think no more of it, Patrick. I must go now. Goodbye and good luck.' And with a quick look to make sure there was no one about she was gone, darting across the yard like a fleeting shadow.

\*     \*     \*

Although still early evening it was dark when

359

Patrick made his way out through the gates of Denmark House stables for the last time. He had said goodbye to Seamus, promising that he would somehow get word to him as soon as he was settled. The old man had asked no questions but he was no fool. He had seen the growing tension in Patrick over the past few months and he had also seen the hold that Miss Caroline had over him. He would miss the lad sadly but he was glad he was making a break for it. If he stayed, all the manhood and the spirit would have been drained out of him.

With his bundle over his shoulder, Patrick walked quickly along the street. The *Mary Ann* was due to sail with the early morning tide at three o'clock and he intended to be aboard. Tom would not refuse him, knowing well that he would pull his weight. But first there were things he must do. He must see Kathy, to explain and to say goodbye. And he must call on Jonathan Nichols too.

When he reached the cottage in Mill Row he hesitated at the door. He had not been back since that afternoon in October. Although Kathy had asked him, he had not returned to meet Will Harrap, hating the thought of seeing Kathy at the side of the man she had wed. Now he wondered how they would react to each other. He raised his hand and knocked on the door, which was opened to him by a pale-faced man with a crutch under one arm.

'I'm Patrick Reardon, Kathy's step-brother,'

360

he said in answer to the man's enquiring look. 'I have to go away for a while and I've come to say goodbye. Can I see her?'

The man held the door open. 'Come in. I'm afraid you can't see Kathy at the moment. She's above—with the midwife.'

In the dim light from the fire Patrick saw that the man's face was strained and troubled and his own heart missed a beat.

'Is it the child? Is she all right?' he asked anxiously.

The man shook his head. 'I'm glad you're here. I'm worried to death about her. All day yesterday she was in pain—all night too and now all today. She's suffering so—and still the child don't come. I don't mind telling you I'm feared for her.'

At that moment there was an anguished cry from above and in an instant Patrick had dropped his bundle on the floor and was bounding up the bare wooden stairs two at a time. At the top he threw open the door of the only bedroom and stood on the threshold.

Kathy lay on the bed, her arms above her head, pulling on a knotted towel which was tied to the rails of the iron bedstead. She was half-covered by a blanket under which the mound of her stomach was huge and grotesque to his eyes. Her hair lay damp and matted on the pillow and her eyes were huge and filled with pain. When she saw him she cried out and held out her arms to him, tears

361

spilling from her eyes.

'Patrick! Oh, I've prayed and prayed that you'd come to me.'

The midwife spun round in horror. 'Get you out of here this instant!' she shouted. 'This is no place for a man. It ain't decent!'

'What are you doin' to her?' he thundered. 'Why is the child not born? Why do you let her suffer like this?' He thrust the woman to one side and took Kathy in his arms, stroking the damp hair back from her brow and murmuring words of comfort. But a moment later she arched her back and let out another of the heart-rending animal-like cries, her face contorted with agony. Shocked and afraid, Patrick laid her gently back on the bed and looked helplessly at the midwife.

'Christ! What's wrong? Is there nothing any of us can do?'

The woman took his arm and drew him to one side. 'You're her kin, are you?' He nodded and she continued in a low voice: 'The child's breeched—d'you know what that means?'

Again he nodded. 'It's many a mare I've foaled. I know well enough. It needs turning.'

The woman sighed. 'I know that, man and I've tried, but it's no use.' She glanced at the bed. 'She'll not last much longer like this. It would've been better if the child had died but it's too strong for her. They're fightin' each other for life and the poor lass is losin'.' She lifted her shoulders resignedly. 'Ah well, it's the Lord's will. All we can do is wait and try an' help her out of the world as easy as we can.'

Patrick stared at her. 'What are you sayin' woman? You can't let her die—you *can't*! Why haven't you sent for a doctor?'

She shrugged. 'There's only him downstairs to go an' with that hoppy leg o' his he'd be a week gone! He'd never get here in time now anyway.'

'He will—he's got to. I'll go for him meself this minute.' Patrick turned again to the bed where Kathy lay limp and exhausted after the last bout of pain. He bent and touched her cheek. 'I'm goin' for Dr Nichols, Kathy, darlin',' he told her tenderly. 'I'll be as quick as I can. Will ye try an' hold on a bit longer?'

She managed a frail smile for him and he straightened again, unshed tears stinging his eyes. 'I'll be back,' he said briefly and ran down the stairs, past the astonished Will Harrap and out into the frosty night air.

It was a distance of a mile and a half to Jonathan Nichols' house and Patrick ran all the way. When the doctor answered to his frenzied hammering on the door all he could make out from Patrick's breathless incoherent speech was Kathy's name. But he was well used to such calls and it was only minutes later that he was leading his horse out of the stable whilst Patrick held the lantern for him. As he mounted he looked at Patrick's sweat-streaked face apologetically.

'I'm sorry I haven't another horse I can lend you.'

Patrick shook his head. ' 'Tis all right, Doctor. I'll walk back. I shan't worry once I know you're there.'

Jonathan reached down and took his bag from Patrick who had been holding it. 'Why don't you wait here for news? My wife will make you some tea,' he said kindly.

But Patrick was not to be put off. 'I'm rested now, Doctor,' he said. 'I'll take me time walkin' back. I want to be there with her.' He stood and watched as the man he trusted most in the world rode off into the darkness, his whole being aching with fear for Kathy, and for the first time in many a long year he offered up a prayer to a God he had long believed to be dead.

\*         \*         \*

Henry Quincey paced his study. He was angry—very angry. When the brougham had come to collect him from his office he had found Seamus driving instead of Patrick and when he had asked why the coachman had been oddly evasive. Finally he had managed to browbeat the old fool into telling him the truth—that the lad had absconded. At first it had puzzled him. Once there had been trouble with him, he had been unruly and

364

insubordinate, lately though he had seemed to settle down, and there was no denying that he was a good worker. Why would he choose to run off at this time of year? And where would he find work enough to keep him going? Then it struck him like a pole-axe. Of course! Caroline and her recent obsession with riding! He was the man! And he'd gone off with two hundred pounds of his—Henry Quincey's—money in his breeches!

At first it angered him to think that Sophia had known and not told him, but after a while he thought he saw her reason for this. She knew him well enough to realise that he would have had the fellow thrashed and that could have led to repercussions. The rogue had threatened to go to Victor Jellings with his story, had he not? If he had followed his first impulse it could have had disastrous effects. However, the more Henry thought about it, the more incensed he became. Not that he blamed Sophia, she had undoubtedly acted for the best—but the Reardon fellow! To think of him getting away with two hundred pounds! It made Henry's blood boil.

Finally he sat down and wrote a letter, sealed it, then rang for Simpson.

'Get one of the grooms to ride out to Drove End Farm with this,' he ordered. 'It's to be given to Jim Petch, the bailiff. Tell him it's urgent and he's to make haste.'

When Simpson had withdrawn he felt better

and poured himself a glass of port. That should fix the young bastard—and get him his money back too with a bit of luck. Now tomorrow he'd go and see the vicar and Victor Jellings. The wedding must take place directly after Christmas. Warmed and relaxed by the port, he leaned back in his chair and fell to the more pleasant anticipation of seeing Sophia at dinner. She had sent him word by Parkes that her cold was better and that she intended to dine downstairs this evening. He hoped that it meant she had considered and was about to give him an answer to his proposition.

She looked lovelier and more desirable than ever as she sat opposite him at table that night and afterwards in the drawing-room, when there was no more likelihood of intrusion from their servants, he moved over to sit beside her, looking expectantly into her eyes.

'I hardly dare ask you, m'dear, whether you have thought any more about what we discussed the other night.'

She smiled at him. 'I believe you know, Henry, that I find your suggestion very tempting—I might almost say irresistible. But I am afraid of what would happen if you were to tire of me as Charles has. I must think of my own security.'

He grasped her hand and pressed it to his lips. 'Tire of you? Never, my dearest! If you only knew how much I long for you. If only you and I had had the good fortune to meet when I was still a free man, you would, I assure you, have become my wife. As it is—' He shook his head sadly. 'I'm afraid that Amelia is very jealous of her position—if not of my affections!'

Sophia sighed, leaning closer so that he could catch the full benefit of her perfume and the low cut of her gown. 'It is a very hard decision to make, Henry. If I were to agree what would my position be? Apart from you I would have no friends.'

He drew a long breath. 'As long as you remain married to Charles it would all be perfectly proper. What is wrong with a father buying a house for his son and daughter-in-law? I am sure that Charles could easily be persuaded to remain in London. He could even go to university as he has always wanted, then we could be together as often as we both wished—and without a breath of scandal. What do you say?'

She smiled and lowered her lashes. 'You are very clever, Henry—and very devious—but I am still not sure that your affection would last.'

Frustration tore at his nerves. 'What can I do to convince you?' he cried. 'Tell me how I can prove my love and I will gladly do it. My God, Sophia, don't torture me any more. I want you so much I can think of nothing else!'

She wound her arms seductively round his neck and kissed him, her lips opening invitingly beneath his. 'Tomorrow,' she whispered against his cheek as his arms closed convulsively round her. 'As soon as you return from your office. I will wait for you upstairs in your room—then I will tell you what I have decided.'

*      *      *

Will Harrap and Patrick sat one on each side of the fireplace. Will, who had been up all of the previous night, kept falling asleep, but Patrick sat tense and rigid, his ears alert for every movement and sound from the room above their heads. Kathy had stopped crying out now and although he was thankful that the heart-rending sounds had ceased, he knew in his heart it was because she no longer had the strength to utter them. Every sheet in the little house had been commandeered by the doctor and kettle after kettle of hot water had been carried up the stairs. What if Kathy died? He had to force himself to face the fact that it might happen. How could he go on, knowing how and why she had died? How could he prevent himself from killing the man who had caused it all? He had long since ceased to judge her or even to wonder why she had not asked for his help. He knew now only too well, the humiliation of forced submission. It would be a long time before he had his own self-respect back again. 'Oh God!' he prayed. 'If only ye see us through this I'll never doubt ye again.' But even in his contrition he cursed Henry Quincey and knew he'd die cursing him.

A feeble wail came from above, bringing him instantly to his feet. The child was born! But what of Kathy? He took the stairs two at a time and then stood staring at the closed door, suddenly chilled with fear. 'Kathy!—Oh, Kathy, my Kathy!' he murmured, his eyes blinded by tears.

The door opened and Dr Nichols stood facing him, shirt-sleeves rolled above his elbows and sweat standing out on his forehead. He reached out and clapped Patrick on the shoulder.

'Don't look like that, man. It's all over. Kathy has a daughter, Patrick—small but healthy. She certainly put up a fight to get into this old world of ours, God bless her.'

'And Kathy?' Patrick asked, his voice hardly more than a whisper.

'Weak and exhausted, but she'll do. She'll need rest and care, but she'll be herself before long.'

'Can—can I see her?'

Jonathan nodded smiling. 'When the midwife has tidied her and the child up.'

'What is it? Is it all right?'

They both started as Will's anxious, sleep-creased face peered up at them from the bottom of the stairs. Jonathan began to descend, rolling down his sleeves as he went. 'Your wife has a fine little daughter, Will,' he said. 'They'll both be fine with a little rest. Have you the kettle on? I think we could all do with a drink of something hot.'

Patrick stood for a moment at the top of the stairs, watching the growing relief that spread over the man's face. In that moment he felt he had lost Kathy for ever. It would be this man who would nurse her back to health, work for her and the child and watch them both grow in strength and beauty because of his efforts. It was clear that he loved Kathy in spite of the difference in their ages. She would come to love him too—she must. Would she also learn to forget him—Patrick—after he'd gone out of her life?

As Will brewed a pot of tea in the kitchen Patrick looked at Jonathan. 'Can ye tell me the time, Doctor?'

Jonathan took out his pocket-watch and glanced at it. 'Just on two. It's been a long job. Shouldn't you be getting back to Denmark House now? You've a day's work to do tomorrow.'

'No. I've left Denmark House for good,' Patrick told him. 'It was to say goodbye that I came here tonight. I'm sailin' on the *Mary Ann* with the tide an' that's at three so I'll have to go in a minute.' He glanced towards Will's back, then took the package with the money out of his shirt and handed it to the doctor. 'Will ye look after this for me, Doctor? Do as ye did with the other—as ye think best. I'll be back when it's safe—when me bond time is up.'

Jonathan took a brief look inside the package then raised his startled eyes to Patrick's. 'There is a great deal of money here, Patrick,' he said. 'Is there anything I should know—anything you want to tell me?'

Patrick read the unasked question in the doctor's eyes and shook his head. 'Ye've no need to worry. I'm not in any trouble and the money's mine right enough. I'll be back in the spring.'

'But if you're going away won't you need it?' Jonathan asked.

But Patrick shook his head. 'If I took it, it'd get taken off me; an' I won't need it for I'll work me passage. No, I want you to put it where it'll work for me just like ye did before.'

When he went up to the bedroom to see Kathy she wept and clung to him. 'You'll come back—promise me you'll come back?' she begged.

He nodded, holding her frail body close. Relieved of her burden she seemed so fragile. He could feel her bones through the thin stuff of her nightgown. Her skin was like wax and there were purple smudges beneath her eyes. He looked at the child lying in the makeshift cot by the bed. It was the image of Kathy: huge blue wondering eyes and already a thick bronze down on the tiny head. He could see no likeness to her hated father much to his relief.

'Sure I'll be back, darlin'.' He kissed her tenderly. 'One day I'll be rich, just like I've always promised ye, an' then I'll see to it that ye have everythin' ye've always wanted.'

She smiled and looked at the child, touching the tiny curled fingers. 'She's beautiful, isn't she, Patrick?' she whispered. 'All these months I've wondered how I'd feel—knowing how she came to be here. But now I see her—so tiny and helpless—all I feel is love.' She looked at him. 'It can't be wrong to love her, can it, Patrick?'

He looked into her eyes and shook his head gravely. 'No, Kathy. It can't be wrong. Sure none of it is her fault.'

She lay back against the pillow, his words seeming to comfort her. 'I'm goin' to call her Mary,' she said sleepily.

He pressed her fingers and stood up. 'I have to go now, Kathy. I have to say goodbye, my love. I'm glad ye've got Will. He's a good man.' But when he looked he saw that she was already asleep. He turned towards the door, grateful that she wouldn't see him walk away.

As he walked towards the river his thoughts were mixed. Would it be better if he left Kathy alone and never came back at all? He had meant what he had said: Will was a good man. He wouldn't want to cause him any pain. Yet Patrick knew now without any shadow of doubt that he could never in his life be near Kathy without loving and wanting her. Maybe it would be better for all of them if he faded out of their lives.

The moon had gone behind thick clouds now and a thin sleet had started to fall. Patrick pulled up his collar and lowered his head, thinking of the *Mary Ann*'s snug cabin and Meg Craven's home-made broth. He had just reached the end of Bell Lane where it joined with the Herring Wharf when a figure stepped out of the shadows in front of him.

'Is it you, Patrick Reardon?' a voice asked.

He lifted his head in surprise. 'Who is it?' But the words were hardly out of his mouth when something blunt and heavy hit him on the side of the head. He reeled sideways against the wall. Another figure appeared as from nowhere and struck him a blow in the stomach which doubled him up. Then it was as though all hell had been let loose. He seemed to be surrounded by dark, hostile strangers, all bent on his destruction. He tried desperately to fight back but there were too many of them. Blows rained on him from all sides. Some of them seemed to be armed with clubs and at last he staggered back, stunned, against the wall and slid slowly to the ground. Heavy boots pounded into his ribs and, when he instinctively curled his body, they crashed into his head and face. Flashes and whorls of brilliant light blinded him until finally the blackness closed in, mercifully blotting out everything.

He awoke to a violent twist of savage pain that seemed to engulf his whole body. It was still dark and fine flakes of snow were falling, covering him with a blanket of wetness. He put his hand up to his face and found it stiff, caked with dirt and blood. With an agonising effort he pulled himself into a sitting position against the wall. His stomach heaved and he vomited violently on to the ground. He felt like one huge mound of living pain. His eyes were so swollen that he could hardly see. He was fairly sure that his nose was broken and both of his hands had been stamped on till they were numb and bloodied, the fingers three times their normal size. All he could think of was the *Mary Ann.* She couldn't be far away, but could he manage to get to her? Then he heard the church clock strike the hour. He counted: one—two—three—*four*! With a surge of despair he realised that Tom Craven would have set sail more than an hour ago!

\*        \*        \*

Sophia listened for the sound of the brougham. She was confident that Henry would be returning early from the office, eager for her half-promised consent. She was ready for him. As soon as she saw him arrive she would slip into his room at the other end of the landing to await him.

At last her patience was rewarded. She

heard the clip-clop of hooves and, looking out of the window, she saw Henry descend from the brougham and hurry up the steps, his breath making gusty plumes on the frosty air. She turned, a smile on her lips, and whisked out of the room.

Henry gave his top-coat and hat to Simpson and made straight for the stairs.

'I do not wish to be disturbed, Simpson,' he called over his shoulder. 'If anyone calls you can tell them I am not at home, do you understand?'

The butler nodded, his face expressionless. 'Very well, sir.'

Outside the door of his room he paused, his hands smoothing his hair and nervously fumbling with his cravat, hardly daring to open the door in case she might not be there. Taking a deep breath he threw the door open. The room was empty. His heart plummeted. Stepping inside he closed the door quietly and looked around. He had been so *sure*. She had given him such hope. Slowly he took off his coat and began to unbutton his waistcoat and loosen his cravat. Going to the wardrobe, he opened it and took out a bottle of whisky and a glass, which he proceeded to fill. He had taken one sip when a voice behind him almost made him choke:

'Aren't you going to offer me some too, my love?'

He spun round in time to see Sophia step

out from behind one of the floor-length velvet curtains and he gasped at what he saw. Her hair, black as a gipsy's, hung loose to her waist and her feet were bare. She wore a house-gown of some light material which clung to the curves of her body in a way that set his pulses racing.

'Sophia!' he whispered hoarsely. 'I thought you had changed your mind—that you did not wish—' he crossed the room and took her eagerly in his arms. 'Your answer is to be yes, then?'

She threw back her head and wound her arms around his neck. 'It is, Henry. I wanted to tease you a little but it is no use, I cannot hold out against you any longer. I am yours if you still want me.'

'Still want you? How could you imagine otherwise?' He was easing the gown from her shoulders, kissing the satin skin while his hands slid down to cup her breasts. His breath was ragged against her ear as he whispered: 'Now, Sophia—now, please *now!*'

She laughed deep in her throat and began to unbutton his shirt. 'Do not be too hasty, my love. For us the first time must be perfect. I want us both to be naked.'

It was as she pulled the covers from the bed that she heard the post-chaise outside, then the far off jangling of the bell somewhere in the distant servants' regions. Henry was far too preoccupied to notice. The last of his clothing

376

removed, he threw himself down beside her, drawing her close and covering her with kisses while his eager hands explored every inch of her body. His breath rasped in her ear as he whispered fevered words of love, his passion rising tumultuously.

Parkes met Amelia and Caroline in the hall and took their outdoor things, twittering round them both like an agitated hen.

'Oh, you must be so cold, madam. Was the journey *very* uncomfortable? I'll have some tea sent up for you. Will you have it upstairs or in the drawing-room? The Master's home. He doesn't know you're coming though. Mrs Charles thought it would be a nice surprise for him.'

Amelia waved her away wearily. 'Leave me for a while, Parkes. I wish to rest and so does Miss Caroline. The journey was very tedious indeed. You may have some tea sent up in half an hour and then you may come yourself and unpack.'

She went up the stairs, Caroline trailing sullenly behind her. She felt numb with cold and she was glad to find a good fire burning in her room. But when she had warmed herself she decided to look in on Henry. She couldn't wait to tell him of Charles's success with Great-Aunt Graves. Not only was he back in her favour, but she had offered him the position of financial adviser and secretary. His future was assured. Mr Jarvis had been hopeful of procuring an annulment too. All in all it had been a very successful visit.

She crossed the landing and opened the door of his room—to freeze in her steps a moment later. The sight that met her eyes was so incredible that at first she could not take it in. Clothes were strewn everywhere and on the dishevelled bed lay two entwined naked bodies—one her husband's, the other, her daughter-in-law, Sophia's. Her hand flew to her mouth to stifle a cry of horror as she turned and fled.

\*　　\*　　\*

Christmas that year in Elvemere was the coldest in living memory. Snow lay like a thick white blanket over everything and the river froze like a sheet of glass. But for some there was more than frost and snow to chill the season.

At Denmark House the atmosphere inside was icier than outside. After the first stormy encounter between them, Henry and Amelia ceased to speak to each other unless absolutely necessary. Amelia had made it clear that she and Paul would join Charles in London as soon as decently possible after Caroline's wedding.

Sophia kept to her room on Henry's advice and after Caroline's hasty marriage on Boxing Day, Amelia kept her word and departed with her younger son, leaving the field clear for Sophia to make herself mistress of Denmark House, just as she had planned.

Kathy knew little of Christmas that year. Three days after the birth of her baby she contracted white-leg. Kind neighbours helped to bring her bed down to the kitchen where Will could minister to her and the baby, which he did as tenderly as any woman. Melissa Gage came to visit her daily, though she herself was now pregnant with her first child. Jonathan Nichols treated Kathy's leg with the salve he made from the tubers Patrick grew for him in the herb garden; the ones which produced a carpet of tiny white flowers in the early spring which his wife called 'snowdrops'. And soon it began to respond satisfactorily to his treatment.

Jonathan had another patient who needed his care that Christmas. It had been breakfast time on the morning after the birth of Kathy's child when he discovered Patrick's unconscious body slumped outside his door. At first he had thought him dead, half from exposure and half from the severe beating he had suffered. For a while he had feared for Patrick's sight, so battered and swollen was his face. He had also wondered whether he would ever regain the use of his hands, but after weeks of care and diligent nursing by Jonathan and his wife, Dora, Patrick began to recover his health and, with it, a new determination to make a better life.

As the old year died and the new was heralded in there was a growing feeling of restlessness in Elvemere. The old order of things was soon to be changed. For some there was great prosperity in view, for others, stark ruin. Only one thing was certain: the town would never be the same again. The railway, that great revolutionary machine that swept all before it, was coming to Elvemere as surely as the day of judgement.

# Part Five
# Elvemere

# CHAPTER THIRTEEN

*March 1850*

Kathy sat by the window with her sewing, her needle flying in a race against the fading light. She was in the little sewing room at Holbrook Lodge, a pleasant room on the first floor whose long window looked out on to the river. The door opened and Melissa Gage came in, checking a little in surprise at seeing her still here.

'Why, Kathy! I thought you had gone home long ago. Your husband will be wanting his tea.'

Kathy looked up with a smile. 'I wanted to get Clarissa's dress finished ready for the party. Will won't mind waiting.'

At twenty-seven her features were softer and more rounded. She had an air of serenity, yet those who knew her well still recognised at times the dreamy yearning in the large blue eyes. Melissa took the little dress out of her hands and held it out of reach. 'You shall do no more today!' she declared.

Kathy laughed. 'You're right, I won't—for it's finished.'

Melissa shook out the dress with its froth of dainty lace frills and laughed with her. 'So it is! Really, Kathy, you spoil Clarissa quite dreadfully, but I know she'll be delighted with this.' She laid the dress carefully over the back of a chair and tugged at the bell-rope beside the fireplace. 'You must have some tea before you go. It may be March but the wind is still cold and it's quite a step to Mill Row.'

Kathy sighed and looked out of the window. The willow trees trailed golden fronds in the ruffled water of the river and a pair of swans sailed majestically by. Soon spring would burst forth once again. It was a time of nostalgia for her.

'Do you know, it's twelve years ago this very day that we first came to Elvemere?' she said reflectively.

Melissa sat down opposite. 'Is it really?' She smiled. 'It seems such a short time ago that I first saw you standing there in the doorway of the drawing-room at Denmark House, looking so lost and bewildered.'

Kathy agreed and they laughed over it together, yet to her it seemed as though it had all happened in another world. So much—so very much had changed since then. She voiced the thought and Melissa nodded and fell silent for a moment, thinking of Denmark House, her old home, once the hub of Elvemere society run by her mother like clockwork. Now it was drab and neglected, half the rooms shut up and all of the servants gone except for old Seamus and the slatternly Sarah, who between them looked after Henry Quincey as best they could. Sophia, his mistress, had left him four years ago after he had suffered the seizure that had broken his health. During the six years they had been together Henry had sold off most of his business interests one by one. His esteem in the town had diminished when it became known that his wife and sons had left him and that he had taken his daughter-in-law as a mistress. The scandal had rocked the whole town, but Henry didn't care. His blinding passion for Sophia had obscured everything else. His hopes of gaining control of the town's commerce; his dream of knighthood—all was eclipsed by Sophia, her beauty and his feverish need of her. Now that she had gone he lived the life of a near recluse in the lonely, cold house, his mind dwelling on days gone by.

'How is Mrs Jellings? Have you heard?' Kathy asked.

The question brought Melissa back to the present and she looked up with a smile. 'I think she is well enough in view of her condition,' she said. 'It is almost her time I believe.' She shook her head. 'This will be her seventh child. I cannot imagine such a family. My three are enough for me!' She laughed. 'Victor has certainly made sure she had no time for getting into mischief since they were wed.'

It was true. Everyone—not least Caroline herself—had been astonished at the unflagging energy of the willowy Victor. Now, with nine years of marriage behind him, he was vicar of a village church four miles out of Elvemere where he ruled his parish, his wife and family with a will of iron. His former slim figure had broadened into portly dignity and the thin, pale hair had given way to a shiny pink pate. As for Caroline herself, she was surprisingly contented. Plump and matronly at twenty-eight, she adored her boisterous brood of children and looked up to her masterful husband with awe and admiration.

The door opened to admit a maid with the tea-tray. Behind her peeped three small faces: nine-year-old Francis and his two small sisters—Claire and Clarissa. As usual Francis spoke for all of them: 'May we come in and have tea with you, Mama?'

Melissa's eyes danced. 'What does Nurse say?'

The little boy advanced into the room, his brown eyes solemn. 'She says we may if you agree.'

Melissa held out her arms. 'Then I do.'

With a whoop the two little girls threw themselves at her, but Francis stood in the middle of the room, solitary and dignified. He bowed to Kathy.

'I hope you are well, Mrs Harrap.'

She returned his bow. 'Very well, thank you, Master Francis.' Her face broke into a smile. 'Well—don't I get a kiss today—or are you too grand now that you're going away to school?'

His little face relaxed and he went to her and kissed her cheek. 'Where's Mary today?' he asked looking round. 'Didn't she come with you?'

'No, she's gone to work for Mrs Nichols,' Kathy told him. 'She's to help in the house two days a week to get her into the way of it till she's old enough to be a "tweeny".'

'And on the other days?'

'School!' Kathy said firmly. Ever since the British school had opened its doors four years ago she had made sure that Mary attended. Will had been in favour of it too, since the school was attached to the 'Iron Church' and run by the charity of local wealthy non-conformists. 'I've never been able to read or write myself,' she told the boy. 'But I'll not have Mary growin' up ignorant!'

When the children had gone, collected by their nurse, Kathy got to her feet and began to put on her bonnet and shawl. Melissa looked at her.

'Kathy—have you thought any more on what I spoke to you about last week?' she asked.

Kathy sighed. 'Sure I've thought of little else, Miss Melissa. But I still don't know what to do.'

'You're the finest needlewoman in Elvemere,' Melissa told her. 'All the ladies adore your work. I know you would bring success to the

387

shop John wants to open.'

Kathy bit her lip. 'What about Will, though? While I do most of my work at home it's all right, but he's getting worse all the time. He can hardly get out of his chair now without my help. Dr Nichols says his spine is twisted. Something to do with the accident he had all those years ago. Besides that though—how could I run a shop when I can't read or write?'

Melissa shook her head. 'You would have no need to worry about that, Kathy. John would employ someone to do the accounts. Your job would be to sew and to train two or three apprentices.' She sighed. 'I do see what you mean about Will and I'm sorry. Does Dr Nichols know of anyone who would sit with him? After all, if he is unable to work you will need the extra money.'

'I'll have to think some more,' Kathy said, her face troubled. 'I don't want to speak to Will about it till I've me mind made up. He's always sayin' he's a burden to me and it breaks my heart. He's a proud man for all he's crippled and he was so good to me when I needed help.'

Melissa nodded sympathetically. 'Of course. Maybe John can think of something. I'll talk to him. I know he'll do what he can. He has quite set his heart on having you for the shop, Kathy.'

As she walked through the spring dusk that evening Kathy's mind was full of John Gage's offer. The idea of the new little shop in the market-place, bright and fresh with its bow window and tinkling bell, filled her heart with excitement. In the back there was a room for sewing and fitting, while the front would have a counter and fitted shelves for materials, ribbons, buttons and trimmings. It was even to have her name over the door if she agreed: Kathleen Harrap. Dressmaker and milliner. Oh if *only* there were some way she could do it.

As always her thoughts flew to Patrick. In the old days he would have been the one she would have turned to, but she saw him rarely now. Since he had left Denmark House nine years ago their paths had diverged widely and what she knew of his life she had learned only from hearsay. At first he had worked as a navvy on the construction of the railway, then he and Dr Nichols had gone into some sort of partnership in the building of new houses for the influx of people who came to work in Elvemere. Kathy knew nothing of how it had all come about but judging by Patrick's new lifestyle he had made a success of it. When they met in the street he was polite, asking after Will and Mary, but he was like a stranger. She could hardly believe they had once shared so much—loved so deeply. Yet the sight of him still made her heart beat faster; she still loved him and she knew she always would.

Although he had not married he lived now

in the Nichols' old house. Jonathan and his wife Dora had bought Willerby Hall after the younger Miss Fairfax had died two years ago; their twin daughters had been born there almost a year ago. Each of their lives had settled into a pattern and although Kathy had been deeply hurt when it became clear to her that Patrick intended to keep the distance between them, she saw now that it was for the best. She was married to Will Harrap and nothing could ever change that. It was wrong to go against God's will—wrong to wish for what could not be.

It was almost dark when she turned into Mill Row and she was startled out of her thoughts by a voice calling her:

'Mammy! I'm here, Mammy! You're home then?'

Mary ran towards her, arms outstretched. She was a beautiful child, slim and tall for her nine years. Her hair was a lighter colour than Kathy's, red-gold and tumbling over her shoulders in a mass of curls, while her violet-blue eyes shone with vitality.

'I've had a *lovely* day!' she said, tucking her hand through her mother's arm. 'Mrs Nichols was ever so kind to me. I cleaned all the silver and I took her little dog for a walk. His name is Rufus. I played with the twins for a little while too, while the nurse was at her lunch.' Her eyes sparkled with interest. 'Did you finish little Clarissa's dress, Mammy? Did you see

Francis?'

Kathy laughed. 'Let me catch me breath, child! Your Da will be wanting his tea!'

'I've made it for him,' Mary said. 'Listen— after I'd done, Mrs Nichols sent me to Mr Reardon's to see if I could help, because his housekeeper is poorly. He has such lovely flowers in his garden, Mammy, yet it's funny because he only grows them to let them die—' She broke off as she saw the colour leave her mother's face. 'Oh, Mammy, aren't you well? Come on indoors and I'll make you some tea.'

'No—wait. You went to Mr Reardon's, you say? Did you see him?'

'Yes, I told you. He showed me his flowers and he told me all about them. We had a long talk, Mammy. It's this way.' She drew her brows together in concentration. 'When the flowers die their strength goes back into the little bulb they grow from, then Dr Nichols makes med—medications out of them. The little bulbs split and multiply so that there are enough for Mr Reardon to send to London on the railway for the doctors in London to use.'

Kathy nodded. 'I know. Soon after you were born Dr Nichols cured me with the salve he makes from those bulbs. I have reason to be thankful to them.'

Mary nodded gravely. 'Mr Reardon told me that too. He said it was him fetched the doctor on the night I was born. Is it true, Mammy? He said he saw me when I was only half an hour old!'

Kathy nodded, putting an arm round the child's shoulders. 'It's true enough. We owe him our lives, you and I.'

'But how? I mean—we don't know him, do we—at least not very well?'

Kathy looked down at her daughter's puzzled face. How strange that she should feel so distant to the man who should have been her father. She took a deep breath.

'Patrick Reardon and I were brought up together when we were children in Ireland,' she explained. 'My father married his mother. We came here to Elvemere together when we were young and we both were in service at Denmark House.'

'Then he's our kin—like an uncle?' Mary said excitedly.

'No.' Kathy said quickly. 'He's no relation at all.'

'A friend then? He must be a good friend to have saved our lives.'

'Yes—a good friend,' Kathy conceded.

'Then why does he never come and see us?'

Kathy gave her daughter an impatient push. 'Oh! Will ye stop your everlastin' questions, child and let me into the house! Your Da will be thinkin' I'm lost!'

Will sat in his chair by the fire. He was in his mid-fifties now, though pain and his disability made him appear older. As his wife and Mary came in his lined face lit up.

'Kathy! Come and warm yourself. Where've you been? I thought you'd never be home!'

Kathy gave Mary a reproachful look. 'There—what did I tell ye? It's Mary,' she told her husband. 'Sure she'd talk the hind-leg off a donkey with her chatter and her questions. Now, have ye had enough to eat?'

Will nodded. 'All I'm missing is your company. Come and sit by the fire and tell me all the news from the Gages.'

More than once that evening Kathy was tempted to tell Will about the shop and ask him what he thought but each time she checked herself at the last minute. He knew her so well. He'd surely see the enthusiasm in her eyes and urge her to go ahead whatever his own feelings. The problem went round and round in her mind. Will could do very little work now. There was hardly any strength in his legs and his arms became weaker as the weeks went by. Most of their income already came from her sewing and she knew he felt the shame of it keenly though he never mentioned it.

Later as she lay in bed she thought of what Mary had told her about Patrick. It was good of him to take an interest in the child. Closing her eyes she visualised him. When she had last seen him he had been dressed in a coat and trousers of the finest cloth with a jewelled pin in his cravat. He had grown a fine moustache and side whiskers and at his temples the glossy black hair was frosted with silver, which gave him a very distinguished appearance. Will turned over beside her and Kathy bit her lip, feeling guilty at the direction her thoughts were taking.

*       *       *

Patrick stood on the Herring Wharf and watched his old friend Tom Craven come ashore from the *Mary Ann*. With a sudden pang he saw that the captain had begun to show his years, though the weather-beaten face was as good-humoured as ever. Patrick smiled to himself, wondering whether old Meg still fixed the Excise men with her steely eye while her petticoats bulged with contraband.

Tom caught sight of him and called out: 'Ahoy there old friend! Good to see you! What wind blew you in?'

Patrick smiled. 'I'd a mind to see an old sea captain and have a chin-wag. Will ye have a jar with me, Tom?'

Tom looked at him sideways, a hint of mischief in his pale blue eyes. 'I've a notion to go to the Calcutta, lad. Will you come with me—or are you too grand?'

Patrick hesitated. He had not set foot inside the Calcutta since that night many years ago when he had been so humiliated. But it was so long ago. He had been a boy then. He laughed and clapped his old friend on the shoulder.

'Too grand? I hope I'll never be that, Tom. The Calcutta it is. Sure I'd like to see the old place again.'

As they walked by, Tom looked wistfully at the few boats moored in the port, shaking his head.

'Elvemere isn't what it was in the old days, boy. I've been thinking lately that it's time Meg and I came ashore for keeps.'

Patrick shook his head. 'Never, Tom. There's still a good fishing trade up and down the river. I can't picture the day when I won't see the *Mary Ann* at her usual berth.'

But Tom pursed his lips. 'She's getting old too, like us. Soon she'll only be fit for the breaker's yard. We none of us go on for ever, lad. We've had our day and it was a good un. Yours is just beginning and the likes of us must stand back to make way for you.'

'It's true the town's changed, but it's for the better,' Patrick said. 'There's more folk and more work for them—a better life all round. The workhouse is nowhere near full nowadays and hardly any livin' on the parish.' He still felt a stir of excitement when he thought of the changes he himself had helped, physically, to bring about. The day the railway had been officially opened was still a cherished memory to him. The town was gay with coloured bunting and all the people in their Sunday best, the fine, stone-flagged platform of the station was packed with civic dignitaries as the first train steamed in heralded by the brassy clamour of the town band; whilst the navvies—himself among them—waved and cheered from the embankment just above the town. It had been a great day—and it had marked a new beginning for him. Since then everything he had touched had gone right—and yet—

Tom glanced at him wryly. 'Seems to me you don't need any standing back for. You've done well enough without.'

Patrick nodded. 'Thanks to a good friend and partner,' he said. 'I could never have done it without Dr Nichols. He's the one with the headpiece when it comes to money matters.'

It was certainly true that Jonathan had been astute. Seeing the mounting fever of railway mania, he had sensed the coming crash and had sold the shares he held for himself and Patrick while the price was high. With Patrick's co-operation he had put the money into a building firm and directed the building of new 'model' houses, designed by himself. He had seen enough squalor in the hovels occupied by the working-class to know their crying needs all too well. It was his dream to build a free hospital for the poor of the town one day soon. The railway company had bought the new houses to rent to their workers and now Jonathan was commissioned to build more for George Gage who was interested in rehousing the workers at his expanding engineering works.

Tom had often wondered how Patrick had come by the money he had invested, but he had never liked to ask. He knew the lad was honest, he'd have staked his life on that, but all the same, he must have had a tidy windfall from somewhere.

They turned in at the door of the Calcutta and Patrick saw that here was one place that was untouched by the years of change. True there were fewer customers than in days gone by and of those who sat in the smoky taproom a lower percentage were sailors, but the atmosphere was the same. Tom insisted on buying the ale and they sat over it for a while in companionable silence, as Tom lit and puffed on his pipe. He asked after Seamus and Patrick told him that the old man was well as far as he knew. Of Kathy, he gave only a sketchy account.

As the evening passed the taproom filled up and the girls began to appear, serving ale and food and making themselves agreeable to the customers. Most of them were young, but there were one or two older ones and presently Tom nudged Patrick, chuckling.

'Remember the night Quincey thrashed you, lad? I brought you here for the first time— remember Tabby? I reckon she taught you a thing or two that night, eh?'

Patrick nodded. 'I remember.'

Tom laughed. 'Changed a bit, hasn't she? Like everything else!'

Patrick followed his glance across the room to where a woman stood talking to a group of men. She was fat, her face red and shiny with the heat of the fire where she had been turning meat on a spit. But when she threw back her head and laughed he knew without a doubt that it was her. He stared incredulously at Tom.

'God! I'd never have known her!'

Tom grinned. 'Too much good living! She married the landlord. She's his widow now and owns the place, but she still has her special *customers*, so I'm told!' He winked broadly and before Patrick could stop him he had called loudly across the room in a voice to rival any foghorn:

'Hey—Tabby! Come over here and see what the wind's blowed in!'

As she made her way across the room towards them, Patrick saw that in spite of her bulk she still moved with the remembered hip-swinging sauciness. Her dimpled arms were bare and her bosom overflowed voluptuously at the neckline of her tight bodice. The abundant hair was darker now, though she still wore it loosely flowing like a young girl's and the strings of the incongruous matron's cap she wore were tied loosely under her multiple chins. She stood in front of Patrick for a long unnerving moment, regarding him, then she threw back her head and gave a bellow of laughter.

398

'Well, well! If it ain't young Paddy Reardon—my old beau! Grown up to be a real gent, eh? Welcome to the old Calcutta, sweetheart. Nice to see you again.'

Patrick nodded, trying not to look as abashed as he felt. 'It's good to see you too, Tabby.' He felt the eyes of the other customers on him and wished he had dressed in a less conspicuous way. Tom moved away with a sly wink and Tabby slid into his vacated seat, leaning her elbows on the table and looking at Patrick speculatively.

'Well, this *is* a turn up. Where've you been all these years—foreign parts?'

Patrick shrugged noncommittally.

'You look as if you've done all right for yourself anyway,' she concluded. 'Tom tell you I'm landlady now, did he? Married old Seth Brewster, I did.' She leaned closer till Patrick felt sure that the bounteous breasts must break loose from their inadequate prison. 'I'll tell you a secret: I reckon it was *you* as give me a taste for wedded bliss, young Paddy!' She smiled, showing gaps in her teeth. 'Remember the night you asked me to wed you?'

Again he shrugged, feeling that half the room was laughing at him. She went on, her eyes misting nostalgically: 'I'll never forget it. Not many girls has a chance like that—not my sort anyhow. I reckon I should've snapped you up.' She looked at him wistfully. 'I didn't treat you right, did I?'

He shook his head, eager for a change of subject. 'It was no more than I deserved as I remember.'

Suddenly she laughed good-naturedly. 'All water under the bridge, eh, Paddy? I expect you're married by now with a string of fine sons to your name?'

'No,' he told her.

She cocked her head on one side. 'No! How's that then?'

He drained his tankard. 'There was only ever one girl for me—and she married someone else.'

Misunderstanding, she clapped him on the shoulder and gave a shriek of laughter. 'Ah— go on with you!' She winked and pinched his cheek with plump fingers. 'You're welcome to come upstairs with me for old times' sake, if you fancy it.'

He shook his head. 'Thank you, Tabby, but I have to go now. I've urgent business to attend to.' He stood up and she gave him a wry wistful smile.

'Well, you know you're welcome any time, Paddy. Have a drink on the house before you go, eh?'

But he was already half way to the door, his face burning. As the laughter of the customers rang in his ears he remembered all too well that night many years ago and he couldn't get out of the place fast enough. 'Good-night, Tabby!' he called over his shoulder.

He was walking back in the direction of the river when he heard heavy footsteps behind him and he turned to see Tom hurrying after him, coughing breathlessly.

'What's the hurry? Why can't you wait for me, young Reardon?' he asked reproachfully between gasps. 'What's the idea—walking out like that, eh?'

Patrick hunched his shoulders. 'There was no air in the place. I couldn't breathe,' he said morosely.

'Why don't you come right out with it and say it stinks!' Tom said angrily. 'I suppose if I was to ask you to come back to the old tub for a bite o' supper you'd turn your nose up at that an' all!'

Patrick stopped in his tracks and looked at his old friend. 'I wish you would ask me, Tom. Sure, sometimes it seems to me that I haven't a soul in the world to call "friend".'

Tom stared at him, his eyes still hurt and angry. 'You've an uncle and a step-sister in the town, yet when I asked you about them tonight you hardly knew whether they were alive or dead! Can you wonder if you're friendless?'

Patrick sighed despairingly. 'Oh Tom—if you only knew.'

The old captain took his arm, his face softening. 'Come on, lad,' he said gently. 'We'll see if Meg can fix us up with some of her good hot broth. I know you were always partial to it.'

401

In the tiny cabin of the *Mary Ann* the two men sat quietly over their supper and afterwards Patrick told Tom about the night he had asked Tabby to marry him. Tom's hearty laughter soon put the incident where it belonged for Patrick—in the past, and when their laughter had died down Tom wiped his streaming eyes and asked:

'But what ever possessed you, lad—asking a lass like that to wed you?'

Patrick shook his head. 'I'd hoped to marry Kathy—and it seemed she didn't want me after all. I'd been in more trouble at the house and I'd been to the hirin' fair to try and find other work. I'd failed there too. Worst of all was Henry Quincey, Tom. He and his damned family damn near finished Kathy and me. That night I'd have done anything to get away from it all, I reckon.'

Tom nodded with a sigh. 'Ah—so that was the way of it?'

Patrick looked up. 'Did you know he had me beaten and left for dead the night I ran away? Dr Nichols saved my life and it was many a month before I dared show my face in Elvemere.'

Tom sucked at his pipe reflectively. 'I reckon he always thought you were a thorn in his flesh, lad. You'd too much spirit for his liking.'

Patrick looked up, a triumphant glint in his eyes. 'Maybe—but I thrived in spite of him.'

'Aye, you did,' Tom nodded. 'A thriving thorn you was—like the haws they planted round the fields after the enclosures come.' He looked at Patrick, one eyebrow raised. 'But has it brought you peace, lad? That's the important thing. You've a fine house and you've made money, but you say you've no friends, so what good is any of it?'

Patrick drew a deep breath. 'Once I thought it'd be enough to make my fortune and know I was as good as any man—but now I wonder.' He straightened his shoulders. 'I've a mind to go in for farming, Tom, and I've heard tell that Henry Quincey's last farm is coming under the hammer soon. Should I make a bid for it?'

Tom tapped out the contents of his pipe and pulled down the corners of his mouth. 'Since them "Rebecca riots" farming's not been too popular. You might get it cheap. But I thought Dr Nichols was your adviser, lad. Why don't you ask him?'

'Because in some ways you know me better than he does,' Patrick told him. 'Dr Nichols is fine with the money side of things, but this'd be between me and the soil—a different kind o'gamble altogether—d'ye see?'

Tom smiled wisely. 'I do—but are you sure you don't want the farm just because it's Quincey's?' he asked shrewdly.

Patrick sighed. 'I suppose I have to admit that's part of it, Tom—but not all. I itch to work with me hands again; to tend horses and live in the open air. I've no family—no one of me own. It's an empty life and I must fill it.'

Tom looked keenly at his young friend. There was a kind of haunted longing in his eyes and he didn't understand it.

'Why don't you marry, lad?' he asked. 'I've seen the way the lasses look at you. You're a fine handsome feller and there's not one o' them wouldn't jump at the chance. You need a wife.'

Patrick shook his head. 'There's none I want. Kathy was the only girl for me, Tom— and now it's too late.'

'Then buy the farm—and good luck to you,' Tom said decisively.

As Patrick made his way home that night his thoughts turned to Mary Harrap. When he had seen her helping Mrs Tate, his housekeeper, that afternoon his heart had skipped a beat. She was so like Kathy. Showing the child his garden when she came out to gather vegetables he had quite forgotten who her father was and her interest in his bulb garden had captivated him, making him see them afresh through her eyes. He hadn't realised until today how lonely he had become. Jonathan and Dora were good, kind friends and he would always be grateful to them, but he was no fool and he knew quite well that he would never fit into their way of life. He didn't fit in with his own sort any more either though, and circumstances kept him from Kathy and Uncle Seamus. He

404

found himself hoping wistfully that the child, Mary, would come again tomorrow.


*April 1850*

Mary burst into the kitchen bringing a gust of spring air with her. Her cheeks were pink with excitement and her hair a disordered red-gold halo round her glowing face.

'Mammy! Mammy! You'll never guess what happened this morning!'

Kathy put down her sewing and looked up with a frown. 'Quiet, child. You'll wake your Da.'

The child's hand flew to her mouth as she swung round to look at the bed in the far corner of the room. Will's slight body hardly made a mound under the clothes now. He did not stir and Mary relaxed and came closer to her mother.

'I went with Mr Reardon to the railway station this morning,' she whispered. 'To take the boxes of bulbs to be sent to London. Before we went he let me pick some of the flowers, snowdrops and narcissus and do you know what happened? There were people on the train and they asked if they could buy them. I sold them *all*, Mammy, and I got a whole *shilling*! I tried to give it to Mr Reardon but he said I should keep it—or give it to you.' She held out her hand to show the coins.

Kathy frowned. 'But they were his flowers. We're not entitled to it!'

Mary's face fell. 'They were meant for you—and he said it was *me* who sold them—with my bright hair and eyes—he *said*!'

But Kathy was adamant. She stood up and, taking the coins from Mary, pushed them into a vase on the mantelshelf. 'We don't earn our bread in that fashion, my girl,' she said sternly. 'I'll take the money back to him tomorrow, so I will! I'll go meself. Now take off your things and help me get your Da's tea, the kettle's on the boil.'

She went over to the bed and looked down at Will. In repose his face looked even older. The ivory-tinged skin stretched tightly over the bones and the eyes were deeply sunken. She had sent for Dr Nichols this morning when Will's speech had become slurred and now she saw that the corner of his mouth drooped ominously as he slept. 'A slight stroke', the doctor had called it. A chill clutched at Kathy's heart. If Will were to die what would she do? She wouldn't know how to begin to live without him. It was true that for some time past she herself had been the breadwinner, but he was always there, lending her his own particular kind of strength and support. There was the cottage too. It was only Will's for as long as he lived. Of course she knew that the Gages wouldn't see herself and Mary destitute, but she hated the thought of living on charity of any kind. It was worrying and her anxiety made her sharp with the child.

She touched Will's thin shoulder. 'Will—are ye awake?' she said gently.

He stirred and opened his eyes, smiling up at her. 'I had a dream, lass,' he muttered. 'I was in this beautiful place—all flowers and trees and the like. The only thing was—you weren't there.'

She bent and kissed his cheek. 'I'll always be here, love. I'll never leave you. Try and sit up now. Here's Mary with your tea.'

It seemed there was no strength in his back but between them Mary and she propped him up with pillows and fed him with his tea. Afterwards he sank back again, exhausted. She sent Mary out to play with the other children and sat by the fire, taking up her sewing again. It was a pity she couldn't have the little shop John Gage had offered her. It was quite out of the question now. But she'd earn a living for them all somehow—*and* she'd see that Mary got her education too—if she had to sew till her fingers were raw. She'd not take charity from anyone! Her eyes strayed to the vase on the mantelshelf. First thing tomorrow after Mary had gone to school she'd take that shilling back to Patrick. She'd managed without him all these years, and she'd take nothing from him now!

\*　　　\*　　　\*

407

She was slightly awed by the grandness of the house and by the time Mrs Tate had shown her into the parlour and bade her wait, some of her indignation had evaporated. She should not have come—or at least, she should not have waited to see him. She should have given the money to the housekeeper woman with a message. Or would that have been rude? No— she must see him herself and explain to him how she felt.

When he opened the door and came in she started as though she had been bitten, leaping to her feet, her heart hammering in her breast and her cheeks burning. But when he saw her his face broke into a spontaneous smile which completely disarmed her.

'Why Kathy! When Mrs Tate said a Mrs Harrap had called I couldn't think who she meant.'

The colour heightened in Kathy's cheeks. 'I don't wonder!' she said sharply.

He looked at her sadly, his smile fading. 'Is there something wrong, Kathy?'

She delved into her skirt pocket and held out the coppers she had taken from Mary. 'I've brought back your money. The money Mary got for selling your flowers.' She thrust the coins into his hand. 'And while we're about it—I sent her to work for Mrs Nichols, not you—at honest housework—not to grovel like a beggar on the railway station!'

His eyebrows shot up in surprise. 'Sure it

wasn't at all like that, Kathy. She came to the station for a ride—and the flowers—they were intended for you. It was an accident that they were sold. The child thought she'd done so well. I couldn't have taken the money from her and put it in me own pocket!'

She looked away, unable to meet his eyes. 'The flowers weren't hers to sell,' she insisted.

'No,' he said quietly. 'They were yours—so have the money. Sure 'tis little enough.'

Her head swung up to look at him, her eyes blazing. 'Little enough to you, Patrick Reardon, with your fine house and your fancy clothes, but I haven't forgotten when we begged for crusts with hardly a rag to our backs and I'll not let my Mary come to that!'

He frowned and took a step towards her, putting his hands on her shoulders. 'Kathy—Kathy—surely you know I'd never do anything to offend you or bring you pain?'

'I know nothin' about you,' she said bitterly. 'Ten years ago ye cast me out o' your life entirely and since then you've become a stranger—an' I want no charity from strangers!'

He shook his head as though she had dealt him a blow. 'Oh, Kathy, don't ye know why I kept away?' he said quietly. 'I'm no stranger. I haven't changed. When I made up me mind to better meself it was all for you—for your sake.' He lifted his shoulders. 'I didn't do it in time to be of any use to you, that's all, so I reckoned

I'd best leave you be.'

She bit her lip, looking around her at the bright fire reflecting its blaze in the brass fender; the soft carpet with its pattern of roses; the plush upholstered chairs. Suddenly tears filled her eyes. Patrick took her arm and led her gently towards a chair. She sank into it gratefully, all the strength seeming to ebb away from her.

'Sit awhile, Kathy,' he said. 'Will I ask Mrs Tate to bring you a drink of something hot?'

She shook her head. 'I'll have to get back to Will. He isn't well.' But she didn't move. Patrick sat down opposite her, his face relaxing as he looked at her.

'Please believe me, Kathy, when I tell ye that I've no intention of makin' Mary into a flower-girl. It was just as I told ye—an accident. A happy one as it happens. It gave me an idea, you see. Those folk on the train— they snapped up the flowers like starvin' creatures snatchin' at crusts. It struck me that flowers don't grow in cities and there'd be a market for them there. There are always too many bulbs for the physic trade. I could try a few boxes of flowers at Covent Garden. If they go well I could grow more next year.'

She frowned. 'Covent Garden—what's that?'

'It's in London,' he told her. 'A big fruit and vegetable market. Now that we have the railway we can send produce there for the city

410

folk to buy.' He smiled. 'I could make a lot o' money, Kathy, and all because a handful of people fell in love with a pretty little girl with a basket o' flowers on a railway station. Does that sound like beggin'?' She smiled tremulously and shook her head. He pressed the money back into her hand, closing her cold fingers over it tightly. 'There—now let's hear no more of it.'

They smiled into each other's eyes for a long moment till he said suddenly: 'She's the livin' image o' you, Kathy. She's a beautiful child—such happy company.'

She nodded, her cheeks pink. 'She's a good girl right enough. I'm glad if she's been a help to you.'

He reached out to touch her hand lightly. 'Are ye—happy, Kathy? If—if there's anythin' ye need—'

'We manage fine,' she said proudly. 'Will can't work now, but I've the sewin'. Patrick—' she hesitated and he looked searchingly at her.

'Yes—go on. Is there some way I can help?'

'It's just a bit of advice I need—somethin' that's been worrying me.' She bit her lip. 'You know I've always kept in touch with Miss Melissa—Mrs Gage, I mean? That I do all her sewin'? Well, Mr John has asked me to take on a new little dressmaker's shop he's opening.'

He smiled. 'That's wonderful, Kathy. Aren't you pleased?'

She shook her head. 'I would be, but I can't

411

leave Will. He needs someone with him all the time now—yet we *do* need the money.'

'I see. Is there no one who would sit with him?'

'Not unless I paid them and I couldn't afford that. Besides, he's so dependent on me.'

He chewed his lip for a moment, then his face cleared. 'I know the premises you mean and surely there's living quarters above it? I'm sure John Gage would let you move in there. His father will be pulling down the cottages in Mill Row anyway, to build new houses for his workforce.'

He walked with her down the long drive to the road and before he opened the gate for her he took her hand and looked solemnly into her eyes.

'Will ye come again, Kathy?'

She looked away. 'No. I've no place in your life now.'

He held on to her hand tightly. 'I wish it could be different, Kathy,' he said huskily. 'Will ye at least promise me that you'll come to me if ye need help—for old times' sake?'

She nodded. 'I will. Thank you, Patrick. I'll not forget.'

On the way home she went to the butcher's and bought a piece of prime beef for Will's dinner with the flower money. She felt happy—happier than she remembered feeling for a very long time—light-hearted almost. Why had she not thought of the rooms above the shop before? There were three, plenty of room for her and Mary and Will. She would ask Miss Melissa about it the very next time she went to Holbrook Lodge.

She thought about Patrick too. She had almost forgotten how tall he was, how broad his shoulders. The fine new clothes he wore now suited him as though he had always worn them. He had grown handsomer with the passing years too, the wild, trapped look had gone out of his eyes. She wondered if there was a woman in his life. Surely he must be one of the town's most eligible bachelors. If he did not marry soon it would not be the fault of the middle-class mamas of Elvemere, she thought wistfully.

She let herself into the cottage and mended the fire. Thank the Lord the weather was warming up at last. Soon she would only need the fire for cooking and would be able to save a little on wood and coal. She took off her bonnet and shawl and turned towards the bed in the far corner of the room.

'Will—are you awake? Could ye drink a cup of tea?' she asked cheerfully. 'It's warmer out today. Sure it'll soon be spring and . . .' She broke off. There was no sound or movement from the bed and a chill crept into her heart as she stepped up closer to take a look.

He looked peaceful, a half smile on his lips as he lay back against the pillows, but even before she laid her hand against the sunken

413

chest she knew that he was gone. Silently she sank to her knees beside the bed. He had gone all alone—while she was with Patrick—arguing about a shilling. Her foolish, stubborn pride had taken her from him just when he needed her most.

'Mother o' God! Will—oh, Will!' The tears slid silently down her cheeks as she laid her head on the hand that lay outside the covers. 'Forgive me, my poor love—forgive me!

*October 1850*

Henry Quincey sat in his usual place by the window, a rug around his knees. He had long since given up the notion that Sophia might return but somehow the habit of watching the street had stuck and now it hardly seemed worth the effort of giving it up. Besides, he had nothing else to do. He could watch people come and go from here and see the few ships and boats that still moored in the port. Although he seldom went out, or indeed left this room, his former study, he was well aware that Denmark House had gone to seed. The paint was beginning to peel and weeds were showing green shoots between the paving flags on the front path. The manicured lawns were high and rank with rye-grass and all the windows on the top floor had been bricked up against the window tax. But in spite of Henry's drastic cuts in expenditure he was falling deeper and deeper into debt. Even the sale of Drove End Farm to that whipper-snapper, Reardon, had not lifted him out of the mess he was in and Melissa and her husband, John Gage, constantly nagged at him to sell up and go and live with them. But Henry refused to listen, preferring to hide his head in the sand like an ostrich, hoping his problems would go away or somehow solve themselves while he sat all day at the window, dreaming of what was past.

It was not of his wife and sons that he dreamed, of his days of success and the former glory of Denmark House, but of the handful of years he had spent with Sophia. They had been the happiest years of his life and the fact that he had paid so dearly for them mattered nothing to him. What times they had had together! How beautiful she had been and how she had pleased him! For six years they'd lived a live of indulgence and pleasure until the break-up of his health had precipitated Sophia's departure. Not that he blamed her for that. He would never have wished her to waste herself on a helpless invalid. He often amused himself by reliving the afternoon when Amelia had returned unexpectedly from London to find them naked in each other's arms. He chuckled now at the memory. It must have been the best thing that had ever happened to Amelia. It would have done her good to see how a *real* woman behaved in a man's arms!

He was still chuckling and muttering to himself when the door opened and Seamus shuffled in, followed by Dr Maybury. The old coachman was bent almost double with rheumatism but the eyes in his weather-beaten face were as alert as ever. He turned to the doctor.

'There—what did I tell ye, sir? He's too much on his own. He's always talkin' to himself like that.'

Henry shot the old man a venomous look. 'Hold your tongue, you old fool! You're the senile one! If you don't keep your mouth shut I'll have you thrown out bag and baggage. Who'd employ an old goat like you then, d'you think, eh?'

'Who'd ye get to do the throwin'?' Seamus retaliated. 'An' who'd look after ye when I'd gone—tell me that?' He turned to the doctor. 'There's not many'd do what I do, sir!'

Doctor Maybury stepped between them, smiling blandly. He was well used to these two and their bickering. 'Perhaps you would be kind enough to ask Sarah to make us some tea, Seamus,' he said. 'I would like to talk with Mr Quincey for a while alone.'

The old man withdrew, muttering, and the doctor pulled up a chair, smiling at his patient.

'He's right, you know, Henry. You are far too much on your own. Why don't you accept John and Melissa's kind offer? It would do you good to have your grandchildren about you.'

'Couldn't stand the noise!' Henry shook his head. 'And as for the Jellings family—!' He raised his eyes to the ceiling. 'How many have they got now? I've lost count! The girl seems to have dropped another brat every time I turn my back!'

Doctor Maybury cleared his throat. 'Caroline and Victor have seven children now. Four boys and three girls. I delivered Caroline of a fine new son last March. I'm serious though, Henry. I believe strongly that it would be to your advantage in more ways than one to sell this house. You cannot keep it as it should be kept. It must be a constant worry to you as well as being far too big. If you were to sell it you could pay off your debts and—'

'What do you know of my debts? I suppose it's your own bill you're worried about?' Henry glared ferociously at his old friend through greying whiskers but the doctor smiled back benignly.

'Come now, Henry, I think you know me better than that. I have only your best interests at heart. I understand that an enquiry has been received regarding this house. Why don't you let it go while you can still ask a good price?'

Henry grunted. 'If I did as you ask what'd happen to my servants? Seamus and Sarah have given me good service. A man in my position has a certain loyalty to his retainers.'

The doctor laughed. 'Face facts, Henry! You

417

know as well as I do that Seamus is long past retiring and you haven't paid him anything for months! Melissa would see that he was looked after. As for Sarah—she's an able-bodied young woman and would have no trouble finding another post.'

Henry muttered to himself, mulling the thought over. 'Why didn't that fool Muxworth come and tell me about this enquiry?' he snapped suddenly. 'He's supposed to be my solicitor, damn it!'

The doctor shook his head. 'You know quite well that you quarrelled with him over Drove End Farm, Henry, and told him not to speak to you again. He asked me to mention the matter to you as the offer he has received seemed a generous one under the circumstances.'

Henry's eyes narrowed suspiciously. 'Who wants it? It's not George Gage is it? He's had the brewery and the mill! If that silly cow of a daughter of his had had the sense to marry my son Charles she'd have been mistress of Denmark House now! Instead of that she married that popinjay—what's his name—?' He frowned. 'Who *did* the silly bitch marry?'

'She married my son Robert as a matter of fact.' The doctor smiled wryly. 'But that is beside the point, Henry. Will you at least promise me to give the matter some thought?'

Henry sniffed. 'Oh—all right, damn you! Why can none of you bear to see me at peace?' He glared at the doctor with fiery resentfulness. 'Well, man—are you going to sit there chewing the fat all day, or are you going to examine me? Maybe you've given up doctoring in favour of worrying folk to death!'

Dr Maybury saw himself out half an hour later, noticing as he passed through the neglected hall the thickness of the dust and cobwebs on the furniture. It was true that one woman could not be expected to keep on top of a place of this size but Sarah obviously made no attempt at doing so. She had not even brought the tea he had asked for. He hoped sincerely that Henry would take his advice and sell up. He himself was growing as neglected as the house and there was a marked deterioration in his physical condition too. True, most of his troubles had been brought upon himself, but he surely did not deserve to be deserted so cruelly. The doctor sighed as he closed the rusty gates behind him, lifting an arm to wave at the grizzled figure at the window. Ah well, he had done his best. He could not do more.

## CHAPTER FOURTEEN

*May 1851*

Kathy closed the door and turned over the sign so that the word 'Closed' faced the street.

Today was something of a special occasion and she was closing early. It was one year today since she and Mary had moved into the apartment over the shop and begun to work and trade there. It had been the happiest year of her life. With all that there had been to do, the sadness of Will's passing had been dulled for her and with most of the fashionable ladies of Elvemere planning to visit the Great Exhibition with their husbands, she was soon kept busy with as many orders for new dresses as she and her two apprentices could cope with. Now the orders were almost all completed and she could relax a little. It had been a highly successful year and this evening she was giving a little supper party to celebrate. She hurried upstairs to put the finishing touches to the preparations.

There would be six of them at the party: John and Melissa Gage, Dr Nichols and his wife, Dora, and Patrick, who through the past eventful months had been both friend and adviser to her. Mary had left earlier to spend the night at the Nichols' house, to help the nurse with Dora's delightful twin girls.

At the top of the stairs she stopped and surveyed the room with satisfaction. It was a large, sunny room overlooking the market-place and she never tired of its ever-changing view. Opposite was the White Hart, once the town's coaching inn, which now did a brisk trade in the hiring of post-chaises, ferrying passengers to and from the railway station. Lately there was the spectacle of the new experimental omnibus too. It seemed to Kathy that the town had adjusted to its new way of life remarkably well. Indeed, it was difficult now to imagine Elvemere without its railway!

The meal was to be a cold one: a collation of cold meats with pickles and home-baked bread, followed by an apple pie, cheese and fruit. Mrs Janes, the woman who came in daily to clean and cook, had laid everything out in the kitchen, covered with a snowy cloth. All Kathy had to do was to lay the table—in the way she had learned at Denmark House—and serve the supper.

The Gages were the first to arrive, John bringing with him three bottles of wine from his own cellar with which to drink the health of 'my partner' as he smilingly called Kathy. Dora and Jonathan came next and, lastly, Patrick, who bore an enormous bouquet of flowers, grown in the newly erected glasshouses at Drove End Farm. Kathy took them from him with a cry of delight, burying her face in their fragrant blooms.

'Oh, Patrick, they're beautiful!'

He smiled proudly. 'They've done better than I'd ever have dreamed. Next year I'm going to have more houses and several more acres of them.'

It was a happy occasion with all of them reminiscing over a year which had seen many changes. That winter had taken its toll, with old Seamus following Will to the grave, but after the shop had opened, life had begun to look up for Kathy. Mary had taken it upon herself to teach her mother to read so that now she could manage her own books as well as the sewing. She was proud of her achievements and when glasses were raised and her health drunk she blushed prettily, her eyes shining. Patrick thought she had never looked more beautiful in her life.

At ten o'clock the Gages' carriage arrived and they left amid much laughter and good wishes for the future. The Nichols followed a few minutes after, and Patrick and Kathy were left alone. Kathy began to clear the table.

For a while he watched her pensively, his eyes tender, till at last he said: 'Kathy—will ye leave that and sit down a minute? I want to talk to ye.'

She looked at him, her cheeks pink. She felt oddly apprehensive with him tonight. All evening he had been looking at her strangely, almost as though he were seeing her for the first time and it made her shy of him suddenly. Although he had been a regular visitor in her home over the past months this was the first time they had been alone together since she had visited his house on the day of Will's death. She folded the cloth carefully and set the vase with Patrick's flowers in the centre of the table, standing back to admire them.

'Thank you for the flowers, Patrick. They're lovely,' she said, her voice trembling a little.

He held out his hand. 'Come here, Kathy.'

Hesitantly, she crossed the room and sat beside him on the sofa.

'You've been here more than a year now,' he said slowly. 'I've tried to be a help without getting in the way—to be a good friend to you.' He chewed his lip, searching for a way to say what was in his heart. 'I've not spoken of the way I felt because I knew you grieved for Will.' He cleared his throat. 'I know there's Mary to consider—though I think she and I are friends.'

Kathy smiled. 'She worships you, Patrick, you know that.'

He nodded. 'That only leaves you, Kathy. How do you feel after all these years? What I'm really askin' is—will you marry me?' His eyes searched hers, dark with longing, and when she did not answer at once he hurried on: 'I've done well for meself, you know that— an' I'll do even better now that I'm plannin' to turn half the farm over to the flowers. I'm going to make this corner of Lincolnshire into the garden of England, Kathy, an' I'm askin' you to be the queen of it—' He shook his head, not understanding her silence. 'Well— it's not the first time I've asked you,' he said, his voice rough. 'Eleven years I've waited for ye—well—what'll it be?'

Her throat was too tight for words and her

heart felt as though it would burst with joy. For a speechless moment she looked at him, her eyes brimming with tears, then she threw her arms round his neck, burying her face against his shoulder.

'Patrick—Oh, Patrick, of course I'll marry you,' she whispered. 'In all these years I've never stopped loving you—no, not for one minute. How could you ever think I might have?'

As his arms folded round her it was as though the pent-up longings of a decade were released in both of them. His arms crushed her body to him and his mouth searched hers hungrily, pausing between kisses to caress her eyelids and throat with his lips—pulling the pins from her hair till it tumbled about her shoulders, then his fingers were deftly unhooking her gown, easing it down to encircle her breasts with tender hands.

'Kathy!—oh my Kathy!' His voice was almost a groan as he lowered his head to kiss the creamy skin and she buried her face in his thick black curls, cradling his head in her hands, tears of joy coursing down her cheeks. Sliding one hand under her knees he lifted her and carried her into the bedroom, laying her gently on the bed. But as he lay down beside her and took her in his arms once more he heard her catch her breath and felt the rapid beating of her heart.

'Patrick,' she whispered. 'I—I never have—

not since Mary was conceived. Poor Will never could. I—I'm—'

He covered her trembling lips with his. 'Don't be afraid, darling,' he said, his lips moving against hers. 'I'll not hurt you.'

He took her as gently as he could and after the initial moment of pain she relaxed, closing her eyes as her arms crept around him. Her heart swelled with joy. Now they truly belonged to each other. Now they were one as they were always meant to be. She could not believe that such bliss existed. Her body relaxing she moved instinctively with him, her pleasure mounting to match his until finally it was as though a million stars exploded inside her, filling her mind and body with brilliant sensation that made her cry out with sheer ecstasy. As they lay still in each other's arms he whispered over and over:

'Oh, Kathy, I love you—I love you so.'

And she smoothed his hair with tender fingers, murmuring soft words in his ear, feeling happier and more at peace than ever in her life before.

They slept for a while and she awoke to see him dressing by the light of a candle. She watched him sleepily for a while, then spoke his name softly. He turned and came to sit on the edge of the bed, taking her hand and placing a kiss in its palm.

'I must go now, love,' he said. 'But I'll be back tomorrow. We'll have a lot of plans to make. The wedding must be soon—as soon as possible.'

She reached up and wound her arms around his neck, drawing him down beside her again. 'Stay a bit longer, love. I can't bear to let you go. There's so much I want to ask you. Where will we live? And what about the shop here?'

He kissed her. 'As for the shop, you must do as you like. I know you're proud of it and rightly so, but maybe when your apprentices are trained you can leave most of the work to them.' He raised his head to look down at her. 'I'd like us to have some babies before it's too late—wouldn't you?'

She smiled. 'Our babies—a family of our own—oh, yes! But do we have to live at the farm? It's such a long way from town.'

He raised himself on one elbow, his face alight. 'There's something I have to tell you, Kathy. It was to be a surprise. No one knows about it yet. I was just waiting to see if you'd say "yes". I've already bought a house in Elvemere. I signed the final papers last January. That's where we'll live.'

'Oh—where is it? Which house?' she asked, catching some of his excitement.

He drew a deep breath. 'It's Denmark House, Kathy! Denmark House itself. Now it's mine—and yours too soon!'

She stared at him in speechless disbelief. '*You've* bought Denmark House? Everyone's trying to guess—but I never for a moment

426

thought—'

'Yes—and now that we're to be married we'll have it made as grand as you like!' His face glowed with happiness. 'We'll have it done out with the new wallpapers and paint—new furniture and carpets. I'll take you to the Great Exhibition and maybe—' He broke off at the look of horror on her face. 'What? What have I said? What is it, Kathy?'

Slowly she shook her head. 'I couldn't live there, Patrick. I *couldn't*,' she whispered.

He shook his head uncomprehendingly. 'But—it's been my *dream*! All these years it's what I've worked for—all that's kept me going. To be able to buy it and give it to you. Now you say you don't want it?'

She grasped his hand and placed its palm against her cheek, his pain hurting her. 'Don't you see, love?' she said gently. 'I couldn't be happy there—where so many bad things happened to us. I couldn't put our child in that nursery—look into the room where he—where it—that nightmare happened.' She broke off, shaking her head. 'I'd never be happy there, Patrick. I'd never feel right or at home.'

Slowly he nodded. He had never looked at it in that way. To him Denmark House was a citadel to be stormed and won; enemy ground to be fought for and made his own. But now he saw it through Kathy's eyes and he realised that she was right: there would be too many ghosts, too many unhappy memories there

427

forming a barrier to their happiness.

'I dare say I'll lose money on it,' he said disappointedly.

She kissed his cheek. 'I'm sorry, Patrick. I can see why you did it and I do appreciate it. No woman was ever more honoured and I'll never forget that you wanted—and *got* it for me, but—' she sighed and looked at him helplessly.

He put his arms round her, drawing her close. 'I was a fool,' he said, his lips against hers. 'I should've stopped to think how you'd feel. I see it now. We'll live at the farm till I've built you a fine new house that we'll make our own and no one else's.'

She kissed him gratefully. 'Thank you, Patrick—for understanding—and for loving me too,' she whispered shyly. 'I never dreamed that anything could be so beautiful. I don't care where we live just as long as we can be together.'

All that day as Patrick worked among his flowers he thought about Kathy and Denmark House. He could hardly believe that she was to be his at last, but what was he to do with Denmark House? He had always sworn to own it one day and to lay the ghosts of the misery he had suffered there. Now it seemed that he must let it slip through his fingers again. He could only compare it with the feeling he had when a spirited, proud horse he had broken was sold to a new owner.

That afternoon he called on his friends, the Nichols, and gave them the news of his betrothal to Kathy. He went on to tell of his purchase of Denmark House and how his plan to make it their new home had misfired. They were sympathetic, each of them seeing both sides of the question, then suddenly Jonathan's face cleared dramatically and he brought his fist down on the table with a triumphant cry:

'I have it! The very answer to your problem, Patrick, and a wonderful one if you agree to it.'

Patrick listened to Jonathan's plan with interest and slowly his face began to beam its approval. It was the perfect answer. He could hardly wait to put it into action!

*September 1851*

The last rays of the afternoon sun slanted through the window overlooking the market-place, catching in Kathy's hair and burnishing it to richest gold. Melissa and Dora stood back admiringly as she turned towards them, the last hook in her wedding dress fastened by Mary.

She had made it herself of soft lemon silk trimmed with creamy lace at throat and wrists. The skirt fell in layered flounces and the tight bodice fitted smoothly over the shoulders while the sleeves belled out to reveal lace inner sleeves.

Mary stood back and walked to the front of her mother.

'Oh, Mammy,' she sighed. 'Tomorrow you'll be the prettiest lady in Elvemere!'

Melissa smiled. 'So you will, Kathy dear. Patrick is a very lucky man.'

'He is indeed,' Dora agreed. 'Tomorrow will be a very happy day for both of you and I think you know that all our love and good wishes will go with you.'

Kathy sighed, her heart full. John Gage was to give her away and Jonathan Nichols was to be Patrick's groomsman. It was to be a quiet ceremony followed by a wedding breakfast given by Dora at Willerby Hall.

'You think I'll do then?' she asked shyly, picking up her matching bonnet with its silk and lace lining.

Dora and Melissa looked at each other and laughed. '*Do?* Patrick will positively burst with pride,' Dora told her. 'But you must take it off now, before he arrives and catches you. It's bad luck for the bride to be seen in her dress by the groom before they meet in church!'

The tinkling of the shop bell downstairs threw them all into a flurry as Kathy whisked away to the bedroom to change out of the dress. She and Patrick were to take a walk this evening. He had something to show her—a surprise—an extra wedding present, he said, though what it was she couldn't imagine. The new town house he was building for them was growing fast and would be ready soon after Christmas. It was nothing to do with that, she knew, so what could it be?

Dressed again she came out of the bedroom to find Mary laughing with her new step-father to-be but when Patrick saw her he stood up.

'Are you ready then, Kathy? I can hardly wait to show you the surprise.'

'Can I come too?' Mary asked. But Dora took her hand.

'You'll see it later. This is just for your Mama and Uncle Patrick. You're coming home with me to help look after the twins.' She looked meaningly at Melissa. 'Shall we go now?' They kissed Kathy, promising to be back at ten next morning to help her dress, then they took their leave with the slightly protesting Mary in tow.

Kathy turned to Patrick, laughing. 'It's a shame. She hates to be left out when there are surprises.'

He pulled her into his arms and kissed her lingeringly. 'Much as I love my new step-daughter it's good to have you to myself awhile.' He looked into her eyes. 'I can hardly believe that in a few short hours you'll be mine.'

'I'm yours now,' she whispered. 'I always have been.'

'Really mine—in church with the priest and everything—like in the old country,' he said. 'I never realised it meant so much to me till now.'

'What about this surprise?' she asked, her eyes dancing.

'I was almost forgetting!' He tucked her hand into the crook of his arm. 'Come and see.'

They walked through the quiet town, mellow with evening sunlight; across the High Bridge and along the High Street. A small suspicion crept into Kathy's mind and she held back a little, looking enquiringly at Patrick, but he took her arm firmly.

'Trust me, sweetheart. You'll like it, I promise.'

They passed by Denmark House, its windows blind and shuttered, then Patrick took out a ring of keys and unlocked the gates to the stable-yard. He held one of them open for her to pass through, which, after a moment's hesitation, she did. Inside, he closed the gate firmly and led the way to the coach-house. Unlocking the door he took her hand and walked inside.

There was no coach inside now, but against the far wall something large and square stood propped and veiled with a sacking cover. His eyes on her face, Patrick drew the cover off to reveal a large stone with words chiselled on it. Kathy stepped up closer and began to spell out the words:

Denmark House Hospital Donated to the people of Elvemere by Patrick Reardon and Dr Jonathan Nichols. December 1851.

She turned to Patrick, her eyes shining. 'It's

what he's always wanted! Oh, Patrick, what a wonderful idea!' Standing on tiptoe, she threw her arms round his neck and kissed him.

'We're hoping to have it open by Christmas,' he told her. 'And we all agree that you shall be the one to unveil the stone at the opening ceremony. After all, if it hadn't been for you it would never have happened.'

The sun had almost gone as they came out into the stable-yard again and Kathy shivered a little as she looked around her. Patrick slipped an arm round her.

'Are ye cold, darlin'?'

She smiled and shook her head. 'I was just remembering.' She looked up at him. 'When I'm old and look back on this time it'll be this evening's memory I'll love the most,' she said softly. 'Oh tomorrow will be grand, right enough, but I'll always remember this as the real proof of your love. This is our real wedding—our time of vows.'

Solemnly they joined hands and stood for a moment in the silence. Around them the neglected stable-yard with its rusty pump and weeds pushing up through the cobblestones seemed to shrink, and it seemed to them both at that moment that all they had ever suffered in this place dissolved and faded with the dying light. Patrick bent his head and kissed her cheek.

'Come, Kathy—Kathy Reardon,' he said. 'Let's go home.'

We hope you have enjoyed this Large Print book. Other Chivers Press or Thorndike Press Large Print books are available at your library or directly from the publishers.

For more information about current and forthcoming titles, please call or write, without obligation, to:

Chivers Large Print
published by BBC Audiobooks Ltd
St James House, The Square
Lower Bristol Road
Bath BA2 3BH
UK
email: bbcaudiobooks@bbc.co.uk
www.bbcaudiobooks.co.uk

OR

Thorndike Press
295 Kennedy Memorial Drive
Waterville
Maine 04901
USA
www.gale.com/thorndike
www.gale.com/wheeler

All our Large Print titles are designed for easy reading, and all our books are made to last.